Planet of the Winds

A Star Brothers Adventure

Colleen Drippé

Proxima Centauri

ST MARY'S, KS

Copyright © 2024 by **Colleen Drippé**

All rights reserved. No part of this publication may be reproduced, distributed or transmitted in any form or by any means, without prior written permission.

Proxima Centauri
St Mary's, KS

Publisher's Note: This is a work of fiction. Names, characters, places, and incidents are a product of the author's imagination. Locales and public names are sometimes used for atmospheric purposes. Any resemblance to actual people, living or dead, or to businesses, companies, events, institutions, or locales is completely coincidental.

Book Layout © 2017 BookDesignTemplates.com
Cover art by MiblArt, https://miblart.com/

Planet of the Winds / Colleen Drippé. -- 1st ed.

ISBN: 9798340121523

Dedication

To all the science fiction writers who enriched my childhood. May they rest in peace.

CONTENTS

CHAPTER ONE

A pair of ringed suns hung at noon, shedding their pale, amethyst light on the blonde heads of the crowd, tinting the ripening grain and bringing out mingled tones of green and purple in the surrounding foliage. The opalescent sky was of the same hue as the sunlight, a dreamy shade of lilac, while the slightly stuffy air breathed a soporific, vegetable sweetness.

Two tall figures flanked an earnest young Star Brother, poised preaching to the people in a language he had only recently acquired and still managed with some difficulty. Standing patiently on either side of him, his servitors might have been brothers, though as it happened, they were not. Both had thick auburn hair, perfectly straight and trimmed shoulder length with bangs. Their faces were stern with long noses and golden skin. The nose of the one on the right was especially striking, almost lacking an indentation at the top. In keeping with these archaic and chiseled features, their clothing was simple, leggings and tunics, in fashion timeless, though everything had been made for them in the robot-factories of a distant world. Both wore long knives and spring pistols at their belts.

The priest was telling a story, familiar to the two, though not to the colonists who were new converts. "A man went out and sowed seed," he said. "And some fell on stony ground and some among thistles."

Ard Matthew Third-Blade, the man on the right, repressed a wry smile. Ynche Colony was well supplied with thistles as he had recently learned to his cost. His hands still smarted from helping the colonists get in their hay.

Though he had not been stationed here long—less than a quarter of a standard year—it was already plain to him that these people had not prospered during their centuries cut off from the more advanced worlds. They had lost more than the Faith, he would say—if they had ever had it.

The carefully tended grain fields were small, plowed with the help of an animal he had never seen before—ox, maybe?—and a great deal of the work was done by hand. The settlements were hemmed in by a forest that could only be called primeval. There were things to watch for in this place, the people had told him. Perils not yet subdued. Ard Matthew had been shown the bodies of creatures killed on the edges of the fields—and the body of a woman killed by one of them.

At the back of the crowd, men with axes and spears formed a buffer against the forest. Ard Matthew watched them as he stood at attention the way he had been trained. He knew that he and Bis Terence Wolfbane made an impression on the colonists. Their presence at the Star Brothers' mission, both of them being products of such another backward colony as this one, reassured the people they had come to serve that they were not conquerors but only colonists like themselves.

He had often been told the story of how his own forefathers, back on Lost Rythar, had received their first visit from the more advanced people of Net Central. They had made war on the visitors and later martyred a number of missionaries before they were finally converted. At least the people of Ynche had never been hostile. They seemed grateful to know they were not alone in the universe.

The sermon, a veritable string of parables, continued to hold the attention of the Star Brother's listeners. A few glances fell on Ard Matthew and his partner and he nodded ever so slightly in acknowledgement of an occasional friendly smile. He had worked with these people, answered their questions about his homeworld and about the other places he had been—he had lived with them, eaten with them, hunted conies in their fields. He had even been asked to stand godfather at some of their baptisms.

But as the priest's words washed over him and the sultry air tried to lull him into a stupor, he could not help recalling the clean mountain breezes of his father's keep, the steep fields dotted with grazing goats and the towering sunfirs against the hard, blue sky. Two suns had made doubled shadows on the green grass and the snowfields while, further up the slope, the coiling serpent spruce became a lurking place for the highwolves.

Now he wondered what lurked *here*. He had seen the speared bodies of some sort of bear—or maybe it was a giant sloth?—and he had seen the wounds it could make on a man. And there was something catlike, a tigery thing, though not so large as the snowtygers of Lost Rythar. One had been shot with an arrow.

But he had never seen woods so thick as these. Edged by shrubbery, the trees rose in great, branching tangles to form green and mauve pillows, sagging beneath the tinted sky. It would be dark inside all that foliage, he thought. He had never liked going in among the serpent spruce, he remembered, and this would be worse.

He noted that Bis Terence Wolfbane was also watching the forest and the crowd. Once their eyes met and Ard Matthew nodded. Everything was going well so far, but both had served in the Faring Guard—the Star Brother's auxiliary—long enough to take nothing for granted.

"You know about hard ground," the Star Brother was saying. "This is a hard planet. But you have made of your fields a place for nurture. You have put much effort into this and the results are growing around you."

There were a few murmurs of agreement. He was speaking their language, both figuratively and literally.

"Your souls need nurture, too," he went on. "The seeds of the gospel require good soil—and this is something you must work for. Treasure these seeds as you do the seeds of your material grain."

Everyone was listening, even the guards at the rear of the crowd. Ard Matthew narrowed his eyes. Suddenly a hunter's sixth sense had sent the hairs rising on the back of his neck. He scanned the area carefully.

The trees slouched together, festooned with mosses, the forest aisles hidden from his view by the ubiquitous holly or whatever it was. Between the forest and the crowd, a field of grain moved slightly in the breeze. Or did it? Were all those movements caused by the wind? He squinted at a rippling undulation, a gentle sway of laden stalks. Was there a hint of deeper gold beneath the hanging seed?

One of the guards looked up, brushing the hair from his eyes. He held a spear in one hand, leaning on the shaft while the point gleamed above his head. Ard Matthew saw his face in profile, lean and bearded.

Suddenly the man yanked his spear aloft—far too late.

A tawny whirlwind erupted from the grain, moving so quickly that Ard Matthew couldn't make out what sort of creature it was. The spearman was half lifted from the ground and tossed aside, blood erupting in a shower as the thing passed by and leaped into the crowd. It snatched a child, swung about, and took off across the field, making for the forest beyond.

People surged in panic, some running to the aid of the wounded guard, others—more tentatively—after the fleeing predator. Only the spearmen kept their heads as they raced across the field. Ard Matthew shoved his way through the crowd, closely followed by Bis Terence. Behind them, the Star Brother had paused beside the injured man.

The creature's track was easy to follow, the grain trampled now that there was no more need for stealth, crushed in a pattern of leaps interspersed with droplets of blood. Ard Matthew passed the first of the pursuing spearmen, his long legs and runner's body carrying him ahead of these smaller folk. He didn't slow down as he drew his weapon and peered at the forest wall. Where snapped twigs showed the whiteness of their inner wood, he plunged through the gap.

At once he came into a different world, green and dripping with moisture, carpeted with moss. The soil was thin and rocky even here, and the great trees had spread shallow roots everywhere, snatching up all the nourishment there was. It was hard not to trip over them.

It was easy enough to track the creature by patches of disturbed moss and drops of blood—the blood of its victim. Ahead in the gloom, a flash of muted amber. He was gaining on it!

Which child had it taken? He remembered small friends who had lured him into their games, small faces looking up into his as he taught them their prayers and told them stories about other worlds. *Which one was it?*

And all the while, like an echo, he remembered that something like this had happened long before, back on Lost Rythar. An infant had been carried off by wolves. He had been a child himself when it happened, listening to the story as he sat beside a roaring hearthfire. They had never recovered the body.

"There!" Bis Terence panted, pointing to a break in the trees. Ard Matthew heard the sound of running water. He ran a few more paces and skidded to a halt.

The creature had dropped its prey and stood looking back at the pursuers. Formidable teeth grew from an elongated jaw while green, reptilian eyes glittered coldly beneath a swatch of what looked like feathers.

He could hear the child whimpering as he drew up and took aim with the spring gun. But even as he fired, his target had already leaped away. Before he could shift his stance the whirlwind was on *him*, trying to bear him down with its weight. He saw Bis Terence hovering, seeking to get in a shot without hitting Ard Matthew while the colonists came panting up, fingering spears and daggers.

Like all Lost Rythans, Ard Matthew was a big man, a giant among these other colonists. He kept his feet though he was slashed along one arm, the sleeve shredded away. Unfortunately, he lost the spring gun.

A misdirected spear grazed his side as he twisted about, struggling. Everything was happening so fast! Avoiding a claw aimed at his face—he lost a strip of scalp—he snatched the knife from his belt and thrust again and again at his attacker, trying to reach its vitals. Long teeth bit deeper into his knife arm. The pain was excruciating and his own cries of rage matched the shrieks of the animal. In another moment, he knew his arm would be useless.

With a desperate heave, he shoved the blade further into the belly of the creature while blood poured from his own wounds, making his hand slick as he struggled to hold on to the knife.

Suddenly the monster's grip loosened. Bis Terence had drawn his own knife and now he straddled the thing, one hand twisted in the feather crest as he swung, nearly taking off its head.

Their eyes met for a moment and then Ard Matthew was on his feet. The child! Where was the child?

He staggered toward the place where the monster had dropped its prey. Two of the colonists were already there but he pushed them aside. A small girl looked up at him, blue eyes mindless with terror, wriggling away from her rescuers as the Lost Rythan's blood splashed down on her. One small arm had been half ripped off, the collar bone showing above shattered ribs.

He knew her. He had been carving dolls' dishes for her and her sisters just the day before. She could not be this ruin! Helplessly he clenched his hands. "Don't," he begged hoarsely in his own language. "Don't die! Don't!" He scarcely knew what he was saying.

But the light went out of her face and, with a final shudder, she lay still.

"Oh God!" he cried, beside himself. "Damn! Damn! *Damn!*"

He was still cursing and weeping when Bis Terence drew him to his feet. Ignoring the apprehensive colonists, Ard Matthew turned his gaze up to the alien sky and whispered one last protest.

"Why? Why did You let this happen?"

Later as he lay on his bed in the cabin he shared with Bis Terence, the image would not leave him. If he had been faster—but no, the damage had already been done. Killing the creature did no more than ensure that it would not offer the final indignity of eating its victim.

He writhed, biting back a groan. He had seen death before. More than once, he had been the cause of it. But that was in clean battle—all save the killing that had earned him exile from his home colony. And even *that* had at least been a duel—a fair fight with axes. Not the senseless slaughter of an innocent child.

Why did little Catherine—for that was her name, he recalled—have to die so horribly? Why hadn't God helped him to save her? Now she lay on her bier in the makeshift chapel, awaiting burial in the Star Brothers' newly consecrated cemetery. She had only been baptized a few weeks before. Her Christian name was his own suggestion in memory of one of his younger sisters lost long ago to a fever.

He squirmed onto his side, taking refuge in the pain of his wounds, as he stared hopelessly about the room. Aside from the two bunks on either side of the narrow space, and a fireplace on the end wall with a crucifix above it, the cabin contained only a hearth bench. Yet somehow, it reminded him of his father's hall in miniature.

He and Bis Terence had visited stranger worlds than this. Dangerous places where he had survived worse wounds. But those were wounds of the body, he reminded himself bitterly. This time he was wounded to the soul.

Whenever he closed his eyes, he saw little Catherine lying among the leaves, staring up at him in terror as she died. He saw again the shattered bone, the marks of fangs and claws on her body. No man had done this, no one would do penance for this crime. It was only a mindless beast—one more howling, shrieking ravening *thing* among so many others that prowled the colony worlds. A freak of nature.

It did no good to remind himself that all worlds had their monsters, that death was a part of life. His own small sisters had lived or died safe in his family keep. They had not had their innocent bodies shredded by the wolf or the snowtyger. Even in the grip of the fever that had killed them, they had been surrounded by their family. *They* had not looked into eternity with the disbelieving stare of the betrayed.

The Star Brother had told Ard Matthew not to get up. He had been given speed heal and there was bread and dried fish on the bench which he was supposed to be eating to help the stuff do its work. But he got up anyway though the floor rocked beneath his feet. He fought for balance, bare toes clutching at the packed earth, swaying as he reached out to grasp the end of the bunk. He barely made it to the door before someone barred his way.

"Father Epinay." He looked down in confusion.

"Hello, Matthew," his superior said, steering him gently back into the room. "I don't think you are ready to go out yet."

Abruptly, the Lost Rythan sat down on the bunk. "No." He turned toward the other man, a grim smile twisting his lips. "But I got up. I am guilty of disobedience."

"You are."

Ard Matthew turned away. The world of rules and penances seemed as remote to him as his lost homeland. A Faring Guard was a penitent, an outcast. Even the thought that he might regain his honor through his service here—that he might one day go home—seemed as remote as the promise of heaven.

He felt the priest watching him. "You did everything you could to save that child," Father Epinay said softly. "And now she is with God."

This Star Brother was a little younger than Ard Matthew who had lived something over thirty years subtime. He wondered how many violent deaths the priest had witnessed in his brief career. Who could say—perhaps he *had* seen some action. After all, Star Brothers were sometimes killed. It was a risk they took when they joined the order.

But the priest was waiting for him to speak and he knew he must make some sort of response.

"I know she must be with God," Ard Matthew said at last. "Certainly she isn't with her parents." It was not what he had meant to say and he was sorry as soon as the bitter words came out. But there was no taking them back.

It was the Star Brother's turn to look at the floor. "God will comfort you," he said finally, "as He has comforted the parents of this child. Ynche is a hard world. Most colonies are."

Ard Matthew watched him for a moment. "Yes," he said at last. "I know."

The Star Brother bit his lip. "Matthew," he said, "I have brought something for you. I would not give it to you now while you are recuperating from your wounds, but I don't think it can wait. It is from your chief—Gaed Alfred Snowtyger."

Ard Matthew felt a sudden coldness in his middle, a chill that kept him from speaking. He saw the message cube in the priest's hand and he knew that there was only one message Gaed Alfred would send him.

"It's about Gris Wolfgang," he said in a low voice, "isn't it? He's dying."

As he said this, everything came back to him, his memories of his last assignment on a world called *Treelight*, and all that had happened there. Once more, God had chosen to take a life, had failed to succor the innocent. He must not think this way, he told himself as he turned his face away from the Star Brother—and yet those thoughts would come and he could not help it.

Gris Wolfgang Bloodbear had served with Ard Matthew on Treelight, nearly a year ago subtime. Gris Wolfgang had been stung by an amethyst horror that grew over most of the planet. Those who kept the borders of the colony were often stung. Afterwards, they clung to life—as long as a year or two, sometimes—fighting until they couldn't fight anymore, after which they died.

The priest laid the cube in his hand and he forced his fingers to close around it.

"We've arranged passage for you," Father Epinay said. "Our own ship, the *Baltasar*, will be here in a few days and they'll send a shuttle for you."

Ard Matthew nodded, still not looking at the other man's face. The thing that made this worse, the almost unbearable thing, was that the Star Brothers had compelled Treelight's former owners not only to poison the wildwood and begin terraforming the wilderness, but to develop an antitoxin for the infected. Gris Wolfgang was one of the very few for whom it had not been effective. He had been granted permission to remain on the planet where he had been received by the Brothers of St. Hubert. He was with them now.

Ard Matthew imagined him there, pictured the priory on the edge of the alien forest. The Brothers of St. Hubert had been the ones who kept the wildwood back. They had been the guardians of the fringe and they had been the ones who died, one by one, in that terrible battle. He had seen them, marked with the vine-like tattooing caused by the disease, welcoming their guests from the stars, living out their time in service to the colony. And now Gris Wolfgang was truly one of them, branded by the dying forest and preparing to die himself.

"Would you like—that is—" the young priest faltered. "I am so sorry," he said. "Gaed Alfred told me that your friend was a good Faring Guard, a good man. But he is resigned to God's will and so must you be."

"God's will. Yes." Ard Matthew clutched the cube. "I think," he said, "I would like to be alone." He knew the priest was offering to give what comfort he could. But there was nothing he could do.

"Of course," Father Epinay said now. "You must ask God for the strength to bear this. Ask for resignation to His will."

The Lost Rythan nodded, but when the Star Brother had gone, he did not pray. He only thought about Treelight and about Gris Wolfgang.

And the child who had died in the wilderness of Ynche.

After a time, in his exhaustion, he fell asleep.

Perhaps it was inevitable that he would have vivid dreams, nightmares even. He was back on his father's keep, high in the mountains of Lost Rythar Colony. Without surprise, he saw that his parents were alive, though both had been killed in an avalanche not long after he had disgraced himself and been exiled from the colony. Not only his parents were there, but also his sisters and two younger brothers he barely remembered since both had died in infancy.

It was winter and the evening sky was covered with a heavy bank of cloud, no stars visible as the dusk deepened. Something in the air spoke of coming snow and he and his sisters were trying to get the goats under cover. His mother had already borne in the milk and his father was hauling down wood from the mountain side.

He knew he should be happy to be home again. But he was not. A dread was growing in him, a foreknowledge of disaster such that he hurried the girls, hurried the goats, driving them into the sheds as quickly as he could. Once he looked up at the silhouette of the mountain and saw, not the pointed tops of the sunfirs, but the more chaotic outline of an alien forest, black against the shrouded embers of the final sunset. Something made humps in the snow, moving down the slope.

At the last moment, he snatched up a spear, but he was too late. The unseen thing had seized one of his sisters and was streaking away toward the labyrinth of the serpent spruce. For a moment, he hesitated, remembering that she had already died—she was years dead of the spotted fever—and it would be no use to go after her.

And then it came over him that this was cowardly. He began to run, plunging through the snow, the spear held aloft as he shouted his despair—and woke.

Bis Terence stood beside his bunk.

For long moments Ard Matthew stared up at the other Rythan, trying to remember where he was. And then everything fell back into place in a stark desolation from which there was no refuge. He sat up. "What is it, Bis Terence?"

"I—I came to see how you were. I mean, they told me the message had come in. From Gaed Alfred."

Bis Terence Wolfbane had not been with him on Treelight. They had met later, when Ard Matthew was reassigned. Bis Terence had never seen the disease that was killing Gris Wolfgang.

For long moments, he and his partner stared at each other, fellow colonists, both cast out from their homeworld. He did not know what Bis Terence had done to earn his exile, but it probably involved bloodshed. That's how things were on Lost Rythar—violence and repentance and an invitation to join the Faring Guard.

Suddenly he was gripped with a great pity for this, his fellow exile. Neither of them had ever spoken to the other about their homes and the friends and kindred they had left behind. And yet, here at his bedside, in the person of this fellow Rythan, was everything he had lost—the mountains and the Sunbrothers—Rythar's two suns. The wolf hunt, and the towering trees, the joy of firelight and beer drinking in log-walled keeps while the wolves howled outside.

"I—I'm alright," he told the other man. "Just a nightmare."

Bis Terence nodded. "It was bad out there," he agreed. "But now she is with God—that child."

At these words which he had already heard, Ard Matthew felt a rage begin to rise in him. He clenched his hands, feeling the pain of his injured arm, wanting to throw himself on the other man and throttle him. "With God?" he nearly shouted. "When her body lies in the church, ripped to pieces! When she looked to us to protect her?"

Bis Terence stared at him open-mouthed. "We did all we could, Ard Matthew. It was God's will."

"I do not," Ard Matthew said, spacing his words so that he would not lose control, "want to hear anything more about God's will!"

When the other man had left him, he lay back down and turned his face to the wall.

But by the time the shuttle arrived, he was well enough to board and he had made his peace with both his partner and the Star Brother, if not with God. There was nothing left but to prepare himself for his meeting with Gris Wolfgang.

***

Six days later, subtime, he was on Treelight.

The smell of the air, the soil beneath his boots and the long, dying shadow of the false forest behind him, brought everything back as though he had never been away. He trudged along a path from the rough shuttle field, staring about him to see if anything had changed, until the outbuildings of the priory came in sight.

A fenced pasture held cattle and a few horses. He slipped over the palings, noting that the animals looked healthy, none of them stricken. Ard Matthew remembered how the Brothers of St. Hubert had once been forced to inspect their herds every morning to make sure the forest had not put its mark on them. Thankfully, all that was in the past.

Soon he saw a familiar figure approach. Familiar and yet changed, for this was Wells, a former corporate bodyguard whom he had last seen in secular clothing. Now Wells wore the habit of the priory.

"Ard Matthew Third-Blade," the other said as they met. "Welcome to Treelight. Though, I don't suppose this is a welcome visit for you," he added.

"No," the Lost Rythan replied. "Is he very near the end?"

Wells gave him a quick look of sympathy. "It is good that you did not delay."

At this, Ard Matthew came to a stop, forcing the other man to halt with him. "Is it like it was for the others?" he asked in a low voice. "In the days before the cure, I mean."

"I suppose it is," Wells told him. "There were only three here for whom the antitoxin failed. Gris Wolfgang is the last."

The Faring Guard started moving again, his long legs eating up the remainder of the distance between the fenced area and the main house. "What about that other fellow," he called over his shoulder as Wells caught up. "That nobleman—*Master* Frayle?"

Frayle had been another of the infected, a villain who had changed sides at the last moment to save the life of Marja Sienko, the agent Pesc corporation had sent down and then double-crossed.

"Master Frayle recovered. He and Dr. Sienko were married as soon as it was certain that he would live."

Ard Matthew looked away. "May God bless their union," he said sourly. But that, too, was part of a story already told. The company representative who had fallen in love with a colonist. They deserved each other. He shook his head, wondering at his bitterness. Shouldn't he be glad that *someone* at least had a chance at happiness?

The priory itself was as he remembered it. They entered a long chamber used as the refectory with a doorway at one end leading to the chapel. On one side, another door led to the cells. Marshal Pwyll met the visitor there.

The Lost Rythan recognized him at once, a middle aged man, his face prematurely lined with the cares of his office. The marshal was one of those cured by the serum. The marks of the wildwood toxin had faded to no more than a few faint, whitish lines on his arms and hands.

"I will take you to Gris Wolfgang when you are ready," he said. "But perhaps you would like to visit the chapel first?"

Ard Matthew shook his head. "I am ready now," he said. The last thing he wanted was to drag God into this affair.

Marshal Pwyll gave him an odd look but he said nothing more except, "This way."

Dumbly, the Lost Rythan followed him into the corridor of the cells. Behind them, the former bodyguard was no more than a grey-clad, yet somehow comforting shadow, the coarse cloth of his habit swishing softly as he paced. Wells had been a corporate slave, freed as part of the Star Brothers' treaty with Pesc. No doubt he was happier here at the priory than he would have been trying to build himself a life out among the settled worlds.

A faint odor of sickness met them even before they entered the place where his friend lay. A curtain was drawn aside and without giving himself time to think, he stepped inside.

Ard Matthew didn't know what he had expected—a fallen warrior? The face of a hero about to enter eternity? A Faring Guard at the terminus of his service to God and his own honor? But all he saw was a young man dying—a young man who had been his friend.

"Gris Wolfgang," the Marshall said gently. "Ard Matthew Third-Blade has come."

The man on the pallet moved a little, and as he did so, the purple vine markings etched onto every visible inch of his skin, seemed to writhe like specters of the dead forest. His eyes, opening in that ravaged face, glittered with fever. Some of his hair had fallen away leaving patches of mangy looking scrub. The marks showed through on his scalp.

"Ard Matthew." The sick man's voice was threadlike, hoarse. "I was afraid—you would not come—in time."

The Faring Guard hurried forward, to kneel beside the pallet, though the smell of Gris Wolfgang's dying hung over them both. "Yes, I've come," he muttered. "I'm here. I hope—that is, you haven't been alone all this time, have you?"

"The brothers have been very good—"

"Your superior, Gaed Alfred was down a month ago," the Marshall told him. "But he is away now on an assignment."

Ard Matthew could not take his eyes from Gris Wolfgang's clawlike hand, marveling at the ridges the toxins had made. It scarcely seemed real to him that *this*—this horror had been slowly and remorselessly coming about as the disease advanced out of control. He and the others had been getting on with their lives while Gris Wolfgang Bloodbear had been left alone in this wretched place, to watch himself die.

He saw the other man struggling to smile. "It is well with me, Ard Matthew, now that you are here. You bring—you bring our homeland—with you. The spirit—of our people."

At these words, Ard Matthew tried to see his friend for one moment as he had been before the disease—another tall warrior such as himself, another penitent, another exile cut off from the snowfields and the mountains of Lost Rythar. They had fought together, drunk beer together, seen the longing in each other's eyes for the home they had lost. He had never asked why Gris Wolfgang had joined the Faring Guard.

Then the vision was gone and only the sick man lay before him. Ard Matthew didn't feel much like the bearer of his people's heritage. He felt like a burned out husk of a man who had seen too much evil and too little good.

But those eyes were still seeking his—looking *into* him with the stark and inescapable command of a soul on the brink of departure. And meeting that gaze, he forgot the other people in the room. "God help me," he said in a low voice. "Gris Wolfgang, I can bring you nothing. Only that I am here."

Still, those eyes searched his. "Where two of us are—" the other man murmured. "Lost Rythar is *here*." They were speaking Rythan and the others in the room did not understand them.

"We will leave you friends together for a time," the marshal said abruptly. "You have only to call and the infirmarian will come at once."

Ard Matthew looked up. "Yes, yes, of course. Thank you," he said, knowing that he spoke at random but unable to put his thoughts in order.

He turned back to the other man. Gris Wolfgang's gaze had begun to wander as though already he saw those far off mountain slopes, the sunfirs and the serpent spruce coiling along the ground. Perhaps he heard the howling of the wolves and saw the doubled shadows of Rythar's suns, shadow on snow.

"You comfort me," Ard Matthew said humbly, watching him. "I who should be bringing solace to you."

"You do bring solace."

They were silent then, while memories of all they had lost hung between them—the familiar faces of fathers and mothers and all their kindred fighting to live on a world not meant for humankind. But then they were not quite human any more. Not like these others. They had mutated somewhat away from the original stock.

Perhaps an hour went by during which the brother infirmarian came twice to check on his patient. The second time, he leaned over his Gris Wolfgang, taking one wrist—the other one, for Ard Matthew would not release his friend's hand—and checked the pulse.

"Is—is he in pain?" Ard Matthew asked softly.

"Oh no. That stage is all past. A priest will be coming soon—he's already had the Last Sacrament, but that was yesterday. You were almost too late, you know." The brother of St. Hubert gave him a kindly smile. "He has lived beyond the others, beyond what is usual in a case like this. He was waiting for you."

Ard Matthew winced but said nothing.

"It is a shame," the infirmarian added, rising to his feet. "We had so hoped for his recovery. So many did respond to the antitoxin. Almost all, in fact."

Ard Matthew barely noticed when the brother left him alone with the dying man. But the disturbance had roused Gris Wolfgang. He moved his head slightly, looking upward with his eyes unfixed. "Ard Matthew?"

"Still here. Feel my hand?"

The dying man's fingers clenched weakly. "Yes." Then, "Do you remember fighting the bandits here on Treelight?" Gris Wolfgang whispered suddenly. "Crossing the colony and—and seeing it all. Everything so strange—"

"The gypsies," Ard Matthew said. "And the druids. Yes. I remember."

"And the bishop. He came to see me here. He comes whenever he can." A pause. "He reminded me of—my courage."

A nod. Ard Matthew recalled their last journey across Treelight, guarding the young Star Brother who had been sent to check on Pesc's dealings with the colony. Gris Wolfgang had been betrayed and stung by one of the rootlets carried by a druid. The signs had soon manifested themselves.

His friend had been afraid, Ard Matthew remembered suddenly. They had already seen what the venom did to the Brothers of St. Hubert. How it marked them and slowly brought them down—to *this*. He ground his teeth. It was not right for a man to die this way. A Lost Rythan should fall in clean battle.

The hand in his begin to tremble, to clench a little and unclench. "Has my mother come?" The words were barely audible.

Did he call for his own mother—or the Mother of God? Perhaps both. Likely they were together by now, two ladies watching over their child. The words of the prayer drifted through his mind—*Salve Regina, mater misericordiae*—

He watched his friend's face. The expression was hard to read beneath the scrolls of tattooing left by the poison. Gris Wolfgang's eyes were immensely dilated, their grey nothing but a rim, the whites occluded by yet more lines of purple. The damned stuff was everywhere!

He leaned over further, hoping the other could still see him. But Gris Wolfgang was beyond seeing anything in this life. He made a low sound, almost a whimper, his brow furrowing like that of a troubled child. "Storm coming," he murmured. "Over the mountain—I hear wolves. Where is—my spear—?"

His hand tried to wriggle free of Ard Matthew's and he struggled as though to rise. "Must fetch—weapons." Another brief struggle, after which he lay back, panting. "Can't you hear them? The wolves—"

"I'm here, Gris Wolfgang. We'll fight them together."

"Yes—you are—so good. Ard Matthew—I am sorry for all—I have killed—in battle. I will meet them now."

"You will meet God." He realized he said it automatically because that was what a Lost Rythan must say. The thought did not bring him much comfort.

The other man stiffened, trembling slightly, staring at things Ard Matthew could not see. "The wolves—on the mountain—but I am not—afraid!"

The hand went limp within his grasp. Behind him, the priest was just coming in the door.

***

Everything became a blur after that. Someone guided him from the room and he was given a place in the guest house where he collapsed on a bench, head in hands. His wounds were troubling him; they were not all the way healed. Sometime later, Wells was beside him. The other man did not offer the usual platitudes and for this he was grateful.

Somehow he got through the next few days, visiting the chapel when it was his duty to do so and meeting Frayle and Marja, who had come for the funeral. The landowner was still handsome, his keen eyes missing very little, but he was changed. The arrogance Ard Matthew remembered with distaste was muted, if not gone, and he turned to his wife sometimes for guidance.

As for Marja, she, too, seemed a different person, radiantly happy and, apparently, soon to be a mother.

But these things remained on the fringes of his awareness. His clearest moments were when Wells took him walking between the newly planted fields. Ard Matthew told him about the child on Ynche. On one side of them, the forest had become a withered ghost of itself and its non-arboreal basis was clearly visible. It was an alien thing, struck now and poisoned.

Wells did not try to comfort him. He only listened.

Once Ard Matthew looked over and really saw the other man, lean-faced, his formerly long hair cut off. He held himself differently now than he had when he was a slave, but even then, the Lost Rythan was sure, this new man had lain just below the surface. "You're staying with the brothers?" he asked suddenly. "I mean as—as one of them?"

"Yes."

"And what about—" He hesitated, remembering that Wells had been doubly a slave—held by law as well as by certain compulsions that impaired his free will. "Maybe it's not my place to ask," he floundered, wondering if this conditioning had been done away with.

Wells met his look with a kindly smile. "My adjustments? I can never be entirely free of it," he said. "It goes too deep. You must remember I have been a corporate slave since I was a child."

"So—Pesc?"

"I will always wish my former owners well. I have no choice." The other man grew more serious. "I think that I would want the best for them even if I were truly free. I cannot help but pity those who must stoop to—the things they did."

Ard Matthew was silent for a time, thinking of how Wells had had to be restrained at the last, his training warring with his conscience, unseating his reason.

"Wells, I cannot stay in the Faring Guard."

The other looked at him. "No," he agreed. "Perhaps not."

Ard Matthew stared back at the forest. It reminded him of a dead behemoth—limbs and tendrils sprawling on the freshly greening ground.

"You will not be alone, Ard Matthew," Wells said hesitantly. "Wherever you go, my prayers will go with you. You will be healed one day."

But Ard Matthew did not believe there would be any healing for himself—no more than there had been for Gris Wolfgang.

CHAPTER TWO

He chose a vile place to match his mood. It was one more outpost for the overflow of the human race, one more marginal world, haphazardly colonized by outcasts, fallen back to an almost pre-technical level, and mostly forgotten by everyone else. He had funds of his own, enough to travel and to live on for a while, credited to his account among the stars. And so he had traveled the net to this world and to this settlement and to this inn.

Warmish drafts leaked between unchinked boards as the evening rain dripped dismally from the eaves. But it would do—all of it would do. His lips twitched into a bitter smile as he waited for what he knew was coming, watching the gang move in on him, catching sight of the knives in their hands, marveling that they didn't have guns as well. But such things were hard to come by here in this place. He watched the other patrons of the dive—for it could hardly be called anything else—slipping away one by one. They also knew what was coming—or at least they thought they did.

An empty mug stood before him on the table and it had not been his first. He had drunk enough that he no longer minded that the beer was bad. Or that the people were rogues and cowards and that he was light years away from the honor he had lost.

Someone brushed against the hanging lamp making shadows dance and swing about like tormented souls. The faces of his would-be killers flickered in and out of the gloom; too common to belong in hell, they would make mediocre demons at best. Eyes glittered as he watched them watching him.

He had been warned, grudgingly, by the innkeeper. He knew he was a foreigner and that things happened sometimes to foreigners. To tall foreigners who looked as though they were worth challenging. Who looked as though they might have something to rob.

He had deliberately let things build until they were as they were. At precisely the right moment, he heaved the table onto the two foremost of his would-be attackers. There was cursing in the language of the colony and he smiled a new and savage smile. This was what he had been waiting for—and he rejoiced in it.

As the rest of the gang closed in, Ard Matthew snatched up the nearest figure, feeling a blade rake his arm slicing across the scars from his battle with the monster in the forest of Ynche. He threw the man back onto his fellows. More confusion followed, more cursing.

Two of them were trying to pull him down while a third reached upward to slice his throat. But the Lost Rythan did not go down and the knife did no more than tangle itself in the front of his jacket. He felt the battle madness rising in him and was darkly glad when bones broke in his grip as he snatched up yet another man and flung him aside. Then, kicking away the benches he leaped in among the others, scarcely feeling his wounds as he tore the life from his enemies. Someone howled a Lost Rythan battle song and it was himself.

When reason finally came back to him, he was bleeding from a dozen shallow cuts, his clothing shredded. There were bodies on the floor and much of the furniture lay in pieces.

There were also uniformed figures running in the door. A stun blast hit him and his legs gave way. He groped for these new attackers, still trying to fight as they took his arms and dragged him along. Finally, a blow landed on his skull and the room exploded into light that narrowed and became darkness.

***

Ard Matthew woke sprawled on a filthy bunk. His legs extended over one end and his right arm hung nearly to the floor. His head ached and so did most of the rest of him.

"Quite a night, fella," someone said in Basic. "I was wondering when you'd come to."

With a groan, he rolled over. A uniformed native watched him through a barred wall. At least he thought the man had a uniform, though the jacket was unbuttoned and his wrinkled leggings bagged above filthy boots. He looked as though he had forgotten to shave for some days.

"Coupla those guys won't be botherin' anyone again." The cop spoke around a toothpick and there was a cup of some steaming beverage in his hand. "You won't get off with less than a flogging for this, you know."

"It was self-defense." The words came out in a hoarse croak as he sat up and waited for a bout of dizziness to pass. His throat felt as though he had swallowed sand and now that he was upright, his stomach heaved ominously. When he shifted his position, he seemed to see two of the man.

"Course it was self-defense," the other agreed with a grin. "That's why you prob'ly won't hang. Prob'ly."

There was no answer to this. Ard Matthew had deliberately travelled beyond Net Central jurisdiction, choosing Wolf-Slammer colony for its colorful name. Only later had he learned that the whole colony was a hub for interstellar smuggling—and worse things—and only later had decided that he didn't really care.

He sighed. The truth was he hadn't done so badly since he'd come here, working for different offworld visitors, going with them into the wilderness to bring back boar heads—if that's what they were. Wolf-Slammer's boars were at least as big as the bison he had seen on other worlds and many a prosperous racketeer now had one mounted on his living room wall thanks to Ard Matthew's skills as a hunter. They were a status symbol.

But he was between jobs at the moment and that was always bad. There was nothing to do but drink the colony's abominable beer and try not to dream too much at night.

People left him alone when he drank. Even here where no one had ever heard of a Lost Rythan, his size should have been enough to keep troublemakers at bay. But not last night. He had been so eager for a fight that he must have broadcast his challenge, the heat of his desire for violence fairly coming off his skin in waves.

The cop walked away and Ard Matthew settled back onto the cot. He had had his fight and whatever happened would happen. No sense worrying about it now. Anyway, there was enough to occupy him at the moment—his aching head, his untended wounds, and the thought of the dead he'd left on the floor of the tavern. He always regretted the dead—afterwards. And there was a time when he would have prayed for them. But not now. Not since Gris Wolfgang.

As he shifted about on the soiled covering, the tatters of his shirt pulled open a few of his cuts and he bit back a curse. Definitely, the future would have to take care of itself. But of course it wasn't enough to dismiss the future. He still had the past to deal with—and *that* would not be banished.

When he had told Gaed Alfred he was leaving the Faring Guard, Ard Matthew had been expecting fireworks. At the very least his superior should have reminded him that his service to the Star Brothers was the only way to make reparation for his crime and—at some future time—to be re-admitted to his home colony. Knowing Gaed Alfred, he had been expecting something between a tongue lashing and a contest of physical strength.

It hadn't played out that way. The older man had looked at him thoughtfully for some moments before nodding as though he had been expecting something like this. And that knowledge had hurt. It was as though his superior had already dismissed him from the Faring Guard and ceased to think of him as one who could be saved.

"Where would you like to go?" Gaed Alfred had asked finally, and when Ard Matthew had only shrugged, all he said was, "I will pray for you."

The chief was a simple man—a man of unquestioning faith, like Wells back on Treelight. He really would pray for Ard Matthew and he would expect God to hear him. He would have been praying for

Gris Wolfgang as well, and undoubtedly still did now that the man was in purgatory.

Ard Matthew was not as simple as Gaed Alfred. He had originally been exiled for a killing and in this new trouble, he did not need a god to compound his guilt. He accepted his exile, but as far as his honor was concerned, that intangible thing must look out for itself.

He was still mulling over these matters when they came for him perhaps an hour later. Two policemen, their coats buttoned, though their chins remained unshaven, brought him out to stand before a judge who did not look pleased to see him.

The first thing he noticed was that the judge's bald head resembled a pink hill rising above a grizzled forest. The fellow's eyes were bloodshot as he regarded the prisoner and he paused from time to time to blow his nose. "Another damn foreigner," he growled, withdrawing a grubby handkerchief. "Did you know two of those men were dead when we picked them up? And another one's not going to make it. Got anything to say about that?"

Ard Matthew winced. What could he say? He had done what he had done and now he must stand by it.

"We got people here who bring in money for the colony," the judge went on, "and they need bully boys like you to keep them alive out in the wild. That means we need you. But there are limits." He squinted down at a paper on his desk. "You used your bare hands, it says here, against guys with knives. Broken neck, skull fractures—used a bench for that, I guess—"

Ard Matthew could not help feeling a little shame as anyone would in the aftermath of the battle madness. Any Lost Rythan, at least. It was a known weakness of their people, to go berserk like that, but it had been years since he had given way so completely.

"Take him to the yard and flog him."

The prisoner gave a start and then he straightened himself. After all, the guard had already warned him this would happen—if not something worse. He was surprisingly grateful not to hang, considering that his life had no value that he could see. And yet, he was still Rythan enough to suffer hope. Hope for a future he could not fathom and did not even want.

Because of this, he did not resist as they took him out and tied him to a post. But as the executioner emerged from the doorway, whip in hand, Ard Matthew noticed another man with him. This one seemed to be an offworlder with something in his face that bespoke both intelligence and maybe even culture. Along with this, the stranger also had the bearing of an experienced fighter. He stationed himself by the doorway, obviously prepared to watch the proceedings. Maybe he was a colony official sent to make sure the job was done right?

And it *was* done right. The flogging was pretty bad, though it was no worse than the prisoner had expected. They needed him alive—the judge had said so—and he clung to this half promise as the blows fell on his tormented flesh and he fought not to cry out. When it was over and he was released from the shackles, he even managed to stay on his feet. Barely. The world seemed to narrow down to a blazing pain and the need to put one foot before the other, to fight off the darkness that threatened to pull him down. He had forgotten why it was so important not to fall until he saw the stranger move forward and take his arm.

"Come on, buddy," the man said. "Let's get out of here."

Ard Matthew tried to shake himself free, but it was too much effort. He stumbled and would have fallen if the other had not held him up. "Where—?" he muttered.

"To the hotel. You don't want to stay in that jail. It gets rowdy at night."

"Who—?"

"Your new boss, I hope. I'm called Saler Mong."

It his current state, this was too much to sort out. So he let himself be guided to a ground car where he sprawled in the back seat. Mong set the controls and they moved through the crowded streets of Wolf-Slammer port. Later, someone had to help Mong get the Lost Rythan into the lobby where he had an impression of shabby grandeur, torn upholstery and a filthy carpet.

Later still, he lay in one of the ground floor rooms while a doctor worked over him, applying antiseptic and adding synthoskin where needed. Mong perched on the window seat, watching.

"I suppose you'll be wanting pain medication," he said presently.

Ard Matthew didn't answer.

The other man leaned forward. "I know how you feel, man, and I'm not trying to make you suffer. You'll get something in a few minutes, but I want to talk to you while your head is still clear."

The Lost Rythan managed a nod. He was in no position to argue.

"I've heard of you from some of the other guides, and what I hear is good. Also, I'm told you can fly shuttles and air transport."

"I can do that."

"I've been looking for a good pilot who can double as a bodyguard. Not for here—this is just somewhere I come sometimes. I've got an outfit on Windy-Go, the next world out and there's a place for you if you want it. Interested?"

Ard Matthew thought about this, insofar as he could concentrate. He knew nothing about his benefactor, but it was safe to assume that Mong must operate outside the law. Ard Matthew was technically an outlaw himself so, as long as he wasn't asked to kill anyone—at least not without a fair fight—he shouldn't mind. However, he waited to hear what else Mong would say before he committed himself.

The other probably saw these thoughts in his face. "We'll get you patched up no matter what you decide." A chuckle. "I don't shed any tears over dead robbers and neither does anyone else. Just so you know."

At this, the Lost Rythan managed a grim smile. "Alright," he said. "Count me in."

A week later, he was on Windy-Go.

As it turned out, Saler Mong really was a trader. Some of his clients were smugglers, of course, though others were corporations.

Ard Matthew's main duties were ferrying passengers to and from the space station and out to the lodges. Windy-Go was another wild place a little more advanced than Wolf Slammer, never officially colonized and legally under no one's jurisdiction but its own. The corporations that made use of it maintained a certain order—to their advantage, of course, but it was better than nothing.

He liked the climate better than that of Wolf-Slammer's settled area. Windy-Go's forests might almost have grown on Lost Rythar. The skies were of a deep, cerulean blue, the ruddy sun neither as large nor as intense as it had been on the inner world. There were no moons, which seemed odd to him, and the sun was not the right shade, but otherwise the place was almost homelike.

There was only one town in the port zone, and that was the port itself—Windy-Go Port. Most of Mong's clients had lodges out in the timberland and the trader and others often had business with them. The winds could be a little tricky but he didn't really think the name of Windy-Go was deserved.

When he wasn't flying, he waited about at one of the lodges, went hiking and even camped out in the woods. Sometimes he borrowed a gun to hunt antelope. Down time at the port was not as pleasant, but then he had hardly expected it to be. He took a flat in the town, did a little exploring and some reading. Luckily, most of his time was spent either flying or waiting at the lodges.

He had recently returned to his flat after a return trip from one of the finer homes out in the wilderness and knew he must wait a day or so for his next assignment. He was just taking his dinner out of the unit and had already poured a beer—the beers of Windy-Go were almost palatable even by Lost Rythan standards—when he heard the chime. He called out an activation and Saler Mong's face looked in at him from the viewer.

"Admit." A few moments later, the trader was at the door.

"I see you got those pirates delivered," Mong said as he accepted a beer. He chuckled. "They really were, you know. Pirates."

"I didn't think they were executives." He had, since his departure from the Faring Guard, discovered within himself a dry sense of humor. Humor of any sort was an oddity in a Lost Rythan and he took this as one more sign that he was becoming one with the people of the stars—the lost and the dishonorable, as he had always heard. Well so be it.

"You're free for the moment?" his boss said.

A nod.

"There's a starship coming in from Archangel. Kessler Corp. They're got their own shuttle but they need you to fly some people out to their lodge."

Ard Matthew gave him a sidewise look. He hadn't heard of Kessler before.

As usual, the broker's face remained blandly noncommittal and the Lost Rythan knew better than to ask any questions. But though Mong's features revealed nothing, there were signs to be read. Maybe it was the way he gripped the mug, or an involuntary twitch of one hand as he lifted it to his lips. Ard Matthew suspected this was not an ordinary assignment.

He waited.

"Big shots," Mong said at last. "Not crooks. Or no more so than most executives." He drank and did not look at his host. "You know the type."

Ard Matthew nodded. He knew.

But still the other man remained ill at east as he gave directions for pickup. Finally, with a shrug, he rose and took his departure.

Ard Matthew was frowning thoughtfully as he finished his meal and opened another beer. Had he been out on the slopes of Lost Rythar's mountains—or anywhere except his flat in the town—he would have said that something was tracking him. It felt like that, his sixth sense. It raised the hairs on the back of his neck.

He took his dishes to the disposal, thinking of his father's keep. Of all the familiar things he had once known, both dangerous and comforting. And he wondered what stalked him now.

Suddenly, shivering in his loneliness, he finished his beer in one gulp and let himself out onto the walkway. Above him, the evening sky was an uncertain blur. Though the settlement was not large, there were lights enough to dim most of the stars. Only a few of the brightest were visible here at the port—not enough even to make a constellation. Absently, he speculated—as he always did when he visited other worlds—in which quadrant of the sky he might find the double star of Lost Rythar. Or if it would even be visible.

But this served only to deepen his depression. He shook himself and turned instead, to scowl at the groundcars and the few people out walking. Lost Rythar might as well lie in a different galaxy for all the good it would do him. He was doubly exiled now and besides, he had been away long enough that most of his kindred would have ceased to think of him. How many years had it been, subtime? At least ten. It might all have been a dream, that other life.

With an angry shrug, he brought himself back to the present. Mong had told him once that he should find a woman, recommending the idea as though proposing a tonic. "The local girls are willing enough," the trader had added, looking him up and down with a sly smile. "Big guy like you—next to the rest of us, you're practically a god to them."

Ard Matthew had said nothing at the time, but the look on his face must have warned the other that he had gone too far. Strangely, it was not the idea that he should entangle himself with one of the sloe-eyed beauties of the port that sickened him—it was the word Mong had chosen to describe him. A *god.* Had he fallen so low as that? Would he be sliding into idolatry next? Making of himself the center and the heart of his miserable existence?

His scowl deepened as he strode away from the housing block, head down, hands in his pockets. Around him, the shuttle port was no different from those of other worlds, a bit less refined than some, but the ambience was the same. It had another name, he recalled, besides Windy-Go Port. He seldom heard it used—Keme Wapun Port. It was named after a prospector who had died here some two centuries before. The same prospector had named the planet Windy-Go. A whole planet. Even now, after all this time, almost none of it had been explored. It was just a place—

He looked up from time to time as a few Panhandlers accosted him—burned out travelers whose journeys had ended here. They were men—and women—long exiled from their own home colonies and waiting only to die. Would he find himself among them one day here or on some other dead end world? Or would he perish in a brawl—or even at the end of a rope? This no longer seemed impossible.

A pimp approached him, two girls leaning against a building as they waited for a deal to be struck. The man looked like an addict and, disdainfully, the Lost Rythan brushed him off. At least he hadn't fallen *that* far. But would he? One day?

The crowd thickened as he approached the commercial district. Bars and cafes—he had patronized some of them—crowded together in tawdry splendor. The people he passed were of all races, from all colonies, dressed in every conceivable style—though the climate of the place, by no means tropical, placed some limits on the amount of flesh they could leave uncovered. As a Lost Rythan, he towered over most of them.

He had not gone far into the lighted center of the town when he ran into someone he knew. Rolf bor Stein, another pilot he sometimes saw at one or other of the lodges, was nearly as tall as a Lost Rythan. Nearly. Though he was a native of Sachsen, bor Stein's mother had come from Miller's world, another colony of giants.

They greeted one another and stood together for a moment as waves of smaller folk broke apart and flowed around them. "Shin's?" bor Stein said finally, gesturing toward a fortress-like structure set incongruously between two dazzling establishments, one of which sported red lights in the windows.

With a shrug, Ard Matthew followed him into the central building. They both had to duck to get through the doorway, but once inside, there was space enough. The walls were of faced stone and the floor was the same. Unfinished rafters crossed the ceiling and the rest of the décor reflected the rugged theme. It was curiously homelike to a Lost Rythan. Maybe bor Stein felt the same way.

Actually, Shin's was popular among all the pilots and other servants of the corporations. It was a place where a man's past was never mentioned, where camaraderie was the equivalent of friendship and where there was no risk of undue familiarity. Better still, it was somewhere their employers never came.

Before long, Ard Matthew found himself sharing a table with bor Stein and two other pilots while the talk ranged from local flying hazards—Windy-Go's unpredictable turbulences—to the hunt for a lost expedition to the so-called ruins.

"You think they're still alive?" the man on Ard Matthew's right asked bor Stein. "The Becker party?"

Bor Stein took a gulp of his beer and set it carefully back on the table. "Who knows? You know how it is out there. Get away from the lodges and you're on your own. I'm surprised anyone cared enough to get up an expedition in the first place."

"That's true," the other man agreed and someone else said, "You crash too far out there, and even if you're not killed outright if your locator goes, that's it."

"Assuming they crash landed," bor Stein said. He looked at Ard Matthew. "What do you think?" he asked. "I know you spend time in the woods. Would they stand a chance out there?"

The Lost Rythan shrugged. "I don't go far from the lodges. Maybe a day's hike, camp overnight, and then return. Who can say?" But he was thinking of the people of the lodges, city folk mostly, and he doubted any of them would survive long in the wilderness.

"No contact with the party," the fourth member of the group, an asteroider named Barzek, said. He reached for the pitcher and poured himself some more beer. "What else could it be but a crash?"

Ard Matthew nodded. A flyer should have been able to signal its position, he thought. Unless it was too badly damaged, of course, which would mean probably no survivors.

"It is hard to imagine," Barzek said, glancing at the Rythan, "going by yourself so far from civilization. A world like this—never really settled. We don't even know what all's out there."

"Hard to imagine for *you*," bor Stein told him with a grin. Barzek had come from a place where people crowded within the rock, boring out their planetoid's guts as they sifted their findings for platinum ore. You were never alone in a mining colony.

Ard Matthew turned to Barzek. "I hunt," he said. "Antelope."

The other stared at him. "You *hunt*?"

"He kills them and cooks them," bor Stein explained to the other man. "We used to do it back home. Hunt, I mean." He turned to the Rythan. "You do eat them, I suppose?"

"Yes, of course. And sometimes I bring in meat for the lodges." How could he tell them of the joy of stalking prey, stationing himself to wait for the elusive creatures. He remembered the thrill of slipping among the half familiar conifers of Windy-Go, knowing—and he *did* know sometimes—that he, too, was being stalked. He had never seen those lurkers, whatever they were—only sensed their presence. The forest floor absorbed most prints, leaving him little but a broken twig or two to show that anything had passed that way.

Barzek's wondering gaze did not leave his face. And then the other man, realizing that he had been impolite, turned back to his beer. "I wonder if Becker and his lot know how to hunt," he muttered.

Ard Matthew glanced over at bor Stein and their eyes met. The Lost Rythan had never spent much time on Sachsen and that, generally in Bloomhadn, the main city. Were there places on that world where a man might take up a bow or a spear and trust his life to his own strength and skill? Did they use guns? Were there wolves on Sachsen? He was too shy to ask.

When Bor Stein went to fetch another pitcher, the other two began talking about cities on other worlds, comparing them with the wretched port of Windy-Go. They spoke of slideways and gravity free ballrooms where couples danced literally on air. Of women and of satellites where they could enjoy days of drug-induced dreamtime in freefall.

Suddenly Ard Matthew got up and pushed his chair back. With a nod to bor Stein, just coming back with more beer, he left the table and made for the entrance. The others were used to the Lost Rythan's abrupt departures and none of them tried to hold him back.

Once more in the street, where music played and the crowd grew ever denser, he stared from side to side as though he were an antelope himself—or a wolf trapped and waiting for the final spear thrust. Then he turned and pushed through the throng until the brightness dwindled behind him and he came to a district of warehouses and small factories. Soon he reached the rustic fringes of the port where the sidewalks were of wood, the street packed earth and gravel and streetlights few and far between. He passed small houses, cabins mostly, and presently a larger structure, roughhewn and surmounted by a cross.

As he passed, "You are the first Lost Rythan I've seen in this place," a voice exclaimed, and he froze, looking back toward the church.

A cloaked figure moved away from the doorway and he did not need to see the emblem on the man's habit to know that this was a Star Brother. He hadn't known they had a mission on this godforsaken world and the knowledge that they must, filled him with something like fear, quickly hidden.

For long moments, the two looked at one another. Ard Matthew could not see the priest very well in the pallid light, though he did note that the man held a small book in one hand—breviary, most likely.

“Long way from home,” the Star Brother said at last. “Both of us.”

“Yes. Father.”

“Would you like to visit the chapel?” The priest laid one hand on the door as though to open it.

Ard Matthew thought of what was inside. *Who* was inside. The God who had not saved a child from being torn apart by an alien beast. The God who had condemned Gris Wolfgang to a lingering and terrible death. The God of sorrow and pain and bitter disappointment. Of loneliness and death.

“No,” he said and would have turned away.

“Wait,” the priest said, taking his hand from the door. “You needn’t go in.” He pointed toward one of the cabins. “Perhaps you would like to have a beer with me. I know that’s what you Lost Rythans drink and so do I. You might stop a while before you go on to—wherever it is you are going.”

Ard Matthew hesitated. He wasn’t going anywhere. Just away. But away from what, he could not have said. Maybe he was only fleeing from himself.

“Your people don’t often travel alone,” the priest said. “It seems providential meeting you here.”

Ard Matthew stared at him. “Providential,” he repeated, tasting the word. He stared at the church building, at the outline of the cross, stark against the night sky. No moon would ever ride that firmament, only the wheeling constellations, plainly visible now that he had left the lighted areas. Constellations whose names he did not know.

He tore his gaze from the cross and looked once more at the shadowy figure of the Star Brother. It seemed as though a great gulf separated him from this man of faith. As though the church and the Divine Prisoner within—for he knew He would be there—were no more than dreams forever lost to him. He turned on his heel and strode away.

The Star Brother did not try to call him back. Soon even the church disappeared from sight as the road curved and descended into a small hollow. There were no more lights—only the faint glimmer of the stars. He couldn't think of any place this lane might go since all distance travel was by flyer. Maybe it didn't go anywhere at all. The spindly trees crowded in on both sides of him so that he walked through a pool of blackness. Above, the sky became a river of luminescence, blue and silver, brushed to the east by a nebula.

Suddenly, he wanted to howl like the highwolves of Rythar, to surrender once and for all his humanity and the terrible responsibilities that went with it. Instead, he just went on walking, hands in his pockets, startling an occasional scuttling thing, hearing the odd calls of the owls and the croak of something he could not identify . He walked until nearly dawn, but the deteriorating road only curved about, making loops that met and tangled themselves into nothing.

In the chill of the early morning, he returned to the port. A passing floater gave him a lift and soon he was back at the flat. He barely remembered throwing off his clothes before sleep dragged him down into a half world of nightmare visions where alien beasts preyed on the innocent while a great, bearded God stared down somberly at the disorder of His creation and finally turned away with a shrug.

By the time he had fought free of his dreams and come to bleary consciousness, it was early afternoon. He must get ready to meet his passengers.

He stumbled into the main room, wondering if he had time for coffee—or what passed for it here. Probably not. But he would shower and shave. He went over his instructions as he scraped away at his whiskers. Most men used dep cream, but none of the Faring Guards did. Dissolving a beard with chemicals was too unsettling to a Lost Rythan—a form of mutilation. He made a wry face, thinking of this. But he was still a primitive at heart, he decided, and he would keep his razor.

Two ladies, Mong had told him. Both from Kessler Corp, they would be waiting at the shuttleport hotel. They should, according to his boss, have just arrived from offplanet; he might expect them to be a bit under the weather after their trip. They would have come down from the station in a company shuttle but Ard Matthew was to fly them out to the Kessler Lodge using one of the Saler Mong fliers.

He did not see anything odd in this at the time. In fact, it all seemed pretty straightforward. He checked the weather forecast—wind gusts for the rest of the afternoon and evening, but expected to let up in the morning. So he would arrange to pick them up early tomorrow. Meanwhile, he had to make contact, introduce himself as Mong's representative and make sure they were satisfied. Or something like that.

He pushed back his shoulder length hair and studied himself in the mirror. He looked respectable enough, he decided, though there were dark circles under his eyes. He might be a bit haggard looking, but he was clean and neat and that would have to do. He took a robocab to the shuttleport and found his way into the hotel where he called the number Mong had given him. A very crisp female voice answered.

"Star Trail here."

He hesitated, a little taken aback. Then, "From Kessler?" he asked doubtfully.

"Yes. Shami Star Trail, private secretary to Dr. Kessler. Who is this?"

He identified himself.

"So you are not Saler Mong?" she asked. It seemed to matter to her that he was not, though he couldn't imagine why.

He explained that he did most of the local flying for the company.

The secretary hesitated and then, "You'd better come into the dining room," she told him. "We are on the west side. Tell the robowaiter the bor Rijn party."

He acknowledged this and crossed the foyer. He had picked up some of Mong's clients here before and knew the layout of the hotel. The reception area, rather than providing a general lounge, was lined on two sides with a series of alcoves in which guests could meet and confer. A few of these were occupied by half seen figures, hunched together and talking in low voices, but most were empty.

As he neared the entrance to the dining room, however, someone moved slightly in what he had thought was an empty recess. He caught a glimpse of a rather brutal looking face, broad with high cheekbones and dark eyes, watching him as he passed. It was no more than an impression, the figure quickly withdrawn into shadow, but once more the hairs prickled on the back of his neck. Had the man been waiting for him? Of course it might have been a Kessler employee. Corporations were like that—paranoid.

Ard Matthew did not pause, though he seemed to feel eyes fixed on him as he passed. Once in the dining room, he asked the robowaiter to direct him to the bor Rijn table. No one followed him through the entrance, though he glanced back once at the doorway as he walked behind the waiter.

The shuttle hotel made no pretensions to elegance, being only a stopping off place for travelers with business at the colony. There were better inns for more wealthy vacationers. He considered this as he studied the two women at the table, wondering what their business on Windy-Go might be.

One of them, he noted, was middle aged with a grim, competent face, wide-cheeked and dark. She wore her black hair in two thick braids, hanging down over her shoulders on either side. They were tied with what looked like leather, each band sporting a gleaming, silver disk. At first sight, this did not strike him as unusual since women often wore their hair this way on Lost Rythar. But of course, she would stand out in a place like this. Her bright jet eyes seemed to challenge him as perhaps they challenged everyone.

He guessed she was the one he had spoken to earlier. The one with the funny name. The other was much younger, frail and blonde, with eyes as grey as those of a Lost Rythan. She had an air of vulnerability, a look of what might have been innocence. He guessed at once, why she was here, why she was going to the Kessler lodge. Though he normally tried not to think of it, he could not help being aware that such women were sometimes shipped in as courtesans.

He became uncomfortably aware of the older woman scrutinizing him. Both ladies had seemed a little surprised when they saw him, but he was used to that. Not only was he taller than most colonists, but there was something about the bearing of a Lost Rythan that set them apart. He could not see it himself, but he knew that many of the star folk thought of them as primitives.

He pulled out a chair and seated himself without asking. Maybe if he came down closer to their level—but then that was awkward as well, since his legs were too long to sit properly and he had to stretch them out in front of him.

The Star Trail woman noted this with a grim twist of her lips. However, she did not comment. Instead she introduced her companion—Téna bor Rijn—and asked his name, though he had already told her who he was when he called. Miss bor Rijn looked up at him in surprise. "Ard Matthew Third-Blade?" she repeated. "What is your colony?"

He almost didn't answer. What business was it of hers? But then he shrugged. "Lost Rythar," he said.

Star Trail turned toward him. "Are you a Faring Guard?" she demanded.

He gave her back a cold stare. "No," he said. "I am not." He felt the sweat pricking beneath his arms, slicking his hands. He forced himself to sit still, though he felt as though he were some creature of the wilderness, not meant to be indoors.

The secretary shrugged. "So Mong has sent you to fly us out to the lodge?" she said.

He nodded. "Tomorrow. I'll meet you on the plat tomorrow morning. Early."

"Why not now?" Téna asked him. She glanced around nervously. Was she, too, watching the doorway?

He explained about the winds. "It's not really that bad," he added. "Just now and then. They didn't need to name the place Windy-Go. I mean, it's a whole planet. Who knows what the rest is like?" He was talking too much and he stopped in confusion.

Then he caught a faint smile on the secretary's face. "That will be fine, Mr. Third-Blade," she said, and at this, the younger woman smiled too.

Not knowing what else to do, he rose to go. "Tomorrow, then," he said and tried to manage a pleasant expression of his own. But now that he towered over them once more, he felt more than ever like an intrusion into their civilized world. With what he hoped was a cordial nod, he left them as hastily as he could.

As he walked out of the dining room, there was no sign of the man he had seen earlier, but he still felt that prickling as of danger to come. Not immediate, maybe, but coming. He did not sleep very well that night.

CHAPTER THREE

After an hour's struggle, Ard Matthew gave up trying to sleep and wandered into the kitchen where he fetched himself a beer before settling at the table to think about his passengers. Mong had told him nothing about their business on Windy-Go and his first contact with the two ladies had certainly not revealed much.

His employer was plainly not sharing all he knew. Normally Mong was pretty open when he discussed his customers. He had a wry sense of humor that the Lost Rythan, despite his own humorless culture, could appreciate. But none of that had been in evidence; this time, Mong had been all business.

Had it just been a matter of delivering a young lady of the call girl variety to one of the corporate managers vacationing at the lodges, Mong would not have been concerned. It struck Ard Matthew, however, that he himself should have some scruples in the matter and now he marveled that he had not. One more sign, he feared, that he was growing hardened.

He clasped both hands around the bottle and scowled down at the table. It really looked as though something else was going on here. Something that had Mong on edge. And now he, Ard Matthew, had better be concerned about this thing.

How did it affect his passengers—that seemed to be the question. As a man it would have been hard not to take some interest in the younger of the two women. She had been such a vision of creamy skin, faintly blushing cheeks and dark hair. Would he be delivering her to something that might be degrading at the least? Did she know what she had gotten herself into? Who could say?

The other woman had seemed to him like an aboriginal duenna, hard faced and scowling, her dark eyes watching him suspiciously as she spoke. Or was he only reacting like a primitive? After all, both ladies could very well be what they pretended to be, professionals sent out to do some necessary job for the corporation.

He took a swig of his beer and grimaced. It was sure that the older one—the *duenna*, as he persisted in thinking of her—did not think much of *him*. Maybe neither of them did. He had probably looked like a man suffering from a hangover.

He got up and went into the other room where he sat—or rather sprawled—in one of the inadequate chairs. "Activate," he told the wall and was rewarded with a scene of straggling pines with mountains in the background.

"Kessler Corporation," he told it. "Recent news."

Immediately a robot, thinly disguised as a newscaster, appeared on the screen. The pre-recorded "news" it gave was no more than a public relations spiel. There was no mention of the two he had just met, though after the first effusion, he did obtain one piece of real information.

"Elfane Kessler, the elusive head of the corporation is said to be travelling due to overwork. We take you to Julie Ling."

Two heads appeared on the screen now, both female, though one of them at least was another AI. "Rumors are that, after more than two centuries of renewal treatments, the reclusive Dr. Kessler is finally feeling her age," Julie told him brightly. "We hear she has departed her headquarters on Archangel Colony for a rest cure at an undisclosed destination while the bulk of the company's business is left in the hands of board members on Archangel and on Earth."

"No one knows," the AI chipped in, its voice a little sexier than Julie's, "whether this has anything to do with another rumor making the rounds of the networlds, that someone *may* have struck phessite."

"Stories like this come up constantly," Julie put in. "And usually they turn out to be no more than fairy tales." She smiled at the screen. "Phessite is, after all, so rare and precious that more than one seeker has been—*deceived*. So we won't be holding our breath on this one."

No, Ard Matthew thought, they wouldn't. Especially not the AI who didn't breathe anyway. Phessite, necessary to access the mysterious starnet, was only found in conjunction with the presumed relics of what could only have been an earlier interstellar civilization, a civilization so far in the past that its remains were mostly obliterated and archaeologically debatable. Such a find would certainly account for any amount of behind the scenes activity among the corporations.

He turned his attention back to the screen where the anchors were speculating about the company's future should its head become disabled. No one seemed to know what would happen, the AI revealed with a final simper, and the scene was soon replaced with another view of Windy-Go's attractions.

The landscape was wasted on their viewer as, head back, Ard Matthew finally succumbed to his weariness. Presently, the screen turned back into a wall while, in his dreams, the Lost Rythan hunted the hills of his homeland, knowing all the while that he was hunted in turn. Even as he searched for tracks beneath the coiling serpent spruce, he felt the presence of something malevolent. Yet he never caught sight of what stalked him. He only knew that it was nothing he could stab or shoot, nothing he could take in his hands and *rend*.

He came awake with a lunge and had to resist an urge to look behind him as he struggled to his feet. Shaking the sleep from his eyes, he saw that there was just time to make himself presentable. Breakfast—if he got any—would have to wait until he reached the hotel.

When he arrived, there was no sign of Mong's clients—only a lone figure waiting for him on the plat. Ard Matthew gave a start when he recognized him—or thought he did. For this was almost certainly the same man he had seen the night before, half hidden in one of the conversation bays at the hotel. By daylight, the fellow looked more like a typical company guard, a type often seen at the lodges and around the settlement.

But then, after a closer look, he wasn't so sure. Beneath the surface of that brutal face, Ard Matthew thought he detected a light of intelligence in those dark eyes along with something else. A bleak patience, as though the guard had endured many hard things, expected nothing better, and yet held on to a grim sort of loyalty, whether to his company or to something else entirely.

"Onegin," he said as Ard Matthew approached. "But you can call me Babe. Everyone does. I'm from Kessler."

Warily, the Lost Rythan introduced himself. "I was told there would only be two in the party, Mr. Onegin," he said.

"Then you were told wrong."

Ard Matthew gave a noncommittal grunt, wondering what Mong would say about this change of plan.

But when the women arrived, it was plain that Babe's presence was not part of *their* plan. The pilot held his peace. It was none of his business what the company decided—he was only Mong's employee—and Mong wasn't here. So he waited while they wrangled, even stepping away so that the secretary would not think he was intruding himself. After a time it became plain that Babe was coming with them whether the other two liked it or not.

While this matter was being settled, or rather not settled at all, Ard Matthew took an opportunity to really study the three, especially Miss van Rijn. She did not like Onegin, though she showed no especial fear of him. Neither did her companion. So it wasn't *that* sort of problem, at least. Or at any rate, he hoped it wasn't.

Then he turned his attention to the company man. Besides that unexpected depth, something else in Onegin's face caught his attention. If he was not mistaken, it was not a threat he saw there, but rather a half hidden fear. Or not fear, exactly, he decided after a moment, but anxiety—the man was deeply worried about something. Since this fit in with Ard Matthew's own uneasiness, he filed it away as a further reason to be ready for trouble.

The matter decided—that Babe was coming along—the Lost Rythan helped the ladies load their luggage into the flyer. As always, he kept some things of his own in the storage compartments, prepared for a stopover wherever he might fly. One kit, in particular, designated for emergencies, was always kept on hand. None of the others had brought much—Babe, nothing at all—and there was plenty of storage room.

Relieved to be starting at last, he took his place and waited for the others to seat themselves. This they did with some hesitation and a great deal of mutual watchfulness. He didn't take off until the ladies, at least, had strapped themselves in.

At last, the flyer lifted above the settlement and the port became no more than a small, cleared space in a vast, thinly wooded plain. Far to the west, mountains loomed above the treetops, forested slopes rising to snow-capped peaks. Shimmering patches of blue closer in might have been lakes. This landscape was a familiar sight by now to Ard Matthew, though he never ceased to appreciate the beauty that spread out below them.

For one thing, he liked the way the trees did not crowd each other. They were a bit like the sunfirs of Lost Rythar, though not as tall. Not as *massive*. A light wind sent them swaying below the flyer. Once in a while, that wind picked up a little, making the craft wobble and the treetops bend. He glanced around at his passengers and saw that Miss bor Rijn was watching nervously out the window.

"Windy-Go," he told her with a smile. "For what it's worth."

She returned his smile absently, before she sat back, turning once or twice to look at the man behind her. Babe had not strapped himself in and leaned forward in his seat, peering out intently at the empty sky. Across the width of the flyer from bor Rijn, the secretary worked furiously at a tablet. Judging by the expression on her face, she might have been writing a protest to her employer about having Babe Onegin onboard. Fat lot of good that would do now, he thought.

But then he saw that he had guessed wrong. Apparently, she had been looking up the history of the colony. "That man was an Algonquian," she said abruptly. "From Odawa Colony. The one who named *this* colony, I mean."

From the back, Babe grunted. "So what's an Algonquian?"

Star Trail looked up and shrugged. But after a moment, she answered him. "Odawa is one of the united tribal colonies. They were settled by descendants of the original inhabitants of the American continent of Earth." She looked as though she were about to add something more, but then she didn't.

"Ah," Babe said. "And you'd care about that, wouldn't you?"

Star Trail did not answer.

Ard Matthew, meanwhile, turned back to his flying, not much enlightened by this information. So the place had been named by an earthman, he thought, or the descendant of an earthman. But they were all earthmen if you went back far enough. Every last one of them. There were no indigenous aliens.

No one said anything else, which was a relief. The last thing he wanted was a quarrel in the confined space of the flier. When an hour or so had passed, he gestured to a locker which he had stocked with provender for the trip. "Bars and caf," he said. "And fruit. It's local. Help yourselves."

The secretary moved forward and opened the latch. She nodded in appreciation at what she saw and pulled the warming tab on a caf, handing the cup to bor Rijn. After a moment's hesitation, she also gave a cup to Ard Matthew and took one for herself. When she did not offer anything to Babe, he crawled forward and got himself a meal. The Lost Rythan noted that he did not look at either of the women as he made his way past them, though the younger one drew back slightly. So maybe they had a history after all.

Certainly there was tension in the air. Despite the cessation of hostilities, the intruder was not forgiven for forcing himself into the group. Ard Matthew looked at the chronometer and saw to his relief that at least half the allotted trip time had passed. They were making good progress and soon enough he could drop off his passengers and return to the port. He was congratulating himself on these things, admiring the woodland below, and had just accepted an unwrapped bar from Star Trail when everything fell apart.

They all heard a popping sound after which the flyer began to lose altitude rapidly. They were wavering like a bird shot from the sky, threatening to roll as they fell. He actually wondered if it *had* been shot down, though that seemed impossible.

But there was no time to speculate. He forget everything else and became one with the machine as his pilot's training took over. First, turn the fall into a glide—he did this automatically, grazing the tops of the highest trees as the flyer continued to descend. He angled into the wind to slow their speed, keeping them upright with difficulty as he searched ahead for a clearing. They were still going far too fast to risk a collision with one of the conifers.

A broken treetop brushed against their bottom, making a prolonged screech that set his teeth on edge. Behind him, he heard one of the women climb out of her restraints and began to claw her way forward. He could also hear Babe shouting for her to hold still and hang on.

But Ard Matthew tried to ignore these things. Treetops were snatching at them now, branches shearing away with a shriek of tearing wood. Their craft shuddered, wobbled. Then something hit the back of his seat and a hand groped for his shoulder. He shrugged it off.

Concentrate. A clear spot—got to find a clearing. Once, he would have prayed. Now he didn't dare.

Ahead, as though in answer to the prayer he had not made, he spotted a patch of blue and brown. Water? Marshland? At the rate they were losing altitude, could he make it that far?

He turned the flyer's nose toward the gleam, trying to keep it pointing aloft as they shot through the upper reaches of the forest. He had to keep adjusting course while they tore lower and lower through the trees, slamming and ripping the crowns from pines and firs, absorbing shock after shock and plummeting ever downward.

It would be close—close. And then, with a last, desperate wrench of the bar, he sent them plunging through a final belt of foliage to slam against the ground.

Gouts of water sheeted up on either side as the flyer half buried itself in mud and weeds. Flocks of birds rose with a great squawking and rush of wings. But he only half heard their clamor. His ears were ringing and he felt as though every muscle had been pummeled, every joint pulled to the utmost. Dazed, he stared through the spattered windshield, tasting blood on his lips. There was nothing to see except a confusion of pools and beds of reeds, all of it streaked with the muddy water that had splashed the windscreen.

From behind him, came screams and sounds of a struggle. He forced himself to turn, despite the pain that every movement brought. He was still strapped in, half lying on his side at the same angle the flyer had landed. He scrambled to undo his harness, wincing as he tugged at the straps.

As he freed himself, he saw that the metal hull was partly crumpled, water and mud leaking through the tear. Someone lay against the edge of what had been the hatch in a welter of blood and a confusion of limbs. After a moment, he recognized her as the older of the two women—Star Trail. She was the one screaming as she clutched at her legs.

On the other side, still hanging from the straps, her companion seemed to be unconscious. The company man, Babe, was just picking himself up from where he had been thrown when they landed. He had a cut above his forehead and was swearing softly as he wiped blood from his eyes.

Ard Matthew wriggled free of his seat and crawled toward the injured woman.

"My legs!" she cried when she saw him. "They don't—I can't feel them!"

He reached for her, fending off her panicked grip, trying to keep her still as he felt for broken bones. He was no medical expert, though the Star Brothers had trained him in the rudiments of first aid, but he thought there might be cracked ribs, maybe even a broken pelvis. Her body was twisted partly onto one side though her shoulders lay flat against the hatch. He was afraid to try to straighten her.

She stared up at him in a terror she was even now making an effort to control. Her screams had subsided to low, shuddering moans. He could not tell how much of her distress was pain and how much was fear as he tried to shake the cobwebs from his own mind. Got to remember the protocol, he told himself. First, fetch the first aid supplies. Get the analyzer. It would tell him if there was internal bleeding, would identify a bone break. Blood pressure—would she go into shock?

Painkillers. Yes, she would need that. What else?

He peered around, looking for the locker. There it was, near the hatch. The door was bent and jammed. Could he even get it open?

His own head was aching, his vision blurred. But he *must* ignore these things. He had to think beyond the necessities of the moment. Where had they landed? Could they signal for help? Worst of all, *what* had happened to the flyer? Why had it lost power so suddenly and fallen from the air?

His eyes met those of the man called Babe. For long moments he stared at the other man in puzzlement, wondering what it was he read there. To his fuddled mind, it could have been anything.

He shook his head. "Help me with this locker," he said, his voice coming out as a hoarse croak. The other man, after pausing to check on Miss bor Rijn, crawled over to his side. Together, they pried off the warped door of the locker. Ard Matthew hunted out a unit of H-6 which was the strongest pain killer he carried. He had never needed it before, or any of the medical supplies, really. He was seldom injured and when he was, he preferred the simpler remedies of his own people.

He shoved the ampule against Star Trail's neck, hoping it would be adequate.

"Stay with her," he told Babe and began to work his way back to where the younger woman still sprawled, unconscious, in her straps. Babe made as though to forestall him and then drew back, watching while, carefully, Ard Matthew released Miss bor Rijn and looked her over. He could see no injury other than a bruise on her forehead. Even as he loosened the straps, she regained consciousness.

"Where—what has happened?" she whispered, taking in her surroundings slowly, eyes wide and alarmed. "What have they done to us?" She began to struggle, still half entwined in her straps. "Shami? Tell me what has happened?"

"We've crashed," Miss Star Trail told her. "He's gone and crashed the flier." Her voice had thickened, probably from the pain medicine.

The girl turned her gaze back on Ard Matthew's face. "Crashed?" she faltered. "Why?" She seemed to be having trouble taking this in.

"We lost power," Babe said from his station beside the secretary. "He—this man—glided us down. It could have been a lot worse." His voice was gentler than it had been that morning—as though a bear tried to moderate its native growl to a more civil tone.

Yes it could have been worse, Ard Matthew thought. A lot worse. But there was no sense thinking about that now. He had enough on his hands. "Are you be alright, Miss bor Rijn?" he asked her.

"I—I think so," she said. As though to prove she was not injured, she began untangling herself from the straps. "Shami—?"

"She's hurt pretty bad," Babe said. "She wasn't in her seat."

At this, the younger woman pulled herself upright and shoving past the Lost Rythan, she clambered to Star Trail's side. "Get back," she told Babe curtly, gesturing for him to get out of her way.

The other man moved aside after a quick, half apologetic glance at the speaker. "Okay, Téna."

Ignoring him, the girl turned her attention to Star Trail. Ard Matthew heard a sudden intake of breath. "What happened to her?"

she demanded, reaching down to shift the twisted form. "What is wrong?"

"Don't touch her," Ard Matthew warned quickly, moving to her side. "I'm pretty sure she has a back injury."

At this, bor Rijn turned her flawless features up to him, eyes widening in fear. "Oh my God!" she whispered. "What can we do for her? She can't just stay like that!"

At this, Babe, who had been fidgeting and looking around the cabin, spoke up. "The first thing we've got to do is get her out of here. All of us. We need to get clear."

Ard Matthew looked at him in surprise. "What do you mean?" he demanded. "You can see we can't move her."

The other man turned his dark gaze on the Lost Rythan. "This is a company job," he said. "They'll make it clean. Just take my word for it—we've got to get out!"

The girl was staring at him in horror, a look in which loathing was mixed with some dreadful knowledge as though she, too, might have guessed what was coming. "Damn you, Babe," she said, her voice rising into an unbecoming shrillness. "Damn you!" She raised clawed hands as though she meant to attack him. "What have they done? You knew! You knew and you—you never said—"

The Lost Rythan turned to Babe. "What is she talking about?" he asked, keeping his voice low.

Babe shrugged, using one sleeve to mop the blood from the cut on his forehead. "She doesn't know anything. She's just talking." He stopped, noticing the hatch. The frame was bent, the opening warped hopelessly out of shape. "Is there another way out of here?" he asked.

"Floor launching access." Ard Matthew pointed to further damage. There was no exit there.

"Kick out the windscreen!"

Ard Matthew hesitated.

"Do it, damn you! Our time's running out."

Without another word, Ard Matthew turned to the front of the flyer. The plastiglass was already cracked. He hadn't seen the damage at first for the mud. Drawing himself up, he rolled onto his back in the angle of the seat and slammed the plastiglass with both feet. The crack splintered, tributaries angling outward. But still the stuff held. It was meant to hold.

He kicked it again and a great shard fell outside, letting in the wet smell of the swamp and a breath of fresh, cool air. The opening was still too small and he attacked it once more, until the screen was no more than splinters surrounding an opening large enough to admit a human body. It would be a tight squeeze for the men, he thought. Quickly, he kicked away the lower fragments.

At this, Babe turned back to bor Rijn. "Come on," he said, ignoring her resistance as he grabbed her arm.

She blinked at him. "They *can't*," she said, trying to tear herself away. "Dr. Kessler is my cousin! I came as a favor to her. You know that! Because of the genetics—Get your filthy hands off me!"

"Sorry. No time to talk about all that, girlie," Babe told her roughly. "Can you get up?"

She opened her mouth, closed it, and struggled silently as he wrestled her around and onto her hands and knees. Seeing that the struggle was useless, she relaxed. "But how can you move Shami?" she asked.

"We have no choice," Babe said. He turned toward Ard Matthew and the Lost Rythan saw a trickle of sweat running down one side of his face, dyed pink with the blood that was still oozing from the cut on his forehead.

"And if her back is broken?" the Lost Rythan asked, his mouth dry.

Babe let go of bor Rijn and looked up at the other man. "Will *you* believe me when I say we must move her? That she'll die if we don't?"

Ard Matthew met his look. Once more, he felt the hairs rising on the back of his neck, the urgency—

"Yeah," he said. "I believe you." Yet he still wondered how he could move the woman without doing more damage—even though he knew that he must. Something had gone terribly wrong here and his instincts were crying out to act—now! That there was no more time.

Babe had turned back to the girl. Though Téna still flinched away from him, he caught her arms once more and pulled her forward. "This way," he growled, easing her over the lifeless controls. "Out you go."

She still hesitated at the empty hole that had been the front window, gripping the frame.

"Careful," Babe told her more gently. "Don't put your hands on the sides." He was boosting her through the aperture while Ard Matthew turned back to Star Trail. The woman was staring at him glassily as he gathered her up as gently as he could. Though she clung with her arms and seemed to be cooperating, her legs were dead weights, dragging as he pulled her to the front.

Ahead, Babe had released the other woman who managed to slide through and onto the nose of the flyer. "Jump down," he told her. "Get away. I'll help with Shami." He came back to join the other two.

"Easy," the Lost Rythan told him, as they took hold of the secretary. "You climb out first and help me get her through."

With a nod, Babe backed himself feet first through the windscreen, twisting and shrugging his shoulders as he worked his way through.

Carefully—but probably not carefully enough, he was sure—Ard Matthew eased his burden through the hole, until he felt the other man taking the weight of her torso. As he did so, he heard a sudden loud click somewhere in the guts of the dead flyer and a low humming sound as though some hitherto unknown machinery had engaged. He had a bad feeling about this—

"Babe! Got her?" He almost shoved her feet through, turned to snatch up the knapsack beside the seat before he plunged feet first into the opening. For a moment, he was afraid he wouldn't make it through. Then he felt someone grab his legs and, throwing his hands above his head, not relinquishing the bag, he let Babe pull him out.

He was covered with sweat—more than sweat, for there was blood on his arms where he had scraped the shattered edges of the frame—

The sound came again. Louder this time; they could all hear it.

"Run!" Babe shouted, shoving bor Rijn.

Ard Matthew picked up Shami and loped after the other two, splashing through the weedy water in the direction away from the lake, his kit swinging from one shoulder as he tried to keep from jostling the injured woman.

Ahead of him, he saw Babe and bor Rijn fighting their way through sucking mud, each step squelching. Within moments, he, too, had to slow down, struggling onward, his efforts adding to the strain of gathering exhaustion.

Behind them, the flyer sat—or rather, hunched—on the edge of the standing water, spattered with mud, dead and seemingly parked for good. But he had heard—*what had he heard?*

After what seemed an eternity to the Lost Rythan, carefully balancing his load, the mud yielded to solid ground. They began to climb, first on sand, then on gravel and finally, looking ahead, he saw trees and brush.

He had time for only one look before the ground made a leap beneath his feet. Simultaneously he heard a thunderclap of sound and a hot wind threw him forward up the slope where he staggered to his knees, fighting to protect the woman he carried. He heard someone cry out—bor Rijn—and Babe began to curse again.

Ard Matthew eased his burden carefully to the ground before he turned to look back at the flier.

What he could see of it—there wasn't much left—was burning with a white flame almost too bright to bear. He blinked and had to look away.

For a moment there was a stunned silence broken only by the sound of flames. Then Babe spoke. “Won’t be anything left,” he said matter-of-factly. “Nothing to find. No evidence.”

Ard Matthew looked at him. “There isn’t any smoke,” he said. “No one will see it from the air.”

“That’s right, Third-Blade,” the other man agreed. “And maybe that’s good.” He and Ard Matthew turned once more to view the wreckage. Already the glow was dissipating and, just as the Lost Rythan had observed, there was no smoke. “I guess everything went up with the flyer?” Babe added. “Food, medicine, medical supplies? The works?”

“Pretty much. The communicator, for sure.” Ard Matthew shook his head. “The one I’m wearing won’t reach back to the port. Besides that, all we’ve got is my camping gear.” He looked down to make sure he still had the satchel. He had dropped it when the flier blew and it lay nearby, the strap torn loose. He did not remember that happening.

“But they *will* come for us, won’t they?” Téna bor Rijn asked. “Someone will come looking for us.” Ard Matthew looked at her. She was wearing a dark green jumpsuit spattered with mud. Or was that blood? She had had a nosebleed and no longer resembled the unattainable beauty he remembered from the hotel. He liked her even more for these imperfections.

“I don’t know,” he told her gently. He looked at Babe. “What do you think?”

The other man shrugged. “It could have been worse, Téna,” he said. “If Third-Blade here weren’t a damn good pilot, we’d all be dead.” He left the greater questions hanging in the air—who had sabotaged the flier? And why?

Ard Matthew turned to the woman on the ground. Her eyes were closed. Was she going into shock? She was certainly pale beneath her naturally dusky skin.

“We may die anyway,” Téna persisted. “We’re lost out here, aren’t we?”

"We won't die," Ard Matthew said, still looking down into Shami's face. "Not all of us anyway," he added under his breath. He came to his feet and studied the hillside. Time enough for the greater questions later. Now he was looking for a level camping spot, somewhere higher above the swamps where he could deposit the injured woman and perhaps do something for her.

He set off walking, but hadn't gone far before he found what he sought. The trees stood like pillars, their tops interlacing delicately high above a forest floor dry and matted with their fallen needles. Beds of very pale moss grew near the base of each tree and here and there, dropped branches mingled with what looked like shed antlers. There was nothing else to be seen.

He turned, seeing Téna bor Rijn behind him. "Babe stayed with Shami," she explained. "I—asked him to." She looked up at him with wide, frightened eyes. Had she thought he was going to abandon the others? Or was it just their situation that frightened her?

"We'll camp here," he explained, hoping to distract her from her fears. "This is a good spot."

"C-camp? Yes—until someone comes for us. Of—of course." Somehow she had got a scratch on one cheek and she kept tracing the line of it with one finger.

"Things will be alright," he told her. "I mean—I've camped out before. Hunted." He felt her gaze on him and wished he could do something more to help her. "We have to get your friend settled," he said. "See if there's anything we can do for her." Maybe this would take her mind off their predicament.

The girl continued to stare at him. "Shami—yes. My—my cousin's secretary. Dr. Kessler is my distant cousin, you know. She—she wouldn't—" But she did not say what her cousin wouldn't do. "You mustn't think—she'll come for us. I know she will."

"Let's get Miss Star Trail," Ard Matthew said. He started back down the hill.

But Babe was coming up, the secretary in his arms. "Here?" he asked.

The Lost Rythan indicated a mound of moss and needles. Together, he and Babe eased Star Trail into the makeshift bed.

She opened her eyes at this and stared up at the others, her mouth working. Then, "Where are we?" she whispered.

"We're in a safe place," Ard Matthew told her. "We're going to camp here."

"The flyer? I remember—but it's all like a dream."

"Crashed," Babe reminded her. "It's gone."

Téna moved forward to kneel beside her. "Shami," she said. "Babe said we had to get out and then it—it blew up!"

Shami's eyes moved until she caught sight of Babe. "How did you know?" she rasped, still staring at him. "How did you know that would happen?"

Ard Matthew thought he saw him wince. Whatever this was, he decided, there might be multiple betrayals here. He must be on his guard.

Babe shrugged. "That's how these things are done," he said flatly.

"An enemy," Téna faltered. "A rival corporation."

Babe didn't answer.

"So what…now?" Shami whispered. She was looking at the Lost Rythan.

He shook his head. There was no answer to this.

"Are you in pain?" Téna asked her. "Can you move your legs?"

The other woman struggled a little and then lay back. "I'm not… going anywhere," she said. She seemed calmer now, but it was probably only the medicine.

"Where would we go?" Babe said, looking down at her. "We're stuck here, Shami. Wherever here is."

Ard Matthew stood up. "Maybe that isn't so bad," he ventured. "Now your—your *enemies* will think we are dead."

Téna looked up at the Lost Rythan. "We might as well be," she said. "Alone on a strange world with nothing to eat but pine needles and moss. And what will we do when the sun goes down? Who knows what—what *things* live out here?" Already she was making him responsible for their survival.

Suddenly Shami reached up and clutched her arm. "Stop it!" the secretary ordered, using a stronger voice than she had yet managed. "Third-Blade is correct. If someone wanted us dead, they must think they have succeeded." She did not look at Babe. "We can try to get back to civilization, but it will be safer to do that on our own terms."

Babe stared at her, his battered features working, his slightly tilted eyes trained on her face. "Sure. That should be easy enough." He gave a small bark of laughter. It was obvious to the pilot and probably to Babe as well that the secretary, at least, would never make it back—not on any terms.

Ard Matthew frowned, studying the trees and the higher hills beyond. His mind was working clearly now, assessing their immediate danger, thinking like the hunter he was. He *was* responsible for the party and though he did not like the role, he forced himself to speak.

"First," he said, ignoring Babe's sarcasm, Téna's fear and Shami's determination—though he admired her for it—"we must get through this night. There *are* predators here, though I have never been attacked. But something eats the antelope and—and other animals. I have seen tracks."

"What kind of tracks?" Shami asked, her voice a little slurred, though she was plainly fighting to stay focused.

He frowned, bringing to mind his few forays into the woodlands of Windy-Go. "Paws," he said uncertainly. "Like cats, maybe." But the tracks hadn't really looked like that. He was uncomfortably aware that his experience with alien fauna was limited. "And—and I think something else," he added. "Something like a bird, though that might only be a scavenger. I've only seen their spoor once or twice near the lodges." *Big* birds, he might have added, but did not. No sense adding to their worries. He remembered the thing he had fought back on Ynche. At least he had seen nothing like that here.

"Well since you seem to know your way around out in the bush," Babe said, "you'd better tell us what to do." He gave the other man a half quizzical half challenging look from beneath bushy eyebrows as he squatted beside the injured woman.

Ard Matthew did not respond to that look. These were corporation people, he was thinking, not prepared for a sojourn in the wilderness. He really *would* be responsible for them.

"We'll make a lean-to for Miss Star Trail," he said. "It needn't be much. Just set up a frame with some of these branches. I've got a tarp in my kit. And we must clear a place for a fire." He looked at Babe. "You're armed," he said. "Will you lend me your gun?"

Babe looked at him in surprise. "What the hell for?"

"Dinner. We can save the ration bars for an emergency. I haven't got many." Ard Matthew drew his own long-bladed knife. "I'll give you this while I'm gone," he said. "Though you probably won't need it."

Babe came to his feet. For some moments, he stood there, looking nonplussed. Then, "Go ahead," Shami told him. "Third-Blade's right. If he can live off the land, so can we. It's our best chance to survive."

Reluctantly, Babe handed over a laser pistol.

"Start gathering branches for the fire and the lean-to," the Lost Rythan told him. "I'll try to be back before sunset."

He turned away and started down the hill.

CHAPTER FOUR

At first, it didn't seem right to leave the others behind this way, as though he were abandoning them. But when he had showed them how to use the collapsible bucket to fetch water from one of the streamlets near the swamp, and demonstrated to Babe how to brace up a crude framework of fallen branches, padding it over with moss, there wasn't much else he could do except find food for the party. For what it was worth, they had given him their trust—and he must not fail to deserve it.

He considered. This was no time to stalk anything as wary as an antelope, which meant his best choice was to bag a few of the water birds so plentiful in the swamp. Turning back in the direction of the campsite, he fixed the scene in his mind—the forest verge, the glittering line of a rivulet crossing the otherwise barren hillside and then, just to make sure, he paused to build up a tall mound of moss and pine needles against the base of a tree. After that, he turned and followed the edge of the reed-bed.

There were plenty of birds out over the lake, but without a boat, he would not be able to retrieve any he shot. What he needed was to scare up a few from the reeds. But he walked for nearly a half hour before anything turned up.

Finally, a flock of mottled geese—or at least he thought they were geese—took wing practically in his face. He set the gun on wide beam and dropped some five or six of the birds. He hurried to pick them up and wring their necks. There wouldn't be much meat on these, but the sun was moving toward the horizon and he would still need to clean and cook his catch.

For a moment, he paused, gripping the dead birds by their legs in one hand, as he gazed out over the lake. The late afternoon tinted the hazy far shore with mellow gold while the water stretched in a barely moving plain of broken greys and greens. There was no sign of the remains of their flier. Above the lake, the blue sky was empty—both of clouds and of any indication that human beings had ever visited this world. They were indeed alone here, he and the others, and though he knew they would be more of a burden to him than anything else, he was suddenly glad that he had them to go back to.

As he turned, he stumbled over something half hidden among the coarse grasses and the reeds. It turned out to be another set of shed antlers. Unlike the bits he had found near the lodges, these were intact. It was puzzling, for he had yet to see a deer on Windy-Go. But by the look of this rack, their owner might not even resemble the deer he had seen on other worlds. Something about the base was wrong—perhaps they were not antlers at all but something else.

He dropped the rack and hurried on. As the light turned reddish, a chill had come into the air. Would the others have lit a fire? Gathered extra fuel? He could only hope so.

One by one, his companions passed before his mind's eye—*his* people now, until they were rescued or until they rescued themselves. He didn't think Shami Star Trail would make it. But that girl should be alright, though he still wondered about her relationship with Babe Onegin. As for Babe, he looked like a survivor for sure. He liked the way the man had in the end, loaned him the gun, taking the knife in exchange. Babe knew they must work together and, if he was not mistaken, knew also how to use the weapon.

But still, there was the way he looked at Téna and the way she looked back at him. She did not welcome Babe's attentions. So, would Babe have sense enough not to endanger their survival by forcing himself on her? There was no way of knowing.

He frowned, going over these impressions. There were other things that bothered him as well and these, too, must be faced. For one, Babe had been edgy from the moment they left the port—apparently expecting trouble. As a Lost Rythan, Ard Matthew Third-Blade knew that his own warnings were a peculiarity of his race. He had been told so by the Star Brothers. So, what were the odds of Babe also having a sixth sense? It was possible, he supposed, but not likely.

But Téna had seemed nervous, too. Whether that was only a result of whatever lay between herself and Onegin, he could not tell. Had she—or Babe—any grounds to expect an attack? And if so, from whom?

Ard Matthew was used to flying corporate types like Babe and Shami. But Téna was not of this sort; she was only a young lady being taken to one of the lodges. She did not act like one of the joygirls he had seen at the port and he doubted that she was one. So what was she? A family member? That still didn't explain much.

He sighed. Whatever lay behind their present situation, he had no time to sort it out. Right now, he needed to know whether someone would be hunting for them. An enemy of the corporation, perhaps. If so, they were safe only as long as they didn't try to reach civilization. And of course that was no solution. A Lost Rythan could live off the land indefinitely but these were not Lost Rythans. And even *he* would probably go mad if he had to remain alone in the wilderness for the rest of his life.

He smiled grimly. It was easy to look down on those not of his kind. Yet he had nearly been hanged on Wolf Slammer because of his own ineptness, so how dared he judge the others' ability to survive?

Ahead lay the moss pile he had left for himself and he began to climb the hill, wondering what he would find when he got there. To his relief, however, the campsite looked better than he had expected. Babe and Téna had built a good enough shelter around Shami, who lay in her bed of needles and moss just as he had left her. She seemed to be unconscious.

Téna spotted him first. Then he saw Babe at some distance, breaking up fallen branches. They had not, he noted, made a fire, though there was a light-cutter in the pack. Probably Babe didn't know what it was.

He held up the birds. "Do you know how to skin them?" he asked and surprisingly, Téna said she did.

"I grew up on a farm." She didn't say where.

Wordlessly, he handed her his catch and set off to meet Babe. "There's a skinning knife in the pack," he said over his shoulder. "Help yourself."

Babe looked up at his coming, letting fall a load of broken boughs. "I was wondering if you'd come back," he said, reaching out a hand for his gun.

Ard Matthew met his look. There must have been something in the Lost Rythan's expression that warned the other he had made an error, because Babe drew back. "No offense," he said. "It's just that we're in a bit of a fix here. Some men would have run out on us."

The Lost Rythan curled his lip. "Some," he said. He reached out his own hand and received his knife back. He ran one thumb over the edge. Luckily, Babe had had sense enough not to use it to cut branches.

"That's quite a weapon," Babe said, changing the subject. "Almost a sword. Local?

Ard Matthew shook his head. "Wolf Slammer. They make good knives." He did not add that he had bought it because it reminded him of those of his own colony.

"You ever have to use it? In a fight, I mean."

Ard Matthew shook his head. "Not this one." No sense telling the other man about Lost Rythar. There had been plenty of sword-play there.

They stood side by side for a moment, looking back at the lean to. Then, "I'll help you with the wood," he said. "It gets chilly here at night." He went back to fetch the mini laser cutter and this speeded up their work.

After his second load, he cleared an area in front of the lean-to. Luckily, the needles weren't as flammable as they looked and the dewfall would make them even less likely to catch. But he was taking no chances. He swept the area down to the soil, leaving a broad margin of safety around the fire. He wished there were rocks to lay, but in their absence, he scooped out a depression with his hands before putting in a layer of finely broken twigs. Carefully he shredded a pile of bark and set this on top.

Satisfied, he put the light cutter on its lowest setting and applied it to the tinder. The invisible beam caught the stuff at once and he fed the little flame slowly with more bark until he was satisfied.

Before long, they had a good blaze going and as soon as there were coals, he took the cleaned fowl and set them to broil. Finally, he went over to look at Shami.

The secretary remained comatose. Her face was very pale, as though she might have internal bleeding. His own experience with medical emergencies was mainly restricted to wounds and all he could remember was that you had to keep things clean. He rose and turned to Téna.

"If I get you some more water, could you sort of—you know, wash her a little?"

The girl looked up at him in surprise.

"I mean," he floundered, "seeing that she's a—a woman. It might be better if—"

Babe laughed out loud. "Better let it go, Third-Blade," he said. "If she messes herself, she won't know it."

Wordlessly, Ard Mathew fished the collapsible bucket and walked away from the camp. A moment later he heard footsteps behind him. "Wait," Téna called. "You mustn't think—I've never been in a situation like this, Mr. Third-Blade. Never seen—anyone die."

He stopped and waited for her to catch up.

"She is dying, isn't she?"

He shrugged. "We'll need a cloth," he said.

"We can use some of her clothing." She looked down at the bucket he was carrying, her hair half hiding her face. "This is all so—so ridiculous. She needs a hospital and we have nothing—*nothing*—"

He didn't answer. What was there to say?

She hurried to keep pace with his longer legs. "Why do you think this happened? If Dr. Kessler's enemies thought she was aboard—"

"Why would they think that?" he asked, as he forged through the brush beside the streamlet.

"I was impersonating her," Téna said. "She is my cousin. Our DNA is similar and this would give her a chance to do some traveling of her own. Incognito, I mean. She gets tired of the people following her about, you know. She has no privacy." The girl looked at him sidewise as she said this.

He glanced at her as he washed and filled their makeshift water carrier. She was still attractive, he decided, despite everything they had gone through. The final gleams of sunset struck incongruous ruddy lights in her hair and made her cheeks glow. "You were *impersonating* Dr. Kessler?" he repeated slowly. "Do you resemble her?" The idea was preposterous.

Téna shook her head. "But I didn't need to. Robots don't scan us that way. They aren't very intelligent, you know. My genetic resemblance is enough."

"And now," he said slowly, "whoever had done this must think she is dead?" He stood up, lifting the bucket from the stream.

"You don't understand," Téna persisted, biting her lip. "There is no reason for anyone to kill her. They would want her alive. She's the only one who knows—"

He looked at her sharply. But she did not say what her cousin knew and, seeing her confusion, he thought it better not to ask. Later, perhaps. What did Téna's cousin know that put her in danger? Some corporate matter? Or something more sinister?

He led the way back up the hillside. The local version of bats were out and in the twilight the trees seemed larger than they really were. In the distance, a night bird gave its booming cry while ahead of them, the campsite was a reassuring haven.

There was no time for questions. In the end, he must help Téna with her patient. The secretary's skin was cool and clammy to the touch, her limbs unresponsive as though the paralysis might be creeping higher. "I think," he said when they had finished, "that I had better sit up with her tonight." His own experience dealing with the wounded was certainly greater than hers.

Téna shivered a little. "If we only had some tea or something," she said.

"We do." He got up and went over to his pack. First he removed a roll of thermal sheeting, deceptively thin and light but virtually indestructible. He tossed it to Téna. "Wrap it around yourself," he said. He rummaged further. It was mostly camping gear never meant to be a survival kit, just stuff for when he had to wait at one of the lodges. But he had been thorough and now he was grateful for that foresight. The truth was that though he knew he could always bunk with the servants at a lodge, he preferred the privacy of the woods and prepared accordingly.

Unfortunately, since he could always raid the larder wherever he stayed, he didn't usually carry much food. A few ration bars, a couple of beer cubes—that seemed to be all he had. But he did remember putting in a packet of tea. He dug down further. A coil of rope, a very basic first aid kit—good thing he had that—collapsible shovel, more knives and a few other odds and ends. It wasn't much for four people.

He needed something to boil the water for tea. Finally, he located a fabric pot and a collapsible cup. He decided to save the beer—reconstituted wasn't all that good anyway. "Feed the fire some more," he said over his shoulder.

He carried the first aid kit and the other things over to the light. "Go through that," he told Téna, handing her the kit. "It should have an analyzer. And there might be more pain medicine if she needs it."

He dipped the last of the water from the bucket and raked aside enough coals for the pot. It wobbled as he placed it.

Téna emptied the kit onto her lap. "I'd be afraid to give her any pain killers," she said. "She seems so—so weak." She handed him the analyzer. "Universal antibiotics—but likely she's had shots. Synthoskin. Some sprays. Bandages. That's about all."

He shrugged. "I never needed any of that." And truth was, he hadn't. One more twitch of pride, he thought wryly.

He hefted the analyzer. "It's still got power," he said. "I'd better scan her."

"What can it tell us?" Téna asked, looking up as Babe ambled over after dropping off a final bundle of firewood.

"Let me," he said to Ard Matthew. "Unless you know how to use the thing?"

Silently, the Lost Rythan handed it to the other man. He *did* know how to use it, but hopefully Babe had had more training.

Shami was no more than a dark shadow beneath the lean-to as Babe stretched out his arm and held the little device above her head. Slowly he moved it down her torso and then along one arm—the other was beneath her—and down each leg. He brought it back and spoke aloud. "Diagnosis," he said.

Whatever the diagnosis, this particular machine was not set up to give it. Instead, they were instructed not to move the patient, to call in emergency services and to give her a stim spray.

"Have we got a stim?" Téna asked.

"If we do," Babe told her, "there's not much point in using it. We can't get her to a hospital."

Téna turned on him. "You heartless bastard!" she said angrily. "I know you never liked her! And she sure didn't like *you*!"

"Do you really want to wake her up with a stim? When we can't do anything?" Babe said, ignoring the jibe. "She's better off as she is."

Silently, Ard Matthew took the birds off the coals and pulled them apart. He knew very well that Babe had told the truth even as a Rythan would. There was nothing they could do. But on the other hand, it was plain the company man had done nothing to earn the regard of the ladies. His official position was still a mystery.

The meat was shared out. The birds were tough and tasted of the swamp, but no one complained. They had not eaten since that morning. When the last bone had been picked clean, there was tea, and they passed around the cup, to wash down the taste of their dinner. Afterwards, Babe stretched out in the moss while Téna wrapped herself in the thermal sheet and Ard Matthew settled himself beside the secretary. He thought about setting a watch, then decided it was not necessary. Presently he laid his head on his knees and slept.

Hours later, he was wakened by a scream.

The fire had burned down to coals and in the uncertain light, he saw Téna fight free of the wrapping he had given her. His ears still registering the echoes of the terrible cry, he leaned over to check on Shami.

"What is it?" Téna whispered, coming up behind him. "Is she—?"

"No." He said, reaching out to lay one hand on Téna's arm. "It wasn't her. It came from further away."

Before Téna could respond, they were startled by yet another scream, followed by the unmistakable sound of Babe's weapon set on high.

"What…is he…shooting at?"

"I don't know." Beside him, Shami stirred and opened her eyes. He could see the faint gleam of them in the remains of the firelight.

"What…" she persisted, her voice barely audible.

"Stay with her," Ard Matthew told Téna. "And put some more wood on the fire."

Téna nodded. He felt her watching him as he hurried out into the darkness. When the new wood caught, he saw Babe, holding the gun as he peered out nervously at the trees.

"What is it, Babe?" The other man seemed shaken but Ard Matthew thought he would be alright. "Is it gone now?"

"It had horns on its head," Babe told him unsteadily.

"A deer."

"I thought—I thought it was part of the trees. I mean it seemed to come down from a tree. And it *screamed*!"

"It had to be a deer. They live on most of the habitable worlds." But the Lost Rythan was not so sure. Certainly he had yet to see one on Windy-Go. He remembered the rack he had examined earlier—would that have fit on the head of a deer? He stared up into the treetops, at the ragged silhouette of branches against the sky.

"It was *screaming*, I tell you! You heard it! Where I come from, deer don't sound like that."

Ard Matthew caught sight of the other man's face, scarcely visible in the uncertain light. "You—you're a city man, aren't you? What you heard—what you saw flying—it might have been an owl. A big one." He fingered his knife, trying to put conviction into the words. "I've heard them near the lodges," he added. "Not this close, maybe, but they scream like that."

Babe looked at him blankly. "What the hell is an owl?"

"A predatory bird. They've got them on a lot of the colony worlds. Sachsen. Maybe not where you come from."

Together, they started back for the campsite.

"Owls and deer," Babe said. "That will have to do—for Téna, at least."

Ard Matthew grunted and went over to check on their patient.

Shami was still awake, though there was no telling how much she understood of what was going on. He told the two women what Babe had said and offered his own explanation.

"An owl," Shami repeated slowly. "We had them—I remember. When—when I was a child."

"Are you in pain?" Téna asked her. "We have some medicines. Stim, I think, and pain killers. You've got to tell me what you need."

She was answered by a dry chuckle. "I need full restoration. In a hospital."

That was about what the analyzer had said. "You still can't move your legs?" Ard Matthew asked her.

"They're gone. Pretty much everything up to my chest. And my arms are starting to go, too. I tried to lift them. No pain, just nothing."

The Lost Rythan glanced over at Babe who was standing by the fire, his attention on the hillside above them. He was at a loss. What comfort could any of them offer?

From the shadow of the lean-to, Shami's eyes met his when he turned back to her, the flickering shadows making them seem as deep as the sockets of a skull. Suddenly he wanted to promise things he could not give. "Yes, we'll save you. You'll have that restoration treatment. Just hold onto life while we solve a few problems."

But he did not say these things.

Instead, it was Téna who spoke. "Do you think you can sleep? I could get you a drink if you'd like."

"You might be Dr. Kessler's cousin," Shami told her, "but you're not at all like her. She would have taken charge here. She always had an answer to every problem."

"Well she didn't prepare for *this* particular problem," Téna said. "At least, I don't see how she could have." She had her back to the fire and Ard Matthew could not see her face.

A dry chuckle from beneath the lean-to. "Didn't she? I wonder now." The words were very faint, blurred as though the secretary spoke in a wandering dream.

But Ard Matthew heard what she said and he also saw Téna give a start. After that, however, Shami closed her eyes and seemed to be unconscious once more.

Ard Matthew studied both women, pondering as he went over the few facts he had. Téna had impersonated her cousin. She had been mistaken for the head of the corporation. Someone, perhaps, had taken the word of an AI. Had Dr. Kessler known her life was in danger? Had Babe?

He thought of Babe. The man must have feared something. Otherwise he would not have forced himself into the party. But at this, his own thoughts trailed off. Where did it go from here? Nowhere.

The remainder of the night seemed interminable. Babe lay sprawled in the moss but Ard Matthew did not go back to sleep. He lay on his side, propped up on one elbow as he stared out over the darkened landscape. On the other side of the fire, Téna slept.

As the night drew on, a chill crept into the air and Ard Matthew was aware of a rising wind. Streaks of cloud passed over the sky, dimming the starlight and making it hard to see the patterns of branches overhead. He became aware that Téna was muttering in her sleep as though she dreamed ill dreams.

He huddled himself together, pulling his jacket around him and, despite the chill, finally drifted into dreams of his own. He remembered little of these when he woke sometime later with the rising sun in his eyes. For long moments, he remained where he was, stiffened and aching as he tried to remember what he had dreamed. Something about strange gods of the forest, gods hungry for sacrifice.

But then it was gone and there was only the wind as it sent twigs and pine straw skittering along the forest floor. A broken branch had fallen nearby. When he looked up, the treetops were thrashing, the wind screaming and great clouds moving in to finish covering the sky. Within moments, the sun was completely hidden.

Wrapped in the thermal sheet, Téna slept on. The fire was mostly ashes. Should he try to get it going again? Probably a waste of time with the wind blowing as it was. He saw Babe sit up and look around blearily.

At this, he remembered Shami. But the secretary was still sleeping. He didn't think she had changed position at all during the night. Her face was a blur in the muted light, but her chest was rising and falling. He thought her breathing seemed irregular, as though she were straining to draw each breath.

He leaned over to have a better look and when he did so, the other woman woke. At first her eyes wandered, not seeming to see anything. Then he saw awareness slowly return.

"Water," Shami whispered, and Ard Matthew fetched the cup. Luckily, there was a little water left in their impromptu tea kettle.

When he reached Shami and held her head up to drink, the secretary choked a little and let the liquid run out of her mouth. "Can't—swallow," she said. The Rythan could barely hear her over the wind. With an effort, she drew another breath. "Put me—down."

He did so and turned to Babe who had come awake at his movements. "Can you get me the analyzer?" he asked.

Wordlessly, Babe found the necessary item and handed it over.

He passed it above the secretary's body and asked for audio. The mechanical voice came on: "Emergency. Emergency. This patient requires immediate hospitalization. Emergency."

Babe gave a snort. "Lot of good that thing is," he said.

Téna roused at this and came over to look at the gadget. "Recommend first aid," she ordered it. "Hospital is not an option."

"Emergency," the thing repeated. "Delay will result in death."

"Tell me what to do!" she cried, snatching the machine and giving it a shake. "What can we do for her?"

"Careful," Babe said, taking the analyzer from her hand. "We might need that later."

"Here," Ard Matthew said. He put it back in the kit and turned to Téna. "Can you stay with her while I look around?" he asked. "Babe can guard the camp."

Without looking at either man, Téna nodded.

Babe looked as though he were going to protest but then he shrugged.

Ard Matthew stood up. The sky was thickly overcast, the trees shadowed beneath. He searched about until he found the trail they had used to bring in wood. It led to a deadfall between two leaning trees.

Slowly he worked his way around the perimeter of their camp, looking for tracks and examining the tree boles until he spotted a raw gouge where Babe had been shooting in his panic. He oriented himself in the direction of the shot and began to walk away from the camp. Once or twice, he saw places where the carpet of needles had been disturbed, but that could have been any animal.

As the light broadened and the wind hit him, he paused to fasten his jacket. During the time he had lived on Windy-Go, the weather had been neither warm nor cold. There was sometimes a tang in the air but this sudden windstorm seemed to promise more. Was the season changing? Not for the better, he was sure, and wished he knew more about the local climate.

Meanwhile, there was no sense in going too far from the campsite, he decided. If Babe *had* seen anything, it would have been nearby. But at first glance nothing seemed out of the ordinary. Before turning back, though, he paused to examine a few fallen branches. It was only natural to look up to see where a branch had broken off—and that was when he saw what he had missed. A long strip of bark was peeled away from the tree, leaving the bare wood, yellowish white against the dark bole. No! There were actually two strips gone, almost parallel to one another.

He leaned back and studied the treetops. It wasn't long before he spotted the same markings higher up on a different tree. He kept scanning until he had found three more sets. Certainly no deer had done this. But as to what could have made the scratches, he had no idea. This he must file away along with the other unknowns and hope he could deal with whatever threatened himself and the others.

A sudden gust of wind threw up a shower of debris as he turned, blinking, and raised one arm to shield his eyes. The clouds were turning ominous. There was rain on the way.

His original plan had been to go fishing in the stream after his reconnoiter, since there was nothing for breakfast. But now he hesitated. If this were to be an ordinary rainstorm, then the fishing might be good. It had been that way on other worlds. But on this strange world, it might prove to be something else.

He paused, studying the sky. As a Lost Rythan, he was inured to discomfort but he had noticed that not everyone was. Was there anything he could do for his companions if the storm should prove heavy?

Suddenly he repressed a grim chuckle. Who had appointed him caretaker of this group of castaways? He was only their pilot, hired by the corporation to fly them to the lodges. He would fish because he was hungry and anyone who wanted to join him could do so. Throwing back his shoulders, he breathed in the wind, taking the gusts as they came, and savoring the smell of the trees. Almost he could imagine himself back on Lost Rythar.

But as he strode into the camp, the illusion vanished. There was Babe, scowling at the clouds, and there stood Téna, scowling at *him*. It didn't take much perception to know they had been quarrelling. He walked past them and knelt beside the lean-to.

Two sunken eyes looked up at him from a ravaged face. The skin seemed stretched over the secretary's broad forehead and wide cheekbones and her lips were drawn back a little from her teeth. She was gasping.

He leaned forward and touched her hand. "Is there anything I can do for you?" he asked gently.

She only stared at him, her mouth working as she tried to speak. "You… know," she said, "how it… is with me."

He knew. A sudden memory of Gris Wolfgang's dying came over him and he almost dropped her hand. He wanted to flee.

This again! And ever again—and yet again. Death and suffering. For this we were created, he thought bitterly. *You* created us for this.

But he remained where he was, cursing the training that had made him what he must be. Responsible, decent—even civilized, though there were many who would not have given such a label to a Lost

Rythan. "Yes," he told her quietly, "I know. I am sorry I can do so little."

"Third-Blad… do you believe in… anything? Lif… after death?"

He was so taken aback at her words that he was startled into speaking his own outraged feelings. "I hope not," he said passionately.

"Why?"

"After all this, it would be too cruel."

As he felt her gaze fixed on him, he was suddenly overcome with self-loathing. It was as though he had struck some helpless thing, as though he had betrayed a child. "No," he said quickly. "I was lying. Of course there is something to hope for. Don't be afraid."

But now her gaze wandered, taking in the skyscape behind him. "It's evil—this place. Something… evil… is here."

He shuddered. She was putting his own feelings into words. Her eyes closed and once again she drifted into unconsciousness as the first raindrops hit the shelter. Rising to his feet, he pulled out his pocket imager and took a picture of her, as though to preserve at least something of the life that was passing. To make up for what he could not give.

Babe had come back to the ashes of the fire and Téna held up the thermo sheet. "I guess we can make some kind of shelter with this," she said.

Ard Matthew noticed that she was shivering. Though he wore his usual rugged clothing, the others were not really dressed for the out of doors. He wondered what Téna would think if he gave her his jacket. Instead, he looked at Babe.

"Come fishing with me," he said. And to Téna, "Wrap that around yourself for now and stay with—with your friend."

She glared at him. For a moment he thought she was going to remind him of his status as an employee. But then she only nodded as though it were not worth the effort to protest, and settled herself next to Shami. "What if she dies?" she asked in a subdued voice.

"We won't go far," he told her. It sounded like a foolish thing to say—as though death would stay away if there were too many people in the vicinity. But it was all he could think of.

Téna worked at spreading the sheet to protect herself and Shami.

"Let me fetch the gear," Ard Matthew said to Babe. He went over to his pack and took out hooks along with a bundle of rod sections he had placed at the bottom. Among the remaining bits were two simple reels and plenty of line. Quickly he assembled two rods out of the pieces. What he had wasn't fancy, but it was as good as anything his home colony could offer.

Babe took one of them in his hands with a half smirk. "Aren't you taking something for granted?" he asked.

The Lost Rythan looked at him.

"How do you know I know how to fish?"

"I'll teach you."

Babe chuckled. "As a matter of fact, I do, though I've never used anything this primitive before."

Wordlessly, Ard Matthew led the way toward the streamlet. Of course the water was too shallow here, and he did not want to eat anything from the swamp. Instead he turned in the opposite direction, hoping to find a pool.

"You ever fish on Windy-Go before?" Babe asked.

"Once or twice."

The other man stared at him, shaking his head. "A real outdoorsman," he said. "What colony did you come from?"

But the Lost Rythan did not answer that directly. Instead, "A little like this," he told Babe. "Which means we may survive if we're lucky."

After that, they did not speak. Presently Ard Matthew found what he was looking for and they each settled down on a tree root and baited their hooks with segmented worms the Lost Rythan found beneath a fallen log. The rain continued, though the wind had abated somewhat. Still, it was cold work and only their hunger kept them at it.

It was Babe who pulled in the first fish, something that might have been a medium sized trout but wasn't. It fought them when they unhooked it and Ard Matthew had to cut its throat. Both had stinging cuts on their hands from the sharp fins.

Luckily the rain lessened as the morning drew on and the fishing was good. Ard Matthew strung their catch together with some of the long grass that grew along the verge. They still did not talk much and neither alluded to Téna and her lone vigil, though the Lost Rythan was feeling more than a little ashamed of himself for leaving her there.

The memory of Shami's question and his own cowardly answer continued to haunt him. If they ever got out of here, he vowed, he was going to find a better use for his skills. Surely there must be *some* sort of job he could do that didn't involve him in the crimes and the quarrels of others. Or were violence and savagery all he was good for? Angrily, he stalked back to the camp, Babe pacing silently beside him.

He saw at once that Téna had relit the fire. Then he noticed that she had draped the thermosheet over the woodpile. She must be cold and wet, he thought, but he admired her resourcefulness. She must have used the little laser from his pack to light the kindling. He should have given it to her for protection when he and Babe had left her alone with Shami, he told himself. But she had found it for herself and that was good.

He held up the string of fish so she could see.

She ran forward and took them. "I'm hungry enough to eat them raw," she said. "Give me your knife."

"Get one from the pack," he said. "It looks like you have coals already." He tried to put some of the warm approval he felt into his voice.

Soon they were all busy cleaning the fish.

"How's Shami?" Babe asked as he worked free the skin of what could have passed for a catfish.

Téna looked as though she were going to say something spiteful, but instead, she turned to Ard Matthew. "She's still alive," she said. "Barely. I tried to give her another drink, but she can't swallow."

The Lost Rythan nodded. "I'll look at her," he said, wondering why he insisted on punishing himself this way. He had no obligation to this corporation secretary. He had known almost from the beginning—right after the accident—that there was no hope for her. And certainly, he thought with some bitterness, if their positions had been reversed, she would have been the first to consider *him* expendable.

To his relief, he found the secretary unconscious and likely to remain that way until the end. Her breathing was stertorious at best and her lips were already turning blue. Even as he watched, that breathing stopped, only to resume half a minute later with a hitch and a gasp. He forced himself to remain where he was while, behind him, the others set the fish to broil. It was not right that anyone should die alone.

For a time, he only watched, deliberately blanking his mind, as he tried not to think of other deaths he had seen. He had been old enough to remember when his mother had died quietly in a firelit room with the wolves howling outside. The priest had heard her confession and given her the Sacrament while Ard Matthew and his siblings knelt weeping beside the bed. And later, two of those brothers had been killed fighting—and two sisters had succumbed to the same sickness that took their mother.

Was there no beginning for him? No time of innocence and peace before the sufferings of life? If so, he had forgotten.

The bluish tinge was spreading rapidly over the rest of Shami's face.

CHAPTER FIVE

When the fish was done—or at least thoroughly scorched—Babe took it off the coals and laid it on a fallen tree. He looked at Ard Matthew.

"Go ahead and eat," the Rythan said. "I'll join you later." He was hungry but he could not eat. He knew his vigil was useless; probably the secretary would not even regain consciousness before she died. But still, he stayed with her.

After a moment, Téna came over to join him. She didn't say anything, though Babe looked up.

"Still alive?"

Ard Matthew nodded.

"How much longer, do you think?"

A shrug.

"Is she—has she said anything at all?" Téna asked.

The Rythan did not turn. "I don't think she can," he told her.

Then he froze while Téna turned to see what he was looking at. For Shami had opened her eyes and was staring up at both of them.

"Sh-Shami?" Téna faltered, slipping down beside the other woman. "Can you hear me?"

The secretary made a faint gasp as another breath of air was forced into her failing lungs. "Elfane—" she whispered fiercely. "Elfane!"

"M-my cousin?" Téna faltered. She turned to Ard Matthew. "She is mistaking me for Dr. Kessler."

But Ard Matthew wasn't listening. He was only watching Shami's face. The dark eyes did not focus so he could not say whether she saw him or not.

Her faced strained with the effort to speak again. "You—*murderess*!"

Téna winced and drew back. "What do you mean?" she demanded.

The secretary fought for another breath. "I know—what you did. You and Babe—"

At this, Ard Matthew leaned closer. "Tell us, then," he said. "If you want justice. What did they do?" But already he thought he knew. He had an explanation for what had happened, though he didn't yet have all the pieces of the puzzle.

They waited as, for long moments, the secretary said no more. Indeed, she closed her eyes—and her breathing stopped. The Rythan reached over and pressed on her abdomen, forcing air in and out.

"Don't—don't do that," Téna said suddenly. "Let her die."

He removed his hands. But Shami was breathing once more. Her purplish face was ghastly. One last time she opened her eyes, focused on some inner vision. "They think—you're dead, Elfane," she gasped. "You pulled it off, damn you."

This time the breathing did not resume. Ard Matthew reached over and gently closed her eyes.

Beside him, Téna knelt, staring at the dead face as though she never wanted to move again.

"Your cousin betrayed you," Ard Matthew said quietly. "She arranged for the flyer to fail. For the evidence to be destroyed. At least that is how I understand the situation." He hesitated. "But why would she want to kill you?" he asked.

Slowly Téna turned. Her face was white, her eyes wide.

"Why would Dr. Kessler do something like that?" he asked her again. "What reason could she have?"

"I—I don't know. I mean—we were never close. She took me in when I came to her from Sachsen. I had been in some trouble and I thought she would give me a job. But she said I had to learn the ropes first. So—so I was trying to learn."

"She wanted other people to think she was dead," he persisted. "Didn't she? Was it something to do with the Rumors—the phessite?"

She looked at him blankly. "The phessite?" she repeated. "But that's only—I mean, there are always stories like that. About the corporations."

But Ard Matthew had already turned away from her. "Babe?" he asked. "What do you know about this?"

Babe stood up and came over to look down on Shami's corpse. "I didn't think she knew anything," he said. "Téna."

"What wasn't she supposed to know?" Ard Matthew asked, still wondering if he could be on the wrong track. After all, if Shami had thought the flier was sabotaged, why hadn't she said something before they left the port? She would hardly have boarded the thing.

Beside him, Téna was glaring at Babe. "Were you going to jump?" she asked him "Did you forget to bring a parachute? Is that it?"

Babe spread his hands. "I didn't know the flyer was sabotaged," he said. "I guessed—I mean I had reason to think something was planned and I tried—earlier, back at company headquarters—I tried to tell you not to go." He was speaking to Téna now. "You know I tried, but you misunderstood me."

She stared at him. "I thought it was more of your nonsense. Another come on."

Babe flushed. "I know better that to try something like that. You've made your feelings plain enough," he said bitterly.

"Babe," Ard Matthew interposed, "just tell us how you know—what made you suspect that something would happen on the flight."

Babe's features twisted into a mirthless smile. "Because I knew Dr. Kessler. I worked for her, after all. We had each other's measure. Or at least she thought she had mine." He shrugged and looked away. "Oh what's the use? She told me she needed to disappear, that her enemies must think her dead. And I agreed to—to bring Téna and Shami here."

"You agreed to see them killed?"

"She never said they'd be killed. Only that they would disappear. That they'd be put up in one of the lodges for a while."

"She had a hold over him," Téna said with a sneer. "Didn't she, Babe?" She turned to Ard Matthew. "It was about something that happened on his home colony. Graft and some missing weapons. I never knew the details, but I think they'd be happy to know where he is." Her sneer turned into a smile that was even worse. "Oh they'd like to get their hands on Babe alright," she said. "If Cousin Elfane ever decided she didn't need him anymore, I don't think his life would be worth much."

Ard Matthew looked at her. It made sense. To save his life, Babe would have done his share of dirty work for the corporation, including murder, no doubt. But he must have drawn the line somewhere.

"So you came along with us," the Rythan said. "You forced yourself into the party—because you didn't trust your employer?"

Babe nodded without looking at either of the others. "She said they'd be taken to one of the lodges. That it would look like a kidnap—or an accident of some sort. That you—" he indicated the pilot—"were in on it. When I met you, I saw at once that was a lie. You're not the type. So I was expecting an attack from outside. An attack from another flier, I mean," he said. "And of course Dr. Kessler didn't know I'd be with you."

He might be telling the truth—and then he might not. The Rythan frowned. Though Babe might claim that he, Ard Matthew, did not look like a criminal, he could not return the compliment.

"You were watching," Téna said suddenly. "All the time, you were watching from the back. Is that why?"

Babe nodded.

"And you were not supposed to be in the flier at all," Ard Matthew added. There was that in his favor.

"I wasn't even supposed to come down in the shuttle."

"But you did."

Babe shrugged. "Maybe I just wanted to get back at her," he said wearily. "Foil her plans for once. Looks like a wasted effort, doesn't it?"

But Téna would not let this go. "I overheard you and my cousin quarrelling," she said. "But I didn't know what it was about. She was threatening you, I suppose."

"You can suppose all you like," Babe growled, stung. "I'm here, aren't I? We're in this together."

"But what exactly *were* you supposed to do?" Ard Matthew asked. "What were your orders?"

"Bring them here. Send them down. I told you."

"And that was all?"

Babe did not answer this directly. "I—arranged with some people," he admitted. "We've used them before. I thought they would attack from outside, kidnap the women and make it look like they had had an accident. I thought I could handle things."

"So you had no idea they would sabotage the flier itself?"

Babe shook his head. "I should have," he admitted. "But at the time, I didn't know how far Kessler would go. I thought she wanted to keep them alive."

Ard Matthew frowned. "It is hard to believe someone would sacrifice lives this way—people who trusted them—and only for convenience. For gain."

Babe gave him a sour smile. "Welcome to the real universe, Third-Blade."

Ard Matthew flushed. So he had been stupid. He was a long way from home and the clean customs of Lost Rythar. A very long way.

But these two—they had lived with the ways of the offworlders. They were citizens of the galaxy, or at least the small part of the galaxy where humans lived. And they had been duped as well as he. He could see that the girl was having trouble digesting the fact that she had been betrayed—almost murdered. He didn't think she had been bred to the ways of the corporations any more than he had.

On an impulse, he put an arm around her shoulders, aware that Babe was watching him and, for once, not caring. "Come and sit down," he said. "You are safe now. Safe from *them*, at least."

"You couldn't save Shami," she said, not looking at him. "She was my cousin's private secretary. I can't believe she would sacrifice her." But she let him guide her to a seat on the log by the fire.

"I guess it had to look convincing," Babe said. "Both of them at once. Kessler and her secretary travelling together—going down together."

Téna ignored him. At that moment, Ard Matthew was distracted by the beeping of his miniature com. He pulled it from his jacket pocket, surprised he hadn't lost it in the crash. But now he looked at it suspiciously—the port was too far away for a good signal and he had not heard another flyer pass overhead. "Babe?" he asked. "What do you think?"

"I don't know," the other man said. "They could be checking to make sure they got us. But I don't think so. That isn't how they work—and anyway, there was no other flier out there."

Lost Rythan frowned. "A ground crew could not have known where we'd crash. Or how far we might travel afterwards if we survived."

Babe nodded. "That would be stretching things, wouldn't it?"

"But who could it be?" Téna asked.

While Ard Matthew did not dare respond to the barely audible signal, he held the com up to his ear. "It's a distress call," he said after a moment. "Set on automatic, I think."

It could still be a ruse. He looked at the others.

Babe shrugged. "If someone else has crashed out here, we might do better working together. But you know this place better than we do. Are we likely to hook up with anyone we can—deal with?"

Ard Matthew knew what he meant. For the most part, Windy-Go was an almost lawless wilderness.

"Did you know of anyone else who took off the morning we did?" Babe asked.

"My employer would have been the one to register," Ard Matthew told him. "There was no reason for me to know about all the flights." He was thinking furiously. Mong had set up this trip. Mong had been in charge of the equipment—the flyer. Mong. He was almost afraid to finish that thought but now that he had begun, he must. He clenched his teeth. It *hurt*—he had to admit that it did.

"You don't see how my operatives could have got to the machine," Babe said, looking at him with almost uncanny percipience. "Unless your boss was in on it. Am I right?"

Ard Matthew looked away. Saler Mong had been the man who got him away from Wolf-slammer, Windy-Go's sister planet. And Mong had dealt fairly with him, had been a good employer. Almost a friend. Of course, among the offworlders, friendship did not mean what it did on Lost Rythar and he had never thought it did. But *this*?

He clenched one fist and let his breath out in a long exhalation. "Yeah," he said at last. There was nothing else to say.

Babe nodded. "Looks like we've all been sold out, doesn't it?"

Ard Matthew nodded. But along with his anger—a desire to come to grips with his enemies that nearly approached the battle madness—he felt the beginnings of a resolution more powerful than even this.

"We will survive," he said, speaking his thoughts aloud and not knowing how fierce he looked. "We will have justice."

"I see murder in your eyes," Babe said lightly.

The other looked at him in surprise. "Death, perhaps," he said more temperately. "But not murder, I hope."

A nod. "So what shall we do about this signal?"

"Answer it," Ard Matthew decided. "It's a risk we must take. There may be someone out there in trouble." He looked a question at Téna, who gave a grudging nod.

He flicked the switch and put out an answering call.

"We all know this is risky," Babe said as Ard Matthew set the signal. "And because it is, we need to be ready to move."

Téna looked up. "Do you really think they—that anyone will be hunting us?" she asked.

The Lost Rythan let them talk. He didn't think, considering the weakness of the signal, that there was any immediate danger. Whoever had set up the accident would have to be obsessively paranoid to have left people on the ground. But on second thought, maybe that was not to be depended on. Someone—perhaps Dr. Kessler herself—would want proof that her plan had succeeded. Once more he felt his fury rising and stifled it. Later would be time enough, he told himself grimly.

Because Babe and Téna were watching him, he tried to smooth his features. I need a shave, he thought inconsequently as he put one hand to his cheek. Was there a razor in his kit? He couldn't remember if he had put one in or not.

With a sigh, he turned to the others. "We aren't ready to move on," he reminded them. "First we must bury our dead."

Téna give a start while Babe frowned. "We could cremate her," he said.

"Not that," Ard Matthew told him, wondering why the idea disgusted him so despite the fact that he had cut his ties with the Star Brothers. What did it matter what they did to the corpse?

But Téna's face showed her own repugnance at the idea. Babe was not making any points with her, Ard Matthew thought.

"We shall bury her," Téna said firmly. "Isn't that right, Mr. Third-Blade?"

Why did she turn to *him*? He wasn't supposed to be the leader of the party. He gave Babe a speculative glance, but the other man had picked up his gun and was busy examining its charge.

"Yes," the Rythan said at last. "We'll need to bury the lady. Do you know her full name?"

"Shami Star-trail," Téna said. "That's all I know. She was from a colony where they have names like that." She looked over at the corpse. "A little like your own, I suppose. But she left the place when she was young."

Ard Matthew gave a grunt, thinking of all the Bloodbears and Wolfbanes he had known. Firespears and Sunspears and of course his own clan, the Third-Blades. He felt a momentary kinship with the dead woman and was sorry he had not tried to comfort her as she died.

Suddenly, the com began to vibrate and he pulled it back out of his pocket, flicking on the audio. The immediate result was not very enlightening. First, there was static, and then what sounded like words fading in and out. He turned up the volume so the others could hear.

"… f you… never… you can… all you like…"

Babe shook his head. "Have to do better than that," he said.

Ard Matthew regarded the instrument thoughtfully. "I can," he said, remembering what he had been taught about reception. "But I'll have to climb a tree." It had all been part of his training, years ago when he joined the Faring Guard and learned to use the offworld gadgets.

First he had to find a tree that would bear his weight. Luckily these were very much like the trees of his home colony. Maybe Windy-Go's evergreens were not as tall, or as bright a green, but many of them could have passed for sunfirs just the same. He slipped the radio back in his pocket and, selecting one he thought might do, he grasped the stub of a broken branch and began to haul himself up.

In boyhood he had often shinnied up a tree this way in order to get a better view of the valley where he lived. The Third-Blade keeps were always located in the higher regions, where thin forests alternated with alpine meadows. Boys were left in the meadows during the daytime to mind the goats. That was fine because guarding the goats meant hunting predators—and the sight of a wolf or a snowtyger was a fine excuse for a hunt. Once in a while, they even saw a bear, though they were not allowed to hunt these by themselves.

He smiled a little at the memories. This was an excellent tree, he thought. But as he got higher, two things became quickly evident. First, it was not really a sunfir. The bark was much rougher, fissured and loose. He had to grip hard with his knees, hugging the bole tightly as good sized pieces loosened and came free. And second, he was larger and heavier than the boy who had once herded goats in the mountains of Lost Rythar Colony.

Once he looked down into the staring faces of the others and gave them what he hoped was a reassuring nod. Téna's eyes had gone wide, her mouth slightly opened in surprise while Babe was looking at him as though he had gone crazy. Then he turned back to his climb, peering upward as he came at last into the sparse foliage of the tree. He would have to be more careful now as the trunk narrowed.

He reached up for a bough and felt it bend beneath his grip. Could he trust it to haul himself up? He edged himself higher and clutched the bough with both hands while he wrapped his legs more tightly around the trunk. With a loud crack the branch came away in his grip.

He let it go, reaching frantically to wrap his arms around the main trunk. For a moment, he clung there shaking with reaction, as he stared upward at the broken stub. He did not dare to look down at the others.

"Come on," he muttered to himself. "This is no different than what you've done before." But he had, as it happened, broken a leg once falling from a sunfir. He could not afford an injury like that now.

Gritting his teeth, he clung where he was, keeping one arm wrapped around the tree while with the other he fished out the radio. Better not drop it now, he thought sourly and almost did.

One-handed, he keyed the transmit function. "Can you hear me?" he asked. "I've got some height but I still think we're almost out of range."

Static.

Patiently, he shifted one leg to ease a cramp, and tried again. "We're down somewhere about grid 7H," he said. He didn't dare use their names for obvious reasons. "Where are you?"

This time, the transmission was clearer. "In hell," a hoarse voice said. He thought it was male.

He wasn't sure how to respond, but he had to say something. Finally, "Do you have coordinates?" he asked, knowing how inane this sounded.

"You're real, aren't you?" the voice said. "I wasn't sure."

This admitted of an easy answer. He risked giving his name. "Ard Matthew Third-Blade," he told the voice.

"That sounds real." A pause. Then, "You can't get any more solid than a Lost Rythan. That's what you are, isn't it?"

"Affirmative."

"Are you up a tree?" Another pause. "*They* climb trees, too."

Obviously the man was either feverish or drunk. "Up a tree," he said. "What about you? And who are you?"

"John Solomon, of the Becker Party. Or at least I *was*. Once."

The Becker Party. The other pilots had been discussing them. The Becker Party had been yet another of the many offworld university groups seeking evidence of non-human sentience. Heading for the so-called ruins—

"But they disappeared over a month ago," he said aloud. "No one knew whether there were any survivors."

"Has it been only a month?"

"I think so." He shifted his grip once more, feeling an ache in his thighs. No, he was definitely not the boy he had been. "Can you tell us where you are? And how many of you survived?"

His answer was a strange sound which Ard Matthew finally realized was laughter.

"Mr. Solomon? Can you give me your co-ordinates?"

"Can I give you—whatever you like, Mr. Third-Blade." And the man went off into another gale of mirth.

Ard Matthew held on to both his patience and the tree. He was aware of someone shouting up to him from below, but he could not make out the words. Hopefully it was something they could handle without him.

"Is your flyer's transmitter working?" he asked carefully. "You seem to be using a personal com."

"Oh the flyer. I'm a long way from there. You would be too."

"What do you mean?"

There was a longish silence.

Finally, Ard Matthew broke it. "Are you still there?" he asked.

"Watch out for—*them*," the other man said. "And don't try to find the flyer."

"Are you alone?" Ard Matthew asked Solomon. "Is there anyone else I can speak to?"

"Sometimes. I am alone sometimes." Then, as though getting a grip on himself. "If you have a PND, you can use my com to get a fix. I've lost just about everything else."

Cursing himself for leaving the PND in his pack, Ard Matthew repeated his question. "Is there anyone else with you? I mean now—anyone else who will speak to me?"

"I—I'm not sure. I don't think so. I haven't been well. Not since…" There was no more. The transmission had been cut.

So. Ard Matthew was pretty sure he could get a fix even if Solomon wasn't using the unit. Grimly he set himself to climb down, even more aware of the awkwardness of his great frame. He slid part of the way, as he had done in his boyhood, but it wasn't as easy as it had once been, and he had a few scrapes and bruises by the time he reached the ground—not to mention splinters in his hands. And he faced another climb back up! He'd need altitude to get a real fix on Solomon's location.

He landed on his knees and Babe helped him to his feet. Luckily his pants were kevlas, bought at the outfitters at the port, and his jacket some kind of leather, or he would have been in rags after that descent. He told the others what Solomon had said.

"Sounds wacked out to me," Babe said.

"I wonder if their flyer exploded," Téna mused.

Ard Matthew went back over his conversation with the man. "I don't think so," he said. "He said we could find *him*—wherever he is—with the PND using his com. I *think* I can do it, though I'm not sure coms were meant for that sort of thing. But as for the flyer—"

He trailed off. Solomon had said not to look for it. And certainly he had not detected any transmission. But somehow, he had an idea it had not been destroyed. Something else was wrong—some other reason not to seek it out. Though of course the man might have been delusional.

Babe grunted. "They're not," he agreed. "Coms, I mean. How about trying to locate the flyer instead? If it didn't blow, you might get a reading."

"Yes," Ard Matthew said slowly. Babe was sharp and he appreciated that. He did not tell him everything Solomon had said. "I guess I'll try now," he said instead.

But Téna shook her head. "Before we go looking for these people," she reminded the others, "we have something else to do."

Babe gave a shrug.

"Of course," the Lost Rythan said quickly, before Babe could say anything. He had been glad enough to forget about the dead woman while he was climbing the tree, but now the weight of all that had happened and what they must do about it settled back on him. "Let's find a place to bury her."

"Right." Babe said, glancing at Téna. "Have we got anything to dig with?"

Ard Matthew fished the folding shovel from his pack. It wasn't very big and he had seldom used it. "This isn't much, but we can burn away tree roots with the laser," he said. He cast about for a clearing where the soil wouldn't be too rocky. The trees never quite made a forest, but neither did they leave many open spaces. He didn't want to make a grave near the swamp.

Finally, they located a promising site not too far from the camp. There were a few larger rocks nearby which they could pile on top of the grave when they had finished.

Leaving Téna to prepare the corpse, he and Babe set themselves to dig.

Of course the arrangement had not been that simple. When she understood what they expected of her, Téna's initial reaction was to refuse. There was no reason she could not help dig the grave and every reason she should not be forced to clean and wrap the body. She told Ard Matthew this in no uncertain terms.

He only looked at her. "She's a woman," he said. "It is more fitting that another woman should do this for her."

"You *are* a primitive," Téna told him in disgust. "A complete barbarian."

He sighed. His legs were aching from the climb and the time he had spent gripping the tree bole and his hands were sore from the bark. He was in no mood to argue with this offworld woman. But he supposed he must.

What would persuade her? He looked at Babe, and there was no help there. But that gave him an idea. "You knew her," he said, choosing his words carefully. "Would she want to be prepared for burial by—by Babe and me?" He looked at her earnestly.

This hit home. She glanced from one man to the other and shook her head. They all looked down at Shami's body. The secretary's face was very still and her normally dark skin had taken on a sallow cast. There were drawn-in places beside her nose and her mouth was slightly open. At least he had remembered to close her eyes.

Gingerly, Téna slipped one arm around the other woman' shoulders and turned her partway over. It was plain she had not done this service for anyone before. Likely she had not known how quickly a body would begin to stiffen after death.

They had nothing to use for a shroud except the thermal blanket which they couldn't spare so Ard Matthew told her to use the lean-to covering. If it rained, they could all huddle beneath the thermal—or else he would think of something else.

So he and Babe did their work, toiling over the alien soil until they had made a serviceable though very shallow grave. It would have to do since they had no better tools.

The rest of the burial went smoothly enough. When the grave was filled in and the rocks laid on top, Babe turned away, leaving Ard Matthew and the girl staring at one another over the mound.

"I—I think we should say something," she ventured. "Some words."

He gave her a long, brooding look.

"Well don't your people do anything to honor the dead?" she demanded angrily.

He glared at her, taken off guard. "What my people do—" he began. Then, "Find your own prayers," he told her roughly. "If you know any."

He turned away, but not before he saw her kneel at the grave and make the Sign of the Cross. For some reason, this made him even more angry.

Babe was waiting. He had cleaned up the site, stowing things in the pack. The sun had some way to go before setting. The morning's storm had been succeeded by sunshine, though a cool breeze promised a chilly night.

"What now?" Babe asked.

"I've got to get a reading on the PNG. If I can."

"Back up the tree?"

Ard Matthew nodded. He wasn't looking forward to another climb. "But I'm going to try it on the ground first," he said. "I don't have to talk to anyone to get this."

Babe grunted. "Should I try and catch more fish?" he asked. "Before it gets too dark, I mean."

He didn't mention the screams they had heard in the night, but he didn't have to. Whatever had made those sounds—and probably the paired scrapes in some of the trees—might very well return.

"We'll need more firewood," Ard Matthew decided. He looked at Téna as he said it.

"I'll go," she said. "But we need food as well. Fish if he can get it."

"I don't know," Babe said. "Hadn't I better come along?"

Téna shook her head. "I can manage," she snapped. "Anyway, isn't that women's work? Gathering wood?" She wasn't far from tears, Ard Matthew thought.

Babe gave her a gloomy look but didn't say anything.

"Go ahead," the Rythan told her. "You should be safe enough by daylight. I'll join you as soon as I have a fix on that comm."

Téna headed back up the hill to the place where she and Babe had gathered wood before. "Wait," Ard Matthew called suddenly. "Take the laser."

Wordlessly, she turned back and picked up the tool.

"Do you know how to extend the beam?" he asked. "Just in case."

He showed her.

When she had disappeared, he got out the PNG and fiddled with the controls. He wasn't as confident as he had led the others to believe—he still might have to climb that tree. But before he could even look for a reading, he heard a loud commotion in the direction Téna had gone. Thudding hoofbeats and then the sound of running.

He surged to his feet, his task forgotten as he pulled the knife from his belt. Téna came leaping down the hillside and skidded past the ashes of the fire. Behind her came two oversized birds, beaks opened to emit their strident cry. Eyes wild, she was gasping and holding her side as the birds veered off and disappeared.

He ran toward her, watching her pursuers vanish among the trees, still squawking. Then he turned to the girl as, trying to catch her breath, she collapsed onto the log. "I—I saw an antelope," she gasped.

"Was coming—to tell you. And then these other things—Wh-what were they?"

He resheathed his knife. "They would have been our dinner if I had had the gun," he said. "They looked like turkeys though I have never seen any so large."

"Were they—I mean would they—have hurt me?"

He frowned. "The ones I hunted were smaller," he said. "On some other world. And I don't know what they ate. Maybe bugs and grain. But these could probably take on something bigger."

Téna looked back up the hill toward the deadfall. "There could be *anything* out there! Isn't that right? You don't really know much about this planet, do you?"

"Not this far from the port and the lodges," he agreed. "No one does. But all habitable worlds have similar life forms. Because of the starnet. Things get transferred from world to world. It just happens."

"Similar," she repeated.

He shrugged. "I've seen some strange animals," he admitted and then stopped as the memories flooded back. Yes, he had seen horrors. But he did not expect to meet anything here that he couldn't handle.

He turned back to the PNG. It looked like he was getting a reading. After a moment, he set the thing to remember. Then he turned to Téna. "I'll help you get wood," he said.

They started back up the hill. The light was slanting now, and their lengthened shadows stretched beside them. In the distance, an even deeper shade was poised ready to gather into darkness beneath the trees.

They worked swiftly. He did the cutting while she tugged out the pieces. She and Babe had already harvested the easy wood and what they found now was mostly tangled together. They had to pull away a lot of useless stuff to get to the larger branches. But soon enough there was a respectable pile. Each of them shouldered a load of cut limbs and headed back for the camp.

Suddenly Ard Matthew heard another rustling sound behind them.

This time he was determined not to lose whatever presented itself. He was hungry and the others must be hungry too. He raised the laser cutter as an antelope came streaking past—only to stumble and fall a few feet away as he used the blade on its longest setting. For a moment, he hesitated, watching the deadfall, but nothing else came out. Only when he was sure they were safe did he go to look at his kill. He had taken it in the neck and the head was twisted at an angle where it had fallen. There was a lot of blood.

"Young one," he said. He slung the animal over his shoulders. "Can you manage the wood?" he asked. "We've got to hurry before it gets dark."

Obediently, Téna took up her load and some of his, staggering a little as she moved beside him.

They were lucky to have the game as Babe had returned empty handed. He watched Ard Matthew gut his kill. "You get that with the laser?"

The other nodded. "I wasn't sure I could," he said. He gave Téna a half apologetic look. "It was a chance."

She turned back to feeding the fire. The warmth felt good.

Babe threw himself down beside it. "Getting cold," he said. The sun had already vanished, and the sky flamed red. In the east—or whatever direction it was—a few stars were already showing.

Taking out his knife, Ard Matthew cut steaks from the antelope. They would need more firewood—the rest of the bundle he had cut. He suggested this to Babe. Then to Téna, "You can start the meat cooking as soon as you have coals enough. We won't be long."

But this was too much for her. "Come on, Babe," she said, rising. "You've got your gun in case we need it."

Surprised, Babe got up and followed her into the twilight.

Ard Matthew was a little startled himself. His experience of women was not extensive, considering his age, for he had been scarcely out of his teens when he joined the Faring Guard. As a penitential society, the Guard had imposed celibacy on its members, something that, with only a few lapses, he had tried to observe.

Now he frowned as he sliced off strips of meat. Somehow he had angered this woman, though at first he had thought she was even less pleased with Babe. He could guess what she thought of Babe—judging by his general coarseness. But Ard Matthew himself had tried to treat her as he would a Lost Rythan woman. Apparently that wasn't what she wanted either.

Well she and the other man were together now. And Babe had a gun. And, come to think of it, those birds should be roosting for the night which meant the two would be safe enough. He began to thread their dinner on sharpened sticks and angled it over the coals.

As the juices started to drip, he realized that he was ravenous.

CHAPTER SIX

The smell of broiling meat mingled with the scents of evening and Ard Matthew felt some of his tension begin to ease. Babe and Téna seemed to be getting along and for this he was grateful. In their absence, he could almost pretend he was alone on one of his own impromptu camping excursions. Before—

But he would not let his thoughts go that way. Before his employer had sold him out was what he meant. Before he had been forced to dispense with yet more of his innocence—his Lost Rythan belief in the basic decency of humankind. The honor of friendship.

Shrugging this off, he turned to his pack. There were still the two beer cubes. He'd save those for an emergency. And a few ration bars. He still wasn't hungry enough to bite into something that tasted like sawdust stuck together with grease. But maybe the others would be less particular? They could be used to food like this for all he knew.

He moved the bag nearer the fire and poked around inside. He was looking for something else, and there it was—his razor. So he had brought it after all. Maybe he would shave before they set off to find this Solomon—Dr. Solomon?—and whatever was left of the Becker party. He must look like a veritable savage by now. He ran one hand over his emerging beard.

He sighed, thinking about Solomon and his message. They would have some miles to cover if they were to locate the man. It could take them several days, moving even further from the lodge district. So far the terrain had not seemed all that different from what he was used to, aside from the giant turkeys and whatever screamed in the night. There was plenty of game here, and the trees seemed about the same.

If it weren't for his responsibility for Babe and Téna—and of course, the death of Shami—he might almost enjoy the chance to explore this new country. It would give him a chance to process recent events. *All* the recent events.

He saw again in his mind's eye the child back on Ynche Colony. He had seen other children die on Lost Rythar, but not like that. And as for Gris Wolfgang—but he let that thought go. It wasn't the death, nor even the torment he objected to. Not really. It was the *innocence* he had seen in his friend's eyes. Gris Wolfgang had accepted it all, had made no complaint. It would never have occurred to him that his suffering had no value.

And then there was Shami's death. He had not comforted her. Instead he had spoken to her out of his own pain and bitterness, had put brutal honesty before kindness. Even now, he would not admit that he could have done anything else. After all, what did he have to offer her? What blessing to give—he who had lost himself?

Slowly he shoved everything back into his pack, setting aside the ration bars and the razor. He was reclosing the flap when the others returned, both burdened with cut wood. Babe managed the gun with one hand while he balanced his load with the other. It was fully dark beneath the trees, while little more than a pale memory of the sunset still lingered in the sky.

As a Lost Rythan, he could never get used to the idea that there was no moon here on Windy-Go. What oceans there were—somewhere on the other side of the planet perhaps—must rely on the sun for their tides. He peered out into the starlit darkness, blinking but unable to see anything at all.

"Sure smells good around here," Babe said as he and Téna came up. He dropped his load and squatted down to examine the cooking meat. "Done yet?"

"Pretty much," Ard Matthew told him. He took off a couple of the makeshift skewers and blew on them. He saw Téna grimace as she watched him and wondered what he had done wrong now. Some failure of offworld etiquette?

She walked over to the fire and tried to pull off another of the crude spits. But the heat had weakened the wood and even as she tugged, the meat fell into the ashes.

Babe managed to retrieve it, though Ard Matthew didn't think anyone would want to eat the smeared and gritty morsel. He offered Téna one of the pieces he held.

"I wish," she said in a low voice, "you hadn't blown on it." But she took it anyway. He could see that she was famished, that she only spoke out of reflex.

Babe laughed and took off another couple of skewers. In the end, they ate every bit of the cooked meat, manners forgotten as the grease ran down their chins. When they had finished, Babe offered to fetch another bucket of water for them to wash.

Ard Matthew threw more wood on the fire. His instincts were telling him that sending Babe off alone was not a good idea. Instead, he took up the flicker torch and turned to the other man. "We'll all go together," he said. "You take the gun, Téna can have the light, and I'll carry the bucket." He didn't want to alarm them, especially when he had no real explanation for his feeling.

Babe raised one eyebrow. "Okay," he said. "We might as well all wash in the stream and save the bucket for drinking water." Neither of them looked at Téna.

Ard Matthew handed her the torch. "Stay together," he said. "I've got the laser as well." He still didn't know why he was so nervous—only that he was. He doubted that these more civilized people could feel what was so clear to him. Most likely Téna would be reminding herself that the turkeys would have gone to roost by now and she would be wondering what else could be out there to make him uneasy.

He shrugged. Let her think he was over-careful. And that was not such a bad thing; after all, he had seen what happened to those who were not. He noted that Babe was looking from side to side, gun at the ready. Good.

He led them down the slope to the brook, pausing once or twice to glance back at the campfire. It was burning well and did a good job illuminating the little clearing they had made into a temporary home. He could not help thinking of the woman who had died there and of the lonely grave they had made for her further up the hillside. A dozen Rythan folk tales came back to him—stories of the restless dead. He shivered slightly with an atavistic uneasiness that predated the Star Brothers' coming to Rythar.

Then he shook himself and resumed his stride. Ahead, the brush made a dark barrier appearing, in the wavering light of the torch, even thicker and taller than it was. He could hear small animals scrabbling about and an occasional plop as something jumped into the water.

Babe, who now brought up the rear, hustled Téna forward so that they closed ranks as they came nearer the water. "Let's see if we can find the path Third-Blade and I made when we went fishing," he said. "Point the light over here." He gestured to his right.

Obediently, she directed the beam to a place where the brush seemed thinner.

Ard Matthew strode forward and pushed aside the branches. He was still holding back a mat of foliage when he froze. Behind them, the darkness was shattered by a scream, drawn out and harrowing. With a little cry, Téna dropped the torch.

The light rolled and bounced before coming to rest against a clump of flags. In the oblique reflection, he could make out Babe pointing the gun back at the camp. Beside him, Téna was a half shadow, her hands spread out on each side.

Without taking his eyes from the hillside, Ard Matthew bent down and retrieved the torch from the flowers. But when he aimed it back in the direction of their camp, he could see nothing moving in the murk. Then, remembering the slashes on the tree boles, he looked upward into the tops. Against the star-crowded sky, branches made clear silhouettes. He doused the light.

He heard Téna gasp as the darkness returned.

"Quiet," he told her. "We are safer this way." He continued to watch the trees.

Once more that scream, no less harrowing because they were expecting it, and then silence. It was not the silence of tranquility. For the first time, he realized that the normal sounds of the night—amphibians croaking, insects chirping, even those furtive movements in the brush by the creek, had ceased. Everything seemed hushed. Hushed and waiting for something terrifying to happen.

That was when he saw what he had been looking for—a dark blot against the stars. It resolved itself into a flying, rushing shape, high among the treetops, moving from tree to tree just as he had thought it might move. If it had wings, he couldn't see any. Perhaps it gripped the branches like one of the apes he had seen in Bloomhadn's zoo. Or did it glide? Some animals did that, he had heard.

But this thing seemed far too large to glide. He could hear branches breaking and see an occasional treetop sway beneath its weight. However it progressed, it was certainly coming down the hill.

Babe had backed up, pulling Téna with him. For once, she did not object. Ard Matthew braced himself, the laser set on its furthest extension. Would it be enough? An antelope leaping practically in his face, was one thing, but this—this shadow beast might well be more than he could handle with such a limited weapon.

"Wait," he cautioned Babe. "Wait for a good shot. It may be our only chance."

"Yeah."

They continued to watch the treetops move, darkness passing against the sky. He still couldn't tell how the thing was propelling itself. He could not even get a clear idea of its shape. The tree branches blocked his view, so that at one moment, the creature seemed to possess elongated spider legs and at the next it was reduced to nothing more than a pattern of tree limbs itself. Already, it was halfway down the hill and there was no sign or it slowing down.

They were all watching so intently that at first they did not hear stealthy movements behind them until Ard Matthew whirled suddenly at the sound of a snapping branch. He brought up the laser, felt something smash into him and went down. There was a low growl and heavy jaws snapped at his leg. In the darkness, all was confusion.

"A bear!" Téna screamed and the Lost Rythan felt the brush of an airbolt pass near his head.

"Don't shoot!" he cried, and rolled over, grabbing the torch. But when the light came on, his attacker was nowhere in sight. Quickly he shone the light back up the hill, trying to catch the treetops in its beam. But there was nothing to be seen there either.

"Back to back," Babe murmured. "All of us. You still got the laser, Third-Blade?"

Ard Matthew realized that he did not. He hunted around desperately until he found it.

"Let me have the torch," Téna said and he gave it back to her.

They waited tensely, while Téna flashed the light all around them. He half expected the beam to catch a pair of animal eyes, but there was nothing more threatening to be seen than a low mat of bushes. In the distance, an animal bellowed and he felt himself tense. But the sound was not repeated.

Once more, he studied the treetops, seeking motion where there was none.

"Let's get the water," he said at last, picking up the bucket. "I think you frightened that bear away. And as for the other—it may have got distracted."

They moved together through the brush, Téna keeping the light on their passage. Ard Matthew knelt and let the bucket fill from the running current. But all the while, he was watching upstream. The rushes were not high enough to conceal anything threatening—or at least he hoped not.

Presently, he stood up, aware for the first time that the bite had bruised his thigh. He was going to be sore, but luckily the teeth had not penetrated the fabric of his clothing. Once more he was grateful for the offworld stuff. It had probably saved him a nasty wound.

"Back to the fire?" Babe asked and he nodded.

"I'm pretty sure it's gone," he said, looking up again. "Whatever it was." He did not add that he had ceased to feel the pricking of his hairs, the intimation of danger, but he took that as a good sign.

"That was no bear in the treetops," Téna said suddenly. He could hear the tremor in her voice. "It was—something else, wasn't it?"

"Yes," the Lost Rythan agreed. "Whatever we saw was new to me." Mentally he went over his impression of the thing, wondering why he had seen no spoor of it in the woods near the lodges. It had seemed almost fluid as it moved among the foliage, but he hadn't got anything like a good look. If it hadn't been for the screaming cries, he might have thought he had seen no more than a trick of the rising wind. A mix of shadows and starlight. But it had seemed so *purposeful*, advancing down the hill toward them—and he had heard the branches breaking. That much was real.

"We'll have to take watches," Babe said as they neared the campsite. "And keep up the fire. Good thing we brought in that extra wood."

Ard Matthew nodded. Yes, it had been lucky. He had a feeling they would indeed have to keep up a fire all night. And, as Babe said, they must take watches. "Is anyone sleepy?" he asked aloud.

No one was.

When the others had settled themselves near the flames, the Lost Rythan opened his pack once more. Babe might use dep—and that was fine until the last treatment wore off and he had no more of the stuff. But Ard Matthew was going to shave.

The wind came up once more, a chilly breeze. Luckily, there were no clouds. As usual, the sky was a mass of stars, almost too crowded to make constellations. There were several smears of color that might have been nebulae.

Babe went over to feed the fire. "So, you've run into bears before?" he asked Ard Matthew. "They seem to show up on a lot of worlds."

Ard Matthew was rummaging once more. He found what he wanted—a piece of soap. It was another anachronism he had found in the market place at the port. He wet it from the water bucket and began lathering his beard. """Yes, I've seen bears on other worlds," he said. "But not exactly this kind. I think," he added, "that we might be the first humans these animals have seen and that's why it attacked. It was different nearer the lodges. I never saw any there. Or—or those other things."

"Well I guess that makes sense." Babe settled himself, the gun in his lap. "But that works two ways, doesn't it?"

Ard Matthew, who had picked up the razor, turned to look at him.

"They have no reason to be afraid of us," Babe said. "They think we are animals. But the hunting should be easier."

"Yes." He thought about the antelope—and the turkeys. "Of course." At least they were not going to starve. He wondered if Babe had ever hunted anything before. But even if he hadn't, that skill would come—Babe was a fast learner.

He took up his razor, aware of Téna watching him. A lifetime's practice made the task seem easier than it was and he tried not to smile as he saw her eyes widen in the firelight. For a moment, he wondered why he bothered. But it was his custom—to keep himself clean shaven. Or at least somewhat clean shaven. Maybe he was civilized after all. Or vain.

Dexterously, he finished the job and wiped himself off. Then, "This is new country to me," he reminded the others. "To all of us, of course. We've got to be prepared for surprises."

"Nasty ones," Babe agreed. "So what do we do now?"

"That should be obvious. Find whatever is left of the Becker Party and then try to get back to civilization."

"I dunno, Third-Blade," the other man said. "If that Kessler bitch wants us dead, I still think we'd better stay dead. At least for a while."

Ard Matthew saw Téna wince. Babe had not minced his words, but he was right. They had all been used as the pawns they were, Téna and Shami betrayed by Dr. Kessler and Ard Matthew by his own employer. And even Babe, he remembered belatedly. They were all expendable and soon to be forgotten ciphers. Unless they came back to life, of course.

He imagined how it would be if they all showed up at the port, telling the authorities what had happened, making accusations that might or might not be believed. Possibly not believed. And then finding a way back—back to *where*? Where would they be safe? They probably wouldn't live long enough to leave the planet.

No, Babe was right. They could not go back just yet. Though just what they were to do, he had no idea.

"You think the rest of that antelope might attract bears?" Babe asked suddenly

A pause. Then, "It might," Ard Matthew said. Once more, Babe had surprised him. "But I don't know what we can do about it. We'll need that food."

"Then we'd better guard it. Keep it close to the fire."

Ard Matthew got up. He went over to the half butchered animal and dragged it nearer the center of their camp. "I can cook more of it now," he offered. "It will keep better."

"Okay," Babe said, eyeing the carcass.

"You want to sleep first? I can grill the meat while I'm watching."

"Sure." After a moment, Babe handed over the gun.

Ard Matthew carried it to Téna. "You hold this," he said, handing her the weapon. "And I'll start cutting."

He was aware of her watching him as he sliced meat from the bones. "You're good at that, aren't you?" she said. "I mean you must have done a lot of this sort of thing."

He didn't look up from his work. "I have," he agreed.

"This is all new to me," she told him hesitantly. "I mean I *did* grow up on a farm. But this is only the second planet I've visited besides my own. It's all so—unreal."

"I guess it would be," he agreed reluctantly. He tried to imagine how it must be for her. Obviously, she hadn't been bred for this, but then likely neither had Babe. They would all have to make adjustments to survive.

Presently he held up a strip of meat. "We'll need something to hold this," he said. "A rack of some kind. Those skewers didn't work very well." He turned to look at her. "I think I understand some of what you are feeling," he added. "There is a first time for all of us to leave the things we know. To lose our innocence not only in—in small things but in greater ones as well."

"Yes," she said, looking at the meat. She laid down the gun and got up. "I'll look for some twigs," she said. "In the woodpile."

"Good. If any are green, they will be best."

He watched her walk over to the pile. She had left the gun behind, but he could reach it quickly if he had to. "How many worlds have you seen?" she asked when she had selected what she needed and come back to the fire.

"More than I wanted to." He gave her a grim smile.

"Have you always been a pilot?" she asked.

At first, he didn't answer. He accepted the wands from her and began weaving them into a sort of rack. Finally, he set this over a bed of coals and laid on the meat. "No," he said at last. "I was not trained for that until later. When I had left my home colony."

"And do you go back?" she asked. "Do you visit?"

His hand clenched on the knife handle as he went back to work on the carcass. "No," he said in a low voice. "I do not go back."

They worked in silence after that until finally he told her they had enough. "Even cooked, it won't keep more than a few days. Even in this weather."

It was growing colder. Perhaps there might even be a frost. He rose and fetched more wood for the fire, saving a bed of coals to one side to grill the meat.

"You need to get some sleep," he said. "Take the thermal blanket."

"What about you?" she asked.

"I'll wake Babe in a few hours."

She picked up the sheet and he saw that she was shivering as she wrapped it around herself. "Don't forget to give me a turn watching," she said.

He was arranging the meat and didn't answer. Presently he thought she was asleep.

How many campfires had he tended on how many worlds, he wondered. How many alien constellations had looked down on him over the years? And yet—and yet even here, those stars were the same stars that shone on other worlds. Hadn't the Star Brothers taught him that? That God was everywhere in all the universe and no world was hidden from His watchful providence.

He heard a slight sound and turned. Behind him Téna sat up, still clutching the thermal sheet around her. "I guess I'm not sleepy," she said.

"We have far to walk tomorrow," he told her. "You will need your rest."

She shrugged. "Talk to me a little, Mr. Third-Blade. Tell me about these other worlds you have visited. Were they as bad as this one?"

He tried to make out her features in the firelight. "This is one of the better ones I've seen," he said at last. Though he would not admit it, he was glad to hear another human voice in the night. Glad that he was not alone with his thoughts.

She nodded, the light catching on her cheekbones, gleaming a little on her hair. "You do seem to be at home here," she said almost accusingly. "I think you like it."

"I'm sorry your friend died," he told her. "I know that would not have happened if we had been somewhere with more facilities."

She did not answer at once. Then, "This place," she said. "Does it remind you of your homeworld?"

"You are fishing," he said with a grim smile. "And so I will tell you that it does. But we have moons and a double sun."

"And your world is called?"

Reluctantly, he told her the name and it was one she had heard.

"Lost Rythar," she repeated. "Something to do with the Star Brothers, isn't it? Do you—are you connected with them?"

"No," he told her calmly. "I am not."

"But your world resembles this one? Are there bears?"

"A few. Our own variant."

"And other things, I'll bet. You learned to hunt there, didn't you?"

He nodded.

"And the trees and—and things?"

"Most habitable worlds have similar lifeforms," he said. "The greatest differences seem to be among the animals but a lot of the trees and things are the same."

"But we don't exactly know what we're facing here, do we?" A little breeze ruffled her hair and she shivered visibly.

"Not exactly, but—" He hesitated. "I don't think you need to be too worried. We are armed and I hope we will be joining forces with others when we find the wreckage of the Becker party."

"And then? What will we do?"

He looked back into the fire. "Then we will face whatever we have to face," he told her. "Isn't it always that way?"

There was a silence of some moments before she spoke again. "This colony of yours," she said suddenly. "What is it really like? Why did you leave?"

He didn't want to answer. Above them the stars—perhaps the double star of Lost Rythar was among them?—made of the sky a silver spattered sea while the darkness of the forest seemed to draw in around their small fire. And yet he wanted to tell the truth. Something was compelling him to be honest.

"I left because I deserved to leave," he said finally, knowing that his voice sounded harsh. He was breathing hard and had to wait until he had some control. When he spoke, however, the anger still throbbed in his speech. "I will tell you what it *isn't* like," he said. "It isn't a place where people are betrayed and killed for the profit of those they have faithfully served. It isn't a place where kindred sacrifice kindred, where falsehood and double dealing are the coin of human affairs."

He paused for a moment. "That woman Dr. Kessler may be your cousin. Yet whatever it is she is trying to hide—whatever requires her simulated death—is of more worth to her than your life. Than her own honor.

"On my world, a *man*—for I did not know that women could be so evil until now—would be cast from a high rock for such a thing. His broken body would be eaten by the wolves, his bones dragged away by scavengers until there was nothing left to remember him by. That is what my homeworld is like."

He turned back to mend the fire. At first he was afraid to look at her, but when he finally turned around, she had wrapped herself up once more and lay curled on the forest floor. He hoped she would sleep now and he was sorry for his bluntness. The Rythan way, he told himself and managed a rueful smile. It always came back to that.

***

The meat crackled as it broiled. The antelope had fed well in life and laid up fat for the coming winter. He turned it carefully, using his long knife, watching to make sure his makeshift grill did not scorch through. After a time, he rose and paced the perimeter of the fire's glow, looking out for pairs of eyes, listening for sounds of stalking predators. Once or twice, he thought he heard a scream in the distance but there was no sign of anything in the treetops. Could that other business have been imagination? Might the screamer be something much smaller, something harmless?

He tried to recall the shadowy movements against the sky, the dark form within the branches. Thinking of the parallel scrapes on the bark, he tried to construct an image of an animal that leaped from treetop to treetop—an animal big enough at least to leave marks like that. In all of his experience dealing with alien fauna, nothing matched.

When the meat was done to his satisfaction, he took it off. This should last them days if need be, though he hoped they wouldn't have to live on it that long. Still there was no way to know what they would find at the end of their journey. He tried to picture the members of the lost expedition—wounded, helpless city men, scientists most likely, starving and frightened. Though perhaps, since it was unlikely their craft had been sabotaged, they would have supplies of their own. He could only hope they had.

Should he try to contact Solomon again before they set off in the morning? Since the man was not calling from the flyer and had warned him not to look for it, the party must have moved some distance away. Were they, after all, afraid of an explosion? *Don't try to find the flyer,* the man had said. But he might not have been in his right mind—starving or injured or both. Alone? The Lost Rythan tried not to think of that possibility. He had no idea how large the expedition had been but surely there would be more than one survivor.

He was getting sleepy. Better get moving, he decided. He got up, stepped over Babe's sleeping form and set off once more on his round. After a moment, he decided to use the torch and check further. It was a strange feeling to be the only one awake. Funny how he hadn't minded being alone on his solitary camping trips. He hadn't thought so much about the unknown. In fact, he hadn't done much thinking at all.

That was best, he thought as he took out the torch and flashed it about. A man should not be forever peeping beneath the surface of things. It was enough to deal with wild animals and the evil that lay within his fellow men. God knew that should be enough—

God. He frowned in irritation. What did *God* know—if there even was a god. But here, alone in the wilderness, in the face of deceit and worse, he found it harder to hold onto his grievance. The thought that God, too, betrayed His people was one thing, but to consider that there might not even *be* a God, was far worse. It meant that he, Ard Matthew Third-Blade was no more than an accident, walking the night beneath enemy trees and enemy stars, with nothing to look forward to but annihilation.

He shuddered and peered up into the treetops, flashing the light among the branches. The wind was moving them, but there were no shadowy *things* to be seen. No nightmare silhouettes.

He was halfway down the hill when he heard the scream. It came from above him, from the place where he had just been. He whirled, flashing the torch up the hillside toward the grave. The treetops were moving, but he could see nothing up there save branches tossed by the wind. The scream came again.

There was gooseflesh rising on his arms, the hairs standing up on the back of his neck.

He knew where the screams were coming from. They were not coming from the trees nor from the wilderness. They came from Shami's grave.

He pulled up short. He was an educated man, not a savage. This fear he felt was unworthy and must be brought under control. Steadying himself, he raised the gun and waited. Below, he could see the others stirring by the fire, Babe looking about frantically.

"Up here!" he shouted and waved the light. "Stay by the fire."

The scream came again.

He began to back his way down the hillside toward the campsite, setting each foot carefully lest he fall and drop the light. Far ahead—

but that may have been his imagination—he thought he heard the crackle of breaking branches. He stopped and set the light on the ground beside him, pointing the beam toward the sound. He held the gun ready, straining with all his senses for whatever was up there.

Suddenly he heard a new sound—a clattering and rattling of stones. At first, he could not imagine what it was—and then he remembered piling those stones on the grave. Something was digging there!

He froze in place knowing that he must go back up the hillside and knowing that he had not the courage to face whatever waited for him on that cursed slope. Below, he saw that Téna had risen and now she went to stand beside Babe. He knew they would both come running up to him in a moment if he didn't do something.

"Wait!" he called and sprinted back toward the grave.

A stone rolled across his path. He realized that he had left the light behind, still turned on, though the illumination was fainter as he moved away from it. He sidestepped another stone and stumbled in the semi-darkness, recovering himself with difficulty. Ahead, the commotion continued.

He rounded another tree and emerged into the starlit clearing. He could just see them now, two shadowy forms barely visible in the feeble light, moving about on top of the grave. The stones had all been knocked away and he thought they were digging.

"No you don't!" he roared, except that his voice came out as a croak. He raised the gun and fired. The airbolt sang and something screeched. For one moment, he was sure they were both looking at him. Then with a wailing shriek, they disappeared. He hurried to the site.

The earth was disturbed, as he could tell by feeling it. But he didn't think the things had penetrated far. He paused for a moment, not knowing what to do.

And that was when they struck. Something fell against him, toppling him to the ground. He dropped the gun, heard it clank against the rocks—out of reach. Turning over onto his back, he made out lean shadows against the sky, seeming to tower over him. Limbs like tree branches swung and he felt the sting of them even through his clothing. He tried to shield his face.

They made no sound now. A head dipped and he felt something pierce his jacket, gouging into his flesh. He rolled aside, snatching the knife from his belt. This was more like it, he thought, remembering the wolf hunts of his homeworld. He felt his veneer of civilization fall away as he slashed at his attackers. "Come on," he growled, "and by all the nonexistent gods of Lost Rythar we'll see whose bones will lie here!"

Another stab penetrated his jacket and then his knife sheered through some sort of flesh, slid off bone. Another shriek. The creature scrabbled beside him, throwing up dirt clods as it fought for balance.

He swung again and heard another scream. Suddenly the other one was on him, grappling him from the back, talons raking his clothing and his flesh. He wriggled around, using his weight to knock it loose. He smelled a carrion smell, reached upward and tangled his knife in a thicket of branching bone. He felt another jab and knew that he would die here if he could not kill the thing.

And that was when he dropped yet further into his Rythan heritage. For he felt the battle madness rising and let it come. Snarling, he grappled with his attacker, one hand gripping the bony mass to yank its head back. He had lost the knife so he seized its throat with his other hand, ignoring the pain of his wounds and the slashing of its flailing limbs. He felt the other, the wounded creature, clawing at his back as he pulled on the head of his victim, dodging a long, sharp beak, straining with all his strength.

They strove together for what seemed an eternity before he felt the thing beginning to give way. At last, something cracked and he wrenched with all his strength until the body went limp. At that, the weight on his back disappeared and he heard a distant scream as the other creature departed.

He tried to sit up, untangling himself from the corpse. But it was too much effort. Slowly he returned from the battle madness, that primal place beneath what little sophistication he had left, and looked around dazedly. Only then, did he realize that he was bleeding. Only then did he feel the pain of his wounds.

A moment later, the clearing was bathed in light as Babe came running up, snatched the gun, and hurried to his side. "What the hell, Third-Blade! What happened here? What *were* they?"

"I—I don't know," Ard Matthew said dazedly. "I—"

Suddenly he looked down in horror at the wrapped bundle below him and realized he was actually lying in Shami's opened grave. He rolled away in disgust, throwing himself back among the scattered rocks.

"Oh God," Téna cried. "You've dug her up!" The light wavered in her hand.

"Hey," Babe told her. "He's hurt, can't you see? And what is—" He grabbed the light from Téna and shone it on the creature that lay sprawled where Ard Matthew had killed it. It really did look like a tangle of tree branches.

For long moments, all three of them stared, trying to make sense of what they saw. Ard Matthew's mind simply refused to process what his eyes told him was there, even though he knew he must. But nothing was coming through very clearly and the trees kept moving in circles and the stars would not stay in their places.

After a moment, he closed his eyes and let the darkness come.

CHAPTER SEVEN

When his consciousness returned, the other two were still speaking.

"Come on," Babe was saying. "We've got to get Third-Blade back down to the fire."

Then Téna's voice sounding oddly flat in the night air: "What about Shami?" she protested. "We've got to cover up this grave."

"She isn't going anywhere," Babe said impatiently. "Get over there and help him up! If we lose this guy, we won't survive!"

He saw her leaning over him. "Third-Blade? Mr. Third-Blade?" Her face was a pale smudge in the darkness.

"Dead." he whispered. "My enemy is dead."

"Right," Babe said. "You killed that sucker. Now can you get up?"

Ard Matthew wasn't sure he could do that. But the others could hardly carry him while also managing the gun and the torch. He forced himself to sit and then to stagger to his feet where he swayed a little, blinking in the light.

"There are holes in your jacket!" Tina exclaimed.

He looked down. They looked like knife wounds. "Beaks, I think," he said. Then, "My knife," he remembered. "Can't leave it here."

"I'll look for it," Babe said, laying down the gun. He clambered over the rocks and returned a few minutes later with the weapon. "You use this to kill the thing?" he asked. "Looks like they've got real blood."

Ard Matthew shook his head. "I cut one of them, but then I used my hands," he said. He didn't tell them about the battle madness.

"Okay, let's go down," Babe grunted. He gestured to Téna who took Ard Matthew's arm. "Lean on me," she said, handing Babe the torch. Together, they staggered behind Babe, leaving the grave and its new denizen behind. They could deal with it in the morning.

But long before they reached the campsite, Ard Matthew had become too heavy for her. By now he was barely stumbling along, fighting to remain conscious. Babe gave her the gun and the light as well, before throwing one of the Lost Rythan's arms over his shoulder to half drag him the rest of the way.

When they reached the fire, Téna hurried forward and threw on more wood. The new fuel kindled into a flame that drove away the encroaching darkness.

Apparently Babe knew a certain amount of first aid—at least the sort needed to deal with something like this. He had Ard Matthew's jacket off almost as soon as he laid him down and Ard Matthew shivered in the sudden cold.

"How—how bad is it?" Téna asked as Babe examined him.

"Not too deep. Just punctures. As long as there isn't any poison, he should be okay."

"Universal antitox," the Rythan muttered. "Should be some in the first aid kit. Swab it in."

Téna fetched the kit and handed it to Babe. When he had finished cleaning out the puncture wounds, Téna threw the thermal blanket over the pilot. He looked up at her sidewise for a moment as she tucked it around him. The firelight flickered on her face, showing her widened eyes. "We'll get through this," he told her. "We will find a way for—all of it."

He closed his eyes.

Somehow they got through that night. Each time he woke, he saw Téna or Babe adding wood to the fire and wondered how their supply was holding out. There were noises on the hillside and he tried not to think about what was probably happening up there.

Finally the darkness began to give way, but in the crepuscular light, the forest seemed even more threatening than it had during the night. The tree aisles were pale, gauzy paths leading to uncertain realms of mystery, while the tops themselves remained hidden in mist. *Anything* could have hidden up there.

He shifted about to ease his wounds. They had all survived the night, he told himself, when the sun's first ruby light touched the treetops. The fog shredded away to reveal a clear sky, but even near the fire, it was a cold morning. He could feel the dawn wind passing over him.

"How is he?" Babe asked, coming over to stand above Ard Matthew.

"Alright, I think," Téna said. Then, "Babe," she ventured, "we need to—you know. We need to put things back on Shami's grave."

He gave her an odd look. "We can check on it later," he said.

Both of them looked down at the Lost Rythan. His eyes met Babe's and he nodded slightly. He didn't look forward to what they would find.

"Can you get up?" Babe asked finally.

For answer, Ard Matthew threw aside the covering and levered himself into a sitting position. "I'm alright," he said, hoping he spoke the truth. At least the things had not poisoned him.

"Then we start this morning as planned?" Babe asked.

He nodded.

But Téna would not be ignored. "I'm not going anywhere," she said, "until we have reburied Shami!" She picked up the laser cutter and hunted around for the shovel. "If no one else is coming, I'll do it myself."

"Hey," Babe said. "We're all together in this. Just let me make sure Third-Blade is okay."

"I'm fine," the Lost Rythan said again. "In fact, I'll come along." He did not look at Téna.

In a few minutes, Babe led the way up the hill. Téna followed with the laser while Ard Matthew brought up the rear, his knife in his hand. When they reached the grave, there was little to be seen except their own tracks in the forest floor where Babe had half hauled him back down to the camp.

Remembering this brought back the memory of the creature he had killed. What would it look like by daylight?

Babe reached the mound first. They saw him stop at the edge of the grave, staring downward, his shoulders unmoving as he cradled the gun and waited for the others. Something made Ard Matthew set his hands gently on Téna's shoulders. "Wait a moment," he said, and moved up to stand beside Babe.

But there was nothing there. The remains of the creature had vanished—and the grave was empty. Of course the ground was disturbed, soil kicked aside, a few more rocks out of place. That the thing he had killed might not have been dead after all seemed well-nigh incredible.

"Are you sure you finished it off?" Babe asked as Téna came up and stared into the grave.

"I broke its neck," the Lost Rythan told him. Wincing a little, he hunkered down and began to examine the displaced dirt. Then he motioned Babe to one side and crawled across the open grave, pausing from time to time to look more closely at the signs. Finally, he stood up, brushing himself off. "Bears, this time," he said. "You can see where they've been digging and where something was dragged away."

"Bears?" Téna echoed incredulously. "Do you mean they—?"

Silently cursing himself for not keeping silent, he didn't answer.

"I guess that's what we heard in the night," Babe said.

"But if you heard them, why didn't you do something?" Téna demanded, her voice suddenly shrill. "Why didn't you go up and drive them off?"

Both men stared at her and she subsided. "I'm sorry," she murmured.

"Let's go," Babe said. "We can't do anything for her now." He turned away from the grave and started back.

Téna matched her pace to Ard Matthew's. He found he was limping a little and his wounds pained him. He wondered how much speed he could make in their search for Solomon and his party. But that would be as it turned out, he thought grimly. He had no wish to stay *here*.

Back at the camp, they ate some of last night's broiled antelope and shoveled earth over the last of the coals. He packed the cooked meat in his pack and rolled up some of their tools in the thermo sheet which he gave to Téna to carry. "You can sling it over your shoulders," he said and showed her how.

The day's tramp was long and grueling. The signal led them back up the hill past the empty grave angling away from the swampland. Ard Matthew had filled the two inflatable water sacks he carried and hoped that would be enough until they found another creek.

The others were not equipped for a long trek. Téna at least had boots, but Babe's footwear didn't look nearly as sturdy. Still, neither complained as they struggled and clambered over the rough ground, Babe was limping as the day wore on.

They covered about a fourth of the indicated distance that day, found no water, and drank sparingly of what they carried. Luckily, as it seemed now, the sun was no longer hot, the winds a little chilly. As they gained altitude, the promise of autumn—whatever it might turn out to be on this particular world—crept into the air.

Ard Matthew chose their camping spot—another clearing among the sparse trees, different from the last only in that the trees were even further apart. He brushed away the needles, dug a little and started a fire. Luckily, there was another deadfall nearby and this they harvested plentifully. When they had eaten of their leftover meat, the Lost Rythan demanded to see Babe's feet. Reluctantly the other man showed him.

"Synthoskin," he said. "It's the best I can do for you, Babe." When he had done what he could, he got up. "I want to look around a little before it gets dark," he said. "But first, I must try and contact Solomon."

"Climb another tree?" Babe asked.

"We're closer now and higher up. I think I can reach him from ground level."

But when he tried, there was no answer at all, not on any of the bands. He got nothing but static with no shadow of a signal, which meant climbing a tree wouldn't help. After this, he left the others and walked further into the woods, taking with him the laser cutter. Almost at once he ran into a flock of turkeys and brought two of them down before they scattered. He wrung their necks and headed back to the camp.

Téna told him Babe had gone to fetch more fuel. But as he looked around, Babe came hurrying back bearing a load of wood.

"Ashes," he said when he had caught his breath. "Someone's had a fire up there." He pointed toward the deadfall. "On the other side. A campsite."

"How old?"

Babe shrugged. "It's cold. There's some bones."

Immediately all three of them started for the spot. When they got there, Ard Matthew saw nothing more than a mound of ashes mixed with a few small bones. Birds? Maybe a survivor of the Becker Party had stopped here, he thought.

He dropped to his knees and began to examine the bones. For some time, he held them up one by one, tracing one finger along their charred edges. Something was odd here.

"What is it?" Babe asked.

The sun had set and shadows gathered beneath the trees. He was aware that they should not stay so far from their own fire. He stood up. "Let's go back," he said.

"But what were you looking for?" Babe asked.

"I was looking for signs that these birds had been shot or lasered," he told the other man. "But they weren't. They died by impact—I think someone threw a rock to bring them down."

Babe frowned. "Solomon?"

But there was no answer to this and he did not try to make one. He was frowning, however, as he set the game to cook. Once cleaned and skewered, he left them for Téna to tend. It was good that she was learning the skills she needed to survive—or at least some of them. He really admired her pluck, but he doubted the feeling of admiration was mutual, though he had been even more careful after the events at Shami's grave to tread carefully in his dealings with the girl.

He was still thinking about Babe's discovery. That someone had camped—and recently—so near their own line of march was unsettling at best. He wanted to examine the area more thoroughly for tracks, but now it was dark and he was sure he'd miss things even with the torch.

But even earlier, in the remains of the light, he hadn't noted any disturbance in the surrounding carpet of needles. Just those ashes and the remains of someone's dinner. And their own party's tracks, of course. Could they have effaced something? He longed to go back out there, even now, and glean what he could.

And there had been one other clue, though it probably led nowhere. He reached into his pocket and retrieved something he had found. Two small stones had been lying near the ashes, both of some dark type he had not seen in the area before. He had examined the bones very carefully and he had seen what looked like broken ribs on one and a broken neck on the other. True, that might have happened in the course of cleaning and cooking—but one of the birds had not been cooked. It had only been skinned and eaten raw.

He stood at the edge of the firelight, fingering the stones, wishing Windy-Go had a moon. Just one would be enough, he thought. One full moon to give him light to examine the site once more.

He looked around as Babe came up to stand beside him.

"What have you got there?" the other man asked.

Ard Matthew showed him.

"Rocks? You think those are what killed the birds up there?"

"Yes. I think so."

"How? Someone use a slingshot?" Babe touched one of the stones. "This Solomon guy must be pretty resourceful."

Ard Matthew turned the stones over, rubbing them against each other, as he stared out into the gathering night. "Slingshot," he said. "I hadn't thought of that."

"You don't really think it was Solomon, do you?" Babe said.

"Do you?"

The other man half turned, staring back at the fire where Téna was cooking the birds. "Third-Blade," he said, "I bet you could come up with something like that if you had to." He turned back, his sturdy form, outlined against the fire glow. "We don't know how hard it's been for the Becker Party out here or even what kind of people they are. But if they ran into—whatever that was—or even a bear, they could be pretty hard up."

Ard Matthew nodded. He had been thinking the same thing. "We'd better go back out there and have another look," he said at last. "Do you think—she will be alright by herself?" He didn't know whether to refer to Téna as Miss bor Rijn or Téna and didn't want to risk another faux pas.

Babe had no such hesitation. "Téna should be fine," he said. "We can leave her the gun if you like."

Ard Matthew let Babe deal with this. Meanwhile, he picked up the laser cutter, made sure his knife was ready in its sheath, and fetched the light. When Babe came back, they set off.

"Did you see any bear tracks as we came?" the other man asked as they left the area of the firelight. "I don't think she'd hesitate to shoot, but—"

"Not many. And the fire should keep them away."

They walked on in silence for a minute or two more, Babe's footsteps crunching lightly on the needles while Ard Matthew made no sound at all. Babe's clumsiness irritated him, but there was nothing to be done. After all, this was probably all new to him.

When they reached the first of the brush piles, he shone the torch around, carefully checking the ground. He saw their own footmarks, coming and returning. No surprise there. Then, something shone in the light. Bending down, he picked up a small clip he had seen in Téna's hair. Nearer the ashes, he slowed and began to search more carefully.

The needles had been brushed away, though not as thoroughly as he would have done it. He could see that some of the surrounding groundcover had been scorched and burnt. A few places showed where someone had stamped out the escaped fires, perhaps kicking the smoldering straw back toward the center.

He hunkered down, shining the light directly on one of these spots. After a moment, he found what he sought. A clear mark showed in the uncovered earth, a small, bare foot with toes widely spaced. He leaned back on his heels and looked up at Babe. "See it?" he said.

Babe bent over. "Looks like—a woman? But what happened to her boots?"

Ard Matthew frowned at the print. "I don't know," he said, tracing the outline with one finger. It was a stubby foot, he thought. Small even for a woman. Perhaps a child?

"Could they be hiding?" Babe asked. "Spooked and afraid to approach us?"

"Why?" the Lost Rythan asked him. "Why would they be afraid? If it's the Becker party, I mean."

"Well—something might have happened. This lady might have seen the others killed. You know—those screaming things." Babe stood up, staring around at the surrounding darkness. "Or someone could have flipped out. It happens."

"Do you think she killed the birds?"

At this, Babe was silenced. Ard Matthew saw the other man's brows furrow as he thought about this. "Okay," he said at last. "Maybe you're wrong about those stones, Third-Blade. Maybe she did use a laser or—or something. And maybe she's not alone."

The Lost Rythan grunted and went on searching for prints.

"Maybe she—they're watching us right now."

Ard Matthew looked up at him. "I think I would know," he said, but he did not try to explain how he would know.

Babe gave him a sharp look and then shrugged. "Okay. So someone maybe had a slingshot. Who? And where did they come from?"

The Lost Rythan got to his feet. "Come on," he said, and led the way around the ashes, shining the torch on the ground as he went. It was easy to see where their own party had circled the site, stirring up the ground cover and leaving boot prints right up to the edge of the char. And there, to one side lay the gnawed bones. Cooked ones scattered, the uncooked still attached, though the skin had been pulled free. It was almost as if the scene had been arranged.

Slowly, he began to work outward in a spiral, seeking the slightest disturbance of the needle carpet. The few bare spots he came across looked natural, irregularities in the ground, humps and fissures. He thought about this. Someone had built that fire. Someone had cooked and eaten. There had to be some sign of how they got there.

It was Babe who spotted the first clue, though he did not know what it was. He picked up what looked at first like a twig, studied it, and handed it to the Lost Rythan. Ard Matthew examined the piece. "Antler," he said. "Sharpened on one side."

"Are you sure—that it's sharpened, I mean?"

Ard Matthew nodded. He remembered where he had last seen a rack of bone, had grasped it as he pulled and twisted until he broke its owner's neck. He would have cut himself if it had been sharp.

Now that the thing had been found, he studied the ground with new eyes. He thought he could make out faint indentations in the forest floor as though someone had walked lightly with great care—and skill—careful not to break the needle carpet. Not even animals walked this way.

He stood up. "I'll finish this in the morning," he said. "At least I know which way she came. We can search further by daylight."

Babe turned back with him to the ashes. Neither said anything as Ard Matthew played the light once more over the remains of the fire. He really didn't know what to think. This was not a colony world, though there could be a few lone homesteads hidden in the wilderness. But he had never seen anything that looked like a cabin during his flights to the lodge district.

They were still out of sight of the campfire when Babe stopped him with a hand on one arm. "Hold on a minute, Third-Blade," he said.

Ard Matthew turned, shining the light on the ground at their feet.

Babe, who was carrying the laser, shifted it to his other hand. "I—I wanted to ask you something," he said. "About our chances of getting back to civilization."

The Lost Rythan waited, not looking up from the ground.

"I mean, I think we will get back," Babe went on. "But—what then?"

Ard Matthew shrugged. He had been wondering about this too. Would there be someone waiting to make sure they did not resume their identities if they should survive? It was certainly possible.

But, "I don't know," he said at last. "I mean I can probably get myself offplanet without too much trouble." With his Faring Guard training, he added mentally. "And maybe you could too," he told Babe. "But I don't know about—"

"Exactly," the other said. "The old girl has a real stake in Téna being dead."

"Do you have any ideas?" Ard Matthew asked him.

"The only thing I can think of is to slip back into the port and arrange a different identity for her. To come back with a flyer and take her out."

"Could you do that?"

Babe thought for a moment. "I have funds," he said. "But I would have to retrieve them under my own name. Or at least all but one account. My emergency reserve. It's set up with only a password."

"You are skilled in these things? Trained?"

Babe grinned. "Curious, Third-Blade? But that's okay. It doesn't matter if you know. I was Kessler's chief of security. And before that—before that I was something else."

Ard Matthew waited.

"Hell, you haven't told me any of your secrets," the other said suddenly. "I know you're more than just a damn pilot. What are you running away from?"

God. He almost said it out loud. Instead, he let the silence stretch until it seemed a part of the night. Finally, he looked up from the ground. "I was a Faring Guard," he admitted. "With the Star Brothers."

Babe whistled. "So that's it. And they kicked you out?"

"I left."

"Good enough. But that might be a place to turn. I've heard they have a hand in just about everything that goes on."

Ard Matthew nodded. "They have. In fact, there is someone at the port. Or at least there was." He remembered his brief meeting with the priest the night before he picked up his passengers. He wasn't sure what the man could do, but most Star Brothers were resourceful. They were trained to be just as he had been.

"Mr. Onegin," he said at last, "Babe. I will help you if I can. I am not—I am no longer one of their people, but that won't matter. They won't hold that against me."

Babe looked up. "Thanks, Third-Blade. I have a feeling I can count on you."

Ard Matthew did not answer. Luckily, Babe could not see the flush that suffused his cheeks. "Let's get back," he said.

They heard the scream just as they rounded the deadfall. Between them and the fire, things darted, skeletal, almost shimmering in the faint illumination. Even as they watched, there came another scream and something shot past, leaping from tree to tree.

They were trapped.

He heard an intake of breath. "Téna's there," Babe said. "Alone."

"She has the gun."

The other man hesitated. "She wasn't brought up for this. She'll never—" He started to run forward.

"Wait. You won't help her that way. And besides, she's braver than you think."

In the treetops, something screamed, a high, wailing sound like a damned soul shrieking into the wind. Even Ard Matthew shuddered.

The scream came again. Ahead, the half seen figures rose and fell, moving with uncanny swiftness as they leaped and gamboled about in a bizarre dance. What were they doing? There was almost something ceremonial in their actions. But so far they seemed to be focused on the campfire.

And now he could make out Téna's form as she stood with the gun aimed. But she wasn't firing. Maybe she had seen the torch?

Then suddenly she did fire. He saw her pause, staring at the creatures in the firelight. She fired again. This time there was a swirling of limbs, a turning, as the whole company began to advance in her direction. She fired two more times, but the creatures did not slow.

Ard Matthew marveled as their antlers caught the light, great, branching racks of them almost too large for their heads.

Then could hear Téna screaming. "Get back! Get away!"

Of course her cries had no effect on the monsters. They just kept on, no longer running and leaping as they had, but almost floating. They seemed to disappear in one place and reappear in another.

As he loped across the intervening distance, Ard Matthew saw her drop the useless weapon and run back to the fire. She snatched up a brand—two brands! Whirling them about her to make them flare up, she made a desperate run at the advancing creatures.

Babe was beside him exclaiming something in a language the Rythan didn't know. Cursing, he supposed. Ard Matthew saved his breath for running.

Ahead of them, Téna held her ground while the monsters swirled around her. She swung desperately, thrusting the brands at anything that came close. And then the men were among them, Babe with the cutting laser and Ard Matthew with his knife. Between them, they chopped and burned, hearing a different screaming as their enemies strove to get away from them.

Within moments, the things were airborne as they dove back into the treetops, still shrieking, propelling themselves from tree to tree until their cries faded in the distance.

Babe had dropped the laser and now he took Téna by the shoulders, forcing her to let go of the brands. "Are you alright?" he kept repeating. "They didn't—didn't hurt you, did they?"

She shook her head, half dazed. "No," she said. "They didn't touch me." She was trembling, almost sobbing as the Lost Rythan came up. Unwillingly, Babe released her but Ard Matthew could see that he was trembling as much as she was.

"I—I dreamed of monsters," she said. "When I was a child. White blobby things with arms like tree branches, hiding in the woodshed. But that was only a dream. There were no monsters on Sachsen."

"You're alright now," Ard Matthew told her sharply. If she or Babe cracked, their position would be a lot worse than it was now.

"Hey. Are you really alright?" That was Babe, reaching one hesitant hand toward her.

But Ard Matthew could see she didn't want that. "I'm fine," she told him curtly. She turned back to the fire. "Your dinner is burnt," she added.

Indeed, the birds had fallen onto the coals, as a not very savory smell attested.

Ard Matthew reached down with his knife and hooked one of them out of the fire. "It's alright," he said. "Or at least this one is. I guess it's too late for the other one." He did not look at the others. Things had been revealed in those few moments that he didn't want to think about just now. Instead, he divided the meat, being careful not to look at Babe.

As they huddled together near the fire, munching their scorched dinner, he seemed to feel the heat of Téna's sudden anger. Anger at Babe? Just what sort of history did these two have? But, whatever it was, as long as it didn't interfere with their survival, it had to be none of his business.

They had barely finished eating when the wailing screams resumed. At first the sounds were distant and then, as the creatures swept from tree to tree, the clamor echoed all around the campsite. The party was surrounded.

Ard Matthew stood up, seeing Téna glance at the wood they had gathered. Luckily, they had been able to accumulate a larger pile than the one they had the night before. As she walked over and picked up an armful to add to the fire, the Lost Rythan could only hope they had enough.

"Looks like it's going to be a long night," Babe muttered and no one disagreed with him.

"We'll be okay with the fire," Ard Matthew said. "Or anyway, I think we will." He hoped he was right. At least there were no limbs directly overhanging the campsite, which was a plus. But in the surrounding forest, branches swayed and shadows moved among the foliage. Occasionally something passed through the air from one tree to another. And all the time, the eerie sounds, screams and wails were coming from all sides.

Babe had retrieved the gun and now he took an occasional shot at anything he could see. But in the Lost Rythan's opinion, he was wasting charge. The creatures were so tenuous—so wraithlike that you had to be practically on top of them to strike a blow.

"But what are they?" Téna breathed. "Mr. Third-Blade, do you know? Are you sure you've never seen anything like this before?"

Ard Matthew shook his head. He supposed they must be some kind of bird, but until he had a chance to really examine one of the dead ones, he couldn't be sure. Of course, birds didn't have antlers. He hoped that in the morning he'd get his chance to dissect one of the things, if something didn't carry off the ones he and Babe had killed there should be plenty. He had seen little in the way of bear tracks on their day's trek and none at all near their present camping place. That was hopeful, at least.

"Babe and I can keep up the fire," he told Téna. "Why don't you take the thermo sheet and try to get some sleep?"

"Why don't I—!" She glared at him. "I'm the one who went after them with fire," she said. "After you had left me alone with a gun that was no use against the damned things!"

Ard Matthew winced. What now? Maybe he and Babe should not have left her alone, but why hadn't she told him then that she was afraid?

"I'm sorry," he said humbly. "But I promise you will be safe now. We've got weapons and Babe and I will keep up the fire."

"We'll all keep up the fire," she snapped. "I'm not helpless—as you seem to think!"

At this, the Lost Rythan heard Babe chuckle and turned to him in bewilderment.

"It's okay, Third-Blade. Anyway, we're all going to be needed to deal with this bunch."

He was right. While they had been talking, the things had crept closer, leaving the trees to circle the clearing just beyond the light. Ard Matthew caught glimpses of them moving singly and in groups, long necks weaving, heads thrust forward to show the gleaming rubies of their eyes and the glittering racks of bone that crowned their heads.

They had elongated beaks and it was these that had jabbed him when he fought them back at Shami's grave. And now he could make out their upper limbs as they moved. They stood upright, but were so preternaturally thin that they seemed scarcely to have torsos at all.

"They look like they're nothing but skeletons," Babe observed as he made a small rush at one that got too close. He and the creature both leaped back at the same time, though it raked his arm with one clawed limb while he thrust a flaming brand in its face.

Ard Matthew looked at the bloody gash. "Bad?" he asked.

Babe grunted. "Can you get me the first aid kit?" he asked Téna.

She fetched what was left of their supplies, but then she paused, looking at the Lost Rythan. Whatever was going on here, Ard Matthew had had enough. "Help him with it," he said and there was something in his voice that got through to her.

Ungraciously, she took out the cleanser and a strip of synthoskin. Ard Matthew didn't see what happened next because he had his own incursion to deal with. The things were definitely getting bolder. He swung a brand, being careful to keep his own arm out of range. When he had repelled the attack, he quickly snatched up more wood and threw it on the fire. The resultant flare-up drove the creatures back a little and gave him time to drag more of their fuel supply in closer.

When he could again check on the others, he saw to his relief that Téna had done what she could for Babe. Both held flaming sticks and Babe had moved to the other side of the fire. Ard Matthew powered up the laser and set it on longest beam. It wouldn't take off any heads at that extension, but it should give a nasty slice. He swung it at the nearest creatures and was rewarded by an increase in the noise level. He struck again and the things moved further off.

"Good for you," Babe said as he tossed his stick back into the fire and got another one.

The Lost Rythan didn't answer this. He was too busy watching the swirling mass as it gyrated just out of range. Suddenly he became aware of Téna beside him. "I wonder what they eat when they can't get people," she said.

"Antelope, probably." But he was wondering uncomfortably whether this was what Solomon had been referring to. "They," he had said. No name. Maybe the party had been attacked. Maybe he really was the only one left. It was not a cheering thought.

At some point near the middle of the night—or at least he thought it must be—the creatures drew off. They were practically invisible in the shadows, but Ard Matthew could still hear rustling in the treetops. The wind had come up, however, so it was hard to tell for sure. The air was growing colder.

"You think we'll have a frost?" Babe asked.

They were both adding more fuel to the fire. "Maybe if the wind dies down. But I haven't lived here for a full set of seasons yet," the Lost Rythan said. "The year is rather long and I've only seen the summer." He took a sparing drink from of the water sacks. Water was one more problem for him to solve, he thought, as he set it down. They would have to find another creek before very long.

"It feels cold enough for frost," Téna said.

Ard Matthew was about to suggest again that she make use of the thermo sheet but then he remembered that this had made her angry before. With everyone's nerves strained to the breaking point, he must be extra careful what he said.

"Think they'll hold off for a while?" Babe asked.

"No." But they all needed rest and the Lost Rythan knew that no one would relax unless he did. He sat down near the fire, still watching the treetops. One wild turkey had not gone far to feed the three of them and he was almost hungry enough to sample one of the emergency bars. But not quite. He took the two he had set aside—squashed now in his jacket pocket—and offered them to the others. Too bad, he thought, that he had not had time to salvage any of the food supply from the flyer.

Téna gagged after one bite, but Babe chewed on his until it was gone. Ard Matthew saw Téna's lip curl as she watched him eat it, but said nothing. The Lost Rythan was tired and hungry and he was thoroughly sick of playing nursemaid for these two.

Their respite wasn't long. With a swiftness that came near to being everyone's undoing, the creatures attacked once more, leaping in and out of the firelight, coming closer than they had in the last foray. Before anyone knew what had happened, Téna was swept off her feet and half dragged out into the darkness.

As soon as he heard her scream, Ard Matthew leaped onto her attacker, slashing and hacking. But Babe was there before him. Between the two of them, they managed to dismember the thing while she scrambled to her feet and ran back to the fire with them.

"You hurt?" the Lost Rythan asked her, but she shook her head.

She was trembling and her clothing was ripped, but he could see no blood. Babe hovered beside her but did not approach any nearer.

After that, they were kept busy for a time as the things leapt in and away with almost blinding speed, never stopping their attacks though the party fought them with fire. Ard Matthew could not have said how long this lasted, only that he felt a creeping weariness that slowed his reflexes and set his head to aching. Jump, swing, dodge. Jump, swing, dodge. Over and over again.

After what must have been about two hours, though it felt like days, the things drew off once more. This time, the party knew better than to let down their guard.

"You know what I think?" Babe said, watching the shadows. "I think they're playing with us."

Ard Matthew didn't want to believe that the creatures were intelligent. Not only were they grotesque in his eyes, but their heads didn't seem large enough to house a thinking brain. As he listened to them out there—tossing the treetops, wailing and screaming—they seemed more like animals. Then he caught sight of a couple of them scrabbling about on the ground, as though to attract attention. Could this be some sort of challenge?

That's all the further he got in his speculations before the attack began again. He and Babe took turns with the laser. Other than that, they settled into the same, grim routine—feed the fire, swing their brands, watch for sudden leaps. When he had a glimpse of the others, he could see the exhaustion in their faces and knew that the same weariness must show in his own.

And still their enemies did not let up.

The sky began to pale. After a time, Ard Matthew found he could better see the creatures as they came. Then, after another time that felt interminable, their attackers began to move off until, with a chorus of wailing cries, they took to the treetops and disappeared as suddenly as they had come.

Babe tossed a flaming stick back into the fire. "Looks like that's it for now."

Ard Matthew wasn't sure, though it looked like the things must be nocturnal.

"I'll watch for a while," Babe said after a few minutes' peace. "You two get some sleep."

With a nod, the Lost Rythan settled himself as near the fire as he could get. There had indeed been a frost and now that their ordeal was over, the cold seeped through the rents in his clothing. A moment later, he felt something thrown over him and realized it was the thermo sheet. "Not that," he mumbled. "Keep it for Téna."

After that, all was darkness until, the next thing he knew, the sun was up and he lay on his back, covered. Téna lay nearby with part of the sheet over her. He sprang to his feet. "You should have wakened me," he said to Babe.

The other man shrugged. "They're gone, Third-Blade. Until tonight, anyway."

Ard Matthew looked around. "I had better hunt us some breakfast," he said when he had satisfied himself that the creatures had indeed, disappeared. Hopefully, he could find more turkeys up near the deadfall.

Carefully, he rearranged the sheet without waking Téna. In repose, she was once more the pretty young woman he remembered, her face flushed with sleep, her brow relaxed. He still had no idea what had gotten into her the night before to make her so angry.

"Want the gun?" Babe asked.

"Sure." He expected to see the ground torn up where the things had paraded around the fire, but the needles lay undisturbed. He did find the bodies of the ones they had killed. Grotesque in the sunlight, they lay scattered here and there, looking like mummified, wingless birds. Except for those antlers. He shuddered and stepped over them.

As he approached the brush heap, he thought he could hear the sounds of small animals tunneling within. Nothing large enough to make a meal. He skirted the pile until he came in sight of the ashes where he was brought up short, staring at something on the ground.
There were two of them—animals that looked like hares. Both had apparently been killed the same way the birds had been killed. He could see small stones lying beside the corpses as though left there on purpose. He made a full turn, studying the sparsely wooded country. But nothing moved save the branches in the wind.

CHAPTER EIGHT

As he led the others back to look at the mysterious campsite, Ard Matthew noticed Téna scuffing, actually stomping, the needle-carpeted soil as though she were deliberately leaving her mark on this alien world. Somehow this seeming show of spirit heartened him. Let her turn her anger on their surroundings instead of on her companions—but either way, anger was better than fear.

Surrounding their own camp, the dead creatures lay scattered at awkward angles, looking as though they had been dead for hundreds of years. Once more, he picked his way among them and tried not to look into their faces. Were the things intelligent? he wondered. If so, it was an evil intelligence.

Presently they left the corpses behind, rounded the brush pile and came upon the ashes of the other fire. There were the dead hares, just as he had seen them a few minutes before. And there were the stones. He could think of only two ways to interpret the scene: either someone had been forced to abandon the place or else the game was left for them as a gift. This latter possibility was even more disturbing than the former, for it would mean they had been trailed and watched by someone with more woodcraft than he possessed.

Babe stepped forward and poked one of the hares. "Fresh," he said. "I bet they were brought here while we were sleeping."

"Brought here," Ard Matthew agreed. "Laid out but not killed here. So why the stones?"

Babe looked at him.

Téna knelt down and touched one of the rounded pebbles. "Maybe someone wants us to know," she guessed, "that they can—can defend themselves. That they wish us well but don't trust us."

"Maybe," Babe agreed. "So do you think we're being watched now?"

The Lost Rythan turned, scanning their surroundings. "I don't see how," he said. "Unless she's hiding in a treetop." He thought of the night creatures.

But the nearest trees looked too thin, their foliage not dense enough to hide anything bigger than a roosting turkey. Whoever had left that footprint could not be concealed there—at least not in broad daylight.

"I don't see any more footprints," Babe said. He started around the ashes and then stopped. "But I don't want to mess things up if there are." He grinned a little sheepishly. "You know I'm no woodsman."

But Ard Matthew hadn't found any more prints. He passed one hand over his eyes, trying to concentrate. He was still pretty tired and now here was yet another puzzle for him to solve. He saw Téna watching him and straightened up.

"Do you think that really was a human footprint?" she asked suddenly.

He looked a question. Everyone knew there were no real aliens—not sapient ones, anyway. Strange as they were, even the bird creatures could only be animals.

Babe scratched a bite on his neck. "We'll have to assume it is," he said reasonably. "But what really matters is whose is it—and where they came from."

Ard Matthew nodded. "I think," he said, "that whoever it is has already had a chance to harm us and did not do so." He reached down and picked up the hares. "Which means that these must be a gift."

"But why?" Téna demanded. "Why doesn't it—or she show herself?"

"Maybe we'll find out later," Babe said. "But I'm hungry enough to take the food on trust." His face was looking drawn, probably with both hunger and weariness.

"I'll carry those," Ard Matthew offered suddenly. He noted that Babe's injured arm had begun to bleed a little despite the synthoskin. Babe had fought all night with that wound and then kept watch while the others slept.

Swinging the hares by the hind legs, he wondered about the woman—girl?—who had left them these gifts. Was this place her home? And, after all, did it matter whether she was terran standard human or not? Who, after all, was the alien here?

Once more they picked their way over the battleground. Back at their camp, he decided to clean the game himself and asked Téna to gather more wood and build up the fire. As he worked, he thought about their latest perplexity. Why was the offering made? That was the first question. Did their benefactor mean to placate them? Or was there some other reason—something not so straightforward? In view of his recent dealings with the people of the stars, the question had to be asked. This was not Lost Rythar, after all.

He caught Téna watching him and hoped he had not offended her again by asking her to do a menial job. She was, after all, as capable as he was of preparing the meat to grill.

And this brought their situation before him with a new vividness. They would face another night soon enough, and if it went as the last one had, things could well turn out differently. How long could they keep going with little sleep, fighting for their lives hour after hour with nothing but fire and the laser cutter?

All the while, he was constructing another little grill made of greenwood, which he set above a patch of raked coals. Carefully, he laid the meat on top. Babe, meanwhile, had stretched himself out on the ground for some much needed sleep.

"I'd like to get another fix on that crashed flyer," the Rythan said to Téna when he had arranged things to his satisfaction. "And to contact Solomon if I can." He hesitated. "Could you—would you mind—?"

She came over to him and hunkered down by the grill. "I'll watch the cooking," she said. And then, "I—I suppose we'll be off as soon as we've eaten?"

He nodded. "We've got to make sure of the Becker Party. And after that, we'll need to find a better place to protect ourselves at night. Maybe a cave."

Suddenly he thought of something else. The Becker party had been heading for the ruins when they crashed. Now he began to wonder how far they had gone—how far away those ruins might actually be. Perhaps he could get a reading when he checked on the wreckage.

Of course there would probably be no other people at the ruins. But there might be other things—amenities left for the parties of scientists who came to study the place. Did he dare hope to locate a transmitter? He mentioned this to Téna.

"Yes," she agreed, after a moment. "That might be a place to go. The ruins."

He regarded her soberly. "But I can't promise anything, Miss, ah, bor Rijn."

She gave him a surprised stare. She seemed taken aback at his formality and this caused him some embarrassment.

Then she turned aside. "Of course," she said coolly. "I know you can't promise anything. No one expects you to."

Despite her words, there was something so defenseless in the profile she showed him that he wished he really could reassure her in some way. But he could not. "At least, we would be safe there," he said at last. "There should be shelter from—from wild things, even if we don't find people. I haven't heard of any other expeditions bound for the ruins and now, you know, the season must be almost over."

"The—you mean because summer is coming to an end? Or is this autumn?"

"I should think so." He tried to remember how it had been when he first came to the colony. He seemed to recall there had been more wildflowers. Late spring, then. "I told you I haven't seen a full year on this world," he said slowly. "But the weather is certainly changing. In fact—"

She looked at him.

"I was wondering if maybe the reason I had never run into those—those things before, might have something to do with the change of season." He tried to remember what, if anything, he had heard about winters on Windy-Go.

"You—no one ever mentioned those monsters?"

He shook his head. "No reason. This isn't a colonized planet, remember. Most of what goes on happens at the port."

"They said—that is, my cousin said we were to hide in one of the lodges. That is where we were going." She reached down to adjust the meat on the grill. "It sounds ridiculous now. That we believed her, I mean. Such a simple ruse."

Ard Matthew reached for his pack and took out the comm.

"Do you really think we could stay in the ruins for a whole winter?" she asked.

He tried not to look at her. "Probably not," he said. "Not if it is as long as the summer has been." He thought back, calculating. The summer, including late spring, must have lasted a good six months. Definitely longer than the summers of other worlds he had visited. "Food alone would be a problem," he told her. "And maybe fuel." He did not add that three people cooped up together for who knows how long, living as they had been living, would probably go mad long before spring.

After that, Téna didn't say anything more but only tended to her cooking.

***

In the end, he was unable to reach Solomon. Whether the man was out hunting or the radio was not working, he couldn't say. There was static, however, and enough contact to give him some idea of the location. Of the transmitter's location, that is. Where Solomon might he, he had no idea.

There was no sense pretending that the man had been in his right mind, he was forced to admit. He plainly hadn't been. But Ard Matthew didn't want to dwell on this problem too deeply. The whole business made him uneasy. It was a reaction that went back to his own people's history—the idea that madness was somehow dangerous and possibly contagious.

Though he failed to get a response from Solomon, he had had better luck homing in on the crash site. It lay not far to the east of them. Perhaps a half day's walk. The land seemed to rise a little in that direction, forming hills with mountains behind them. The going might be rough but it looked doable.

They'd better be on their way, he decided, as he stood up and stretched the kinks from his shoulders. His few hours' sleep had done little enough for the creeping weariness that threatened to weigh down his limbs and slow his reactions, but he knew he mustn't give in. Another night like the last one would do nothing to recoup his strength.

Once he was sure of his direction, he walked back to the fire. Téna looked up at him and he smiled at her. "That smells good," he said.

"So where are we?" she asked, ignoring the smile. "Did you reach Solomon?"

"No. But we're near the crash site." He sat down beside her, careful not to get too close. "I don't like to wake Babe," he added, "but we don't really have a choice."

Téna looked away. "I wonder how it will be," she said. "Their crash. It could have happened to us if you hadn't been so skilled at getting us down." It was as close as she had come so far to graciousness.

But he cut her off. "At least we know John Solomon survived," he said. "And theirs would have been a bigger machine than ours. Maybe it wasn't so bad." Yet somehow he guessed that it was. If there had been other survivors, then he should have been able to reach them.

The flyer's transmitter was obviously working, but no human voice had responded to his call.

He also wondered why Solomon had left the area. Though in light of recent events, he could make a pretty good guess. If those bird creatures had been there, then it was possible that Solomon himself might even now be dead.

He teased a bit of meat from the grill with his knife. The green wood was beginning to smolder. "Done enough, do you think?" he asked as he regarded the reddish morsal. At least it wasn't dripping blood.

To his relief, Téna answered him civilly enough. "It's fine," she said.

"I'll wake Babe," he told her and got up.

He found the other man sprawled on the thermo sheet, half curled up on the other side of the fire. "Babe?" he said in a low voice. He knew better than to lay a hand on him—after the night they had all been through, he was pretty sure how he would react to someone shaking him awake and didn't want to risk getting shot.

Babe grunted. Then with a jerk, he was upright, staring about wildly until his eyes focused on the Lost Rythan.

"Food," Ard Matthew told him. "And I've located the crash site."

"That Solomon guy?"

The other shook his head. "But we're not far from the crash. We might find some clues there as to the—the rest of the party."

Babe met his eyes. "Yeah," he said. "That. Okay." He climbed painfully to his feet and followed Ard Matthew over to where the meat was cooking.

When they had finished their meal—and there was nothing left but bones—the party set off in the direction the transmitter had indicated. Or at least they tried to. The going was quite a bit rougher than he had thought it would be and Ard Matthew kept having to recheck his bearings as the terrain refused to cooperate. This was a rockier country filled with gorges and dry streambeds which they must either cross or parallel until they could cross. And they were climbing, though the Lost Rythan couldn't be sure whether they were actually in the foothills of the mountains or if there would be more descents. Their water supply was running low, but luckily the sun was no longer as warm as it had been. A cool wind blew in their faces.

At one point, they came upon a crumbling slope. The trees were growing even more sparsely and Ard Matthew was worried. He knew they would need both game and water. He glanced at the sky where the sun hung mostly overhead, though it tilted a little to the south. There was still time for all that, he thought. Hunting for game and water. They must be very near the crash site by now.

Suddenly, Babe, who was in the lead, seemed to waver for a moment before leaping back. He slipped and came down hard on his knees on the gravel. Ard Matthew hurried to his side.

"Don't go any further. It's a drop off."

Sure enough, the hill ended in an abrupt cutting that went down about a hundred feet. The Lost Rythan stood staring into a narrow valley as Téna hurried up behind him. He put out an arm to steady her.

He had already spotted the wreckage at the bottom and pointed it out to her. "We won't get down from here," Babe said from behind them.

Ard Matthew nodded. "I saw water down there," he said. "A stream."

"Then we can drink up what we've got," Babe said.

No one mentioned lunch since there wasn't any. But the Lost Rythan was sure there would be some sort of game near the water. He wasn't worried about that. But first they had to get down to it without breaking their necks.

He moved closer to the edge and studied what he could see of the sheared off rock. A tumble of earth and stones some fifty yards to his left looked more promising and he started off in that direction as the others followed. Luckily, the rockfall proved to be everything he had hoped and he started down, Babe and Téna at his heels.

He was about halfway to the valley floor when a stone moved beneath him. Flailing his arms, he tried to keep his footing, twisted his ankle as another rock gave way, and found himself sliding helplessly to the bottom. He heard Téna scream as he fell and hoped she had not slipped as well. But there was no time to look back. With one wrench, he was able to save himself from a final drop of ten feet or so, and came up half lying on a rim of crusted soil. Presently the others joined him there.

"You okay, Third-Blade?" Babe asked as he knelt beside the Rythan.

"I think so." His jacket had rucked up and there were scrapes on his back, tearing off the healing scabs from his first battle with the creatures. One arm felt seriously bruised, but when he used it to raise himself into a sitting position, the pain wasn't as bad as he had feared. From where he crouched, he spotted another break in the rock and used it to climb down into a mass of berry bushes and what looked like rushes. The others followed.

"Guess we found it," Babe said, pointing toward a break in the foliage.

Ard Matthew climbed painfully to his feet. Ahead he caught sight of a curving piece of metalplast and another further on. "Yeah," he said, licking his lips. For a moment, he was reluctant to proceed. But when Babe cocked one eye at him, he started to walk toward it and the other man followed.

Abruptly he stopped and turned to Babe. "This could be bad," he said in a low voice, nodding toward Téna who was making her way behind them.

"Third-Blade, stop being a chivalrous idiot. She's an adult."

Ard Matthew looked at him blankly and then turned away without answering. The flyer, he saw, had split open on landing, though apparently there had been no fire. He moved closer and stooped to peer inside the broken shell. A rank odor met him but it was not that of decay. He thought it smelled more like the musk of some animal. But it was plain that there was death within.

Scattered bones were gnawed clean. He counted three human skulls. Babe eased around him to look, Téna beside him. He heard her intake of breath.

"I wonder how many there were in the party," Babe said as he squatted down and dug into the remains of clothing. With a grunt of satisfaction, he retrieved another laser cutter, smaller than the one they had. A small colony of beetles, disturbed by his intrusion, ran scuttling from the rags.

As the Rythan had feared, this last was too much for Téna. She drew back, gagging while he glared at Babe. "This is unseemly," he said, echoing the sentiments ingrained in him by his culture. "A woman like Miss bor Rijn cannot be expected—" He stopped, wishing he had not said what he had, but it was too late.

Téna recovered herself in an instant, confronting him with flashing eyes, her face reddening. "I was almost starting to like you," she said, so angry she could hardly get the words out. "But you really are nothing but a damned throwback! Who are you to say what a woman should do or not do? Miss bor Rijn, for God's sake. What do you think this is—a tea party?"

He turned to Babe in helpless frustration but the other man only shook his head. "You blew it again, Third-Blade. Why couldn't you keep your mouth shut?"

Before their combined rebuff he had no recourse but to back down. Feeling his own anger rise, he turned away and left them, striding through the rushes toward what looked to be the nose of the flyer. But there, as he kicked aside the vegetation, a worse sight met him—the remains of a man with an obviously broken leg who had apparently tried to crawl from the wreckage.

The story of what had happened to him was plain enough, for there were neat puncture wounds in his clothing—the marks of beaks. His flesh had not been eaten, however and the wounds did not look fatal.

Ard Matthew examined the desiccated form, and tried to determine how the man had died. The answer to that came when, moving aside the collar of the jumpsuit, he saw a neat hole in his throat. Of course he could not be certain, but it almost looked as though one of the creatures had drunk his blood. Certainly, there was no sign of dried blood on the clothing.

He drew his hand back with a shudder of horror, as he stared down into the drawn face, with its sunken eyes and open, screaming mouth. Would this have been his own fate if he had not fought the creatures off? He imagined the injured man, lost in darkness, hearing the wails of the creatures, wondering what they were—

There were no tales of vampirism on Lost Rythar where the only blood drinkers were goat flies and mosquitoes. Faced with this horror, he felt like throwing up.

Hurriedly, he stepped away from the corpse. Luckily, the others were still examining the bodies in the wreckage and neither of them had come after him. He stood up rather shakily.

"I'm going to try Solomon again," he called, but they both ignored him. "I'll have to climb back up to the top." Still no answer. So be it.

He studied the rock face and soon spotted what looked like an easier path to the rim. Without a backward glance, he climbed it and took off his pack. Luckily, he had been using the shoulder strap when he fell. Nothing seemed damaged and he pulled out the communicator.

Static. Could the man have gone down into another valley? Of course there might be all sorts of reasons why he didn't answer. But Ard Matthew kept seeing the face of that other pilot—if he was the pilot. Whoever it was had died alone and screaming as one of the creatures drank his blood. No wonder Solomon had come apart as he had. Especially if he was the only survivor.

There was still nothing but static. He was about to put away the radio when he heard a change in the background noise. "Solomon?" he said. "John Solomon? This is Ard Matthew Third-Blade. Can you hear me?"

The voice was faint, but it was an answer. "The Lost Rythan! Pray for me! That's what you do, isn't it? You and the Star Brothers—"

It was as though he had been struck. Thinking of Shami, he could not answer a word. Then, as the other man waited, he finally managed to say, "I'm here, Solomon. We're coming to you."

"Too late. Don't you know about the wendigo? They know—the little people. Can't do a damned thing—"

"Wendigo?" He had never heard the word before.

"Do you know what it does? Do you?"

Whatever it was, Ard Matthew was afraid that he did know. "We're coming," he repeated but already the connection was breaking up.

The wendigo. So that was their name? He tasted the word and found it vile.

***

Téna did not look up when Ard Matthew returned after descending the same path he had used to reach the top. She and Babe had drawn off from the wreckage and were sitting on a dry mound nearby. Neither looked up at him, but it was plain that the fact he had alienated both of them had done nothing to make them allies with each other. He saw no friendliness in their attitude.

With a sigh, he turned to Babe. "We can't stay here," he said bluntly.

Babe gave him an unblinking stare. "Why not? There's water. Even if we don't see any turkeys, we can fish."

They had not eaten since that morning and now the afternoon was passing. Hunger pangs did little to sweeten the atmosphere. Téna looked up, plainly ready to add her vote to Babe's.

But, "I have spoken to John Solomon," Ard Matthew reminded them. "He is desperate and he needs us to come."

"Is he the only survivor of the Becker party?" Babe asked. "Because there are sure no survivors here."

"I think he might be."

Babe shrugged. "If he's lived this long, he can wait another day, can't he? We need a rest."

Ard Matthew looked at Téna, who met his look with one of stubborn belligerence. She had not forgiven him for insulting her hardihood.

But he shook his head. "I told him we—I would come," he said. He was determined not to abandon Solomon, as long as there was any chance the man might still be alive. Now he waited, towering over Babe and the others.

Slowly, the other man got to his feet. "I don't know who made you the boss of our outfit," he said coldly. "You were an employee, Third-Blade, the last I heard. Hired to fly us to the lodges."

"There are duties that go beyond those I owe to my—former—employer," Ard Matthew said. "Duties to you and to this other man who is lost and alone." He was all Lost Rythan now, whatever veneer of courtesy and civilized behavior he had assumed, shorn away. "Have you filled the water bags?" he demanded.

At this, Téna also climbed to her feet. "Mr. Third-Blade," she said, "you're not listening. Whatever the customs of your—your tribe—we will not be bullied into acting against common sense. This is a good place to fight off those creatures—we can build a fire and have the cliffs at our backs."

Before Ard Matthew could answer, Babe spoke up. "She's right. It's only one night and the rest of this afternoon. We can go on tomorrow."

"What makes you think you'll be any fitter tomorrow than you are today?"

Babe did not answer this, but Téna did.

"Go yourself if it's so important to you," she said. "Babe has a gun." But she sounded a little less confident than she had.

"Babe can stay if he likes. But not you." Ard Matthew did not explain that he was sure Babe could protect her and that was not the problem. His question was, who would protect her from Babe?

The other man held the gun negligently in one hand. "Look, if you really care what happens to her, then think for a minute," he said. "This really is a defensible place. Hadn't you better reconsider?" This time he raised the weapon slightly.

Meanwhile, Téna continued to glare at him. "Don't you dare speak of me as though I were a child," she said. "Or—or so much baggage! I've had all I'm going to take of your patriarchal attitude! You've treated me as a second-class citizen long enough and now you can go wherever you want to and damned good riddance!"

"I?" the Lost Rythan said. "I have never meant you harm or—or insult." He stared at her in confusion.

At this, Babe intervened, lowering the gun slightly. "Look," he said, in a more conciliating tone. "You can see she doesn't want to go with you. Neither do I. But if you can give me one good reason to leave a safe place like this—"

Ard Matthew frowned for a moment, wondering how to convince this man. After what he had seen, he knew the gorge was not defensible. But had the others seen the dead man? Probably not.

He gestured toward the wreckage. "What makes you think it's safe here?" he asked. "And why do you think Mr. Solomon left? He even warned us not to come here to the wreckage."

"Who knows why he took off," Babe said in irritation. "Maybe he got spooked. But as for these other people, it looks to me like they were killed in the crash. Solomon was lucky."

The Lost Rythan gave him a brooding look. "There are more seats than there are bodies," he said. "Had you thought of that?" After a moment's hesitation, he came to a decision. "Come with me," he told Babe. "I want to show you something."

Something in his face must have alerted Babe, because when Téna started to rise, both men shook their heads. She subsided unwillingly. Perhaps she thought she had made her point, which was fine with Ard Matthew. It was Babe he wanted to convince and if they had not already seen it, the sight of the dead man in the reeds should be enough to persuade anyone that this was no place to spend the night.

But at the look of disdain on Téna's face, he could still not help feeling the beginnings of an answering anger. He had, by his lights, dealt fairly with her and her biting comments rankled. Nor was he especially pleased with Babe's attitude. He didn't think he would ever understand the starfolk.

"This way," he said curtly, pushing through the undergrowth past the front end of the flyer. He followed his own former path until, shoving the last of the reeds aside, he stepped once more into the cleared space. There was the dead man, looking as horrible and pathetic as he had before. The skin was stretched over his screaming face, eyes already gone and the rest darkened with incipient decay. There was also an odor he had not noticed before.

He did not look at Babe though he heard the other man suck in his breath. The sounds of his swishing through the undergrowth stopped abruptly. He muttered something that sounded like "Zaebis!" and then was silent. Ard Matthew had no doubt of his meaning, though the language was unfamiliar to him. It was the exclamation of horror and shock he had expected to provoke by bringing him here.

With a visible effort, Babe holstered the gun and stepped over to examine the corpse. "So what do you think happened to this guy?" he asked.

"As you see." The Lost Rythan bent over and showed him the neck wound.

Babe stared at the round hole for long moments. "It drank his blood," he finally got out. "Is that it?"

"That's what it looks like to me."

"So now we know," Babe said at last. He swallowed. "Of course we knew they were nasty. But—"

Ard Matthew waited.

"Okay, Third-Blade," he said at last. "I admit I don't want her seeing this guy and maybe the wreckage isn't the best place to hang around. Especially after dark," he added in a lower voice. He had to force himself to look away from the corpse. "But whether we'll find a safer place—"

Ard Matthew nodded. "We can only try," he said. "Will you help me to convince—her?"

"Yeah, I'll do that. And Third-Blade," he added. "I've been a jerk."

The Rythan looked at him. "It's what we are now that matters," he said. "At least if we want to survive."

"Yeah," the other man agreed. Once more he looked back at the dead pilot.

When they got back to the main wreckage, Téna looked gave them an enquiring look from her seat on the mound. "Well?" she said to Babe.

"He's right about this place," the other told her. "I think we'd better move on."

Her eyes narrowed. It was not the answer she had expected. "What if I refuse?" she said, though they both knew she wouldn't. "What if I build a fire and stay here?"

Babe ignored her and picked up the water bags. It was Ard Matthew who came over and knelt down beside her. "I am sorry for having offended you," he said, "but I ask you now to set all that aside. My ways—and those of my people—are not yours and I suppose I am what you would call a primitive. Others have said so. But I know no other ways and now we must work together in order to save ourselves. Can you accept that?"

She glowered at him mutely.

"There is a man out there alone and he—he is losing himself. Perhaps he is lost already. But he needs our help. We would be less than we should be if we did not do our utmost to find him."

"Show me what you showed Babe," she said suddenly.

He hesitated.

"This isn't your miserable planet," she reminded him. "You are not among primitives now. On my world, a woman isn't—isn't a grown up child. You may have done the best you know, but it isn't good enough. Can't you see that?" She rose, not giving him a chance to argue further. "Show me."

He glanced helplessly to where Babe had disappeared with the water bags. "Miss bor Rijn—"

"Now," she said. "Or I won't come with you."

In the end, he had no choice but to take her to the place beyond the wreckage where the body lay, shriveled and contorted among the grasses. And there she saw the face—empty eye sockets, mouth gaping in an eternal rictus of pain and horror. And she saw the neat hole in his throat, not much different from the wounds she had seen on Ard Matthew's back. Only this one was deeper, dried at the edges now and shriveling back from the hole. There was no sign of blood.

She stared at this, her face growing pale beneath its weathering, her mouth set and trembling slightly. "What—what did it do to him?" she whispered. "How did he die?"

He told her, already wishing he had not brought her here. Once more, he seemed to be getting everything wrong.

But Téna drew herself up, still pale and set of face. She turned to face him. "Very well, Mr. Third-Blade, I'll come with you," she said.

As they turned away from the scene, Ard Matthew saw that Babe had returned and was staring at her. He turned his angry gaze on the Rythan.

"It's alright, Babe," Téna said wearily. "I made him show me." They could see in her face that something in her had grown harder—a necessary toughening which made it more likely she would survive.

Ard Matthew was relieved to see this, though it saddened him as well. Certainly Lost Rythan women were strong, he told himself. But one tried to remember always that they were women, mothers and sisters. He thought of his own sisters. He would have spared them had he been able to.

Only later, as they waded the little stream and crossed the valley, did he remember their mysterious benefactor. Someone lived here—someone who knew how to survive in the wilderness. And he still thought that someone was a woman—maybe even a girl, running barefoot over the rough ground, hunting with a slingshot.

Colonist? Of course she must be. Likely there was, or had been, a settlement in the area. A lost settlement. He knew that Windy-Go had never gained colony status. Now he wondered if the corporations that used the place might not have something to do with that. Could they have deliberately held things back in order to use the planet for their own purposes? Just what all those purposes were, he had, of course, no idea. Other than the lodges, he did not know of any other use being made of the place. But it was a planet—an entire planet. And almost none of it had been explored.

Still, he thought, as he led the others along the route he had chosen, there were many planets in the starnet. One day they might be settled, but for now most of them were not needed for the advance of the race. Many were just as this one, scarcely touched, barely used—or not even used at all.

The far side of the valley was gentler than the broken rock they had first descended, with a very manageable incline, overgrown with what he now concluded must be autumnal grass and flowers. He paused from time to time to check his direction but didn't try to contact Solomon. They needed to cover as much distance as they could before sunset and he didn't want to slow them down.

It would be good to find a cave, he thought, or even an overhang. But that, too, must wait. First they must find the missing man. And, he thought grimly, it would be good to find him alive, not drained of blood and left to shrivel in the sun.

They came out onto another stretch of sparsely wooded terrain, floored with needles. But now there were larger stretches of grassland, sere and dun colored in the autumn sunlight. He glanced back at the sun, reddening as it began to descend. He had already noted that their shadows were lengthening ahead of them. A chill crept into the air. He forced himself to hurry.

The sun had set behind a fold of the land when he finally called a halt. They had emerged from under the trees and onto a slight, boulder covered eminence. All around them, the forest fell away, shadowy now, treetops soughing gently in the wind. "I think this is the best we can do for the night," he admitted.

Babe glanced around at the rocks. "These might give us some protection," he said. "But we'll still need a fire."

"And those creatures seem to use the trees to get around," Téna said. "So we're better off up here. But shouldn't we gather wood while we can?" She was looking around uneasily as she spoke.

"Of course." He unslung his satchel and laid it on the ground. "Babe, can you keep watch while we bring the wood?" He did not quite look at Téna but tried to make her feel included in the "we."

The other man grunted and followed them to the edge of the trees. There were plenty of fallen branches and it did not take long to assemble a good-sized pile which they dragged up among the boulders. At last, Ard Matthew turned off the laser cutter and paused for a moment, to study their surroundings.

"I'd like to scout around," he said abruptly. "Can you get a fire started while I'm gone?"

Babe nodded. "If you see anything edible, bring it back."

"You'll be okay?" the Rythan asked. He was still a little confused about the relationship between Téna and this man, but she really did not seem to be afraid of him. And it was true that they were all hungry and Ard Matthew was the only experienced hunter among them. Besides, he needed to check for signs of anything dangerous in the area.

And so he set off in no very settled state of mind.

CHAPTER NINE

He had to safeguard both Téna and Babe, he told himself. He was their guardian no matter what. Ard Matthew kept the thought before him as he left the campsite. It was true he had usurped the position of group leader automatically and he was still usurping it, despite Babe's objections which were probably not very serious. But in view of his Faring Guard training, who was better qualified?

Though he had to admit the reasons were more complicated than that. He was a Lost Rythan. Even now that he had fled from the Faring Guard, from his honor and his Faith, that one fact could never be changed. There was something in him that set him above these folk of the gentler worlds—those who had never fought the wolf or the snowtyger, had never climbed the mountains of Rythar or seen the ashfalls and the burning skies. He was tired of pretending that his folk and theirs were equals—or worse, that the Rythans were inferior in some way. He knew they were not.

As he made his way down the eminence, he seemed to be two men, two sets of eyes looking at the same facts and seeing very different things. On the one hand, his companions truly needed him whether they thought so or not. Not only did they depend on his skills in hunting and fighting, but also on his guidance. Yes, he told himself firmly, his guidance! He—and they—must rescue Solomon if they could, not only for the man's own sake but for theirs. For they would all be less than they should be if they did not at least try. Later, even if they tried and failed, he hoped the others would understand this.

But he was, indeed, two men. That first was the Lost Rythan speaking. The other man, Ard Matthew Third-Blade, stripped of everything he had once cherished, had no words. For this man, his true and inner self, there was only the ignominy of failure. He had been tested and he had failed that test—he had denied God. Shami had turned to him when she was dying, asking for the hope he should have given her. But he had held fast to his petty grievance and kept silent. And now he couldn't even become a proper pagan because he did believe and he regretted bitterly what he had done and failed to do.

All around him lay the shadowed landscape. He listened with all of his senses for the sound he had learned to know so well—the wailing scream of the wendigo. But there was nothing beyond the normal noises of the evening—a distant owl and the whisper of the wind among the trees. And the voice of his creator.

The trees seemed larger here, rising like pillars to hold up the fading sky. Even as his feet found what might have been a game trail, he was overtaken by a memory of his boyhood on Lost Rythar. He had missed his way—he and a cousin who died later in one of his clan's many feuds—and they had found themselves on the side of a wooded slope surrounded by sunfirs. The two suns were setting, nearly together at that time of year, the Elder Brother and the Younger. The elder, and brighter, was no more than a reddish hemisphere, stabbed by the peaks above, while the younger, a little higher in the sky, was nearly eclipsed in the glow. Out over the lowlands, the sky had been turning green. He remembered that especially because only rarely did one see the green glow at sunset.

For some reason, he recalled, he had tilted his head back and looked up at the trees, seeing them for the first time as they really were—tall and cold, towering hugely above the two boys like emblems of the coming night. He shuddered still at the memory. And even as he had this revelation, they had heard the first wolf howl high above them on the mountain.

He remembered how they had drawn their puny blades, assuring each other that they would sell their lives dearly. How they had stood back to back, waiting. But the wolves had never come. Instead, they were found by Ard Matthew's elder brother, Gris Andrew. Later that same night, he recalled, they were whipped soundly for leaving the hunting camp. Only now did he realize that the anger he had seen in his kinsmen's faces had really been fear. Fear of what might have happened to the boys if the wolves had found them.

Returning to the present, he gazed down at the trail—if that is what it was. It certainly seemed to be one. But had it been made by antelopes or some other animal? He squatted down to study what he thought were tracks but in the fading light, he could not tell for sure what they were.

He was still thinking about his father's fear. What if the wolves really had come down, slinking among the sunfirs in the twilight? What if the last rays of the sun had caught their eyes and made them glow? And what if Ard Matthew and his cousin had only been found later, a scatter of bones on the forest floor?

But I tried, he groaned. I tried to save that child on Ynche. I would have given my life to save her! You know that.

But God had not asked his life. He had asked something else entirely—his trust, his confidence. He stood up, shaking his head in denial. No—

The hairs were rising on the back of his neck again and he knew that if he turned he would see Someone back among the pines, waiting patiently for Ard Matthew Third-Blade to turn. Commanding him to turn.

But when he forced himself to look, he saw nothing save the darkness crowding beneath the sentinel trees. He stepped over the trail and cast about desperately for any sign of game. In the distance, something caught his eye, a bit of whiteness further down the slope. He moved toward it.

At first he thought it was the remains of yet another survivor of the crash. But then he saw the antlers, more than one set. And there were bones, thin and birdlike, leg bones and upper limbs and a shattered ribcage. He saw a skull, broken as with a blow. And near it, another one. There were stones—

In the forest, something made a woofing noise and he thought immediately of bears. The sound came again and he tried to gauge the direction—was it near the camp? But Babe had the gun. Babe might not have the skill of a Rythan, but he could shoot. He had done well enough so far. So had Téna if the truth were to be told.

But at the thought of Téna facing a bear—or worse, a wendigo—something turned over in him and he found that he was trembling. It was not that he was romantically interested in her, though perhaps he should be. Shouldn't he? The thought came as a shock. But no—it was rather, he told himself, that she was physically weaker than he and innocent.

Out in the forest, the sound came again—*woof! WOOF!*

He had to get back to the camp! It was not a reasoned decision—he simply knew that he must go now. Suddenly the trees became his enemies and, for a moment, he was a child again, bewildered among the sunfirs high on the mountainside. Lost.

He stared hard at the alien landscape, forcing his panicked mind to recall that this was not Lost Rythar and that he was a grown man trained in tracking. A Faring Guard. After a moment, he found his way back uphill to cross the trail in a different place.

Something turned beneath his foot and he paused to pick it up. It was another of the rounded stones, but whether it was dropped on the trail or had rolled here, he had no way of knowing. Still, someone had killed the wendigos and the thought gave him comfort. He straightened himself, then bent over once more, to peer down at the ground, seeking he knew not what, while all around him, the trees had grown silent, and the stars had begun to shed their dim radiance. On an impulse, he drew out his torch and flashed it at the ground.

That was the only reason he saw it, the sharp, contrasting shadows outlining the clear print of a human foot. It was the short, broad track of their benefactor—or someone very like her. He studied the print for a moment, noting the absence of an arch, the stubby toes. He looked for more tracks and found them. Someone had used this part of the trail quite recently.

He raised his head, listening, but there was only the wind. He had no time to follow the tracks now. Instead, he made straight for the camp, passing another set of shed antlers as he went.

The remembered vision of the child on Ynche had left him, but now it was Gris Wolfgang he saw. If he had done what Marshall Pwyll had asked him to—if he had gone with the priest into the chapel and offered himself and his friend to God, things might have turned out differently. Oh, Gris Wolfgang was dying and that could not be changed. But if Ard Matthew had come to him in hope, with the touch of God's grace on him, then maybe the other man would not have had to meet the wolves that way—the spirit wolves that sought to take his soul on the mountain of the dead.

"Yes—" Once more, he knew the shame he would feel later, when he had time to feel. It was the reckoning God saved for those He loved. But that would be later. Now he clenched the laser cutter, listening—and hearing nothing. If he were to die at this moment, he wondered, would he die in courage and hope as his friend had done? He had unconfessed sins on his soul. If he fell to the wendigo, his exsanguinated corpse might lie where it fell as though he were no more than an animal decomposing on the forest floor.

But his soul? an inner voice demanded. He swallowed.

That was when he heard the thing again—this time ahead of him. There was that barking sound and a growl. There was no doubt it was a bear. He could hear it moving among the needles. He began to run.

Shouldn't he see the glow of the campfire by now? When he had left, the others were getting ready to light it. Something must have happened, either bears or the wendigo. He ran harder, remembering the dead child, remembering Gris Wolfgang. He must not fail this time!

But that was laughable. Why mustn't he fail? He was only a man and he had failed before. He had failed because he had done all a man could do and thought it was enough. But it wasn't. He knew that now.

He heard the bear growling just down the slope. And a scream! He powered on the laser, hoping it would be enough as he plunged toward the sound.

Would You aid me now? Even now? I ask! I dare ask—

He heard the whoosh of the air gun and stumbled to a halt as the growl was abruptly cut off. He could just make out Babe and Téna's forms in the starlight, saw the mound of an animal lying at the base of a tree. Above him, something moved and in response, a shadowy form ran forward.

"Don't shoot, Babe," Téna cried. "It's a child."

But it wasn't Téna's voice Ard Matthew heard but Another, far more familiar. "It's a child," the Voice said. With a lunge, the Rythan was there before the girl, reaching up to grasp something that clung to the trunk. Something that shivered and released its hold to fall into his arms.

For a moment he stood dazed, feeling the warmth of it and wondering if he had lost his mind. Surely he had been close to madness up there on the hillside!

But it didn't matter. Not now. "Get the torch from my belt," he said to Téna. "Babe, light the fire!"

Once more Ard Matthew Third-Blade was in charge!

Téna had actually staggered with surprise when she saw him, barely catching herself on the great furry haunch of the dead bear. "Mr. Third-Blade!" she exclaimed. "I—"

"Take the torch," he told her again.

Obediently, she reached over to unclip the tube from his belt.

"Now put the light on," he said more gently as he eased his burden to the ground. "Let's see what we've got here."

Obediently, Téna shone the light on the face of the child. "My God," she breathed.

Ard Matthew reached down to tilt the small head backward. Babe came up and stared. No one said anything as they took in the sight of those closed eyes beneath overhanging brows, the broad nose and generous mouth. The child's head seemed to be all face, for the forehead sloped backward to a shock of wiry hair. Neither was there much of a chin. Ard Matthew had never seen anything like it before and he was at a loss to understand what it was they had found.

But, "Look at the little bugger!" Babe exclaimed after a moment. "I wonder what colony he's from."

Of course. This would be a colonist. A mutation. As he was himself. As all the Rythans were. After a moment's groping, he rearranged his thoughts. "Build up the fire," he reminded Babe. "Before the wendigos come back."

"Wendigos?" Babe said.

"That's what Solomon called them."

Behind him, he heard the rustle as Téna added kindling to the fire space and Babe stepped over to light it.

He brought the child nearer to the center of what was to be their camp. Once the blaze was going, Téna set the torch where it could give him more light. He was already examining their find, who proved to be exceedingly dirty and probably wounded. "I'll need—do we have anything left to clean him with?" he asked. "Look in the pack."

Téna upended the much depleted satchel. "A little antibiotic," she told him. "Nothing else that I can see."

"No cloth—? Synthoskin?" But he knew they had probably used all he had.

"No cloth," she told him. "One more packet of synthoskin."

Abruptly, he shrugged off his jacket and removed the ragged shirt beneath. It would have to do. With the aid of his knife, he tore the much soiled garment into pieces. "Water?"

Babe laid another branch on the fire and fetched him one of the water bags. It was about half full. Without another word, Ard Matthew set to work.

Téna hovered for a moment and then turned to Babe. "The bear," she said. "Hadn't we—I mean—"

"Take the knife," Ard Matthew told her, not looking up from his work. Babe did so and soon he could be heard working away at the hide of the dead animal. They had been hungry so long and here was meat!

"Don't forget the fire," the Rythan said as he worked off the dirt and blood and applied synthoskin to his patient. The boy had not regained consciousness even when he turned him over to deal with the long gashes on his back. "I've used the last of the synthoskin," he said to Téna. "The last of everything, I guess."

"I don't grudge it," she murmured, looking down at the child's wounds. "Especially if—I mean do you think he'll be alright?"

Ard Matthew looked down at his patient. Aside from his strange physiognomy, he seemed normal enough. Maybe his legs were a bit short for his torso—or that could only be a truck of the light. And the back of his skull seemed slightly misshapen, though his abundant hair, held away from his face by a leather thong, made it hard to be sure.

Gently, he turned him back over, carefully wrapping him in the jacket he had taken off. The child had worn very little clothing—a short kilt of tanned hide and a sort of baldric, half torn away. Ard Matthew held up a strip of leather. "The sling," he said. "And he's got some stones in a little bag." There, at least, was one mystery solved.

He stared down at the boy's face for a moment. "I don't think there's much else I can do," he said. "He's been clawed, but the wounds aren't serious. He has lost some blood, though. I suppose he could go into shock."

"Then we should keep him warm," Téna said. "I guess that's all we can do."

The Rythan stood up. "Can you watch him?" he asked. "I mean, unless you would rather help Babe with the butchering." He hoped he was learning how to treat her. His phrasing was a lot more careful than it had been and now he gave her a choice.

Téna stared at him for a moment as though she were seeing him for the first time. Really seeing him. Judging by the look on her face, it occurred to him that, shirtless as he was, he might well pass for such another savage as the child. In the firelight, the ribs showed clearly on his slim torso, while muscles rippled in tight bands across his upper chest and arms when he moved. He turned away in some embarrassment, and then realized that she was gazing at the scars on his back. The results of his fight with the wendigo were not yet healed. And then there were those other marks—from his flogging on Wolf Slammer. Quickly, he moved out of the light.

But Téna had knelt to hover over the boy, brushing his face with her hands. Suddenly there was an intake of breath as a small hand gripped hers. Ard Matthew turned back just in time to see the boy's eyes snap open, gleaming a little in the shadows of his face. He made a soft mewling sound.

Téna did not try to draw her hand away. "It's alright," she murmured. "You're safe now." Then with a sudden scream. "He bit me!"

She stood up quickly, her hand dripping blood. The boy was also struggling to rise.

"No—you've got to stay put," she said, grabbing the jacket and using it to hold him down. "Mr. Third-Blade!" she called anxiously. "Help me!"

In a moment, he was at her side. The child seemed to calm somewhat at the sight of him and he leaned over, risking a bite himself, as he wrapped him in his arms. He was murmuring something in Rythan, he realized—the sort of things you said to calm frightened children. Of course the words would have been unintelligible to the boy, but after a moment, he relaxed and stared up into the Rythan's face with an expression not of trust, quite, but something noncommittal, at least.

"Better clean that bite," he said when he caught sight of Téna's wounded hand.

"With what?" she said. To her obvious disgust, there was nothing to use but the remains of his shirt. Gingerly she sought one of the few remnants not already soaked with blood and water, and bound up her wound while he watched her. What they would do for injuries in the future—if they even had a future—he couldn't imagine.

Babe, meanwhile, was bringing a handful of cut steaks to the fire. "Hungry?" he asked. He sounded almost cheerful.

Ard Matthew glanced at Téna. There was a time when she would have gibed at him—Babe the mighty hunter or something like that. But he had shot the bear and even she must acknowledge that fact. She stood up. "I'll help cook those, Babe," she volunteered and Ard Matthew relaxed.

"Thanks," Babe told her, handing over the meat. "I want to see if I can get that hide off. It might be smelly, but it's warm."

"Good idea," the Rythan said, his opinion of Babe going up a notch. "I'm sure we can use it tonight, at least."

"You think the kid's hungry?" Babe asked, not coming any closer to Ard Matthew's burden.

The Rythan looked down at what he held. "I think he's asleep," he said, easing the limp weight of the child. "I'd like to put him down and get another fix on Solomon, if I can."

Suddenly he looked up. Something had alerted him, his sixth sense again. Without a word, he laid the boy back on the ground, after which, he straightened himself and moved casually toward the half butchered carcass of the bear. A shadowy form lurked in the deeper darkness beneath the trees. He slipped out of the light and advanced into the shadows.

"What the—?" Babe said, but Téna cut him off.

"Something's out here," she said. "Maybe we can't hear it but he can."

And then he passed beyond the sounds of their voices, wishing they would be quiet. He paused, trying to focus in the grudging starlight. Something moved—or was that only a breath where no breath should be? Drawing himself up, he pounced.

There was a cry, cut off, and he found himself holding a struggling captive. Female, he thought, and she was straining to bite him as the child had bitten Téna. He pinned her arms and held her away from him. Half lifting her from the ground, he brought her back to the campsite.

Babe lowered the gun he had taken up while Téna, who had wrapped herself protectively around the child, looked up in surprise.

As he emerged from the shadows, it was plain to Ard Matthew that he had taken another one of the same race as the boy. There was the same overhung brow, broad nose and large mouth—half opened now and snarling. Her hair was tied in a pony tail and she wore a sleeveless, leather tunic.

"What have you got there?" Babe said, laying down the gun.

"Can't you see?" Téna asked. "This is the girl who left the footprints. The one who brought us meat—if it was for us." Her voice trailed off.

Ard Matthew not daring relax his hold on his struggling captive, found himself suddenly at a loss. He looked helplessly at Téna, who had got up and was eyeing the girl.

"Hello," she said. "Can you understand me?"

Those deep-set eyes fixed on her, the receding brow wrinkling with uncertainty.

"Your—your boy is here," Téna said. "You can see him. He's hurt." She turned to Ard Matthew. "She doesn't look old enough to be his mother, does she?"

He shook his head. Relaxing his hold a little, he led the girl over to where their patient slumbered, still wrapped in the tattered jacket. There was a sudden gasp of indrawn breath from his prisoner who resumed her struggle. Before he could regain his hold, she broke free and threw herself down beside the boy.

"Kensh!" Her voice was higher pitched than he had expected, as though she spoke with a different sort of throat. She said a few more words and then repeated the first, "Kensh" which must have been the boy's name. She looked up at Ard Matthew, the skin still wrinkling above her eyes, her lips skinning back from slightly oversized teeth.

He returned that look with great earnestness before he spread his hands and shrugged. Carefully, he reached forward to ease back the covering, showing her the boy's wounds.

At this, the child woke, saw the girl's face above him and smiled a little. Apparently he felt safe enough now and did not try to rise.

Nor did she try to lift him. She sat back, reaching out one hand to smooth his hair. She said some more words in that odd voice of hers and then, quite clearly, she looked up and said, "Shpezz man?"

Ard Matthew looked at her in perplexity, but Téna seemed to understand what she was trying to say.

"Yes," she said. "We come from space. Do you speak basic?"

"Bezz-kik? I shpik—I khear. Zhon."

This was too much for Téna and she looked to the Lost Rythan for help.

He thought for a moment and then, "Zhon," he repeated. "Solomon?"

At once, the girl began to nod her head. "Zhonsomen," she said, still nodding. Then she added something else in her strange, high pitched language. Reaching out one hand, she laid it on his naked chest.

Ard Matthew started. She was looking intently into his face as though she knew that he too belonged here in the wilderness that was apparently her home. For a moment, he forgot himself in a rapport that seemed perfectly natural. Here was someone who meant them no harm—indeed it was likely that she, or else the young one—perhaps her brother?—had been watching over the party for some days, even supplying them with food. He knew the language barrier would be a challenge, but if this girl had met Solomon, then he could be fairly certain the other man was still alive.

Suddenly he smiled at her. "Are you hungry?" he asked as he gestured toward the steaks Babe had set over the coals. He must have given up on skinning the bear and, since Téna was occupied, had taken over the cooking job himself.

The girl hesitated, still hovering over the injured child. He had an idea she wanted to ask what had happened but lacked the vocabulary for it. Gently, he took her shoulder and turned her toward the half butchered carcass of the bear. Then he pointed to the tree and mimed an attack.

Their guest traced one finger over a strip of synthoskin angling over her brother's rib-cage. "Bay-er," she said carefully.

Ard Matthew gave an encouraging nod. "You can stay here," he told her. "I'll bring you something to eat."

He watched her settle herself beside the boy, who still watched everything languidly without trying to rise. On the other side of them, Téna hovered uncertainly.

"You stay with her," the Lost Rythan said quietly. "I'll bring the food over here."

He fetched some of the meat when it was ready, and brought it over to Téna and the girl. "Still hot," he said as he handed each a makeshift skewer. He was very hungry himself, but he had been trained to go without food for long periods and now he forced himself to wait until he saw the others eating.

While they ate, Babe stayed by the fire, holding his food with one hand, his other gripping the gun. "No sign of wendigo so far," he said. "Guess we picked a good spot, Third Blade."

The Lost Rythan shook his head. "They're out there," he said. "I found some dead ones. Killed by stones, I think."

"The kid? He doesn't look big enough."

Ard Matthew came over to the fire and took up his own portion of meat, blowing on it while he considered this. "Might have been the girl," he said at last. "I'll bet she's got a sling of her own." He settled down beside Babe.

"Not much good against a bear," Babe said. "A sling."

"You'd be surprised." He stared at the meat in his hand thinking of all that had happened out among the trees and of the truce he had made with God. Suddenly he switched the skewer to his other hand and with his right, he made the Sign of the Cross. Only then did he begin to eat.

Babe said nothing for a moment while he chewed and swallowed a bite. Then, "I guess you're still a Faring Guard after all, Third-Blade."

Ard Matthew looked at him, still eating.

Babe gave a snort of amusement. "Third-Blade, according to my people, you did that backwards. We're Orthodox."

The Lost Rythan relaxed. "It'll do," he said and grinned shyly at the other man.

"We going for Solomon tomorrow?" Babe asked then.

"I don't know. Depends on how the boy does. He was clawed pretty bad."

"So you have priorities," Babe said. "About who gets helped, I mean."

"Of course I do." Ard Matthew looked at him in surprise. "This is a child."

"Women and children first," the other man mocked. Then, "Sorry, Third-Blade. You didn't seem like that kind of guy—earlier."

"I—was trying not to be," the Lost Rythan admitted. How could he find words for the thing that had happened to him up on the hillside? He felt as though God had taken him by the scruff of the neck and given him a good shake. No, that wasn't it—it was more as though he had been first among all the fools who had ever dared to judge his Creator by the standards of men. He had taken his own small store of wisdom and virtue as the measure of God's righteousness. Now he looked up to see Babe grinning at him.

"It's okay, Third-Blade. I saw through you."

For a moment they regarded each other with the same almost preternatural understanding he had felt with the native girl. "Want to tell me?" Babe said at last. "What happened before you came to Windy-Go?"

And Ard Matthew told him—about the girl on Ynche and about Gris Wolfgang. When he had finished, he got up to feed the fire. Mercifully, the night continued quiet, the star-crowded sky swept periodically by a cloud or two, the tree-tops soughing in the wind. He felt washed clean as though he had confessed his folly at least, if not his sins.

But what about Babe, he wondered. What grounds did Téna have for her antipathy toward the man?

Babe had gone to fetch more meat for them, but both men stiffened at the sound of a distant wail. "They're out there, after all, Third-Blade," he said.

The cry was answered from further away. "Not here. Down in the forest."

"Right. But let's build up the fire a bit just in case." Babe turned to the branch pile and laid on more fuel while Téna watched from her station beside the wounded child.

"Ask that girl," Babe suggested and Ard Matthew went over to where the two women sat together chewing bear steaks. The boy—Kensh?—seemed to have gone back to sleep.

He looked at the girl, then pointed out away from the camp. "Are we safe?" he asked. He wondered whether wendigo was her own name for the things. "You hear them? The wendigo?"

She peered up at him for a moment and then at the darkness beyond. "No shree," she said in her high voice. He was reminded of the cry of a bird.

"Shree?" he asked.

She made a gesture with both hands, outlining something in the air.

"I think she means 'tree'," Téna said. She turned toward her. "You mean there are not enough trees up here, don't you?"

After a hesitation, a nod. "No shree, no scay."

Ard Matthew was willing to accept this, especially as it accorded with his own instinct. After all, that was why he had chosen this spot for their campsite—there was only the one skimpy pine the boy had climbed.

"But we'd better take turns keeping watch," he told Babe as he settled himself again and accepted another chunk of bear meat.

Babe grunted. "You can sleep first if you like."

But Ard Matthew wasn't sleepy. He glanced covertly at the other man, wondering how to broach the subject that was on his mind. There were many things he wanted to know about Kessler Co. and the flyer crash. He was pretty sure that Babe knew at least some of the answers.

"What?" Babe said, reading some of this in his look.

The Lost Rythan settled back, resting his arms on his knees. "After we find Solomon," he said. "Should we still go to the ruins?"

A shrug. "That depends on why you think we're supposed to be dead."

"Why are we supposed to be dead, Babe?"

"I was in that crash too."

"I had already guessed that Téna is a stand-in for her cousin," Ard Matthew said slowly. "Though I could hardly have expected them to try to murder her. I still don't know why it is so important that people think that woman is dead. I mean it should have been enough to have a decoy here so that she could go somewhere else."

Babe nodded. "That's good reasoning as far as it goes, Third-Blade. I've been thinking about that, too."

The Lost Rythan frowned, watching the smoke spiral into the shimmering sky. "You came down in the shuttle. I was told to fly the two women to the lodge." Suddenly he looked over at Babe. "There is only one reason I can think of for killing us here on Windy-Go," he said.

The other man waited, the firelight catching on one side of his face. Ard Matthew could not read his expression. He groped for words as the ideas came to him. "If she died here—then no one would look for her here," he said. "Isn't that so?"

"I think you're right," Babe agreed. "It's my guess Kessler actually came down later and now she's hiding somewhere on Windy-Go. You see, there is phessite. Here."

"And she's the only one who knows where it is? Besides the discoverers, I mean."

Babe laughed harshly. "She's the only one who knows, Third-Blade. The others have been taken care of."

Ard Matthew looked at him. It was on the tip of his tongue to ask him whether he had killed them, but he resisted in time. What was the point?

But Babe seemed to read his mind. "I didn't kill them," he said. "Though Téna would never believe that."

"But you knew?"

"Damn right I knew. And there wasn't a thing I could have done. Just like this balls-up."

"There was nothing you could have done?"

Babe jerked around and glared at him. "Don't you know anything about the real world, Third-Blade? No I guess not. You were a Faring Guard. And that's about one step from being a monk, isn't it?"

Ard Matthew had never thought about it that way, but he supposed the other was right. For all his efforts to damn himself, he was still pretty naïve by Babe's standards. He shrugged. "I guess I don't know much," he admitted.

"Well you can thank God for that!"

Suddenly the Lost Rythan leaned forward. "Tell me," he said. "Why did you work for Kessler? Why did you do the things you did?"

It was Babe's turn to shrug. "I don't suppose the name Oleg means anything to you?"

Ard Matthew shook his head.

"Well this Oleg fellow was what you might call a semi-decent man. He had a conscience of a sort, though I doubt he was as honest as you'd have liked. He didn't come from a place where honesty was much in vogue." There was a pause as they listened to the wendigo screaming in the distance. "One of his weaknesses was that he had a family—a lot of relatives back on Earth. Novosibirsk. And more on Novodny Colony which is where he ended up."

Ard Matthew was wondering what he meant by a semi-decent man. It was not a Rythan concept. His people did not understand shades of gray very well.

"So Captain Oleg got involved in one of Novodny's internal skirmishes," Babe went on. "And because of an arms deal he brokered, some battles were lost. They don't tolerate graft on Novodny. He had to flee and later, he had to find a protector for his family. A corporation head who covered up for him and for them."

Ard Matthew winced. "I suppose," he said diffidently, "this Oleg was grateful to his protector? And maybe he changed his name?"

Babe started to laugh, then, looking over at the girls who had apparently gone to sleep, he struggled to stifle the sounds. "Oleg," he said, "was so grateful that he got himself into even deeper shit, working for the corporation. And later, when things cooled off a little on Novodny, his benefactor still had a hold on him because he'd done so much dirty stuff for her. And," he added, "I'm sure the folks on Novodny wouldn't mind getting hold of him though, by now I suppose they would probably lay off his relatives. But not him. They're very traditional people in Novodny Colony. Oleg could be hanged or even impaled. Probably the latter."

The Lost Rythan, to whom this did not sound as shocking as it would to someone like Téna, digested Babe's story. The man was indeed a scoundrel and he must be guilty of murder among his other crimes. But Ard Matthew was not his judge and for this he was grateful. Something did occur to him, however. "This Oleg," he said. "Was he married?"

"He was." Babe let that hang for a moment. Then, "She died in a skiing accident. Oleg was away at the war."

"Children?"

"Divided up among the relatives. He never saw them again."

No, he decided, he could not judge this man. In fact, he doubted he would ever judge anyone again.

After a time, he curled up next to the fire and slept despite the cold and the fact that he had given up his shirt and jacket. He dreamed of his father's keep on Lost Rythar, but the great hall wasn't as he remembered it. It was much larger and crowded with people as though for some great festival—Christmas maybe, or someone's wedding. And all of the dead were there, living once more and looking on him with kindly faces, his kinsfolk and his former enemies, Rythans and offworlders, even the men he had killed. Both Gris Wolfgang and the child of Ynche Colony were there, smiling and whole.

He was comforted as he had not been in many years.

CHAPTER TEN

Ard Matthew woke covered with dew, shivering beside the dying fire. The rising sun was caught in a band of cloud and in the wavering light, Téna was a mound, covered—Babe must have done it—with the thermo sheet. Even from where he lay, he could see that it was grimy and torn. She sat up suddenly, looking around dazedly.

Across from her, the strange girl still sat where she had settled herself the night before, looking as though she had not moved. In the broadening light, the glaring oddity of her features was revealed even more plainly than it had been by firelight. This girl, it seemed to him now, came of a race so outlandish—so alien—that he found it hard to believe she was human.

Deep set brown eyes blinked at Téna. Above heavy brows, there was that same wrinkling of the forehead, that same intensity he had seen on the boy's face.

"How is he?" Téna asked suddenly and the girl looked down.

Stiffly, Ard Matthew got to his feet and came over to check for himself. Both women glanced up as he stood above them, but his attention was for the boy whose face was turned to one side showing those same bizarre features, rounded a little with childhood, that he saw on the girl. He could not call this child ugly by any means; he was merely strange. He saw Téna look down and touch her bandaged hand where he had bitten her.

Carefully, the boy's—sister?—reached over and pulled Ard Matthew's jacket away, revealing the small body, long torso and bandy legs. "Kensh," she said. "Kensh?" He stirred in his sleep but did not wake.

There was that same fine down he had felt on the boy's face when he held him the night before, just barely noticeable on his chest and arms. The rising sun was throwing everything more and more into relief, illuminating the roughhewn faces of the pair.

And suddenly, as the light broadened, Téna turned to Ard Matthew. "I know what they are!" she cried. "I've seen reconstructions—pictures, I mean, from earth. But that's impossible, of course. They've been gone for thousands of years! Tens of thousands."

He blinked in confusion. "What do you mean?" he demanded.

"They were called Neanderthals," she said. "They used to live on earth."

"Another race? I've never heard of them."

"You don't understand!" she said impatiently. "They've been extinct for over fifty thousand years. There is no way they could have survived to colonize this world."

He gave a shrug. "But if what you say is true, then they must have. Either that or these two are mutants."

Meanwhile, the girl had turned to Téna with her quizzical, slightly anxious expression. "Kensh?" she said. "Kensh have shpeert?"

Ard Matthew reached for the boy, turning him slightly to see how the synthoskin adhered to his wounds. "Kensh is fine," he said with what he hoped was a reassuring smile. "He'll wake up soon."

The girl seemed relieved, though her forehead remained wrinkled above the eyes. It must be a habitual expression, something that went with her deformity—but no, if what Téna believed was true, then she was not deformed. He must remember that she was of another race.

She peered up at him anxiously. "Kensh—shpeert? Leeve?"

"Oh," the Lost Rythan said, understanding her. "You mean spirit? Life?"

She nodded vigorously.

"Look." The boy had opened his eyes and was smiling up at her. "You see? He's going to be alright."

At that moment, the child turned on Ard Matthew another trusting smile just as the first rays of the sun broke free of the clouds. A stray beam caught his auburn hair, drawing out touches of ruddy gold. The Rythan thought it must be almost the same shade as his own.

Abruptly a shadow cut off the sun as Babe appeared, stifling a yawn. He stopped at the sight of the two guests. There was an intake of breath. "So—"

Ard Matthew looked up. "What?" he asked.

But Babe only shook his head. "These people didn't come on any starship," he said. "Unless it was a very long time ago."

Téna swallowed. "We were talking about that," she said. "I might be wrong. There could have been a colony once—and then something changed them."

"This place was only contacted three hundred years ago. Isn't that right, Third-Blade?"

Ard Matthew nodded.

Babe narrowed his eyes. "Anyway, I've never heard of a group changing this much. And certainly not in only three centuries." He looked down at the girl. "You got a name, *zaika*?" he asked.

She gave him an uncomprehending stare.

He thumped himself on the chest. "Me Boris," he said. "You can call me Babe." Then he pointed to the girl. "You?"

After a moment, she pointed to herself. "Lish," she said.

Babe nodded and turned back to the others. "So Lish and her people would have to have been cut off from the rest of the settled worlds for a long time," he said. "A lot longer than three centuries. And even so, she sure doesn't look like any human being I've ever seen."

Ard Matthew raised one eyebrow. "Have you travelled to every colony in the net?"

The other man shook his head. "No one has done that," he said impatiently. "But we have communication with them all. We see pictures."

"There are lost colonies."

"There are," Babe agreed. "And colonies settled before the beginning of star travel. Accidental colonies."

"Oh God," Téna breathed. "I forgot about those. Could there be one here? Hidden in the wilderness?"

Ard Matthew frowned. Of course there were colonies like that. Relics from ancient times when the starnet had touched down accidentally on earth and took whole tribes and villages of people to deposit them off among the stars. His own world was one such colony.

"So maybe something like that could have happened here," Babe said. "A really long time ago. And these people's ancestors never got around to building a civilization."

Téna looked at him. "Do you really think so?" She glanced once more from Kensh to Lish. "But it really does seem incredible," she said. "Fifty thousand years?"

Babe made a small grimace. "We can't know for sure," he agreed. "Maybe not that long. But still, look at how they're dressed. Even if there had been an official colony here—and there aren't any records of one—their technology could never have gone down so far in just three centuries."

"Let's wait and see what this Dr. Solomon has to say," Téna suggested. "He's supposed to be an archaeologist or something, isn't he?"

Ard Matthew nodded. "Yes," he agreed. "We had better ask him. And—" He turned to Lish. "Can he get up?" he asked. "Go to Solomon?"

In answer, the girl scrambled to her feet, followed by her brother, though he winced a little as he came to stand with her. She put an arm around him to support him.

"Guess we can take turns carrying him if we have to," Babe said. "Too bad we don't have any speed heal."

Too bad about a lot of things, Ard Matthew thought. He went over to the remains of the fire to see about breakfast. The cut filets had dried out a little overnight, but when he set them over the coals, they cooked well enough. At least no one complained. After they ate, Babe rationed them water, keeping part of one bag for emergencies.

With a guide, there was no need to get another fix on Solomon's location. They followed the girl down off their eminence, where she made a beeline through the trees until she reached the trail. Ard Matthew walked behind her, carrying the boy and Téna followed behind him. Babe brought up the rear, carrying the gun.

At first, they could not see very far ahead of them. This was partly because the trees were becoming larger and closer together as they continued to descend, but also, a heavy mist lingered in the lowlands, only slowly burning off as the morning advanced. At one point, Lish turned aside from the trail and Ard Matthew, scenting water, set the boy down and followed her. "Bring the water bags," he called.

Soon they were all scrambling down a mossy slope to what proved to be a spring. A small pool lay amid rushes and some thick-leaved plants. When the bags had been filled, they all drank from the pool and laved their faces with the icy water. But all the while, the Lost Rythan found himself eyeing the brush as they drank. He noted that Lish was doing likewise.

They did not stay there long, before returning to the trail. This time, Babe took the boy on his shoulders while Ard Matthew carried the gun. Ahead of him, Téna turned from time to time to look back as she walked ahead beside the Neanderthal girl.

The trail began to curve as the land fell away. They were moving down a slightly steeper slope and must move with the contour of the hill. The trees were different here, with large, smooth boles rising like columns to a mat of greenery that shut out the sky. In this twilight region nothing grew save trees and moss. It was startling to see the landscape change so swiftly from something at least half familiar to this dim and alien wood.

Their guide seemed perfectly at home, however, as she led the way deeper into the gloom. This certainly wasn't a jungle—nothing like the forest of Ynche, Ard Matthew decided with relief. To his eye, the trees still seemed to be evergreens, but now their trunks were blotched with streamers of moss. Increasingly, the party must clamber over rotting logs. On one of these occasions, Téna gave a little scream as her hand touched a great, yellow slug.

Babe looked at her, the boy sliding on his shoulders. "Alright?" he asked.

She gave him an angry nod. With gritted teeth, she swung one leg over the top of the log and slid down on the other side.

Behind her, Ard Matthew vaulted the obstruction, eyeing the slug. "We do not have such creatures on my world," he said. "Or at least, not this large. Is it dangerous?"

This earned him a look of disgust from Téna while Babe chuckled and shook his head. "You have any idea where we are, Third-Blade?" he asked.

"Not exactly." Ard Matthew toed an outcropping of some dark stone, partly hidden by tree roots. "But I think we're getting close to the area of the ruins." Their voices sounded flat in the still dampness of the air.

The truth was he was uneasy and it had nothing to do with his sixth sense. He had begun to feel uncomfortable even before they stopped to fill their water bags. Sure he had known there was water—he was woodsman enough for that. To that extent this was a normal forest. But—

He glanced around at the massive boles of the trees, noting the moss and the colorful fungi at their bases. He had seen similar fungi on other worlds. The vagaries of the net meant that one always found at least some familiar life forms, though the slug had taken him by surprise.

No, it wasn't the moss or the dampness, but rather the ambience of the place itself that unnerved him—the gloom and his feeling of being towered over by the trees. They were so tall, so absolutely huge, that he felt once more like the lost child he had once been. God, however, wasn't going to suddenly cure his acrophobia, if that was what it was.

He was being humbled and he must respond with all the courage he could muster.

Perhaps this was why, when he did begin to feel the familiar prickling on the back of his neck, he dismissed it as nerves. Directly in front of him, he saw Téna moving cautiously among the pillars of the trees, scrambling over fallen logs nearly as high as her head. Once or twice she looked back at him as she did so, and once he reached down to boost her over a particularly big one. Beyond, Babe and Lish were shadowy figures slipping in and out of sight. Whenever he caught sight of Kensh looking back at him from his perch on Babe's shoulders, he tried to give the child an encouraging smile.

Presently, Lish guided them off the trail, onto an indefinite track. "Zhonsomen," she said when Babe caught up with her. She pointed ahead where the forest became a darkened wall.

And suddenly, Ard Matthew knew they were being watched. Something was stalking the party and the fact that the two natives seemed not to care could only mean that they already knew and were not threatened by whatever it was.

The Lost Rythan, however, was as tense as a bowstring. He did not turn his head, lest he give away to the watchers that he knew they were there, but his eyes were never still. Each blot of darkness—and there were many—might hold something or someone. Each fallen log might hide he knew not what. But for all his staring, he could see no threat.

It was only when they reached the wall of holly and yew that made up the forest verge that he would have halted the others. But it was too late. With a low exclamation, Téna stumbled back and he held out one hand to stay her as she fell against him. Still holding her in place, he looked over her head in bewilderment at what lay in the clearing on the other side of the boundary.

Lish had forced her way through a short tunnel in the greenery from which she led the others out into bright sunshine. A few bark shelters were scattered about but at first they seemed deserted. Was

Solomon here? The Lost Rythan studied the clearing intently. But when a head did finally emerge from one of the doorways, he saw only another chinless, slope-browed face, bearded and smiling at them to show snaggle teeth.

He was not surprised to see men appearing from out of the forest while women and old people emerged from the huts. The warriors were skin-clad and bearded, their expressions watchful as they balanced themselves on sturdy legs. Some held slings—and he already knew what those slings could do—while others carried spears and bows.

Lish spoke to them, carrying on a conversation in their high-pitched language which made them all, even the men, sound like a convocation of birds. A few weapons were lowered, though not all. Noting this, Ard Matthew knew better than to make any sudden moves. He continued to rest one hand on Téna's shoulder however, feeling the tremors that went through her.

Meanwhile, Babe had knelt and was handing over his burden to a squat woman with a weathered face and tied back hair. She eyed the offworlder suspiciously as she examined the boy, chittering all the while to a man who had come to stand beside her. Lish, after trying to get in a word or two, was obliged to stand aside while this was going on. Ard Matthew could not tell by her expression whether things were going well or ill, for she continued solemn as always, with her wrinkled brow and an expression of deep patience.

"When I give the word," he murmured to Téna, "drop to the ground and hold still." He still held the gun in his other hand, readying himself for attack and hoping he would not have to use it. If only he could read the expressions in those strange faces. Were they planning violence or were they only puzzled? Who could say? He sought in vain for a reference point.

Then a flash of something white caught his attention and he shifted his gaze to another hut set somewhat to the left of the others, a cobbled together affair half falling down. It looked as though it had been constructed inexpertly by someone in a hurry. A strange figure was emerging from the opening—something like a half draped skeleton, taller than the natives.

"Zhonsomen," Lish said.

Most of the men turned, to watch in silence as the apparition came slowly to its feet. Ard Matthew got a good look at a wild face, bearded like the others, though plainly not of their race. Tangled hair surrounded a pair of eyes that seemed to bulge in contrast with the deep set eyes of the Neanderthals, with a nose that looked almost rudderlike in comparison with theirs. The strange figure stared at the newcomers silently for a moment and then began to totter toward them.

"Solomon," Babe said, echoing Lish. "Right?"

"You are—real? Not another ghost?" As Solomon approached, Ard Matthew saw his face pucker a little. His eyes were as wild as his hair.

"We're real," Babe told him. "Now how do we convince them?" He jerked his chin in the direction of the watching tribe.

Solomon looked around at the Neanderthals as though he had never seen them before.

At this, Lish stepped forward and the madman recognized her with a look of relief. She spoke to him softly in the high key of her people.

After a moment, he turned back to Babe. "You—we talked on the radio," he said slowly. "I couldn't be sure you were not another dream—"

Babe shook his head. "You talked to our pilot," he said, jerking a thumb at the Lost Rythan. "Third-Blade."

At this, Ard Matthew released Téna and stepped out into the clearing. He saw the natives stiffen and felt their watchful gaze on him. He was acutely aware of the bows, loosely held but aimed more or less in his direction. Carefully, he bent over and laid the gun on the ground, stepping back from it while he eyed the bearded faces around him. At this, one of them stepped forward and addressed him in their bird-like speech.

He had never heard a language like this before and he looked helplessly from Solomon to Lish, shaking his head a little to show that he did not understand.

"He says you don't look like the ghost people," the archaeologist said. "Though you carry a weapon like theirs." He gave a shrug. "You understand I haven't seen these ghosts, quite. But I think they might be real—" His voice trailed off. "They shot two of the people," he said suddenly. "These—" He spread his hands to indicate the tribe. "These are the people," he added. "The real people, I mean."

"Neanderthals," Babe said. "Isn't that right?"

Solomon nodded. "If they are really here, of course. It would be as easy to dream Neanderthals as anything else. But I suppose you see them too?"

"We see them," Ard Matthew told him. "But you say someone shot two of them?"

"That's right. I saw the bodies."

"Where did it happen?" Babe asked. "Here?"

"Closer to the ruins. The place is full of ghosts, but ghosts don't carry guns."

The Lost Rythan thought this over, wondering how far he could trust what Solomon said. Yet there was certainly no one else he could question. "Did anyone say what these ghosts looked like?" he asked.

This earned him a grim chuckle. "What does a ghost look like—what is your name anyway?"

The other told him.

"Oh yes. I had forgotten. Then Ard Matthew Third-Blade, have you ever seen a ghost?"

Ard Matthew had to admit he had not. "But you are right that ghosts don't shoot people," he added. "At least I've never heard that they do." He did, in fact, believe in ghosts, within certain parameters anyway, despite his years out among the stars. He was, after all, a Lost Rythan.

Solomon squinted one eye, peering up into his face. "The Kola—that's what these people are called—say they are ghosts. They call us ghosts as well. We are tall and thin and we wear the smooth skins of ghost animals. You especially look like something from the spirit world because you are so tall." He moved closer and Ard Matthew resisted an impulse to draw back from his touch. The archaeologist, in his opinion, really did resemble a ghost—or at least a walking corpse. He repressed a shudder.

"I get it," Babe said suddenly. "You're saying there are more people out there. Offworlders, I mean. Explorers?"

"Not in my party," Solomon said, turning in his direction. "My people are real ghosts, you know, because they are all dead." He chuckled. "I seem to be alive," he added. "But of course I can't be sure."

"We saw the crash site," Babe told him.

Ard Matthew frowned. "So who are these others?" he asked. "And why are they killing people?"

Solomon glanced over at the man who seemed to be Kensh's father. "The people say," he said slowly, "that the killers are guarding the ruins. They say it is their home—the ghost home."

"But you were going to the ruins," Babe reminded him. "Your party. You must have had no idea anyone else was there."

The archaeologist seemed genuinely bewildered by the question. "No one goes there," Solomon said at last. "The gods of the wendigo won't allow it. That's why we crashed. We didn't know, of course, and no one warned us before we left the port."

Téna made a small sound at the word, "wendigo" and the Lost Rythan felt a little chill run up his spine when the things were named. Only Babe seemed unaffected.

"So why were you going there?" Ard Matthew asked finally. "To the ruins, I mean."

"Oh—" Solomon spread his hands and gave them a baffled look. "That was before," he said. "When we were scientists. Then we crashed, you know and I came to live with the Kola and everyone else was dead."

"He's not going to tell us anything useful," Babe muttered. "He's too far gone. But I think I can guess. Either someone's hiding something in there—or else they've found something and want to protect it. And these people came along and got in the way." He indicated the Neanderthals. "No one would have had the least idea they lived here."

Téna glared at Babe. "But you can guess," she said and her words broke off like bits of ice. "Oh yes, you can guess what's in there, can't you? Who is in there, rather."

Babe met her gaze, his own weathered features tightening a little. "Téna, I really didn't know," he faltered. "Maybe I should have. But who would look here—after the crash? Who would think—"

Ard Matthew stared from one to the other putting two and two together. "So your employer really is here on Windy-Go?" At the thought of meeting the woman who had tried to kill her own cousin—who had in fact, killed the secretary—he felt his own anger kindle. And yet something held that anger in check now that he knew what it was like to live without grace. He did not dare to judge even this.

"So she's here," Babe said in a tone that made it clear that he did not share the Lost Rythan's scruples. "She must be." He grinned suddenly, but it was not a nice grin.

Téna looked up in excitement. "But that must mean that—that the phessite is—" She stopped, aghast at what she had revealed.

Solomon only laughed while Ard Matthew shrugged. Of course, he thought. This explained everything. And it also meant that once she knew she had failed to kill the party, Kessler would not rest until she had finished the job. Now, more than ever, their lives depended on secrecy.

As he digested this somber knowledge, Ard Matthew watched the others. Téna looked troubled, Babe angry. There was a glint in his eye that promised vengeance—if he could manage it. But if he could not, then a failed attempt would only put the rest of them in worse danger.

"But these people," Téna said suddenly, indicating the collection of huts and their inhabitants. "These are colonists, aren't they? The original colonists of this world."

"Technically," Babe agreed.

"Legally," the Lost Rythan added, beginning to see where she was going with this.

"They are the first citizens of Windy-Go," Téna said. "I wonder if my cousin knew about them."

"Would it matter?" Babe asked her. "I mean, she probably didn't. But you can see they're no match for modern weapons and that's the only thing she'll care about."

Something else had just occurred to Ard Matthew. "Do you think she was responsible for the crash of the expedition flyer?" he asked.

"We could ask Solomon," Babe suggested.

"He isn't likely to know," Ard Matthew said, going over his former conversations with the man.

But Babe had already turned to the archaeologist. "How well can you talk to these people?" he asked, indicating the Neanderthals.

Solomon hesitated. "They took me in," he said. "They are my friends."

"Right. But how well do you know their language? They must have told you about the killings in the ruins, right? So you can communicate with them."

There was no answer to this, though Lish's father, who seemed to be the leader of the band, was staring hard at the newcomers. He spoke to Solomon, who did indeed answer him in his own language.

"What did he say?" Babe demanded.

The Rythan tensed. If Solomon had told them these were evil ghosts, they would have no way to convince anyone otherwise. He looked at Lish. "Tsayna," she said and turned to her father, drawing Téna with her.

The bearded man studied Téna's face for a moment and then nodded. "Kola," he said at last.

Téna turned questioningly to Solomon.

"He just called you a human being," he said. "That's what they call themselves, so I guess you're not ghosts after all."

Téna gave the chief a shy smile and was just about to rejoin Lish and her brother, when they all heard a strange humming growing louder as they listened. Ard Matthew looked around; it was no natural sound. And then, recognizing it for what it was, he sprang into action. Luckily, so did Babe.

"Get into the woods!" he shouted, while Ard Matthew grabbed Téna and shoved her toward the fringe.

"Tell them, Solomon!" the Rythan cried. "It's an aircraft!"

Solomon called out something, but for some he was too late. Not all of the people made it out of the clearing before something long and flat shot into sight. Looking over his shoulder, Ard Matthew saw the beam descend even as Téna tumbled into the holly with Lish and her brother practically on top of her.

In the clearing, all was confusion, huts burning and several people down. At once, he darted out, hoisted a man onto his shoulder and came loping back to the trees just as the humming sounded again. Once more the beam swept the area and then again until the clearing was no more than a scorched and blackened ruin. A cloud of reeking smoke blew into the woods not unmixed with the smell of roasting flesh.

"Maat! Maat!" someone called and he realized it was Kensh. Téna groped for him and clasped him to her. There was no sign of Lish, though many of the people had already slipped back into the deeper forest.

A moment later, Babe took the boy from her. "Come on," he said, hoisting Kensh onto his shoulders. "You're not hurt are you?"

Téna shook her head. "Where is Lish?" she asked.

"Over here," Ard Matthew said. He had put down his own burden, who proved to be a badly burned tribesman. As Lish came running up, he looked the man over, but he didn't think there was anything he could do.

"Not shay," Lish said, looking around fearfully. "You take."

Wordlessly, Ard Matthew gathered up the injured man again and followed her along a trail he had not seen before. Ahead of them, Babe and Téna were just disappearing. Then he caught sight of Solomon. At least they hadn't lost their interpreter.

"This is the death walk!" the archaeologist intoned when he saw Ard Matthew looking at him. "We are going to our grave, Faring Guard!"

"Shut up," Babe called back to him. "We've got enough problems already."

But Solomon only ran away among the trees.

After a time, Ard Matthew, who was having some trouble following the others as he tried not to jar the man he carried, caught sight of the chief. His wife and daughter were helping him along. And presently when two others took charge of the man he was carrying, the Lost Rythan hurried ahead to look for Babe and Téna.

They had entered a ravine, the great trees hemming them in, the sides walled with a tangle of roots. In the increasing gloom, it seemed to the Rythan as though they were descending, not into death, but into the past. As he caught glimpses of the Neanderthal faces, the squat and sturdy forms of the Kola, he seemed to be revisiting the Motherworld he had never seen. Here surely, grew the trees of the dawn time, in this green murk from which the first men arose. And here, he heartily hoped, there would be no more alien creatures.

When the walls closed in and became a tunnel—mossy at first and then bare—he was not at all surprised. Some of the Kola kindled flaming sticks and, belatedly, Ard Matthew switched on the torch he still carried at his belt. Ahead of him, Babe glanced back from time to time, the light illuminating his broad, Slavic face. From behind, they could hear the faint sounds of bare feet on the rock.

"What is this place?" Téna asked suddenly. "Do you have any idea?"

It was Ard Matthew who answered. He had fallen behind Lish and her family and now he let Babe get further ahead of him so that he could walk with Téna. "I think," he told her, "this is a back door into the ruins. I don't see what else it could be." As the tallest one there, he kept having to duck a little as they continued their descent beneath the forest floor. Above him, the ceiling was of earth and stone, cracked here and there by the roots of trees above.

"Dr. Solomon called this a death walk," Téna persisted. "Do you have any idea what he meant by that, Mr. Third-Blade?"

The Rythan shook his head. "I'm not sure he meant anything especially. I mean, he's not thinking too clearly at the moment." That, he thought grimly, was an understatement, but he did not say so out loud.

Téna had nothing to say to this and they lapsed into silence while the tunnel slowly leveled and then began to ascend once more. Ard Matthew tried to calculate how long they had been walking, but in the unchanging gloom, he found it hard to concentrate. He was worried about the others, though. The tribal chief was not the only one suffering from burns though he had not heard any complaint.

They all proceeded in silence as though making a sacred journey and, perhaps they were. The thought of what this might mean sent a little chill up his spine. He could not be sure he was not on sacred ground and though he was a Christian, as a Lost Rythan he was not free of at least some fear that he was trespassing where he should not. Not that he would allow his misgivings on this score to slow him down.

"How is—the headman?" Téna asked, breaking the silence. "I mean Lish's father. I guess that's what he is? Their chief?"

"He's able to walk," Ard Matthew told her. "They're helping him along. These people are very tough."

"And these caves? Do you think they must come here often?"

"Judging by the torches and striking stones, I'd say so." He had seen several caches of these and the people were now using brands to light their way.

"I wonder if this is where they come to escape from the wendigos," she said.

Before he could answer, they emerged into a larger space, moving single file across a cavern. The light caught what at first appeared to be scattered rocks on either side of their path. Ard Matthew glanced curiously at these until he suddenly realized what they were. The place was a giant ossuary!

"So that's what Solomon meant," he murmured. "By the path of the dead." And then, because it seemed the right thing to do, he paused and crossed himself. Beside him, he saw Téna do the same.

As far as he could see, hills of bones lay on either side, stretching into the shadows beyond the light. How long it must have taken to accumulate so many skeletons! He said this to Téna.

"Yes," she said slowly. "But if their ancestors really came here fifty thousand years ago, then—"

He nodded, trying to take this in. "But surely," he said, "they haven't been coming here to this place for fifty thousand years." It seemed impossible, when he thought of it, that they had advanced no further, that they had built nothing in all that time. He said as much to Téna.

"I don't think Neanderthals were very innovative," she told him. "I read about a place back on earth where they had used the same hearth for ten thousand years."

Ten thousand years. He tasted the words and tried to make them real. And this group would have lived on Windy-Go at least five times that long. Could it even be possible?

He became aware of Téna watching him and remembered that she too had made the Sign of the Cross at the sight of the heaped up dead. He was surprised, even pleased to have seen that—to know that she, too, was a Christian. Perhaps they had surprised each other. Who could say? They began walking again.

After what seemed like another hour, they emerged from the cavern and found themselves in a new tunnel. Suddenly there was daylight ahead. To Ard Matthew's surprise, the sun had set and Windy-Go's star-crammed sky hung above them. He hadn't thought they had walked so long, but apparently they had. He emerged into a narrow valley among hills that looked artificial—almost as though they stood in an ill paved and slightly overgrown amphitheater. He became aware of Solomon standing behind them.

Some of the torches had been extinguished and Ard Matthew put out his light. Solomon by starlight looked a little less disheveled, though his eyes were no more than dark sockets in the pale smudge of his face. Below, his beard trailed into shadow. He seemed to be grinning at the pair as his teeth gleamed faintly among the whiskers. "Ghosts," he said. "All of us together."

"Yes," Téna agreed and Ard Matthew looked at her sharply. But she seemed to be alright.

The people had halted, some of them collapsing onto the rocky ground, others kneeling beside the fallen.

"Have you any idea where we are?" Téna asked the archaeologist.

"Oh, it's the ruins. We're in the ruins. Must be. They shot us down." He paused, combing his beard with one skinny hand. "Something hidden here—don't you think?"

Téna nodded. "Yes," she said, looking around at the walls that hemmed them in.

"Would they—these people's enemies—have a base further in?" Ard Matthew asked.

"They sent—Makena sent people to spy on them," Solomon said. "Only one got back."

"And the others were shot?"

"Oh he got shot, too. Didn't live long. He's in the ghost cave now."

The Lost Rythan was glad he had not looked too closely at the landscape of bones. Any recent additions would have accounted for the musty smell of the place and its undertone of rottenness.

"What did he say—before he died?" Ard Matthew asked, trying to put the other thought from his mind.

Solomon looked up at him, starlight spilling over his features. "He said they were ghosts and that they had killed his companions. What else would he say?"

There was a brief silence.

"Well they were! Evil ghosts."

The Rythan gave him a thoughtful look. "I'm sure these people would have seen them that way," he agreed. "Enemies."

"Don't you?"

Another pause. Then, "No," he said sturdily. "I don't think they are ghosts. I believe they can be killed."

"What are you going to do, Mr. Third-Blade?" Téna asked nervously.

He was already looking around. "Come with me to see the chief," he said to Solomon and when the other man hesitated, he laid one hand on his shoulder. "Now. I need you to interpret."

To his relief, the madman obeyed. Whether he would actually help the two communicate remained to be seen.

CHAPTER ELEVEN

Though he wanted to inspire confidence in the others, Ard Matthew was really at an impasse. Somehow he had taken on the responsibility not only for his original party but also for John Solomon. And perhaps the Kola as well. Who could say? But he needed more information—if he could get it—and he was painfully conscious of the language barrier. And then there was that other, even greater obstacle, that his interpreter was completely insane and had to be watched every moment lest he wander off.

After some searching, he finally found Makena. The chief was allowing his burns to be treated. Or rather, his wife was licking his arm where the flesh had been blistered and cracked. Ard Matthew winced and looked away from this operation though he had heard of such things among his own people in the olden days when they had no antibiotics. The chief's face, where it could be seen above the beard, was drawn with pain, though he spoke calmly to Solomon, looking up at the others over his wife's bent head.

"He is grateful for the care you have shown his son," Solomon translated. "He says the boy told him he tracked your party because he was curious and he wished you well."

Ard Matthew nodded to show Makena he understood this. "Tell him we are grateful for his good will. Tell him that these others are our enemies, too. That we must learn more about them in order to defeat them."

Solomon spoke to the chief in the incongruous, cheeping language of the people and waited as he replied.

"He thanks you that you carried his brother off the field. Cama has died, but his ghost is safely in the caves."

At this, the Lost Rythan gave a start and looked back at their trail. He could just make out the tunnel-mouth from which they had emerged. So Cama's corpse must have joined those others in the ossuary. And probably he was not the only one to have died since the firebombing of the village, though not all the bodies would have been recovered.

"He knows you will want to spy on the evil ghosts. He says that you must not take the path his spies have taken—the men who were shot. You shall go by a darker way. If you have the courage—"

Ard Matthew gave Solomon a sharp glance, wondering if this last bit about courage was an addendum and whether there had been other changes during translation. Perhaps Solomon had said more to the chief than the Rythan had intended. But of course it was true that he must go on ahead to determine who haunted the ruins, what equipment they had and what they intended to do with it.

"You may tell Makena that I go willingly," he said at last. "And that I am not afraid." He tried to sound more optimistic than he felt as he listened to Solomon translating his words. He could only hope the other man was giving Makena an accurate version of what he said.

The chief spoke again, more slowly this time as he paused to rest between his words. The others waited for him to finish, though he seemed to be explaining something at great length.

"Give him your hand," Solomon said when he had done. "He wants to make you one of the people before he sends you in. That way your ghost can join the others in the cavern if you should get killed."

Ard Matthew hesitated, looking into the chief's eyes. But what he saw there reassured him. This man had the spirit of a hunter, of a warrior. He stretched out one hand.

Makena's wife had finished with his burns and now she drew out a small object which she held ready as her husband turned over the Lost Rythan's hand, gripping it in his own. Ard Matthew could guess what was coming for his own people had similar customs. They would mingle their blood, of course, man and Neanderthal, and now he prayed for God's blessing on their alliance. He held himself firm as he felt the sharpened flint against his flesh, never taking his eyes from the chief's face.

But Solomon was chuckling. "You'll get germs from that, Faring Guard," he said. "Nasty, dirty business."

Ard Matthew, who had been inoculated against just about everything the settled worlds could throw at him, only grunted as the chief's wife made a ragged cut on the back of his wrist and on that of her husband. Immediately Makena pressed the torn flesh against his own while uttering what may have been a ritual phrase. Hopefully, he wasn't invoking some heathen god, the Rythan thought and then remembered that he had, after all, invoked his own. For a moment, he felt a true kinship with other man. Hopefully, they would both live to be good friends hereafter.

Once the ceremony was over, the chief became all business. He turned to Solomon and spoke slowly, during which he fixed his serious gaze—which seemed to be habitual with these people—on the archaeologist as though he, too, knew that the man was unreliable and must be treated with care. When Makena had finished speaking, Solomon turned to Ard Matthew.

"They've got tunnels all through the ruins," he said. "They haven't used them much in recent years, but their ancestors did."

Ard Matthew glanced back at the chief. "They didn't build this place, did they?" he asked Solomon. "Or I mean their ancestors." He didn't really think this likely.

Solomon shook his head. "Neanderthals don't build things," he said. "Unless they've changed a lot since they came here from Earth. And I don't think they have or we would have found signs of them before this."

The Lost Rythan frowned. "People change over the millennia," he said. "We changed, after all. My own people, I mean. We do not resemble our ancestors. And it wasn't all that long for us—a few thousand years they say. Not more than that. These people might—just might—have been builders in the past."

The archaeologist laughed. "A few thousand years, Faring Guard? Oh you've changed alright—but not into a Neanderthal. Just look at you—you're something else entirely. Nothing like you ever grew on the Motherworld."

A shrug. "I might not be Terran standard, maybe, but I'm as human as you are." He did not add that while others were usually of shorter stature, who was to say they were not the mutants? Solomon, for instance. Whatever colony he came from—

He drew himself up. "What does Makena want me to do?" he asked, pressing one hand over the wound on his wrist.

"Take the way of the old ones. The hell gate. Sheol, I mean. Ancient powers and all that." He chuckled. "You'll be like one of those heroes of old, travelling to the underworld. Odysseus, Enkidu."

Ard Matthew, who had never heard of either of these people, looked to Makena for some confirmation of Solomon's words. If only he could talk to the man. He could see how much the chief must be suffering from his burns—no language was needed for that—and he wished he could help him, but beyond that suffering, the man's face communicated nothing. Maybe if he could find his way in among the invaders, he thought, he would help himself to some of their medical supplies and bring them back. That was one thing he could do at least.

But first he had to get in there without being seen.

The chief must have understood at least some of the Lost Rythan's frustration, for he beckoned to his daughter, who came at once to stand before the two men. He spoke to her for a moment before she turned to Ard Matthew.

"Come, Shpaesman," she trilled and beckoned him away from the others, guiding him toward another opening in the surrounding rock face. Without a word, he followed her.

When they had crossed the starlit space, they came into a smallish cavern, pitch dark and smelling of something like incense. Groping about, he was finally obliged to switch on the torch. He gasped as the walls sprang to life with a multitude of paintings and designs, some laid on top of others, some so faded that he could not make out what they had once been meant to represent. But everything here—animals and people alike—seemed possessed of an almost iconic quality, timeless and unchanging, from the most faded to the newest and brightest. Or if there were any changes in the style of the work, he decided, these had been so minor that he could not make them out.

He felt a tug on his arm. Lish was directing his attention to an inner chamber and he followed her to the low archway. Once inside, he saw that the smooth walls bore no animal or human figures at all, but only patterns of curving lines done in several tones of pigment—red and yellow, mostly, with here and there some blue. After a moment, he realized he was looking at a map. Lish laid one finger on a reddish area near one edge. After this, she pointed to herself and to him, speaking a word in her own language.

"We are here," he guessed. "Is that it?" He smiled at her as he also pointed at the spot and at himself.

Though she gave him no answering smile—it seemed these people were not given to the same facial expressions as their human kin—she took his arm and turned him back to the map. Now he watched as she traced a route also marked in red. Once she paused to point downward, making gestures at the stone beneath their feet. Perhaps the way lead downward as their original tunnel had done? But then it had climbed once more.

He closed his eyes for a moment, visualizing their former route, remembering the incredible landscape of bones they had traversed. Though he had lived among the colony worlds for nearly half his life, it was not easy to shake off the sensibilities of his people. He might not fear the spirits of the dead, but he wasn't eager for more of their company. However there was no way to ask Lish if he would find another ossuary in this tunnel.

"What is at the other end?" he tried to ask her, pointing to the place where the red line tapered off. Then he looked up and saw that Solomon had come into the cave after them. "Solomon?" he asked. "Can you translate for me?"

Luckily, he was willing to comply, trilling the language of the Kola while Lish watched him impassively with her deep, brown gaze. After a moment, she replied.

When she had finished, Solomon turned to Ard Matthew. "She says the top zone is at the end of the way. That would be where the tourists go, I think." He reached over and traced a line along the upper part of the design. "That is the land of the living," he said. "Scientists and treasure seekers go there. Below—no one told us there was a below." He smiled beatifically. "Below there are monsters. It is always that way."

Ard Matthew ignored this last comment. "Ask her how far it is to this outlet? And is it well hidden? But I suppose it is if no one knows about it."

Unfortunately, the archaeologist had lost interest in the conversation. "Long ago," he murmured. "Eons and eons and things like that. The dead and dusty are mounded up beneath the earth. Eons and eons—"

"I will need to make a map of my own," the Rythan persisted. "Ask her if there are any signs I should watch for. Any turnings or—or things like that."

Solomon nodded wisely. "Spoken like a true hero, Faring Guard," he said. "A regular Theseus. Shall I ask her for a ball of string?"

But in the end, he did ask the girl something because she turned and pointed to a small circle traced in red ochre. Below it a he saw a triangle in blue. She touched the red one and nodded. Then, indicating, but not touching the blue, she shook her head and gave a little shiver of rejection. She said a few words in her own language, almost spitting them out.

"Ah. Evil spirits down there," Solomon said. "And you by yourself underneath all that rock. Just you and the evil spirits and the dark."

The Lost Rythan did not change expression, but the truth was that he felt his courage draining away. No one needed to tell him that this venture would test him to the utmost—and that he might truly fail.

He fished out the pocket imager and shook it into life. The last time he had used it was to take a picture of Shami as she lay dying. Now that picture was the first thing he saw on the screen. Quickly he thumbed the back and began to move the imager over the rock drawings, carefully recording everything he thought he would need.

He was a relief when Solomon finally wandered back outside. Lish, too, had gone, perhaps returning to her parents, leaving him alone in the little cavern. It was only when he had finished recording and checked the result against the painting, that he saw Babe standing in the cave entrance watching him. He wondered how long the other man had been there while he worked over his map.

"You're not going alone, Third-Blade."

Ard Matthew put the imager back in his pocket. "I don't think you have the skills for this, Babe," he said. "We can't risk letting the Kessler people see us. You know that."

The other gave him a steady look. "That would have been true—once. About my skill, I mean, though not as true as you seem to think. But now we have hunted together, you and I, fought the damned wendigo together. You can't say I'll be a liability to you this time because you know I won't."

Ard Matthew fingered the imager before removing his hand from his pocket, thinking. Babe was at least partially right. He was no longer the company thug he had seemed back at the port. He had changed indeed—they all had.

"You do hear me, Third-Blade?" He came further into the cave. "I'm coming along."

"I hear you." He couldn't quite hide the relief he felt, though common sense told him that two people were far more likely to be discovered than one. He had wanted to make a quick trip in and out just to see what the corporation was up to. If there really was phessite in the ruins.

But he dared not look ahead. One thing at a time.

"Alright, Babe," he said. "Are you ready to go now?"

"Ready as you are."

There really seemed no sense in waiting and the Rythan went out at once to find Téna who was, predictably, furious when he told her of his plan. It was Babe who finally persuaded her that her place was with the Neanderthals and for this, Ard Matthew was grateful.

"You've got to try and learn their language," he told her in a sudden inspiration. "Get Lish to help you. You know we can't count on this Solomon guy and we'll really need to communicate with them when we get back."

"Do you truly believe my cousin is here on Windy-Go?" Téna asked.

Ard Matthew didn't say anything, but Babe nodded. "We're going to have to assume she is," he said. "If there's phessite here, then it makes sense this is where she would come. Where else could she be?"

Neither Téna nor Ard Matthew had an answer to this. Or rather, they would have to find one. After a final visit to Makena, during which Solomon's contribution consisted mostly of what Ard Matthew hoped was nonsense, they returned to the cave of the pictures. Makena had not offered to adopt Babe into his tribe—perhaps he did not realize that the other man was going to accompany Ard Matthew into the "underworld".

With one last look at the outside world, the Rythan led the way into the tunnel. At first the going was easy, the stone clean and glittering with minerals in the light. The air continued good, though damp, and for about an hour they made good progress. Then they met their first check—directly ahead of them, the tunnel branched into two.

The Lost Rythan shone his light on the arched opening of each choice, noting that the walls were indeed chiseled, that these were not natural caves. Was it possible that the Neanderthals had after all, done so much at some time in the far past, to accommodate themselves to the ruins? Or was this the work of someone else—the mysterious and original builders?

After a short search, he finally located the red circle high on one side of the left hand passage. It was faded and cracked across, but there was no blue mark on either opening.

"I guess that's a good sign," Babe said when the other man had explained what the colors meant and showed him the crude map he had photographed. "Too bad they didn't give us more detail, though."

Ard Matthew checked the imager again. Both routes were there, he noted, but on the map, the alternate was marked in blue. He showed this to Babe.

"So maybe the sign's worn off," the other man said. "Who knows what they used to make it and how long it's been."

Ard Matthew nodded. "Well we can see the red and that's enough. Let's go."

They set off once more and soon they began to descend. But, the Rythan could not help thinking, if Babe was right about the pigment wearing off, then even the red marks might not always show up. They might have to rely entirely on the imager, their lives depending on that small glowing screen. If anything happened to it—

He looked down at the torch in his hand. This at least was powered for a century or more, but the imager needed light from time to time to charge itself. He fought down a momentary panic as he thought of how dependent they were on these bits of technology. He wished he had thought to bring some boughs for there didn't seem to be any of the native torches stored here. But of course, it was probable that no one had come this way in many years. Perhaps not for centuries. This was, if he understood Makena aright, a place of fear and because of that, any trips into these tunnels by the Kola would not have been taken lightly.

After what seemed another hour, their descent became even steeper. An acrid odor rose from the emptiness below, a reminder that they were about to enter the underworld of Neolithic history. And when the first wall paintings emerged, he was not surprised to see a frieze done in exactly the same style as those he had seen above. Only the subjects were different. He moved closer and shone the light directly on the stone.

The first thing he made out was what might have been a wendigo and around it, crouched as though in submission—or worship?—a crowd of skeleton men. He heard an intake of breath behind him and turned so quickly he nearly dropped the torch.

"I'm okay, Third-Blade," Babe said. But in the light, he didn't look much better than the Lost Rythan felt. "It just surprised me is all. Took me off guard."

Ard Matthew nodded, wondering what the pictures meant. Had the ancestors of Makena's people once tried to work magic here? To placate or control their enemies? Was this part of the reason they dreaded this place now? And yet they knew it—knew it led into the upper ruins. They just didn't apparently choose to go this way.

He shrugged. One more mystery. He and Babe went on until the tunnel branched once more. Luckily the red circle was plain on one side and the blue triangle on the other and this agreed with the imager They were still descending.

Their continual passage down the slanted stone was tiring and the walls and roof of the tunnel were oppressive. When would they begin to rise again? After a time, Ard Matthew found himself remembering some words the Star Brothers had taught him long ago when he was a child.

For though I should walk in the midst of the shadow of death, I will fear no evils, for thou art with me. Thy rod and thy staff, they have comforted me.

They were certainly in that shadow now, he thought grimly, and no sign that they were likely to emerge from it. But that wasn't the point, was it? He smiled wryly to himself. Not the where or even the destination but the fact that he was here now. What mattered was that his courage was for this moment, parceled out bit by bit.

Suddenly Babe's voice jarred him out of his reverie. "I wonder how far we are below the surface," the other man said when the tunnel showed no sign of levelling off.

There was an odor here, not wholly unpleasant, though Ard Matthew could not help thinking of the ossuary and similar possibilities. It put him in mind of some mold or fungus. Mushrooms, perhaps. His father had grown them in a cave near the family keep. But would they grow so deep underground as this?

Then, as he had feared must happen eventually, the next fork in the tunnel was not marked. Neither branch bore either the red or the blue sign, though a few marks of chipping—as though someone had knocked away some rough spots—made the left hand turning the most likely. The imager seemed to agree with this, save that the junction on that map was portrayed as a triple rather than a dual fork. There must have been a rockfall at some time in the past, he thought. If there had once been third branch, there was one no longer.

"So we take the left?" Babe said as he studied the image.

"Looks like it." But Ard Matthew still wasn't sure. The stone way was confused enough what with the tumbled detritus, and he could certainly not make out any entrance to the left of the two tunnels that were open. Lacking a more certain sign, they set off down the lefthand tunnel, still descending, though not as steeply. The smell grew stronger, tickling his nose and making him a little queasy. He decided he didn't like it after all.

After a time, he tried to distract himself by thinking about Téna and the others who were counting on him. He still had no clear plan of how to use any information he obtained when they got into the ruins, but somehow he must not fail the others. He must—

An abrupt, jarring vision of the madman broke into his thoughts. He heard again Solomon's voice. "Into the underworld, Theseus."

Theseus. That was an earthman, the hero of a saga. Ard Matthew had heard at least some of the ancient stories when he was a boy. The Star Brothers translated them into Rythan.

Theseus and the minotaur. Yes. Some sort of monster. Others had made similar journeys. Something to do with the subconscious? Or perhaps a return to the womb? Ahead of him, Babe stumbled a little and groped for the side of the passage.

Ard Matthew shone the light on the floor, but he could see nothing to trip over. "Alright?" he asked.

Before the other man could answer, a roar shook the tunnel. It was a massive sound, more solid than a wind, charging out of the darkness to roll over the heads of the interlopers. It sounded like a giant bull.

The impossibility of any such thing struck him as a last ray of sanity before he felt Babe's hand clutching at his shoulder.

"Mertvets!" Babe struggled as Ard Matthew gripped him in turn. "Vsyeh moy mertviyeh!"

The Lost Rythan had no idea what he was saying or even what language he was using. He gave him a shake. "What is it, Babe?"

"My—the dead. Oh God! He was right! This is the underworld."

Ard Matthew looked around frantically, trying to focus the torch that trembled in his hand. But he saw no one, dead or otherwise. "I—I thought I heard a—" But he could not go on. Of course there couldn't be a bull in these tunnels. This wasn't Earth—or Lost Rythar either. But he seemed to have forgotten just exactly where they were.

"You are in hades," Solomon said. "The underworld. As you should be, for you are Theseus—and Odysseus—and every other hero who has ever made this journey."

But that was impossible. If they were in hades, he told himself, then the Motherworld must lie above them. But he had never been to Sol system in his life! He was a colonist. A mutant. He wanted to tell Solomon that, but the words kept getting mixed up as they came out.

Like Babe, he realized suddenly, he was reverting to his native language.

He must have let go of Babe, for suddenly the other man seemed to be running down the tunnel crashing into walls in panic frenzy. Automatically, Ard Matthew set off in pursuit. "Come back," he called. "Something—something isn't right here—"

Babe staggered and brought up against the wall. As the Lost Rythan reached him, it seemed as though the tunnel had grown into a cavern, dimly lit with torches—the real kind—wreathed in smoke. He blinked. There were figures in the mist.

Slowly one of these drew closer. He recognized a man he had known back on Lost Rythar—Gris Bede Firespear, killed by a snowtyger when Ard Matthew was a boy. The old man gaped at him and shook his bloody head. A vast wound stretched from his chest downward, entrails bulging from the rent as he moved. Without speaking, he turned away.

"Why am I here?" the Lost Rythan demanded loudly. "Am I damned after all?" He knew he deserved to be, for he had denied God. But he had recognized his sin and he had prayed for forgiveness. He would not let himself believe that God had abandoned him!

Behind him, someone chuckled. "This is just a visit," Solomon said. "You've come for wisdom and that can be expensive. Are you willing to pay the cost?"

On the tunnel floor, Babe moved slightly, groaning. "Marfa," he said clearly and then began muttering in the language he had used before. He seemed unaware of the Rythan's presence.

"No wisdom there," Solomon said. To his consternation, he realized the madman had been speaking Rythan.

Ei minth tharkjust seal. Olete tulnud tharkjuse järele ga tharkjus on hallis. Was that really what he had heard? Somewhere deep in his brain, an alarm went off. He blinked, but the sooty flames, the turgid smoke, and the shades remained. He tried speaking, and to his relief, his own words came out as Basic. "Babe? Can you talk to me?"

"She will not see me. She will not speak—"

"Who?" Had Téna joined them in the tunnels?

"My wife. Marfa."

Babe's form was becoming more tenuous even as he spoke. In another moment, he might vanish entirely.

Desperately, Ard Matthew grasped the other man's clothing, trying to reach the flesh. With a groan of despair, he realized that Babe was transforming into a wendigo.

Slowly the thing unwound itself and stood up, towering even above the Lost Rythan. In a nightmare vision, its proboscis like jaw came nearer and nearer to his throat.

Like an antelope pinned by a snowtyger in the coils of a serpent spruce, he froze before the approaching horror, remembering the cave paintings, the people falling down to worship the wendigo. Invisible hands gripped his shoulders, pushing him to his knees.

But this he would not permit, though the weight of ages seemed to press on him, the weight of the consent of Neanderthal exiles who had once roamed these corridors. And perhaps because of this resolution, another glimmering of reason found its way into his mind—for in remembering the Neanderthals he knew that he wasn't on Earth.

The flames and smoke gave way to the light of his torch, lying where he had dropped it. But the wendigo remained.

"Worship me," it said in Rythan, "and you will return to your home."

As he heard the words, he stood on a familiar mountain slope, the two moons and the stars of Lost Rythar shining softly on new fallen snow. He smelled the wind of home, though even here, a fungoid stench overlay the cleanliness of the winter night. Down the mountain, almost at his feet, he made out the silvered forms of the sunfirs, the coiling serpent spruce and the huddled log houses of his father's keep.

"Give me what I ask and this will all be yours," the wendigo said. Once more, he heard the echoes in his own language. *Anthe mulle, mitha ma falun.*

Give me what I ask.

As the creature spoke, such a longing came over him that no price seemed too high to pay for this, his heart's desire. He became one with the people in the cave painting, one among the worshippers of the wendigo, shrinking even into the compact form of a Neanderthal. How easy it might be to forget duty and the demands of honor! There were skis jutting from the snow and he knew that if he strapped them on, he could go soaring down the hillside to where they waited for him—his parents and his brothers and sisters and all of his kindred.

"But what about Babe?" a small, familiar voice demanded. He thought it was Téna's, though why she should be concerned about Babe, he didn't know.

Suddenly he realized he had completely forgotten the other man! Guiltily, he turned back, fumbling for the torch he had once more dropped in the snow. Where was Babe?

Then he remembered. Babe was a wendigo now. They had come for something—to save—Téna. And Lish. But Babe was no good to them in his present form.

He hovered, uncertain what to do. Why couldn't he just go home and forget his unending troubles, his eternal duty? He glanced at Solomon who balanced lightly on top the snow, the starlight catching in his eyes. "Isn't that what you did? Lay down your load of duty?" he asked the archaeologist.

The madman chuckled. "It's your choice," he said. *Tsee on theie falikh.*

The wendigo reached down to turn him around. It had grown taller beneath the sky of Lost Rythar. "Take the skis," it said. "Go back where you belong."

Kuhu huuluth. Where you belong.

But behind the wendigo, other eyes looked down at him. His mother's eyes. He would not find her at the keep, he realized suddenly, for she was with God. She had died. And behind her—that greater Mother he had almost forgotten. *Ave Maria—*

He held the torch in his hand, knowing that if he turned the light on the scene below, he would lose forever the mountainside, the sunfirs and the serpent spruce. His father's hall would be no more.

The wendigo clutched at him. Wasn't it true that if he abandoned his duty, he would only fall into a worse slavery? And yet—even if this were no more than the semblance of his home, would that not be worth it?

"Help me now," he prayed, feeling as though his heart was being wrenched from his body. "Holy Mary, pray for me."

He flashed the torch on the scene below his feet and the light shone on rock. The wendigo had shrunk to a huddled thing sprawled almost at his feet. The clean winter smell was gone and the air was filled with the stench of mold—fifty thousand years of mold.

Weeping, he took up his burden. Duty, like a corpse lay draped over his shoulders—the corpse of the wendigo. He began to retrace his route back up the tunnel.

After what seemed like hours of struggle, bent over with the weight of what he carried, he emerged into a place where broken rock lay piled and scattered. He could go no further. His last thought as he collapsed beside his burden was that Lost Rythar lay where it had always been out among the stars and that it was not lost after all.

***

"Damn it, Third-Blade, wake up! What do you think this is—a hotel?"

There was fear beneath the anger in that voice and in response to that distress, he forced himself to wakefulness. To duty. He opened his eyes, blinking in the familiar glare of the torch. "What—?"

"Thank God," Babe said, lowering the light a little. "I was just wondering how I would ever get your great carcass out of here." Even in the dimness, Ard Matthew could see that the other man's face was haggard, haunted.

"What happened?" the Lost Rythan mumbled, wondering that he could speak at all.

"What happened? Or what do I think happened?"

Ard Matthew closed his eyes, remembering the wendigo. He ran one hand over his head, wondering if he might have fallen and dreamed the whole thing.

"Both," he said. Nothing hurt when he pressed on his scalp, so it wasn't that.

"You turned into a bear," Babe said. "A really big one. With red eyes and long claws."

The Lost Rythan blinked. "A—a bear?"

"That's right. First I saw—some other stuff—and then you started growling. I thought my last moment had come." Babe grinned ruefully. "Nothing like the prospect of being eaten by a grizzly to knock some sense into a man."

Ard Matthew gaped at him. "A bear? Really?" He wondered if he was starting to lose touch with reality again.

"What about you? What did you see?" Babe demanded.

Haltingly, the Lost Rythan told him about the wendigo. "Have you got any explanation for—for all this?" he asked when he had finished.

"It seems pretty plain to me," Babe said, "that we took the wrong tunnel. Any Neanderthal who went down there would have met his ghosts for sure."

"But there are no ghosts—not really."

"Didn't you smell it, Third-Blade? There was something in the air. We were both hallucinating."

He took this in. Of course, that would explain things. But there had been no such substances on his homeworld and he had never encountered such a thing elsewhere. The only time he remembered hallucinating was when he had the lung sickness as a child and thought the wolves had come into his room. "So," he said slowly. "And—then what happened?"

"I don't know. I woke up here."

Ard Matthew looked around as, slowly more of his scattered memories came back. There had been the burden of duty he had carried. A literal burden that must have been Babe. "What do we do now?" he wondered, still dazed.

Babe directed the light to the rock pile on the left of the opening behind them. "We dig," he said. He wedged the torch among the fallen stones and they did this. It did not take as long as the Lost Rythan had expected before they disclosed another tunnel mouth. And there, like a smudged blessing, was the red sign.

"I was careless—before," he said. "To think we might have been lost down there and never got out!"

"We were both careless," Babe agreed. "But we did get out. Thanks to you."

Ard Matthew scrambled to his feet. He didn't feel well and his head ached. But now they must go on no matter how they felt. He could only hope he would walk off the aftereffects of the hallucinogen.

This time he was alert for the familiar musky smell. But luckily, as they moved away from the intersection, it faded away. In fact, the tunnel smelled like nothing worse than wet stone. Even more promising, they soon began to climb. When Ard Matthew checked the imager, he was pretty sure this was the right way. In fact, they should soon come across the first outlet into the ruins above. He told Babe this.

The effect on the other man was immediate—he actually grinned in relief. Though they had said nothing more to each other about their experience in the cavern of the mold, it almost seemed to the Lost Rythan that they had become blood brothers in a far deeper sense than his formal ceremony with the Neanderthal chief. He and Babe had touched souls in a place outside of time—in the underworld—and they had mingled something deeper than blood.

But now he needed to concentrate on the task ahead. They faced a common enemy and, though Ard Matthew had no love for the Kessler Corporation, his feelings paled beside those of the other man. Babe's hatred of his employer erupted once more into a blaze that threatened the success of their mission.

"If she's here—" Babe said once.

"When the time is right," Ard Matthew told him. "She will be brought to justice."

"Justice?"

"Babe," the Lost Rythan said, "are we fit to judge and—and pass sentence?"

A pause while they continued to climb. Then, "But if we are attacked, Third-Blade? If she comes after us?"

"Oh, then." Ard Matthew turned, showing the edges of his teeth. "That's different."

"For Shami, at least." Then a rueful headshake. "Not that we ever got along, of course."

"For Shami. But we must try not to be seen. If they found out about these tunnels, the people would not be safe."

Babe nodded reluctant agreement. And at that moment, they heard voices above.

CHAPTER TWELVE

The language seemed to be Basic, though it was impossible to make out any words. But to Ard Matthew, it sounded very much as though someone was getting chewed out.

He and Babe looked at one another, not daring to move. They were in a wider area of the passage, though the ceiling was low enough that the Lost Rythan had to stoop slightly. It gave him a claustrophobic feeling. So far as he could see, there was no sign of an outlet. Ahead of them, the tunnel continued level or slightly rising until a bend hid the rest of it from view.

"Turn out the light," Babe breathed and Ard Matthew did so. They were left in total darkness.

"Well that's alright, then. If we can't see their light, they can't see ours."

At this, Ard Matthew turned the torch back on and began to examine the roof of the tunnel. It all seemed to be solid rock. But he had been in caves before and knew that the acoustics could do strange things. He told Babe this, trying not to speak above a whisper, though it was extremely unlikely anyone could hear him over the harangue going on above.

"Then they might not be nearby at all," Babe murmured. "If what you say is true."

The Lost Rythan nodded, lifting one hand to silence his companion. The voices had ceased.

They waited, Ard Matthew counting silently to sixty. Nothing.

"We'd better go on," he said at last, his voice no more than a thread of sound.

"Be careful with the light," Babe warned him.

Ard Matthew held one hand over the torch, directing the muted beam to the floor in front of them to avoid any pitfalls. As they neared the turning, however, the passage widened out into a small chamber and came to an abrupt dead end. At this, the Lost Rythan doused the light completely. It was as well he did, because in the sudden darkness, they could now make out a dim glow that seemed to come from somewhere above.

That was when they heard the voices again, though there was still no way to be sure where they were coming from.

"I think this must be it," Babe whispered. "The way up into the ruins."

Ard Matthew stepped into the smaller compartment. The pale illumination still held, but he could still see nothing here except more stone—a forest of what looked like stalagmites. He could make out where the glow was coming from, though. There was a crack in the ceiling, and the light made crazy shadows as the forest of stone broke up the pale beams. It was a confusing mix of twilight and darkness.

Suddenly, they both jumped.

"Don't give me that crap!" came loudly from directly over their heads. "You're not a damned slope-head. Afraid of the dark—"

"I know that voice," Babe whispered. "His name is Shin."

Ard Matthew looked at him sharply. "From where?"

A low chuckle. "Shin was my assistant. At Kessler. Sounds like he's in charge of things here. Probably making a mess of it—he was never too bright."

Well there was his answer—this was definitely a Kessler project. But of course he had had little doubt that this would prove to be the case. The Rythan laid one hand on a stone formation, listening intently as the voice came again.

"Now quit whining! You two are to stay with the supplies and keep those new guys from stealing stuff. You know what Windy-Go types are like—port scum. But we have to use them because we can't get anyone else."

This was followed by silence. And then, "Don't know why I take this shit," a different voice said. "I thought when we got rid of Babe, we could all move up a little."

"Ha! They're all alike. Bosses." This one had a strong colonial accent, though Ard Matthew could not identify the place of his origin.

"Damn right," the other said.

"I always knew Shin was a jerk. Not as rough as Babe, but still—"

Ard Matthew looked around to see how his companion was taking this. It must be a bit like attending his own funeral. Under the circumstances, the thought sent a little shiver up his spine.

Babe was grinning, however. Or at least his teeth were visible in the dimness. Maybe it was a snarl instead. The Rythan signaled for Babe to stay where he was and settled down to wait. He needed more information.

Up above, the grousing gave way to recollections of port time and stories about sexual conquests which made Ard Matthew distinctly uncomfortable. And then, quite clearly, "You think they cleaned out most of the slope-heads?"

"No, I don't. They're still hiding in the ruins somewhere."

"What do you think they are?"

"Who knows? Aliens? Animals?"

"Animals don't use slings and bows. You saw Obuna. Got an arrow in the stomach. Lucky it wasn't poisoned."

Ard Matthew nodded to himself. That was an idea. Makena's people might not be sophisticated enough for such crude chemical warfare, but if necessary, he could help them along.

"Well who the hell cares as long as we get rid of them!" the other man said loudly.

"Yeah, they give me the creeps."

"Look." There were sounds of someone moving about and then the skreek! of something being moved across stone. A chair? "Whatever they are, they don't matter. She'll take care of them. And when the real crew gets here—"

"If those Turks don't find us first."

"You mean Kemal? Yeah, that could be bad. But he won't. She's too smart for him. Way too smart."

"Yeah, it's pretty slick the way she faked her death," the other agreed. "Who'd look here for the stuff? And it's all over the news—the corporation's supposed to be in a real mess with her gone. But we don't know yet for sure yet if Kemal will buy it."

"He will. I think she played it right."

"Hey, you want to light up?"

The conversation trailed off at this point while the two apparently shared a joint.

"What do you think?" Babe breathed. "Do we go up?"

"Why?"

There was a longish pause. At last, the other man chuckled softly. "Okay, you know I want her dead, Third-Blade, but I'm not an idiot. I won't risk people's lives just to take her out. But I—we both—want to know what they have up there and how they plan to use it. If they dump something nasty in these tunnels, it's our skin, too. And that kid—the chief's son. We need to find out."

The Lost Rythan grunted. He knew Babe was right. "So what do you suggest?"

"You know what I suggest," Babe said. "We go up. And we do what we have to as far as these two guys are concerned. Are you game?"

With a sigh, Ard Matthew nodded and began to search for a way to the chamber above. He didn't want to kill anyone, but they had to know more. Could they slip by the two watchmen? he wondered. Or if not, could they leave them unconscious in such a way that no one knew who had done it? He was pretty sure he'd be sorry later if he let them live, but what other choice did he have? He was not a murderer. No Rythan was.

He switched the torch back on, at its lowest setting this time. Using the light as sparingly as he could, he began to work his way around the walls, dodging the stone pillars when that was possible, scraping his skin when it wasn't. After a time, he discovered red markings—arrows painted on the stalagmites—and he followed these until they led him to what he was looking for. A jagged cleft in one wall rose from the floor, moving upward into darkness.

It looked like a tight squeeze for a Rythan, but there was no other way. "Come on," he said to Babe and started edging his way upward.

The narrow space made for hard going—it had obviously been meant for smaller people. Ard Matthew lost some more skin from his arms and torso, but after a brief struggle, he emerged into another rock chamber. He could hear Babe panting and struggling below until presently the other man joined him. Daylight filtered down from a broken roof, illuminating what appeared to be a natural cavity in the rock.

He glanced at Babe, laying one finger over his lips, and then turned back to study their surroundings. There was just enough light to see that the opening through which they had come was outlined in smears of red ochre. He took that as a good sign, though the original map did not include the upper part of the ruins. Not that he needed a map, Ard Matthew decided after a brief search, for there was only one egress from the apartment in which they found themselves—a doorway blocked with a broken slab.

"We'll never shift that," Babe whispered, but Ard Matthew ignored him and moved closer to the aperture.

"We don't have to," he breathed. Behind what looked like a barrier there was just enough space to wriggle through. Space for a Neanderthal, anyway. With an effort that added yet more abrasions to his lacerated skin, he wormed his way into what proved to be a passage partly open to the sky. It looked like morning up there.

Once more he glanced back at Babe who nodded. They moved along cautiously until they could look down over a parapet onto a sort of plaza half overhung by a ledge. Now they could hear the voices very clearly. The speakers sounded more than a little nervous.

Apparently they had continued their conversation while the others were finding their way to the upper level.

"—saw one of the bodies up close. She's got it in the cooler. If that's not an alien—"

Apparently they were still talking about the Neanderthals.

"Mutants. Someone's got a lab at one of the lodges. Bet the slope heads escaped from there. You know what kind of people come to Windy-Go. There's no law. You can do just about anything you like if you don't bother anyone important."

A brief silence, then, "One of them took out Ulvi with a rock" the other man said. "I mean a slingshot, you know? Killed him. Not just arrows. These things mean business."

The other man made a dismissive sound. "Okay—okay. Bad news. That's why we've got guns."

"But what if they're in here now? What if they live in here? Troglodytes or something. What if they've got secret passages?"

Makena hadn't told him that his people had killed any of the offworlders before they themselves were shot, Ard Matthew thought. But then maybe the chief hadn't known. There had only been one survivor of the trio who had come in to spy on the so-called ghosts. But it was good to know that the superstitions of the Neanderthals had not prevented them from taking out their enemies when the opportunity arose. They must have figured out that the so called ghosts were solid flesh.

He eased forward until he could look directly down on the pair. The distance wasn't too great to drop on them—if they were distracted, that is.

He was aware of Babe beside him, waiting expectantly. He considered. Why not? He picked up a stone, nodded to the other man, and tossed it into the rubble beyond the overhang.

The reaction was everything he could have hoped. With a cry, one of the guards leaped to his feet and both were looking frantically in the direction of the sound.

It was all he needed. Ard Matthew dropped onto the still seated man, knocking him unconscious with a single blow.

There was a bad moment when the other one reached for a weapon, but Babe kicked him in the head as he came down. The gun skittered away across the stone and before the man could recover his balance, the Lost Rythan had the weapon and was pointing it at him.

"Babe!" the guard exclaimed, his eyes rounding in shock. "I thought you were dead!"

"I'll bet you did, you bastard."

"Hey, I didn't have anything to do with that flyer business," the other protested. "I mean, when I heard about it, I was as surprised as anyone."

"Me, too," Babe told him. "But we don't have time for a chat. I want to know what she's got planned. And when."

The guard's eyes slid from one face to the other. He didn't seem reassured by what he saw. "Well, you know, they never tell us much," he temporized.

"Who strafed the village?" Ard Matthew asked suddenly.

The prisoner only shook his head. "There aren't any villages here. This is an uninhabited area."

"It wasn't last time we checked," Babe said. "Your lot killed some innocent people."

"Just slope heads. We have to clean them out. Whatever they are, they're sure not human."

"Clean them out?" the Rythan said. "So you can take the phessite?"

Their prisoner gave Ard Matthew a sharp look. "How did you—?"

"What is her plan?" Babe demanded. "After you clean out the inhabitants?"

A twitch at the corner of one eye gave warning. Ard Matthew had barely time to turn before the fallen guard fired at him, the beam searing his clothing. He felt the heat of it on his side.

Continuing his turn, he brought up the other weapon before the man could fire again, and shot him in the neck. It was not as clean a kill as he would have liked, but it did the job.

But their other prisoner had not been idle. Taking advantage of the distraction, he whirled about and fled.

"Shoot him!" Babe cried, scrabbling for the dead man's gun. "Don't let him warn the others."

Ard Matthew hesitated.

At this, Babe snatched up the weapon and fired just as the fugitive passed beyond the overhang, shouting for help. He fell spread-eagled on the stone and lay unmoving.

There was nothing to do except hide the bodies and mop up the blood as best they could. As he worked, Ard Matthew was thinking furiously. He hadn't wanted to kill the men. He hadn't! But there was no other way the scene could have played out and he should have known that. Worse, they had learned almost nothing they didn't know before; they had only had their suspicions confirmed. It was a sickening waste of life.

Babe must have seen some of his thoughts on his face because he paused as he shifted a crate to better hide the results of their work before looking up at the Lost Rythan. "They were murderers," he said. "I knew them. Oh hell." He looked down angrily as he took up the crate once more.

"Babe?"

"Damn it, Third-Blade, I should know! I hired them myself. Renegades, fugitives, what have you. What did you think this was—a damn tea party?"

The Lost Rythan hesitated. "Of course our own hands are not clean either, yours and mine," he said. "But still we must go on."

"I know that."

"Alright. Let's check around some more while we're here. We might as well see how big this operation is. How soon they—when the others are coming, I mean. From offplanet." He could not put out of his mind what had just happened here and he wondered that it should bother him so much. It was self-defense, after all and he had killed before. Was it that they had busied themselves concealing the bodies? As though they were—ashamed?

He tried to shake off these thoughts and looked toward the arch. There was no way to know when the guards would be relieved—or if someone would check on them beforehand. He did not know how much time they had. He said these things to Babe.

"We should be okay. They've just come on—remember? I think Shin's been having his troubles here. More than just the Neanderthals. They're all spooked."

"Then come on."

Carefully, they worked their way through the ruins, the Lost Rythan keeping careful track of their course. It wouldn't do to get lost, he thought with a shudder. There might not be real ghosts here, but it was an ancient place, inimical to his kind, built by unknown star-farers from long before human beings had left the earth. As he moved among the broken stone-ways, he tried to distract himself by imagining how the supplies the other two were guarding could have been brought in through the ruins. The job would have been formidable with all the twists and turns, not to mention piles of rubble, to traverse. There must be a more direct way.

After a time they came to a large, open space where four fibresteel domes had been set up. For some time, they crouched among the rocks watching as men and women moved about, carrying crates and other things from one structure to another. Ard Matthew could not overhear any of what they were saying, but it looked to him as though these workers were assembling some kind of equipment.

Beyond the domes, two flyers perched on the stone pavement. Ard Matthew studied them thoughtfully. He recognized the models. They were good machines, meant to be transported through the net and assembled on the ground. Likely the company ship had brought them and then they had been freighted to the ruins by one of the companies like the one that hired Ard Matthew himself. Maybe even Mong's own. It wouldn't surprise him—now.

He felt Babe's touch on his arm and nodded as the other man gestured for them to pull back. They had done what they came for and it would be foolish to risk anything more. It was time to return to the others.

They were safely back in the cavern beneath the supply dump when someone apparently found the bodies. They could hear the confusion above, a mingling of voices, exclamations and orders. The word "slope-head" was heard more than once.

"They think the Neanderthals did it?" Ard Matthew said. "That they fired guns?"

Babe shrugged. "I don't know. Maybe. It can't make things any worse, whatever they think."

He was right, the Lost Rythan thought. Things were about as bad as they could be already.

***

The return was less toilsome than the initial journey into the ruins. Now that they knew what to avoid, there were no hesitations, no delays. And Ard Matthew wanted to make speed. He didn't think the Kessler people would discover how they had got in, but there was no way to be sure. Only when they had travelled for some time without incident did he decide it was safe to slow down.

He wasn't sure how long they had been walking, though he was exhausted. The hallucinogen had taken its toll on them both and beyond this, they had had nothing but water in all this time, since there had been no food available to take with them. Both were hungry and gritty-eyed and the Rythan, at least, was heartily sick of the dark. His abrasions hurt and the chill was seeping into his bones. Grimly he kept going, setting a pace that probably taxed Babe as much as it did him. Hours later, when they got back to the cave of the map, he only wanted to lie down on the stone and go to sleep.

To his surprise, however, they found Téna waiting for them. Her eyes widened when she saw Ard Matthew who came in first. "Where is Babe?" she asked quickly, trying to see around him into the tunnel.

"Here," the other man said as he followed Ard Matthew out into the chamber. "Can't get rid of me that easily."

Téna stared at him, taking in his battered condition. "Oh," she said, unable to suppress a little cry when she saw him. She looked quickly at the Rythan. In the torchlight, he could not tell if she was blushing or not, but he rather thought she was. "What happened?" she asked quickly, to cover up her first reaction.

Babe grinned at her. "We're okay," he said. "Really. We're just a little tired and hungry."

"Right," Ard Matthew said. "We didn't mean to startle you." But even as he spoke, hunger and exhaustion were sapping his strength and he was finding it hard to stay on his feet.

Indeed, he hoped he didn't look as bad as Babe did. Their journey had pared away whatever original bonhomie the company man had once possessed, accentuating the harsh, planes of his face. But Babe was obviously trying to put the best face on things. "Got anything to eat?" he asked Téna.

She trembled slightly. "Oh Babe!" she cried. "Thank God you're—" And then she burst into tears.

The two men looked at each other in consternation while Téna regained control of herself. Her features, when she looked up once more, showed nothing but anger.

Ard Matthew tried not to look at her. "How are things here?" he asked diffidently. "Any trouble?"

"We're doing alright so far," she told him without looking at Babe. "They've got—there's dried meat. It's all we have." She led the way out of the cave.

It was late afternoon and both men blinked in the sunlight. "I guess it's morning," Babe muttered. But he was watching Téna and not the sky. And when she glared at him, he looked away with a slight shrug and an eyeroll in Ard Matthew's direction.

It didn't help when they ran into Solomon almost immediately. But to everyone's relief, he seemed more rational than he had been. He congratulated them on their journey, and there was no more talk about the underworld.

Encouraged by his lucidity, Ard Matthew took the opportunity to ask him about the ruins. "That's where you were going," he said, "when you crashed. Had you been there before?"

The archaeologist shook his head. "The Kola brought me here once—later, I mean," he said. "To commune with the spirits. I was—a little bit confused when they found me. I still am sometimes, I think."

Ard Matthew winced. He kept forgetting that John Solomon had been through an experience as horrible as anything they had seen in the caves. Almost certainly he had witnessed one of his people being sucked dry of blood by the wendigo. No wonder he was confused, as he put it.

"The question," Babe said in his plain way, "was whether there really is phessite here. If this is the right place. But I guess there really is no doubt about that."

Téna looked at Solomon. "Do you believe in the old ones?" she asked abruptly. "The original star travelers?"

"Got to keep an open mind," the archaeologist said. "But just how many aliens have we ever found?"

As far as Ard Matthew knew, the answer to that was none. And the few so-called ruins scattered among the discovered worlds were over a million years old. Any one of the sites could just as well be natural if it weren't for the phessite. So where was Téna going with this?

She was addressing Solomon once more. "Is it possible, Dr. Solomon—I mean, do you think the old ones could have brought the ancestors of these people here?"

He shook his head. "If there really were any 'old ones' as you call them, they would have been gone long before the Neanderthals. I think these people's ancestors were taken by the net itself, quite at random, as it sometimes does, and deposited here no more than one hundred thousand years ago. Probably much more recently than that."

"And in all those years, they haven't changed? They've just hidden here on Windy-Go and—and that's it?" Babe broke in. "I find that hard to believe. Don't you?"

"No change," Solomon told him. "Or very little. They have survived because they were left alone and the place agreed with them."

"But what about the wendigo?" Ard Matthew demanded. "They wouldn't have been prepared for something like that."

"A challenge. But hardly worse than cave bears and mastodons. I was thinking about the threat of homo sapiens—now that's another matter. But homo sapiens wasn't here—at least not until recently."

Ard Matthew considered this. It made sense, he supposed. So what was in store for these gentle people now? He tried to imagine a race with almost no concept of change, no will to invent—to develop. "They'll fight to survive, won't they?" he asked.

But Solomon's mind had made another of its sudden shifts. "They're dead already," he said cheerfully. "Maybe fifty thousand years dead. Or longer. They just don't know it."

"I won't believe that," Téna said angrily.

"So ask them." He grinned at her. "Do you think they're angry about this attack? Most of them have checked out. It's what they do when things get bad."

Startled, Ard Matthew looked around the open space. Yes, there they were, settled into a state of pure and almost mindless waiting. Groups of them hunkering together on the stone, unmoving. He could easily imagine them dying where they sat, still waiting for someone else to deal with this invasion from beyond the sky.

But as he followed Téna to Makena, he began to see people stirring, brown eyes alert and questioning as they followed her progress and that of the two men. Lish had been dozing beside her mother and now she roused as the others approached the family. Makena climbed to his feet and came forward to greet the pilot. He was speaking, but Solomon had disappeared and it was left to Lish to translate as best she could.

"Ish gud you make come back," she said. "Not be—shpirt."

Ard Matthew nodded and took Makena's hand. "Very good," he said with a glance at Lish. "But now," he added to Téna, "we are going to need Solomon to translate for us. Do you think he'll—be able to?'

Téna shrugged. "He's been like this off and on ever since you left," she said. "But today was his clearest day."

The Rythan glanced out over the seated groups of people, their broad faces turned up to him like flowers opening to the light. He wished he could speak to them, could be whatever they needed to help them survive. Or better still, to lead them and show them how to defend themselves from what must still seem a supernatural force—evil from beyond the stars.

But he was helpless.

Then he spotted Solomon over near the entrance tunnel. Rapidly he strode over to meet him. "We need you to interpret," he said hesitantly, wondering whether the other understood him. For the first time, he really looked at the archaeologist, bearded now and covered with dirt—as Ard Matthew himself was—his eyes haunted with all he had seen and suffered. He was not as old as he had seemed at first. His experiences had marked him—aged him. What must it have been like when the wendigo came? When everyone on his team had died?

He tried to summon an encouraging smile.

To his relief, Solomon smiled back. "I'm sorry. I was afraid you might be ghosts after all," he said.

"No," the Rythan told him. "We're okay." Together they went back to join the others, passing once more among the seated people.

Meanwhile, Babe had been given a few strips of dried meat which he devoured hungrily beneath the cold gaze of Téna. Kensh, the boy, hurried up to meet Ard Matthew and handed him some of the meat. It was wind-dried, stale and tough. But it was just what he needed and he took it gratefully.

He hunkered down with the others and the boy joined him. There was a warmth between them, a fellow feeling. Ard Matthew had known the wilderness in a way the other offworlders hadn't and because of this, he could relate to the Neanderthals in ways his companions probably couldn't. Looking down at the boy, he renewed his determination to save these people—or die trying. But for now, he was so weary. It was good to refuel his body, good to relax.

Meanwhile, Makena began speaking at once and Solomon seemed willing enough to translate. The chief was apparently asking questions in his high pitched language.

"He wants to know if you made it all the way up into the ruins."

"Tell him we did," Ard Matthew said. "And we saw the people who attacked his men. Who attacked the village."

They waited while Solomon translated.

After this, the Rythan gave the chief an account of his and Babe's journey. Some things he edited out and Babe did not correct him. Their visit to the underworld—even the underworld of their own minds—was private. But he confirmed that their guesses had been right and that Kessler Corp was certainly behind the operation. That there was little doubt about the phessite, though they had not seen it.

"But can they do this?" Téna asked. "Just kill off everyone and go ahead? I mean can they get away with it?"

It was Babe who answered, after a moment's hesitation. "They can go ahead and retrieve the stuff," he said. "I mean that must have been the original plan." He did not look at Téna. "No one knew there were people living here," he added. "Not at first. And I guess you scientists had never seen them either?" He looked at Solomon as he said this.

"This is my first trip to Windy-Go," the archaeologist admitted. "There really haven't been all that many expeditions over the years, you know. If the Neanderthals wanted to stay hidden, I'm pretty sure they could have done it. No one remained at the ruins more than a season and they would have been too busy to scout around. I don't think anyone knew about the lower tunnels and the—the wall paintings."

There was a pause while Ard Matthew silently prayed that their interpreter wouldn't lose the thread of his thoughts. So far, so good. "They took me in," Solomon finally resumed. "I was—not myself at the time. I don't think—that is, new ideas come slowly to them. And that's what I was—something new. A possibility."

But now Makena was speaking again, the high pitched syllables coming incongruously from his hairy face and while they waited for the translation, Ard Matthew mulled over the word Solomon had chosen. A possibility. Yes, it all fit. These people had simply ignored what did not threaten them—until one day something happened to make them think that strangers might be people, too. They had compassion. Kensh had had compassion on their own party, he recalled. It was a very human thing.

"He asks what we are to do," Solomon said, breaking in on these thoughts.

"I'd say we go back in and take those guys out one by one, quietly," Babe said. "Before the next load gets here. And see if she's in there."

"You know that's not practical," Ard Matthew said. "Even if we could do it, word would get out. We could hardly hide all the evidence of something like that."

Babe shrugged. "You have a better idea?"

The Rythan glanced down at Kensh, snuggled up beside him with one hand on his arm, gazing up at him adoringly. Téna, he noted, was watching this with some amusement. What, he wondered, was she thinking? Perhaps she, too, had seen the spiritual kinship between the Rythan and the Neanderthals and interpreted it in her own way. The way of the starfolk. Did she despise him for it? he wondered. But he was too tired to care.

Suddenly Babe spoke up. "Did you spot any flyers while we were gone?" he asked Téna.

"No," she said. "But even if they had flown over, I don't think they would have seen us. We didn't move around much and I guess we were half camouflaged. We lit no fires—never did anything to attract attention."

He nodded. "So. And how much food is there left?"

"Not very much," she admitted. "But we have been sharing it carefully."

Ard Matthew grimaced. "You should have told us that," he said. "I'm afraid we were pretty hungry, Babe and I, and we might have had more than our share."

"You hadn't eaten in a day and a half," Téna said.

"So how long do you think the Neanderthals could hold out here?" he asked. "And if anyone came—well I'm guessing Makenna's people could fight if they were not outclassed? Outclassed in weapons, I mean." He pulled a hand gun from his belt. "Babe and I each got one of these while we were up there, so you'd have something at least."

"What do you mean?" she asked. "What do you plan to do?"

He wasn't quite sure what he planned, but he had been thinking all the while the conversation was going on. He spoke hesitantly. "As I see it," he said, "there is only one real hope for us. We need help from outside and we must get it before the company starship returns with more personnel and equipment."

"Help from outside?"

Even Babe looked up at this. "Third-Blade," he said. "You know what would happen if word of the phessite got out. Kessler might lose it but there'd still be a free for all and our friends would be either wiped out or taken as specimens."

"No," the Rythan said. He smiled down at the boy. "Don't you see? They aren't specimens—they are colonists. Just as I am—and Miss bor Rijn." He glanced at Téna. "She may look more like an earthwoman than we do, but it's true, all the same."

Babe frowned. "Colonists. You think they are colonists?"

"Well, you don't doubt they are human, do you?" the Rythan asked him. "And it doesn't matter how long they've been here. The law is pretty clear." He turned to the others. "That's how it was on my own world," he said. "Our ancestors did not come to Rythar on starships. We were not planted by a corporation. We were an accident of the net—not as long ago as this one, maybe, but certainly for a few thousand years."

"Okay," Babe said slowly. "So these people are colonists. And human. But Kessler would argue that one. After the fact, of course. When they were all dead."

There was a small sound and both men looked at Téna who had gone white.

"Sorry," Babe muttered, flushing a little.

"What you said is true," she told him.

He gave her a troubled look. "I guess what I meant was, I'm sorry it's true," he said. "But I shouldn't have said it."

"We all should be sorry," Solomon said. "But that's not the issue. What do you have in mind, Mr. Third-Blade?" To Ard Matthew's relief, he seemed to be following the conversation without any trouble. As for Makena, he only watched the offworlders with what was probably alert curiosity—though it was hard to tell because of his permanently wrinkled forehead.

"Third-Blade," Babe put in, looking at the Rythan. "Just how do you expect to get outside help? All the communicators are lost and anyway, who would help us? And don't forget, Kessler could intercept any message we sent."

"There were flyers at the base," Ard Matthew reminded him. "You saw them, Babe." He was pretty sure he could fly one of them and he pointed this out to the others.

There was a long silence. So long that Makena began to speak once more, questioning as he looked intently at his blood brother.

"He wants to know what we're talking about," Solomon said. He was getting restless and the Rythan was afraid his spell of lucidity might be coming to an end.

He considered carefully what to say. "Tell him I have friends," he said at last. "Tell him I will go for help." He looked at Makena. "You must hold out until I return. All of you."

"I don't like this, Third-Blade," Babe said. "Say you make it. Who will listen to you?"

"I know someone who will." He was remembering the Star Brother he had met that night outside the port. The one who had invited him to come in and have a beer. He felt himself grow hot with shame remembering his curt refusal. He was ashamed to recall how he had actually fled, not from the priest but from all that he represented. From the Host on the altar of the church.

Babe was still looking doubtful. "They've got laws here, even if it's not a real colony. You can't just steal a corporate flyer and land it at the port."

The Rythan gave him a grim smile. "Yes I can. They don't want anyone to know what they're up to. If I make it back to the settlement, they won't dare file a complaint."

"So far so good, then," Babe agreed. "All you have to do is get the flyer, get out of here without being shot down, and then contact—"

He narrowed his eyes. "So who is this hot shot friend of yours who can get Kessler out of here and take on the rest of the corporations? Just who do you think you are?"

Ard Matthew looked down at Kensh and met the boy's deep eyes with his own. "I am a Faring Guard, Babe," he said quietly. "If I can get word to the Star Brothers, they'll have this declared a colony world within days. It would be as much as Kessler's worth to stay here after that."

Looking up involuntarily, he saw Téna's eyes widen. Of course she would have heard of the Faring Guards, though what she had heard was another matter. Servants of the Star Brothers, reformed criminals—who could say what she had been told.

"You? Why?" she burst out, looking at him suspiciously.

He chose his words carefully. "I—I have been away for a time. Some things happened and—well it doesn't matter now. I will go back to them."

Babe regarded him seriously. "Are you sure about all this? They'll only have your word and if you left them, will they still trust you? And," he added, "how will you contact them?"

Ard Matthew told him about the mission outside the port. "And—yes, Boris, my word will be enough for them. Even now."

He had not used Babe's real name before. He didn't know why he did now. He could feel Téna's curious gaze on him and turned away. Babe would believe him, he knew, because they had been through the depths of the tunnels together. As for the others, that must be as God willed.

He leaned back against the stone and closed his eyes. Everything would be as God willed, he decided. And then he was asleep.

CHAPTER THIRTEEN

They didn't let him sleep for long. He hadn't expected to and now he roused guiltily from the brief rest he got. Babe and Téna were arguing, Solomon was staring off at the far wall of the amphitheater and Makena had withdrawn into himself. Of them all, Ard Matthew still felt the greatest kinship with this man who knew when to keep silent and to wait—and it was to him he turned now. The Neanderthal, he was quite sure, would make a good hunting companion.

The other man was looking back at him and their glances met and held. "I will save you if I can," he said softly in Rythan and knew that the other understood, if not the words, then the meaning.

Babe turned to him. "Ready, Third-Blade?" he asked.

Ard Matthew nodded. He hadn't known for sure he was actually going to go through with his far-fetched plan until he said the words. But it was all true. He was a Faring Guard and though he had betrayed his trust, his failings did not change what he was, either in the eyes of the Star Brothers or in God's. He had sinned before, been exiled from his home colony for it, and he had been given him another chance. That was what it meant to be a Faring Guard, servant of the Star Brothers and of all whom they served. A Faring Guard lived by those second—and third—chances.

He turned to Solomon, speaking hurriedly. "Will you tell the chief what we have decided to do?" he asked. "Or did you already?"

It took a while for his words to penetrate. Slowly the other man's attention came back to the people around him and he stared at the Rythan in confusion. "You're going back to the underworld? Alone? I don't think that's in the story. Odysseus never had to do that, you know."

"It is in this story," he said. He laid a hand on Solomon's shoulder. "Can you tell him now? And—pray for me," he added. He strode away before the archaeologist could make another protest.

After all, there was no reason to delay. The little cave lay directly in his path and now he would not let himself falter, though the thought of traversing that darkness once more, alone this time, filled him with dread.

His was an almost supernatural terror made up of the memory of his experience with the hallucinogenic fungus and also of something worse. For he remembered the choice he had been offered—to return to his beginnings, to his home, at the expense of his honor. He shuddered at the bare suspicion that he might have wavered.

It was also true that as a son of Lost Rythar, he could never be completely free from a fear of spirits, pagan or otherwise. The suspicion, however unlikely, that they dwelt below and that his own weakness might put him in their power, caused an inward shudder he could not conceal. Even the fact that he was a Christian and an educated man, did little to dispel his dread, for it was himself he feared even more than whatever forces dwelt in the caverns.

However, he did not let this affect his steady pace as he neared the entrance of the painted cave. In vain, he tried to think ahead to the task he must accomplish, hoping this would help to take his mind off his fears. And he prayed that the Kessler people had not yet discovered the upper entrance to his path. If they had, he'd really have his hands full.

Just as he reached the entrance, he heard footsteps overtaking him and turned to see who it was. To his surprise, it was Kensh who stood there, his face puckered even more than usual. "Shpaeshman," he said and reached out his arms.

"You can't come with me," Ard Matthew said, picking the boy up. "You will have to stay with the others."

It came to him then that he was leaving his friends in a peril little less than his own. He tried not to think what would happen if

Kessler's people found them. So many had died already. Once this became a colony world, the Star Brothers would be able to guide and protect the natives—to do for them what the order had done for his own people on Lost Rythar. But for now they were at the mercy of the corporation.

He set the boy down. Recalling a custom of his father's, he made the Sign of the Cross on the child's sloping forehead. Then he called for Babe.

The other man hurried up to join him and took the boy by the hand. "You good with this, Third-Blade?" he asked.

Ard Matthew nodded. "How about you?" he asked in turn. "Things might not go well here while I'm gone."

"I know." Babe looked down at Kensh. "I've thought of that."

"If only we had some way to communicate."

"You still have that thing you used to talk to Solomon. He must have something."

The Rythan shook his head. "I don't know if he still does," he said. "But anyway, it wouldn't reach very far."

"Maybe not," Babe agreed. "But the flyer must have a communicator—and if I know Kessler, they'll be top of the line. So if you give me your unit, we'll be in touch at least long enough to know you managed to survive and steal the thing."

Ard Matthew nodded. "Of course," he said, pulling the comm from his belt. "And another thing, I just thought of. When I get to the port, I may locate something strong enough to beam in on this one here." He was thinking of the Star Brothers as he said this. Appearances were always deceptive where the order was concerned and there was no reason to think the priest he had met was not as well equipped as his fellows.

Babe sighed. "Yeah. Okay, Third-Blade."

It would be a relief to him to know how things stood with Babe and the others. Though if Kessler found them, there was nothing the Rythan could do. It would be up to Babe. But Babe had surprised him more than once. He would just have to trust to the other man's resourcefulness to preserve the tribe. And Téna's, he added. For she, too, had grown and the truth was, he had probably underestimated her from the beginning.

After that, there was no more reason for delay. He caught Babe watching him and knew the other man must know at least some of his thoughts. He forced himself to turn away, though it felt as though he were breaking his last link with his human family.

This is what it means, a small voice repeated in his mind, when you become a Faring Guard. This.

And then he was inside the tunnel.

At first it wasn't so bad. After all, it was not the first time he had made the journey. But he was very tired, having had no more than a short nap in the last day and a half and, besides, he was alone. He resisted the urge to turn from time to time and look over his shoulder into the darkness. He knew that wouldn't do.

As he drew closer and closer to the place where he and Babe had made their false turn, he smelled the fungal reek and could not control a shudder of remembered horror. If he went down there now, what would he meet? And as he stood at the junction of tunnels and saw the piled rocks he and Babe had cleared from the mouth of the third one, he felt an unaccountable urge to seek once more the path they had taken into the underworld. The true underworld. What would the dead have to say to him this time when he came alone? What wisdom might they share if he asked for it?

But that was a temptation. Necromancy was a sin. He knew that. And this time, he did look behind him, ashamed lest anything, human or spirit, might see him hesitate. Holding his breath, he hurried into the cleared passage. He was remembering the wendigo that had shown him Lost Rythar and he still could not get this temptation out of his mind. He could almost hear the crunch of snow beneath his feet and feel the familiar clean wind on his face. Oh God! To be home!

Suddenly he began to tremble, even though he knew it must be the effect, even at this distance, of the hallucinogen. Had he grown more sensitive to it? One moment, he seemed to be back in the snowfield above his father's keep and the next, he saw the tunnel walls and knew where he was. What if he collapsed? What if he could not go on? He began to pray while forcing himself to keep going.

After that, things got better. As he moved further and further away from the fatal opening, his head cleared once more and left him wondering what he had been thinking of back at the fork. A death wish, perhaps. But he was alright now. At least he hoped so.

Presently, the journey began to seem less difficult and it wasn't long before he was back in the cave of the stalagmites. He entered with greater caution this time, but there was still no sign that anyone had found the entrance. Quickly he wormed his way up the shaft and into the upper chamber where he eased himself out onto the stone and crept over to the edge.

There was no sign of life below. Even the crates had been removed. Unable to determine how the Neanderthals had got in, Kessler's people had probably decided to find another way to guard their supplies.

Dared he lower himself to the stone floor, he wondered? He had left the gun with Babe and was unarmed except for his knife. But then, if it came to fighting, his mission would already have failed. He could hardly take on the whole crew or steal a flyer from beneath their noses once they were aware of him.

In the end, he took the risk, easing himself over the edge and facing the area beneath the overhang, ready to leap aside at any sign of movement. With a jar, he landed on his feet and looked around. But the place really was deserted. Of course Kessler probably didn't have that many people here yet and already he and Babe had reduced their number by two. And that was not counting the one the Neanderthals had killed with a slingshot.

He chanced one half shielded glimmer of the torch to make sure that all of the supplies were really gone. Then he waited for a time, but he heard nothing.

Finally, he moved on and picked his way among the slabs and broken stone, retracing the route he and Babe had taken the first time. Not much light tricked down to where he was and he had no idea what time it was but obviously the sun must have gone down some hours ago. Presently he saw light ahead and beheld once more the plaza of the domes. Glowfloaters hung above, dimmed but sufficient for Ard Matthew to see that no one was about. Even so, there would be watchers somewhere.

Cautiously, he began to work his way around the wall, keeping to the shadows until he crouched opposite the pair of parked flyers. Or what had been the pair. Now there was only one machine remaining. But that would do, he told himself firmly. If he could get into it.

He crouched where he was, waiting until he caught sight of what he had been looking for all along—an almost invisible figure leaning against the fuselage. Now was that the only sentry?

He started to move and then froze as another guard emerged from between two of the domes. The pair met and exchanged a few words. The Lost Rythan could not make out what was said, but their voices sounded querulous. Likely they were bored and tired.

He waited for a time, but the two did not separate. Could he manage both of them? He studied the pair, trying to determine what weapons they carried. Even if he could reach them quickly enough, there would almost certainly be a scuffle—probably enough noise to rouse the people in the domes. He would have to move at lightning speed, disable the two and then take possession of the flyer—if he could get in. Now that he was actually here, the whole scheme seemed absurd.

Even if he could knock out the guards, there was still the problem of the flyer. Of course, he told himself, there was no reason they would have locked it down, not here in the middle of their base of operations. And once inside, his pilot's training should enable him to override the startup code. Probably.

Nevertheless, the whole operation seemed incredibly reckless—enough to make him wonder that he had ever thought it possible. Worse, the night would be passing and the two guards seemed to have settled themselves there beside the flyer to wait out their shift. Ard Matthew continued to watch them, wondering what to do. Time passed.

A faint greyness was creeping into the sky when someone finally emerged from one of the domes. There was a smell of cooking in the air.

What to do? They would all be waking up in a few minutes.

And then he saw his chance. The two guards had finally moved. They were following the other figure to one of the domes. He could hear low voices, still grumbling, as they passed his hiding place. He waited a moment more and then crept out onto the stone. He was halfway to the flyer when one of the guards turned.

He stiffened, knowing the half-light would not be dim enough to conceal his presence, but hoping they would mistake him for one of their own. A second passed, two seconds. Then, "Who's there?" someone demanded.

"It's not a slope-head, stupid. He's too tall."

"Hey—you!"

Too late! He sprinted to the flyer, leaped for the flange and threw it wide. A moment later, the camp exploded into life, but he had already slammed the top. He flicked on the lights, and keyed in the override code.

Nothing happened.

Sweating, he tried another code as running footsteps echoed on the rock. Damn. What model was this?

He tried a third sequence with no result.

"Come out of there with your hands up," someone shouted.

They wouldn't fire on their own machine. Besides, anything powerful enough to breach the metalplast would endanger the domes.

"We're going for a nerve cannon. Come out now or we'll carry you out—"

Nerve cannon. It was the one weapon they could use safely. It would render him helpless, every muscle taut with agony as they came in and pulled him out of his seat. Frantically he punched in code after code, his hands shaking as he worked.

Why wouldn't the thing power up?

"You hear me?" the guard shouted. "I don't know who you are, but you've got seconds to save yourself a lot of pain."

He heard the whine of machinery outside the flyer. They hadn't been bluffing.

And then he saw the switch. This was something new. He shoved it down and began punching in the code once more. But even as he did so, there came a sharp hissing sound from outside and he was seized with a sudden cramp. He half fell over the controls, gasping with pain.

"This is your last chance!" a voice shouted. "Open that hood!"

Feeling as though every joint was being pulled apart, he forced himself to press the keys, fighting for concentration. As the flyer hummed into life, he grasped the lever, hoping for a trajectory that would take him above the ruins without smashing into a wall.

Even as he slammed his hand down on the activate, he was hit with another burst from the nerve cannon. He screamed with agony as his vision became tinged with red. But the flyer rose, skimming over the maze, climbing steadily.

And then, nearly in front of him, one last broken line of stone—

He heard the shriek of rending metalplast as he tore across the final obstacle and shot into the sky. After that, there was only mindless pain, as he rode the crippled machine out above the forest.

After what seemed like hours but must have been less than five minutes, he found he could use his hands. He hunched over in the seat as every move brought waves of nausea and caused the sweat to pour from his tormented body. But he had to get control of his flight, had to determine the extent of the damage.

Slowly, with tooth gritting effort, he steadied the flyer and forced himself to begin checking systems. He was sure his passage over the rock had ripped something in the undercarriage—he would have a rough landing later. And steering was going to be a little trickier as well, especially as he rose into the prevailing winds. But rise he must, well above the treetops—he couldn't afford another collision.

He checked the locator. Four hours at least to the port. He set the flyer on automatic and, after that, flicked on the comm unit. Static. Later, he would try to reach Babe, but for now, he had other things to worry about. For example, would they send out the other flyer in pursuit? Of course, that would depend on where it was. It could be anywhere.

He would not think of that. He must try not to think of anything at all except his mission. All God demands of us, Chief Firespear had told him more than once, is our duty. But of course there really isn't anything left outside of duty, he reminded himself with a wry smile. Not for a Faring Guard.

And so, hanging on, watching the sparse forest unfold beneath him, he began to pray the Rosary, counting on his fingers as he pictured to himself the Mysteries of salvation. At this rate, he would have time to get through the whole thing.

***

He did not, however, get through more than a couple of decades before he fell asleep. Luckily, he had set the flyer on automatic, but still it was frightening to wake suddenly and find that some time had elapsed. But he was so exhausted, suffering not only from fatigue but also from the aftereffects of the nerve cannon, that he could not help himself. Dazedly, he cast about to determine what had woken him.

Then he saw the comm light blinking. He put on the audio.

"...alert, repeat, storm approaching from the northeast. Expect high winds, snow and sleet."

It was nothing worse than a weather forecast, coming from the port. Probably no one there knew the flyer had been stolen. He was still counting on the fact that Kessler's people wouldn't want to attract attention to themselves. And so far he had been right. But he had no sooner congratulated himself on one problem avoided than another forced itself on his attention.

The wind was picking up, as he could plainly feel by the vibration of the craft. He checked his altitude and position and found that he had over two hours more to go. He was already flying as low as he safely could. He would just have to put up with the gusting of the wind.

Next thing was to try and contact Babe.

The small communicator he had given the other man would hardly be adequate for much distance and when he failed to raise a signal, he was not overly disappointed. He would probably have to wait until he had something stronger to call with than the flyer's unit.

Nevertheless, he fiddled with the dials for a moment or two longer while watching the landscape pass beneath him. The sky had grown leaden while he slept, and the hills and forests had taken on an uninviting dun color. He really felt the wind now, shaking the small craft. Soon, he would probably have to put it back on manual.

And then he thought he heard something on the comm. A response to his own calling. It was faint, half obscured by static, but undeniably a human voice. Babe's voice.

He turned up the volume. "Babe? You there?"

A burst of static. Then, "We're here. Back… in the ruins. Saw a flyer… overhead."

Well that accounted for the other flyer. At least he knew it wasn't pursuing him. Or at least, not yet.

"Are you safe now?" he asked.

"So far. People are"—more static—"Got to get them all in here."

"Are you going back the way we came in?" Ard Matthew asked him.

"No sense in that. They would… over the woods. Get us that way."

Yes. There was no point in trying to escape the ruins. Where would they go? He thought of Kensh, of Makena and the rest. On the other hand, what chance would they have if Kessler's people hunted them down—or, worse, released poison gas into the tunnels?

He looked up at the viewscreen. It was starting to snow. Would that help the people trapped in the ruins? Maybe. He didn't know.

"We can hear them, Third-Blade. Flying past the opening."

"You've got guns. Give one to Solomon."

"I gave one to Téna. She says …"

"Téna?"

"Look, Third-Blade, she's an adult." The reception faded out for a moment. Then, "The people are… have to fight. No choice."

"Yeah. Okay." He felt as though he had betrayed his friends. Just what was he trying to do anyway? Did he even stand a chance of getting help for them? And if he did, would it be too late?

He stared grimly out into the storm. Things were in God's hands, now. He had to keep reminding himself they always had been, but it didn't help much.

"These guys…can fight." More static. "… surprised… want to …"

He was losing contact. "Breaking up, Babe."

And then there was nothing more. Was it the storm? His increasing distance from the communicator? Or had something happened to Babe?

Well at least he knew where the other flyer was. But that didn't mean it might not soon be pursuing him. Probably Kessler didn't know exactly who he was or what he intended to do, but no one could miss the fact that not very many people knew how to hijack the codes and steal a flyer. Even if they didn't realizes he was a Faring Guard, they would almost certainly take him for an agent of a rival company. If they did, he decided, that would actually be a gain since it would distract them from Babe and the Kola.

But even so, he knew perfectly well that Makena's people were no more than an annoyance so far as the corporation was concerned.

Vermin to be wiped out. He sighed. What difference would the survival of the tribe make in the end, if he failed in his own mission? And yet he was doing all he could. Sleet sounded on the metalplast while he alternately prayed and dozed, and the flyer rocked in the wind above the treetops. He tried not to think about how he was going to land the crippled machine when he reached his destination.

The beacon alarm roused him fully at last. By now, the viewscreen showed nothing except whirling snow, making it impossible to land by sight. Instead, he brought the flyer down by homing on the signal from the landing plat. The radio came to life once more. While there was at least a traffic controller, Windy-Go lacked any sort of central authority. Law and order were arranged through corporate collaboration.

"Kessler Corp?" A voice said.

"Correct," Ard Matthew replied, stretching a little in the seat. Very few colonies made furniture and equipment that could accommodate a Lost Rythan comfortably and besides, he ached all over from the nerve cannon.

"Then come on down, Kessler," the voice—female—told him. She asked no questions, which meant that probably no one had reported the flyer stolen. Or else that no one in traffic control was interested.

That, however, had been only one of his problems. There was still the damage he'd sustained back at the ruins. The air jets on one side had been sheared off and the others warped. He could try to glide in, but actual contact with the pavement was going to be rough. And, considering the visibility, he stood a good chance of hitting something else as he came in.

He told the woman about the damage without mentioning how he had got it. "I'll need some room to land," he added.

"It's only the thrusters?"

"I think so."

"Take the west side of the field," she said. "And good luck."

That, too, was how they did things on Windy-Go. Someone would clean up the mess if he crashed, but unless he had made arrangements with one of the corporations, he was on his own.

He brought the flyer around once more on a flattened trajectory, buffeted by the wind, flying nearly blind as the blizzard intensified. He had not known that winter could come on so suddenly here—a few days ago it had seemed like early autumn. Hopefully, the weather was helping to protect Babe and the others.

But now he must do his own part and he did it as well as he could. The screen showed him a diagram of the plat. Maybe eight or nine flyers huddled beneath the pelting snow but there was nothing large enough to be a shuttle. At least that meant Kessler's ship had not yet arrived with its second load of workers.

As he approached, he fired the air jets on the left side and felt a response that slowed his descent though it put him very much off balance. The craft began to wobble and slipped off course, while he fought the steering bar. To him, it seemed as though everything was going in slow motion. The snow-shrouded lights of the field, the twitching, crippled machine, the ground he could not see—all combined in a dreamlike sequence that could only lead to disaster.

And then the left jets failed. With a lurch that threw him against his restraints, the flyer dropped, skidding, slewing sidewise as it tore across the field. Hands on the useless bar, he saw showers of sparks outside the viewport and felt a tearing crunch as the machine came to a halt, canted to one side. Once more his piloting skill had saved him, he thought dazedly—but not by much.

He released the bar and clutched the side of his seat, pulling his body upright as he unfastened the restraint. Luckily the hatch wasn't damaged and with an effort, he managed to shove it aside.

He had forgotten about the storm. Immediately he was soaked and blinded, while the roar of the wind deafened him and sought to tear the flange from his hands. With an effort that tore at his cramped muscles, he vaulted the rim and tried to get his bearings. He knew he had to get clear of the Kessler machine at once for they would have people here, even if the others back at the ruins had not called them. The flight controller would have notified them that one of their flyers was damaged and there would be questions—or worse.

He focused on the blurred light of the tower, using it to guide him across the field. In the murk, it was hard to avoid the other vehicles parked there. He edged around a machine that had seemed to leap out of the storm in front of him and, because of this, he didn't see the men who waited for him until two of them grabbed his arms. He felt something cold thrust against the back of his neck.

Luckily, Chief Firespear had trained him painfully and well. Now that training took over. "Don't stop and think," the chief had said. "You might get killed if you act, but you will almost certainly die if you do not."

One moment, he was a prisoner and the next he had thrown himself forward, dragging his captors with him. He whirled, striking out into the darkness and felt his fist connect. A thin pencil of laser light cut the flying snow and he shoved one of the men into its path.

There was a scream but the Lost Rythan was already moving. He ducked in under another beam and tackled the shooter, reaching up to break his neck. Still moving, he avoided another shot and grabbed someone to use as a shield.

"Who are you?" he demanded as he backed away, still holding his hostage. "What is your quarrel with me?"

"That's our question," a voice said out of the night. "Who the hell are you?"

"Someone who doesn't want to kill this man," Ard Matthew told him.

Another speaker. "If he stole it out at the ruins like they said, then he's got to be one of Kemal's people."

They were edging around him. Judging by the voices, he estimated at least three still on their feet. He took another step backward.

"I'm not," he said, still backing and dragging his prisoner with him, "working for—whoever you said. Is that what Dr. Kessler told you?"

He felt the side of another air car at his back. Good. Judging by the position of the tower, he must be near the entrance to the field. Beyond lay the blurry lights of Port Street, a place of warehouses and bars. If he could lose himself in the crowd, he might make it.

But there would be no crowd, he thought. Not on a night like this. Again he made his move as soon as he realized this, throwing his captive toward the others, leaping and rolling over the top of the flyer. There was nothing to do but run and he sped through the gate, veering onto the sidewalk, half blinded by the flying snow.

This was like one of the blizzards of Lost Rythar's high country. The wind was tearing at him, trying to sweep him off his feet. He didn't look back as he rounded a corner and paused, panting. Here he was sheltered from the wind at least, though the air was filled with flying snow.

One more turn ahead, into a courtyard. A beam hit the side of a building, scoring a furrow along the polished surface. He inhaled the reek of melted plastiblock.

Staring around wildly, he made out an opening between two sheds and ran for it. As he reached this shelter, he felt a sudden pain in his left thigh—a tearing burn that left him staggering. With the last of his strength, he worked his way beneath a wooden platform and into the crawl space under one of the buildings.

It was all he could do to drag himself along after that, biting his lip to keep from crying out each time he jarred his wounded leg. Had they seen him? Or had it just been a lucky shot? Did they even know he was hit?

Inch by inch, he moved deeper into the darkness, gripping his thigh with one hand, feeling the blood leak between his fingers. Though he strained his ears, he could hear nothing over the distant tumult of the storm. Finally, he slowed, feeling the cold begin to creep into his limbs, knowing he would die here if he did not move but not sure where to go.

He began to grow drowsy. I should pray before I sleep, he thought hazily. The only prayer that came into his head was that great apology, the Act of Contrition. Oh my God I am heartily sorry—

He was sorry. Sorry for all of it, his failed life and his duty undone. Sorry for the friends who would perish because he had not lived up to his calling as a Faring Guard. Once more, he seemed to stand on the slope above his father's keep and he could hear the howling of the wolves—or was that the wind? The skis lay at his feet—the skis the wendigo had given him. He had only to strap them on to go flying down the mountain and away from all this—all this failure.

But what lay below was a false vision, he remembered. That wasn't the true Lost Rythar. His homeworld was more than just a place—it was the spirit of his people. And that spirit bowed only to God.

With a wrench as great as the one he suffered the first time he had turned away from the wendigo's vision, he returned to his aching body. He could not die here. He must fulfill his mission.

He opened his eyes wide, straining until he saw the faintest hint of illumination. With limbs that felt like so many pieces of wood, he wriggled toward that light. An eternity later, he emerged on the other side of the building, into a snow covered street. The storm had abated somewhat, but there was still no one about.

He lurched to his feet, staggered and fell. The agony in his leg had subsided to a dull ache, but the limb would not support him. He began to crawl. How far was he from the Star Brothers' chapel? This must be the street of hotels, where he had first met Téna and Shami. And Babe.

He didn't dare take shelter here. The Kessler people would certainly find him.

He grasped the side of a building, pulling himself upright and hung, panting for a moment, gripping a railing. There was no time to linger—wherever he was. He found he had forgotten.

He turned to his mother who offered him her arm. “Am I dying?” he asked, speaking in Rythan.

But she only smiled. “Come on,” she said in Basic. “It isn’t far.”

“Do you know where the chapel is?” he asked in that language. “I have to speak to the Star Brother.”

“Come on. You’re freezing.”

He blinked, leaning heavily on his companion, who staggered slightly. “Mother?”

But she wasn’t his mother. She was much too small. In the light of a window, he saw her features pinched with cold, her inadequate clothing and the cheap jewelry that dangled from her ears. “Who—?” he asked in Basic. “Who are you?”

“No one,” she said. “I don’t matter.”

He took in the words slowly. “That can’t be true,” he said at last. “Everyone matters.”

“You need to come with me,” she told him. “I have a place. The bars are all closed and I think you’ve had enough to drink anyway.”

He pulled away. “I’ve got to find the Star Brothers’ mission,” he insisted. “I have to tell them something.”

She shook her head. “You need to sleep,” she said. “You can look for them tomorrow.” She took his arm again.

But he would not go with her.

With a shrug, she yielded. “I can’t let you die out here,” she said impatiently. “Come on, then. I know where they are.”

It was a long walk and several times he forgot where they were going. The storm was abating and as the skies cleared, a wavery sunlight gleamed on the snowy streets. They had left the lights of the port behind.

“You’re hurt,” she said once, seeing that his stumbling walk was more than the reeling of a drunkard. He had ceased to feel the leg and used it as though it were a stick attached somehow that did not belong to him. Hurt? He wasn’t sure.

“I am not,” he said once, “on Lost Rythar. Am I?”

A man stood shivering in a doorway. "No," he said. "But this will do."

With a sigh, Ard Matthew Third-Blade collapsed into the arms of the Star Brother.

CHAPTER FOURTEEN

It would have been so easy to sink into the warmth of the room, to resign himself to the care of the man who had taken him in. He sprawled on something padded, felt a hand raise his head as a hot drink was placed at his lips. But he was afraid to taste it.

"Wait," he whispered. "Don't—that is I need to stay awake. There is something—"

He lost the train of his thoughts and tried again. "Got to tell you. About—about the Neanderthals."

There was a moment's silence. Then, "It's tea," his host told him. "It won't put you out."

Still he hesitated and then he knew he must drink and it was good. After a minute of two, the hot liquid seemed to melt the ice at the core of him until suddenly he began to shiver.

"Here." A coverlet was thrown over him and he felt his muscles contract as his body began to reassert itself. His fingers and toes burned and the wound in his leg came to life. He gasped and clutched at the pallet beneath him.

"Now tell me. Did you say Neanderthals? Do you even know what that word means?"

He had to fight to concentrate. Desperately he stared around him trying to find something to fix his eyes on. The light was rather dim, the log walls bare save for a crucifix and one or two holo scenes of a world he did not know. At last, his gaze fell on the face of his benefactor and he recognized the Star Brother he had encountered all those weeks ago.

"Yes," he murmured. "I know what the word means."

“Then you had better explain,” the priest told him briskly. “Because as far as I know, the last Neanderthals died out on earth rather a long time ago.”

He managed a nod, though it made his head swim. He felt so weak suddenly and the walls seemed to wobble around him while the pain in his leg became ever more insistent.

Abruptly, the Star Brother frowned, leaned over him and twitched off the covering. “You’re wounded,” he said. “I didn’t see this when you came in. Though I should have.” He began at once to work away the bloodied legging while Ard Matthew fought back a scream. In the freezing cold, he had ceased to feel the wound. But now the torn flesh came to life with a vengeance.

“I’ve got to deal with this,” the priest said. “It’s bleeding. Heat beam?”

“Wait,” the Lost Rythan gasped. “Got to tell you—you need to call offworld. Tell the authorities—and try to contact Babe. Can you do it?”

The other man looked up from his work. “What do I need to tell them?” he asked. “And who is Babe?”

At this, Ard Matthew realized he hadn’t been very coherent. “It’s—it’s the reason,” he faltered. “Why I am here.”

The priest nodded. “Then tell me about it while I work on you.”

While the Star Brother sprayed on an analgesic, Ard Matthew tried to get his thoughts in order. The sudden cessation of pain cleared his head a little and he told the other man about the flyer crash and the death of Shami. About contacting Solomon and finding the expedition flyer. About the village and Kessler’s attack on the Kola.

Once or twice the other man put in a question but mostly he listened.

“If these are genuine Neanderthals, then their ancestors must have been transported here by the net in prehistoric times,” he said as he took one more look at the wound in Ard Matthew’s leg. “And it makes sense that their presence would not have been discovered by the few expeditions to the ruins. It is true that this world is mostly unexplored." He gave a wry smile. "Windy-Go has never been anything to anyone except a convenience. Not a homeworld—only a place to make shady deals."

The Lost Rythan nodded. He could hardly argue with this assessment, though he burned with shame when he remembered that it was this very defect that had recommended the planet to him. "About the Neanderthals," he said quickly. "That's what—what Dr. Solomon thought. That they were not found because no one was looking."

"Of course. Who would go looking for a primitive tribe on a world like this? And likely they hadn't done anything that would show from the air. No cities or roads for instance."

"But even so they were here," Ard Matthew said. "They live here."

"And that makes them genuine colonists," the Star Brother agreed. He paused to clean one last bit of the wound before applying synthoskin. "And ipso facto, they own the planet," he added. "But probably you already deduced that?"

"Yes. I thought it must be so. It's the law, isn't it?"

"It's the law, alright. Interstellar law." When the Star Brother had finished, he helped Ard Matthew to sit up.

"You must give me something," the Rythan said earnestly as his head began to swim once more. "I mean I need to get back to them. I've got to stay on my feet. And can you get me a flyer?"

"We'll see," the priest told him. He narrowed his eyes thoughtfully. "I'm not sure you're in any shape to fly back right now even with a stim. But I will contact my superiors at once and get this declared a colony world." He laid a hand on Ard Matthew's arm and tried to force him back down. "In fact, I am already in contact with them."

The Rythan looked at him in surprise. Of course he should have expected something like this, he realized, knowing what he did about how the Star Brothers operated.

The other man smiled slightly. He was a Totwalder, lean and dark, though grizzled slightly with his years of service. Ard Matthew had met one or two of his fellow colonists before and they were earnest folk, not given to levity. Now, the other man raised a reassuring hand. "Not entirely on your account," he said. "You see, I have other business here on Windy-Go—business unconnected with this affair. You could hardly think there were enough people here to warrant a mission, did you?"

"I—I hadn't thought of it," the Rythan said in some confusion. "I mean, I guess I thought the Star Brothers went everywhere."

"We would like to. But we're spread pretty thin." The priest shrugged. "Of course this mission is open to all and there have even been a few, not conversions, but at least reconciliations. It hasn't been wasted." He fixed the Lost Rythan with a sharp glance. "Like your own, I hope. And the woman who brought you here."

At this, Ard Matthew looked around in consternation. "I—I never thanked her," he said. "It was so kind of her to bring me here when I asked. My head wasn't clear, you see—" He faltered to a stop.

"If—when she comes back, I will give her your thanks." The priest stepped over to a basin to wash his hands. "Meanwhile I think your head is clear now?"

"Oh—of course." He flushed. "I am sorry about—before," he said quickly. "That I didn't accept your invitation. To—to visit the church. To stop and have a beer."

"No doubt you had your reasons."

Ard Matthew shook his head. "Not good ones. When I first came to Windy-Go, I was angry. Angry with God." He felt like a criminal admitting this, and even more, like a fool.

The Star Brother nodded. "Would you be surprised if I told you that I know your name? That your Chief Firespear mentioned you to me in one of his communiques?"

"I suppose I shouldn't be." Actually nothing about the Star Brothers should surprise him he realized. "So you are—working with Gaed Alfred?" he asked.

"More or less. I am Father Bauer, by the way. And now as to your friends. My knowing about these 'Neanderthal' colonists changes everything. It was news to me."

"Can you get help to them in time?"

"I hope so. We have our connections." He turned away. "And I should give you speed heal."

Ard Matthew looked at him in confusion. "But how—I mean, what is your real reason for being here?" he asked. "If it wasn't that, I mean."

"Oh well." Father Bauer shrugged. "I've been gathering evidence on a couple of corporations who use this place as a meeting ground. Quite another matter, as I told you, and rather complicated. It involves slavery in one of the colonies, and persecution of the Church on a world far from here. I've about got my investigation wrapped up. They'll come into line." He vouchsafed another thin smile. "Diplomacy. As Chief Firespear would say, I've got the goods on them."

"Yes, that is what he would say." For the first time, Ard Matthew began to realize how very providential his meeting with Father Bauer had been. But then, God's providence was what underlay the universe. He had learned that in school. And then, to his shame, in the face of real suffering, of what he perceived as tragedy, he had let himself forget the lesson entirely. He looked up at the other man.

"Meanwhile," he said, flushing. "That flyer—?"

The Totwalder regarded him for a few moments. "Yes," he said. "I can see where your duty lies. I will give you something first—to strengthen you. But even with force-pills and speed heal for that leg, your body can only take so much. You do understand that, don't you?"

"How soon do you think help can get to them?" he asked, knowing the priest was right about his own limits.

"That is in God's hands, Matthew."

He sighed. Of course the fate of his friends lay in God's hands. Babe and Téna and the mad archaeologist. And the child Kish and all the wonderful people of the forest who might succumb to the casual greed of Kessler Corp. He knew better than to question that now. He gave the priest an anguished look. "Of course," he said. "Sometimes—I forget."

"It may not be as long as you think," Father Bauer said. "I was transmitting from the moment you came to me. Our people already have your story and, as a Faring Guard, your word is enough. They will be acting on it now and the authorities will contact Kessler Corp. Something like this is not negotiable—Kessler must desist immediately or be crushed."

"But how long will that take? Messaging them?"

The Star Brother looked troubled. "A day or two perhaps," he said.

Ard Matthew climbed to his feet, his head spinning so that he had to hold onto the frame of the couch. Sometimes God took people into His hands and used them. This was going to have to be one of those times. "I must get back to them," he said. "I know you see that. And if you have a transmitter that will reach the comm I gave Babe, I'd like to try and contact them."

The other man had already turned away once more. "I think we can manage that," he said, seating himself at a console. His hands played over the keyboard. "Contact code?"

Ard Mathew gave it to him. It had been several hours since his last communication. He remembered Babe saying that the people had taken refuge in the caves once more while a flyer buzzed the entrance. And Babe had given Téna the extra gun, he remembered.

The priest handed him he earphones. Breathlessly he listened as the speaker came to life.

At first there was nothing except a sort of keening sound—interference? And then he thought it was the wind. The storm would have hit the ruins, of course. Was it still raging there?

He tried to calculate how long he had been gone. Hours, it would be, but how many? Had it been late morning when he made his crash landing at the port? Afternoon? What with the storm, it was hard to tell. But he had stolen the flyer at dawn, contacted Babe a couple hours later, and a lot could have happened since then.

"Any luck?" Father Bauer asked and Ard Matthew shook his head.

"But I've got to get back there," he said. He could not put into words his conviction that whatever happened—attack or flight—Babe would not be overpowered as easily as all that. His respect for the other man had been growing steadily as they struggled through Windy-Go's wilderness and he was sure that Babe would protect the Neanderthals to the best of his ability. And Téna. But ranged against all the power of Dr. Kessler and her crew? Two guns and a lot of slings and spears—

Suddenly, picturing Téna to himself, he remembered his mother and how she had once been obliged to kill a wolf that had gone after the goats. How she had wielded an axe after shoving her children behind her as she faced the creature. Ard Matthew had been no more than eight years old, he supposed, and would have taken the weapon himself if she had let him.

But she didn't. And when, later, the menfolk returned from hunting, there was the wolf—and Lost Rythan wolves were much larger than those of other worlds—stretched out in the snow with the bloody axe still embedded in its skull.

But later still, in the clan feuds and the free for all battles of his teens, it would have been unthinkable for a woman to participate. He knew everything was different out here among the stars, but even so, he could not imagine Téna fighting off her kinswomen's henchmen. Hopefully, Babe had given the spare gun to Solomon. But then—

At that point, the static resolved itself into a voice—Babe's voice—and Ard Matthew clutched the speaker with relief. "Babe? What's happening?"

Reception was better than it had been in the flyer and the voice came in clearly. The Star Brother was remarkably well-equipped for a simple priest.

"So you made it!" Babe sounded out of breath.

"Yes. I'm at the port. And you?"

"Okay. For now."

He waited impatiently, almost afraid to ask about the others.

But Babe did not leave him in suspense. "We're all okay," he said. "Really. Only a few wounded. They fired into the tunnels, you know, and that was bad for a while."

He pictured this—beams hitting the stone and bullets ricocheting among the people. Maybe hitting children. "And then?" he asked tensely.

"And then I learned that the Neanderthals could fight after all." A chuckle. "Téna shot at the flyer and, well, she hit something. It had to make a forced landing, actually. Tough luck on the men inside. The Kola were pretty mad when they pulled them out."

Ard Matthew thought of the powerful, craggy faced tribe finally stirred to killing rage. Like Rythans, perhaps.

"So the people have gone under cover now," Babe resumed. "In the tunnels you and I passed through, not the other set. They were afraid, but there was nowhere else to go. For some reason Kessler and her people hadn't found the entrance to those."

"But what about the hallucinogens?"

"I know—and they know. We worked our way around the bad parts. And after that Téna and I went on. We're outside now, on top the overhang where you and I were before."

The whole business sounded risky in the extreme and Ard Matthew could not forbear saying so. What did Babe hope to accomplish?

"Look, Third-Blade, I know what you want to say. Consider it said."

"Sorry."

"So is anyone coming?" Babe demanded. "Did you—you must have got through or you wouldn't be calling me."

Ard Matthew looked over at the Star Brother. "Yes," he said. "I'm told there are."

"My superiors are already in touch with the authorities," the priest said. "Offplanet. There is corruption here, however, and I don't know how much cooperation we can get from the local authorities."

The Rythan knew exactly what the other man meant. Knowing the law and seeing it followed were two very different things on a world like Windy-Go.

"Babe," he said, "help is coming, but not—not right away. Soon. It's complicated."

"There is a ship in the system," Father Bauer said. "I mean a Net Central patrol. They are being notified now, but they have to receive confirmation from their own superiors before they can intervene."

"You hear that, Babe?"

"I heard."

"And I'm coming," the Rythan said with a glance at his host. "Now, I mean. I'll try to get into the tunnels with a transmitter and—" But now that he thought about the matter, he was not sure that he could. If the bad weather continued, he might avoid detection, but on the other hand, he might also crash. It all depended on what sort of equipment the Star Brother could provide.

He looked questioningly at the other man. Luckily, Father Bauer understood at once.

"We keep some things here," he said. "At the port. The authorities don't know they belong to the Star Brothers, of course, but the flyer I can provide you is military grade. It is silent and has some other cloaking features. Unless you are spotted manually, you should be able to get back to the ruins without detection."

Ard Matthew raised one eyebrow. This was stretching things even for a Star Brother.

"Oh," his host said with a small diffident smile, "I'm afraid this is mostly my doing. On my own responsibility, you know. I'm thorough. I wasn't always a priest, I'm afraid." But he didn't say what he had been before and the Rythan didn't ask. Like Faring Guards, Star Brothers often had interesting antecedents and they didn't always talk about them.

"Okay," Babe said. "So far, no one's come into this part of the tunnels. But I don't know how long we have until they figure out that the Kola aren't where they thought they were."

"No." The Rythan wondered what equipment the corporation would have for sniffing them out. But of course they had had no idea of the Neanderthals' existence when they first came into the ruins and might not be prepared to deal with them in any except the most direct ways. Like the poison gas.

"Anyway," Ard Matthew told Babe, "I'm leaving as soon as I can. Meanwhile, the Net Central authorities have been notified and they'll be in touch with the corporation headquarters." He looked at Father Bauer. "Is that right?" he asked.

"Yes. Within hours, I hope, but it may take a day or even more. The people here will be ordered to withdraw as soon as that formality has been achieved."

"Hear that, Babe?"

"I hear. But that doesn't help us much right now. And there will still be a legal fight. An appeal."

The Rythan was not quite sure how these things played out, but it seemed to him that a legal battle on some other world was preferable to a massacre on this one. He said as much to Babe.

"Third-Blade," the other said, "think. What good is a lawsuit if there's no evidence? All she has to do is get rid of the natives. There aren't many of them. This might be the only tribe. And then—as a fait accompli—"

Ard Matthew looked at the priest. "They can't really get away with that, can they?"

The other man frowned. "I don't know," he said. "I have seen worse injustices, Matthew."

For a moment, he felt trapped, stymied by the grim logic of all he knew and had heard about the doings of the starfolk. He was out of his depth and he knew it. "Well we've just got to protect them until help comes," he said at last.

"Yes," the Star Brother agreed. "If they can hold out until the official word goes through then Net Central has to intervene. I'm going to give you a tracer so they can find you as soon as they arrive."

"Okay," Babe told him. "I got that. We'd better cut off for now just in case they pick up our signal."

"Sure—and Boris," Ard Matthew said. "May God protect you."

After that, he had to get ready. And it wasn't long before he discovered that the drugs the priest had given him had their limits. If he was to succeed, it would be a matter of endurance and will.

"I can't give you too many force pills," the other man told him, "without some kind of trade off. You will have to suffer some pain in that leg. It's already coming back, isn't it?"

It was.

"But I will give you concentrate bars to help the speed heal. And—and perhaps you'd better have something you can use as a crutch."

By now the storm—this storm, at least—had abated completely and the late afternoon sun shone in the small windows. They paused to eat and Ard Matthew did justice to several good sized sandwiches and several mugs of beer. It really wasn't too bad, that beer, and the speed heal demanded a lot of calories.

"Now," the priest told him when he had finished, "you must sleep. You can't head out until full dark and we will fetch the flyer at twilight."

"Is it at the port?" He was afraid the Kessler people would we watching out for him.

A headshake. "I keep my things in a large shed further out on this road. It looks tumble down enough, practically a ruin, that it isn't normally disturbed. And I've got safeguards, of course."

And so, despite the force pills—or perhaps because of the beer—Ard Matthew collapsed on a cot and slept for several hours. He was ravenous when he woke and gladly accepted another round of sandwiches and a large bowl of soup.

The sky had cleared and the reddish evening sun was shining down on the snowy fields when he glanced out the window. It wouldn't be long now. He looked over at his host who, he found, was regarding him with some earnestness.

"Uh—Father—"

"Yes, Matthew. I will hear your confession whenever you are ready."

The Rythan looked down. "I have been ready for some time," he said in a low voice. "God knows I am sorry—"

"Yes." The other man made no excuses for him and for this Ard Matthew was grateful. He had failed and he knew it.

Later, when he had spoken of his great anger, his resentment at God's treatment of the child on Ynche and of his friend, Gris Wolfgang, he told about his own dealings with Shami Star Trail and how, by his surly answers, he might have denied her the opportunity for grace she needed. And there were other things as well.

He knelt afterwards by the altar in the small chapel, wondering as he always did, that even here among the stars, so far from his homeworld, the Lord waited. That the sanctuary light was lit as it was everywhere that Christian men had come. Everywhere.

Finally, he rose from his knees, almost crying out with the pain of his wounded leg. It had stiffened just in that short time and was likely to stiffen more. Even with speed heal, he wasn't going to run any races. He picked up the cane which was all Father Bauer had been able to find for him, and limped out of the church and back to the house. It was time to go.

The return flight to the ruins was going to take less time than the trip to the port thanks to the Star Brother's machine. Small and compact—a tight squeeze for a Lost Rythan—the flyer was everything he might have dreamed of piloting. He hadn't known such a wonderful device existed. He accepted the loan along with the priest's blessing, with an abashed sort of gratitude.

Once aloft, he flew low again, skimming the tops of the forest, using sensors instead of lights. In the starlight, the snowy landscape made ghost shadows beneath reminding him of the wendigo. But he could see nothing in the treetops as he passed by.

Before him on the panel, the area was mapped out in a pale, greenish grid. Soon, it looked like he was already one fourth of the way to his destination. Gingerly, he shifted his position in the cramped seat. Would his leg hold up? He supposed that would depend on what he found when he arrived—on what he needed to do.

His host had armed him well and once more he was left marveling at the man's foresight. He was quite sure Father Bauer must have been a soldier before he became a priest—perhaps a mercenary? A pity he didn't dare ask.

It was time to check in with Babe. He called him on the flyer's set, and waited. But this time there was no answer. Nothing but static. Had Babe and Téna taken cover beneath the rock? Was that the reason that there was no reception? But that hadn't mattered before. And now there should at least have been something.

He tried the hand unit. Static again. An empty line. Something must have happened! At once he imaged all the possible mishaps—poison gas, robots, a firefight. Capture.

And then he forced himself to calm down. There could be many more innocuous reasons why he got no answer. Babe might have turned the thing off. He and Téna could have climbed down and gone to look out at the main camp. He hoped not. But they might.

He would try again later.

Again he moved in his seat. The leg still pained him plenty and there was no room to stretch it out. He must bear it. Trying to distract himself, he called Father Bauer to report his location and the fact that he had lost touch with Babe.

"Just keep trying," the priest said. "Likely they have moved their position as you say."

He signed off and began the Rosary. No sense wasting time. He forced himself to pray all the mysteries, taking his time as he flew over the forest. Slowly he began to calm down.

According to Babe, Kessler's other flyer had crashed. Or rather Téna had shot it down. Now they were waiting for reinforcements from the port. And, he reminded himself, so far as Kessler knew, he, Ard Matthew was still afoot—or even dead—somewhere in the port city. They would not be expecting him.

But even so, he would take no chances. It was his plan to drop silently into the open area where the tribe had waited when they first emerged into the ruins. If what Babe had told him was true, and Kessler still did not know about the tunnel system beneath, then with no flyer available, the place would not be watched.

But of course he could not be sure. The machine he piloted was equipped with the latest in sensors and he used these to scan not only the area below him but also the sky above—just in case. Nothing. Even if someone was down there, he knew he would be practically invisible as he eased lower and let himself glide down onto the stone.

At the last minute, he pulled up. There was something in his path. Belatedly, he recognized it as the crashed flyer. The one Babe had told him about. He drifted above the wreckage and came down at last on the other side. Silence. Darkness. No spark of light anywhere.

Slowly he eased open the cockpit and let himself down onto the snow-covered pavement. He could not suppress a small sound as he put weight on his injured leg, but he must endure it. He peered around him, gun in hand, trying to make no more noise. Nothing.

Nor, as a Rythan, did he feel the warning he might have felt at the approach of danger—though that sixth sense, he thought grimly, was not always reliable. He waited, counting to one hundred. Still nothing.

At last he relaxed. Took one step—and nearly stumbled to the ground. With one hand he grasped the rim of the flyer and pulled himself back. The cane—he had to find the cane. He felt around in the flyer until, after a moment, he pulled the thing out. It wasn't much of a crutch, but it was all he had.

Gritting his teeth, he set off in the direction of the cave—the one that led beneath the ruins. He still did not dare risk a light. His progress was slow and he wasn't even sure he could find the entrance as he kept reaching out with his gun hand to feel for the wall, bracing himself with the cane in the other.

And then he remembered that Father Bauer had given him more than weapons. He paused, propping himself with the cane, and reached into his pocket. Goggles. He slipped them on and his surroundings took on a reddish glow. It wasn't much but after the darkness, it was everything. He saw the stone no more than a pace or two in front of him. Now to find the entrance.

For the first time, he realized that he was shivering. A cold wind blew down off the ruins, and the jacket the priest had given him—too short in the sleeves—did little to protect him. Trying to ignore his discomfort, he limped to the wall and began to follow it. He had no idea how far out of his way he might have gone before he remembered to put on the goggles.

Luckily, he found the opening with his hand even before he saw it. Reholstering the gun, he dragged himself inside. Here, at least, he might use the torch at his belt. He set it on low and moved further in. It didn't look like anything had changed. There was the crude map on the wall and he went over immediately to study it. Where would the people have hidden themselves? But the map gave no clue.

Anyway, it was Babe he must find. Babe and Téna. And he knew the way to the secret entrance to the upper ruins. He had traversed it twice now—actually four times if he counted each trip there and back. But before he took that way—and it still filled him with remembered dread—he had to stop and eat a couple of ration bars. The speed heal was making him hungry, even though the pain in his leg was almost sickening. At least he was out of the wind, he thought, as he chewed and swallowed the tough food. One small blessing.

At last he had to admit that he was stalling. Though the thought of one more journey through those tunnels chilled him even more than the air of the cave, he simply must go in, risking the hallucinogenic spores in the air. What if he should be trapped, entangled in his hellish nightmares? What if he could not get out?

But he knew he had to get to the others. It was up to him to safeguard them until help came. He wore a beacon disguised beneath a bandage on one wrist and this would guide in the troopers when they came. And they would come. The Star Brothers would see to that.

But when?

It was no use thinking such things. He swallowed the last of a ration bar and turned resolutely to the back of the cave. Once more he traversed the way, ducking where he must, moving more slowly than he had the first two times because of his leg. He used the cane where he could though he had to be careful of stones and runnels of icy water on the rocky floor. If he should fall, he might not be able to get up and keep going.

As he neared the place where he and Babe had once had to dig an opening, his worst fears seemed realized. He smelled the fungus in the passageway, coming from the mouth of the descending tunnel and shuddered, trying to hold his breath as he hurried by. If it had spread into the other passage, he was out of luck.

It had. Maybe the things were blooming—or whatever they did. Maybe the beginning of winter had set them off. He didn't know, but the smell was all-pervading. He pulled up the collar of his jacket, trying to cover his nose and mouth, and plunged in. His only hope was to keep climbing as quickly as he could and come out above it.

He struggled upward, taking the now familiar way. It seemed to him he almost didn't need the torch. Indeed, there was a shimmer on the walls—he could see it when he looked behind him. But after a time, things moved there, spectral in the strange glow, haunting.

"But this time I am in a state of grace," he told himself firmly, wondering where the thought had come from. And, though he grew somewhat light-headed, there was no return of the terrible visions he had had before. He just might make it!

And then, without warning, something emerged from an aperture on the side—something that cast a wavering shadow in the light of his hand torch. He had no time to draw the gun, no time to do more than drop the cane as he was grabbed by clawlike hands. He was dragged to one knee, his bad leg collapsing under him as he swung the torch at the thing and felt it connect. No specter then! He grasped it by the throat and pulled it down.

"Third-Blade! You're real!" The voice was Solomon's.

Immediately he let go. In the light of the torch which had rolled away and was now lighting up one wall, the other man was no more than a shadowy silhouette, both hands raised to his throat where Ard Matthew had throttled him.

"What are you doing here?" the Rythan demanded. "Where are the others?'

"Down in the bowels of the earth," the archaeologist said solemnly. "Down in the womb of the mother."

"Below us?"

A shrug.

If they had taken the lower tunnel, they would be psychotic by now. He shook his own head, trying to clear it. "And you?" he asked.

"Oh, I'm the watchman. They left me here."

"Who did? Babe?"

The other man picked up the torch and began shining it on the ceiling. "He said to wait for his friend—you, I think. I was going to but then I followed them and—and she made them fast." He chuckled softly. "But they didn't get me. No one saw me!"

"Are you talking about Boris? And Téna?"

But Solomon was busy making hand shadows on the wall. He seemed not to hear the question.

Ard Matthew bit off an oath. He raised himself painfully and reached for the archaeologist. He wanted to shake the other man, but only pulled him closer. "Who," he said, spacing his words, "made—who—fast? What are you talking about?"

Solomon looked at him in surprise. "Some men. They seemed to know Babe."

This didn't sound good.

"So Téna and Boris are prisoners?"

A solemn nod. The light jittered and Ard Matthew let go of the other man. That was a mistake.

With a broken laugh, Solomon leaped to his feet and ran away down the passage, leaving Ard Matthew alone in the darkened tunnel.

"Come back!" he shouted, scrambling around for his cane. "Come back!"

But the light faded away and was lost around a bend in the corridor.

CHAPTER FIFTEEN

He was alone in the dark. For a few moments, that was the only thing he knew. He was alone in the tunnel beneath the ruins and not at all sure that he could even walk.

Slowly his mind cleared as he thrust the rising panic back into its dark place. He was long past the zone of the hallucinogens, at least. Past even the hint of their strange odor—or at least he hoped so. But how could he be sure? the voice of returning panic demanded. In the utter blackness, his mind was already sketching images on the void and he was afraid that if he called for Solomon, he might find himself screaming instead.

He closed his eyes and the darkness did not change. But he felt safer somehow, locked within himself. He drew his body together, hunched against the side of the tunnel. He needed to form a plan. But then another thought came to him—which side of the tunnel was he on? Which way had Solomon gone? What if he tried to follow and went the wrong way? What if there was a turning he had not noticed before and he really lost himself in the depths of the ruins?

But the truth was that when it came to following—or even trying to follow—Solomon, he had little hope that he could. He could not even locate the cane and without it, he knew he would have to crawl. Bracing himself once more, he groped around, finally opening his eyes onto the same stygian night—a night that still pressed in on him, crushing him. He bit his lip and persevered. Reach, slide over, turn, reach again. But the cane was nowhere to be found.

Once more panic threatened to take over and he fought it down. But the attack was followed by a dull despair. He had failed his friends. They were in trouble if what Solomon hinted was true. What mercy could Téna expect from Dr. Kessler who had already tried to kill her once? Or Babe?

And then quite suddenly, out of the darkness, a new thought came to him. I am in a state of grace. And along with that came the reminder of his duty. He was a Faring Guard. No longer a fugitive from God, no longer a fool with a grudge. He must and would succeed because that is what a Faring Guard did.

At this, he began to think more clearly. How far had he come along this tunnel? The final stretch before the cave of the stalagmites—it sloped downward and then upward. Had he begun to climb? He didn't think so. Once more he tried to orient himself, reaching backward to the stone wall, bracing with his legs stretched out before him. If it was too painful to walk, then he really would crawl. But which way?

There was no way to be certain, but he thought Solomon had run to his right when he broke away. And, having the torch, he probably was going in the right direction—the way to the camp. But then, after Solomon had gone, he had sat against the opposite wall which meant that he would have to move leftward. Probably.

Despite the chill in the place, he felt the sweat running down his forehead. It was best not to think ahead too much. One bit at a time. *Spera in Deo*. The Star Brothers had taught him that long ago when he and his brother had been altar boys. Hope in God. It was in the blessed tongue of Old Earth, the Motherworld.

"*Spera in Deo*," he muttered under his breath and, dragging his bad leg behind him, he inched his way along the passage. Hope in God. It was a prayer. All that—the words of the Mass and everything else he had ever learned from the Star Brothers. These things were prayers to shape his life, to bind him to God. That, he thought, was what prayer really meant. Hands reaching out to God and God's own Hands reaching back in the darkness. And somehow that realization seemed more real than the night that surrounded him, more solid than the great weight of stone above.

But when the gloom gave way to what could only have been the faintest of illumination, the shock of it caused him to cry out. A moment later he was blinded by light and a hand touched him from behind. Doubling himself around, he grasped the arm and would have broken it had it been the arm of an ordinary man. But what he held was as strong as a tree root, hairy and rippling with muscle. He heard a grunt.

"Who—?"

"Zhonsoman?"

And then he knew this was one of the tribesmen. He relaxed as two of them came up with him, their shadowed, deep-eyed faces solemn as they studied him in the light of the torches they carried.

"Thank God," he said, still blinking, and meant it. He had never been so glad to see anyone in his life. "Solomon is up ahead. He's got my torch." Belatedly he remembered that they could probably not understand more than a word of two of Basic.

He pointed in the direction he was going. "Solomon," he said.

One of the Neanderthals peered ahead and nodded. "Zhonsoman," he agreed.

"We've got to catch up with him," Ard Matthew said, but he knew it was useless to speak to them in Basic. He could only hope the pair would help him for their own reasons. He reached out to the stone and tried to pull himself to his feet. Almost at once his leg gave way and for a moment he had to clench his teeth and wait for the pain to subside into something bearable.

One of the tribesmen looked at the bandage. Luckily Father Bauer had put on synthoskin and there was no bleeding despite his exertions. The wound was healing at its own rate, he told himself, though he was probably not doing it any good. But whether he tore it open or not, he had to get up.

The others must have understood this. One of them handed his torch to his companion and squatted down to lay both hands on Ard Matthew's leg. The Rythan had no idea what he was doing as moments passed and the pressure continued. But while the pain did not diminish, he felt a new warmth spreading from the touch of the other's hands. It was impossible, of course, and contradicted everything he had been taught about science.

Looking down at the shaggy head of his benefactor, he smiled a little and let all his science go. He was, after all, a Lost Rythan, and his people had never lived by theories but only by what they heard and saw. So be it.

The Neanderthal let go finally and stood up. Reaching out one hand, he pulled Ard Matthew to his feet and the leg held. It was still not good, but it held. He saw them both looking at him, their brows wrinkled, their faces otherwise expressionless and he nodded. He would walk.

But even so, each step was an effort that left him trembling and sweating. Soon one of the others had to help him. He leaned on the man, hunching over because of his greater height, and tried to take as much weight as he could on his good leg. The tunnel was definitely climbing now—they must be nearing the final turn. One of the torches was put out and he squinted ahead into the darkness looking for the telltale sign of the greater, mechanical light Solomon carried. But there was no sign of it.

Had the man climbed out of the cave of stalagmites? Had he been captured? Would Kessler's men be waiting for them? He turned to his companions wondering if they would know. Could they sense danger? His own sixth sense told him nothing, but then maybe that was because he was wounded and suffering from exhaustion.

Both Neanderthal faces, now even more deeply shadowed, still expressionless, looked back at him. "I think," he said aloud, "I had better go ahead without the light."

Neither responded. Of course they wouldn't. They didn't understand his words. He released his hold on the one who had been helping him along and pointed first to himself and then to the tunnel ahead. "Wait," he said and began to creep forward.

Hands on the wall, one foot before the other. He was already learning to ignore the pain. He concentrated on the darkness ahead. Still no least flicker of light. He came to the turning, felt the wall before him, worked his way around the obstruction.

And then he heard something. Voices. Or rather one voice. Some one—Solomon?—was talking in Basic. Speaking softly and—answering himself? It was eerie.

"They won't drink our blood. Not here.

How do you know?

No trees for them. No wind.

They can be silent.

Not here I tell you! We are in the womb. You know about the womb. Every world is a mother."

No doubt he was talking about the wendigo, working out his fears. Ard Matthew resumed his silent approach, using the skills he had learned as a hunter back on his homeworld. He was breathing through his mouth, silently, listening as he approached his quarry.

But the murmuring had stopped. He could no longer hear the other man.

Once more, he paused. He didn't want to stumble over the mad archaeologist in the dark. Was he still ahead? Or had he gone on?

And then, quite clearly, "They put their beaks in your flesh. They drink until you die." The words came from directly in front of him, closer than he had expected.

Without stopping to think, he pounced, throwing his weight on the lesser man as he grappled, seizing one flailing arm, avoiding the ragged nails that would have raked his face. There was a sudden scream.

"It's me, Solomon," he said. "The pilot. You're okay. I won't let them get you."

For a moment, the other continued to struggle, shrieking mindlessly.

With an effort that left him scratched and bleeding, Ard Matthew got a grip on Solomon and pinned his flailing arms. With his other hand, he covered the man's mouth. "Easy," he said. "You're safe."

The archaeologist subsided and Ard Matthew took his hand away.

"You?" Solomon said hoarsely. "The pilot?"

"That's right. You remember. You took the light and ran away." Though the other relaxed slightly in his grip, he did not trust him enough to let go. "Now what did you do with it? The torch? Where is it?"

"I was—afraid to use it here," the other said and the Rythan could feel him trembling. "They might have seen me!"

"We're safe enough out in the passage. There's no crack in the ceiling until we get into the cave at the end."

"No, no. Not them. The wendigo."

Ard Matthew knew it would do no good to tell him the wendigo couldn't get into the tunnels. He would have to play along with Solomon's delusions.

"Oh sure," he said. "The wendigo. But we'll take care of that. Don't worry. We're not afraid of it."

Behind him, the flickering torchlight light approached around the bend as the Neanderthals came up to join him. "Zhonsoman," one of them said and addressed the archaeologist in the language of the Kola.

Solomon was answering them. To Ard Matthew's relief, he sounded rational enough that he dared release his hold. Though of course there was no way to tell what the man was actually saying, he thought wryly.

After a moment he spied his torch lying on the stone near where he had tackled the madman. He reached over and picked it up before turning back to his erstwhile prisoner. "Are you alright now?" he asked as he returned the torch to his belt.

A nod. The Neanderthals were looking at him. If only he could tell what they were thinking. But he couldn't. He must do the best he could, however.

"Solomon, I've got to know what happened to Téna and Babe," he said slowly. "You started to tell me, but—but I did not understand all that you said. Can you tell me where they are?"

Another nod. Ard Matthew eased himself down onto the tunnel floor, biting back a groan as he stretched out his leg. "You said they were captured," he began. "Now I need to know what happened."

"Oh yes, they are captured. Her—minions. I saw. We were up there." he pointed to the roof above. "But I was behind the stone. They didn't see me."

He probably meant the stone doorway in the chamber above the one with the stalagmites. The stone that looked like a barrier unless you got really close to it. Likely they had not explored enough to realize it was a doorway. Why should they? It was plain there were not many guards and they were afraid of the ruins. Or rather of the Kola.

He turned back to Solomon. "So then what happened?" he prompted when the other seemed to hesitate.

"They used a—I'm not sure what it's called. It slowed them down. Slowed their breathing, made them—not move. Not react. It was—horrible."

"Incapacitator, I think," Ard Matthew said. He had heard of the device though never suffered its effects. It wasn't supposed to be fatal, just disabling. But it was news to him that Kessler had such a sophisticated weapon on hand. He wondered what else he would have to look out for.

"Then they came and got them," Solomon went on. "Some men. They knew Babe. I think he used to work with them. Is he a criminal?"

Ard Matthew didn't answer this. If Babe worked for Kessler, then he could hardly be considered anything else. "Go on," he said to Solomon.

"They joked a little. One of them was looking at Téna but I couldn't see her very well. He said he was sorry they couldn't get better acquainted. But I could see Babe's face when the man said that. He was trying to get up, but he couldn't. I think he wanted to kill the guy."

That seemed likely, Ard Matthew thought grimly.

"Then they came over to him and one of them laughed. 'This is gonna be good," he said. 'I can't wait 'til she sees you, Babe. She didn't believe us when we told her you were alive.'"

Solomon paused so long that the Rythan was afraid he had lost his train of thought. "So the guards," he prodded, "knew Babe?"

The other man blinked at him. The Rythan could almost see him retrieving his thoughts. And then, "Oh—the guards. They don't matter."

He frowned and put one hand to his head. "But I saw her. I think she is a monster. That woman—"

Ard Matthew took a moment to sort this out. "Do you mean Kessler?" he asked. "From all I've heard, she most certainly is. But obviously, she didn't see you. So what did she do?"

This seemed to confuse the archaeologist and he blinked for a moment as though not sure where he was.

Quickly, Ard Matthew tried to regain control of the situation. "You saw Dr. Kessler," he said slowly. "Can you tell me what she was doing when you saw her? Can you remember?"

Solomon gave him a dreamy look, his gaze moving to the tribesmen who waited patiently while the others spoke. "There were two people with her," he said finally. "A man and a woman. 'That will be enough, Faber,' she told the guard." Solomon paused for a few moments. "I guess that was his name," he said. "Faber."

"Right. So Dr. Kessler said this? She just showed up and took charge?" He really didn't know which situation would have been worse for the captives, but he definitely feared the outcome of this one. "What happened then?" he asked.

Once more there was a long pause while the archaeologist peered out into the shadows as though he still thought there might be a wendigo in the tunnel. But then he rallied and turned back to the Rythan.

"I saw Babe struggling. He's a killer, isn't he? I mean you get that feeling about him. Like that's the kind of man he is." Solomon, who was most definitely not a killer, nodded his head and went on. "Mr. Third-Blade," he said, "I don't think that woman will survive. I think she will be killed."

For a moment, the other man was confused. Then, "Do you mean Dr. Kessler?"

Solomon nodded.

The Rythan grunted. "Not by Babe," he said. "I'm more afraid of what will happen to him and Téna." He frowned. "So what happened then?"

"Well they gave them stim and then they could sit up. Dr. Kessler said she was glad it was them making trouble for her and not a rival corporation. And she mentioned you. The pilot."

"Me?"

"She said she thought you were wounded and they would have you soon. She said you stole a flyer."

"Well I did," he admitted. "I'm afraid it crashed." But he was thinking furiously as he spoke to Solomon. So Kessler knew he had reached the port but apparently she did not know about the Star Brother. Probably she thought Ard Matthew was still there, hiding among the warehouses while her men hunted for him.

"After that she asked about someone named Shami and Téna said she was dead."

Ard Matthew winced thinking of the secretary's death. "Yes," he said. "But she is responsible for that. Dr. Kessler, I mean. She tried to murder us all."

"So she is a criminal," Solomon said, nodding his head. "I thought she must be."

"And then?" the Rythan pressed. "What else did she say?"

The archaeologist shrugged. "So Téna asked her what she was going to do with her and Babe but she didn't say exactly. She did say she didn't suppose Téna would shed any tears if she got rid of Babe."

Considering the friction that had been between Babe and Téna, this was an obvious conclusion. But it was, in his opinion, a false one. Much had happened since Téna saw her kinswoman last. Now could that be put to use—?

But Solomon was speaking again. "After that she said, 'Come on, girl. I'm not going to kill you. What do you take me for? You'll still have a place in the corporation when this operation's over.' And 'Just let bygones be bygones and chalk it up to experience.'"

"They are not," Solomon added, "nice people. In the corporations."

Ard Matthew had to agree they were not. And he wouldn't give much for Téna's chances of survival if she were stupid enough to believe her kinswoman. But Téna wasn't stupid. He was sure of that. "So what did Dr. Kessler do then?" he asked. "Where are they now?"

"Well she talked about making a fortune on some phessite but she said they had to tidy things up first. Téna asked her what that meant and she said they had to get rid of the people—the Kola. Only she didn't call them people and she didn't know where they were."

The Rythan looked at him. "Do you think she has any idea they are in the ruins below her?"

The archaeologist frowned. Talking about the threat to the Neanderthals seemed to clear his mind. They were, after all, his saviors. "I'm not sure," he said. "She seemed to think Babe and Téna knew where they were. She told one of her people to fetch in someone named Sam. She said he was a modified android and he would persuade Babe that a quick death would be better than a slow one."

Ard Matthew groaned. "What did Babe say?" he asked, fearing to hear the answer.

"He laughed at her."

"So this—this android," the Rythan said, his voice showing his distaste. "What did it do?"

"Oh—that. Well it never showed up. Some lady came in with a message instead. Whatever it was, she was upset. Dr. Kessler, I mean. She told the guards to lock Babe and Téna in one of the storage units and left."

He could guess at the contents of the message. Probably it was an order from Net Central to desist and evacuate her party from the area. At least he hoped that's what it was. If his message had had the effect it should have, the authorities would have no choice except to step in and open an investigation.

"So she put them in one of the storage lockers?"

"That's what she said."

"Then we'll have to find them," Ard Matthew told him. But he had no idea how he was to do that. He glanced over at the two tribesmen. Obviously, he would need Solomon to translate for him. So far the man seemed to be doing alright, but the Rythan knew very well that his mental clarity could not be relied on for long.

Suddenly the archaeologist looked up at him and he thought, here it comes. He's losing it now.

"Dr. Kessler didn't know," Solomon said with a suddenness that was unnerving. "But I saw—I heard."

Ard Matthew blinked. "What did you see?" he asked, wondering where this was going. "What didn't she know?"

"She didn't hate him after all. And he—" The other man shrugged.

The Rythan was now totally at sea. "Who didn't hate whom?" he asked.

"Those two. Babe and Téna. I thought she was—that you—all that," Solomon said with a shrug. "But after you were gone, when she shot down the flyer, they had stopped quarrelling."

Understanding at last, Ard Matthew gave him a rueful smile. He had already guessed that Babe's feelings for Téna were not those of a company hit man for a nice bit of female flesh. That Babe ran deeper than that. As for Téna, he could not have said for sure. He had no illusions that she harbored any romantic feelings for himself, though she seemed to offer him goodwill. But beyond his duty to protect both Téna and Babe, he had never thought of her in any special way.

He did not consider himself romantic, though he enjoyed female company. But what few adventures he had had along those lines had invariably involved nothing but regret and shame. But that was only to be expected of a Faring Guard pledged to celibacy—

And now here was Solomon looking at him with a half smirk that brought the hot blood to his cheeks. He shook his head. "Right," he said briskly. "And it's a good thing Dr. Kessler never caught on." Which was an understatement. He didn't even want to imagine what she would have done if she had discovered that particular weakness in her former henchman. Would she have tortured Téna to make Babe reveal the location of the Neanderthals? Of course.

And would Babe have told her?

He gave a shrug. Who could say?

"She's going to gas the tunnels just in case," Solomon said with one of his unnerving jumps from non sequitur to non sequitur. "Even if she doesn't know where the people are. The guards were talking about it. 'Gonna gas the slopeheads,' they said. 'One way or another, we'll get rid of them.'"

The Rythan looked at him in consternation. "Which tunnels? Where?" he demanded. "She doesn't know how we got in."

But Solomon couldn't answer that.

Once more he looked at the tribesmen. He would have to get into the corporation camp, and soon. But could he now? Sure he had done it before, but they would be more watchful now—and there was his bad leg. "Solomon," he said. "I've got to talk to these guys." He indicated the Neanderthals.

"Okay."

He eased himself back against the tunnel wall, and reached down to massage the bandage on his thigh. He could use the leg, he realized. If he must. And he would do it. But would he be quick enough to succeed in what he needed to do? Could he prevent Kessler from killing the tribesmen before help arrived?

He turned to Solomon. "Ask them why they are here," he said indicating the Neanderthals. "Did they come from—from wherever you left the rest of the tribe?"

Solomon turned to the Kola and began to speak in their high-pitched tongue.

As he spoke, the response took Ard Matthew by surprise. Both looked at him and those looks were full of a mixture of determination and intelligence. One of them spoke while the other nodded and put in a word or two. When they had finished, Solomon translated.

"It is our place," the archaeologist said and even the tone of his voice was different as he spoke. He might have been another man. "From the beginning, it is ours and the marks of our people's shaping are on it. The floors have been worn by our footprints from the dawn of our time. The walls breathe with our breath. We are the Kola and this is ours!"

Ard Matthew stared at them in surprise. "He said that? Ask them if they know about the phessite," he said.

There was a brief exchange before the other man translated.

"The stone of power shines like leaves in early summer. It is sacred."

At this, he realized he had never seen phessite in its raw state before. Was it radioactive? Dangerous? He couldn't remember ever hearing that it was. But these people were familiar with it and that was another shock. They must have known all along that it was here, though not, of course, that it was valuable.

But they were speaking again and he must let these speculations wait for another time. When the two had finished, Solomon turned to him again. "Apparently," he said, "there is more phessite here than Kessler Corporation knows. Deeper beneath the ruins. Whole caverns of it. Or so they say."

The Rythan fervently hoped that both Solomon and the Kola would keep this secret permanently. Even with the law on their side, such a temptation would almost certainly be too much for Net Central and anyone they sent here. Just the portion of the treasure Kessler had located was creating enough problems for the Neanderthals.

Was there some way to make sure they knew this? That continued secrecy was their only hope of survival as a race? He didn't dare to say anything to the two tribesmen now—not with Solomon translating. What guarantee was there that the madman might not talk about it later?

If he ever got back to the tribe, though, Ard Matthew would talk to the girl—Lish. Maybe he could make her understand the danger they were all in. He indicated the waiting Neanderthals.

"Do they have any clue as to how valuable it is?" he asked. "The phessite Kessler found?"

Solomon looked at him. "What is value?" he asked. "To them it is the spirit of the sun on the leaves. Lish told me."

He felt as though he had been struck. Looking over at the half shadowed Neanderthal faces, it was as though he had stepped—not onto higher ground exactly, though that might have been the case—but into a world his own people had once inhabited. One they still visited in the wolf hunt or when they climbed Lost Rythar's volcanic peaks. He had been away among the stars so long, he had almost forgotten the clean purity of his ancestral hearth—the innocence.

"Of course," he said, looking down in confusion. "Of course."

When he dared look up again, he met those deep and shadowed eyes and once more knew them for kinsmen, however divided they all might be by race and time and the cold deeps of space. "Of course."

Then, to Solomon, "Do they know about the gas?"

But the archaeologist's mind had wandered off once more and when he looked up, there was no understanding in his expression. "Are you sure," he said in a quavering voice, "that the wendigo cannot come here?"

Ard Matthew sighed. "I killed some of them, Solomon," he said patiently. "You can trust me to do it again if they come."

There was no reply. The other man was curling up, drawing himself into a fetal position. He made an inarticulate sound and put his thumb in his mouth.

The taller of the tribesmen looked at him for a moment and then reached over to pull the hand away. He said something in his own language.

Solomon did not respond.

When it became plain that he either wouldn't or couldn't, the Neanderthal came over and set both hands on Solomon's shoulders. Ard Matthew was reminded of how they had treated his leg when he thought he could not walk and he watched the archaeologist curiously.

After a time, Solomon whimpered and sat up. "Go away," he said fretfully.

But the other man didn't and, under his patient pressure, Solomon finally blinked and seemed to snap out of his funk. At least Ard Matthew hoped so. He still needed the man's help. "The gas," he repeated. "Do the Kola know about the gas?"

"How would I explain something like that?"

The Rythan sighed and turned to the other two. "These people—the evil ones," he said, striving to reach them. "They will send poison into the ground. Into the tunnels. You must tell your people. You must warn them."

Solomon translated.

When he had finished, the pair looked at Ard Matthew, but did not say anything. And even if they had understood, what was there to say? Obviously, the Neanderthals would have to vacate the ruins, but if they did, where would they go? Where would they be safe?

Then one of the pair spoke up and the Rythan could tell by his tone that there was not going to be any running away. When he had finished, Solomon translated.

"He says this is a place of the people. He says the newcomers will not have it. He says they are evil spirits and they are not welcome here."

Ard Matthew sighed. "Can't you make them understand that these people will kill them all? They will spare no one. Kessler wants them all dead and if she is to secure the phessite, that is how it will have to be."

Solomon blinked at him and translated this speech. As he spoke, the Rythan watched in vain for some facial expression he could decipher. He tried again.

"Tell them, Dr. Kessler thinks they are animals. They are in her way and she will kill them as I would kill a wolf—or a wendigo."

Solomon looked up in alarm at the word, and the Rythan could have bitten his tongue. But before he could try to say anything to reassure the man, Solomon turned to the others and translated what Ard Matthew had said. At least the Rythan hoped he had. And this time there was a reaction.

The other of the two—he wished he knew their names—reached for a stone axe and pulled it from his belt. He spoke for some time, indicting the rock ceiling above their heads. Finally he subsided and Solomon was left to render his words into Basic.

"This is their holy place," he said. "And they are not animals. They will not be driven forth by ghosts and demons from the stars." The native looked hard at Ard Matthew while Solomon was speaking. "He told of the many generations of his people, the memories they have passed on from the beginning of time. I think," he added conversationally, "they really do remember Earth. I have been listening to their stories—"

"They remember Earth? But that's fifty thousand years ago."

"They don't think of time the way we do."

Once more that jolt. Ard Matthew looked at Solomon in consternation—in awe almost. Had he dared to think he understood the Kola just because his own people lived by traditions and memories of their ancestors? By what stretch of egotism did he presume to sail upon the millennia as they had? Rythar had not been settled more than a few thousand years—maybe less. But these people—

Yet he must not think of that now. He pulled himself together knowing that his task was to persuade these men that they stood no chance against the modern weapons of the corporation. That they would be swept aside by those who really did see them as no more than vermin.

But what could he say to them?

As he looked at the Neanderthals and they looked back at him, implacably it seemed now, he knew there was nothing he could do. It was an impasse. If help did not come in time, the Kola were doomed.

CHAPTER SIXTEEN

Ard Matthew was not one to waste time on the impossible. If the Neanderthals refused to flee, then he must find another way to foil Kessler's plans. He never stopped to question whether he could do this; he only took it for granted that he must. It was the next part that was a little harder—deciding what to do and how to go about it.

"We'd better get up above," he said to Solomon. That was the first step, of course.

Whether it was the ministrations of the Neanderthals, the speed heal or just adrenaline, he found it easier to get to his feet this time. The pain was still there but it was manageable. Father Bauer had wrapped and sealed the wound well and he could only hope the synthoskin was beginning to knit itself fast. Though he should, he remembered with a guilty start, be eating more if he expected the speed heal to work properly. In the excitement, he had not felt any hunger. But that, too, must wait.

He directed the torch toward the tunnel ahead. They were not far from the cave of the stalagmites. Solomon pressed on at his side and he was aware of the tribesmen behind him, their gentle breath and nearly soundless footsteps reminding him of the hunting companions of his youth. As they moved in among the crazy stone forest, he doused the light. Above, the familiar crack in the ceiling very faintly illuminated the chamber with lines of light and shadow.

He circled the stone walls and soon located the first of the familiar red arrows, though in the dim light, they looked black. Soon he reached the narrow chimney that led to the upper chamber. And, as it had done before—twice, in fact—the jagged rock scraped the skin from his arms as he wriggled upward. He had to use his shoulders more this time since he could not put any weight on his bad leg. Consequently he took most of the strain in his arms. Below him, someone boosted him up—he thought it was one of the tribesmen and was grateful. The light was better here, coming from a wider break in the roof and this helped him to find what handholds were available.

Once above, he soon located the doorway, hidden by its false barrier of stone, and headed toward it. One of the Neanderthals slipped in front of him and disappeared around the slab. After a moment, the man returned, saying something in his own language which Ard Matthew assumed meant that the way was clear. He followed and emerged into the familiar daylit passage.

Moving cautiously, they gained the open parapet and looked down. In the evening light—for the day was far gone—he spotted three guards moving nervously about and peering at the walls of the ruins. None looked up in his direction and by this he knew that their entryway must not have been discovered. Were there perhaps other entrances down there? Other tunnels? The place might be honeycombed with them.

At this point, one of the tribesmen pulled back from the edge and slipped away. The Rythan did not try to stop him. Hopefully he was reporting back to his chief. Hopefully. Ard Matthew was still afraid for the Kola, afraid they did not—could not—understand the powers that would be brought against them. But he had done all he could and now he must trust in whatever intelligence and common sense had preserved the tribe for all those long millennia. What else could he do?

Suddenly he felt a rage rising within him at the thought of Lish and her brother dying to suit the convenience—the greed—of the corporation. Of the casualness with which they would be dispatched. And of their helplessness in the face of modern technology.

But at least he, Ard Matthew Third-Blade wasn't helpless, he reminded himself. The first thing he needed to do was to take out these guards just as he and Babe had done to the others before. And this time, he had fewer qualms about the matter. But for this, he and the remaining tribesman—and maybe Solomon—would have to work together.

Then came the first halt. For he was remembering the Sacrament he had received back at the port and realized he didn't want to kill anyone if he could help it. Even now, knowing that these were enemies and the minions of an archenemy, it seemed a terrible thing to take the lives of these men by stealth. He beckoned Solomon back from the parapet and told him this.

"Is there another way down?" he asked.

Solomon addressed the remaining tribesman and a whispered conversation ensued. Presently, the man beckoned them back to the way they had come. He didn't stop at the tunnel entrance but continued along the curving wall. After a time, Matthew saw that a rift of deeper shadow was indeed such another crack as the one through which they had emerged.

This time the space was so cramped that he feared his giant frame would not fit. But he turned himself sideways and, fighting down an attack of claustrophobia, began to descend a flight of shallow stairs—stairs he would have sworn were not meant for human feet any more than the space allowed was meant for human girth. Here and there, the stone cracked beneath his tread, crumbling away in bits as he made his agonizing way down.

It felt as though he were descending into the deeps of time, losing himself in darkness—because they soon left the daylight behind and had to grope their way among shadows that were little less than night—into a twilight that seemed compounded of forgotten eons and the dust of the nonhuman builders of this place.

Eventually, the stairs ended and he risked flashing his torch on the floor, keeping it on the lowest setting. Ahead lay a tunnel where he had to stoop and half crouch his way along. The strain of this set off another attack of pain in his wounded leg, but he bore it in silence, biting his lip to combat both the ache and his mounting fear of this dark and claustrophobic place.

At last, to his great relief, they came out onto a sort of balcony that overlooked the camp he had seen before—Kessler's settlement in the midst of the ruins. Quickly, he doused the light which he no longer needed. They were above the huts and the place where the fliers had been kept—empty now since he had crashed one of the machines at the port and the other had been shot down over the Kola's original stopping place.

Otherwise, the encampment looked about the same. He recognized the dormitories, the offices and what he thought must be the galley. Perhaps a few more structures had been set up since last he had been here, but they were smaller and probably meant for storage. He touched Solomon's shoulder. "Do you know where Babe and Téna are being held?" he whispered.

Solomon pointed. "Storage locker?" he ventured. "She told them to do that. To put them in a locker. She was busy, you see. She was upset." He squirmed a little. "They were going to torture Babe, I think. But she got distracted. Do you get distracted sometimes?"

Ard Matthew nodded. "Did you see? I mean do you know which one?"

The archaeologist shook his head. "She was pretty mad," he said. "Do you know why she was mad?"

"I think she just found out that Net Central has been told about the Kola. That she's on the wrong side of the law."

Solomon frowned. "But she already knew about them. She was shooting at the village. I remember."

"That's right," the Rythan told him patiently. "But then she thought she could get rid of them and no one would know." It was like explaining things to a child, he thought.

And childlike, Solomon's focus had already shifted. "I like them," he said. "More than humans. They were kind to me."

"They were," the other agreed soberly. "And now we must save them if we can."

"And Babe and Téna?"

"And Babe and Téna."

He peered out over the campsite. He counted at least three of the smaller structures that hadn't been there the last time he'd come. If Babe and Téna had been confined in one of them, they would be in pretty cramped quarters. And, he thought suddenly, probably not well-ventilated either. But of course, their comfort would be the last thing on Kessler's mind.

So, he would assume they were down there in one of the lockers he could see. It was the only logical assumption he could make and God grant that he was right.

Now where was Dr. Kessler?

As he continued to study the camp, he had the beginnings of a plan. It wasn't a good one, he knew, but it was the best he could come up with on such short notice. He must try to seize the corporate head before she could order her people to release the gas. If he could take her prisoner and hold her as a hostage, then there might be a chance for at least a stalemate—something that would last until help came.

Of course his idea was totally impractical. There were people below moving in and out of the huts, some of them stringing wires while others assembled machinery. Mining apparatus? Or were they preparing something to facilitate the gas flow into the tunnels below the ruins? There was no way he could know, but the presence of these workers would make his own job a lot harder.

"But I don't have any choice," he murmured to Solomon. "There's no time and I've got to find Kessler. Got to get hold of her."

The other man's mind seemed to have cleared again. "Yes, you do," he agreed.

Ard Matthew studied the scene for a few minutes longer. One of the structures seemed to have more traffic than the others. Could it be the command center?

As the evening advanced, artificial lights bloomed around the area, creating dense areas of shadow here and there beside the huts. A smell of cooking drifted to the watchers in their hiding place; Ard Matthew realized that he was hungry after all. The speed heal made its demands on him, but this too must be endured.

"That one," Solomon said suddenly, pointing to the hut Ard Matthew had picked out. "It's the busy one."

"Yes—I think so, too." But how could he know for sure? Only if she came out. But why should she? He looked at Solomon, thinking. If something happened—some threat or seeming threat. That would bring her out.

"I believe I can get down this wall without being seen," he said slowly. "There isn't much light here. But once I'm on the ground, it will be different." And I won't be as fast, he added mentally. My leg cannot be relied on. He laid one hand on the bandage.

The other man seemed to follow his thought. He, too, looked at the wrapping. "You can do what you have to do," he said in a voice Ard Matthew had not heard before. Was this the voice of the archaeologist as he had been before the wendigo? He swallowed, unable to shake off the idea that God was speaking to him through this badly damaged man. Telling him what he should do.

Meanwhile Solomon had turned to the remaining tribesman and the two spoke together in the twittering language of the Neanderthals. The Rythan saw the other man nod several times and then slip away.

"He's going to guide me to another opening further along the wall," Solomon said. "We'll create a distraction. The rest is up to you."

For a moment, Ard Matthew felt nothing but panic. What if he was wrong? What if Kessler was not down in that hut? And what if he could not get to her before someone saw him? He closed his eyes, striving for calm. He recalled something Chief Firespear had said to him once. Something about how a Faring Guard did his duty and God did His part. That it was presumption for a man to worry about the outcome.

When he opened his eyes once more, Solomon was staring at him in a way that he had not seen before. As their eyes met, he was almost blinded by the humanity in the other man, the kinship that lay beneath their mutual suffering. A kinship stronger than Solomon's madness and his own sins.

"Right," he said. "I'll start down."

"Your leg?"

"It's better." He hoped he spoke truth.

A moment later, Solomon had vanished and Ard Matthew slipped over the edge of the lookout. The stone was rough and cracked, much weathered, and probably not too secure. He felt with his feet for chinks and steadied himself, flattening his body against the wall, as he grasped an outcropping with one hand. It was going to be a difficult descent and God help him if he knocked loose any of the stones.

But God would help him, he thought, and released the parapet with his other hand.

He was halfway down and the sky above was dark now, the stars half obscured with cloud, when he felt something loosen beneath one foot. He clutched the rock with both hands, his sinews straining as he took his weight off the unsteady place and sought for another foothold.

Below, people moved in and out of shadow, their voices clearly audible to him as the guards and workers headed for the mess tent. The smell of food seemed to twist something in his vitals and he felt a moment's weakness. At the same time, his foot located an outcropping that allowed him to release some of the weight from his arms.

But the sudden pain in his healing wound as he put weight on that leg, made him draw in his breath. Could he do this? How had he dared to think he could succeed in such a mad plan? And now that he thought of it, he didn't even know what the Kessler woman looked like!

He pondered this as he continued his descent. But of course, he would know her, he told himself. A lady powerful and of a certain age. Ruthless. She should be easy to spot.

Another brief spate of climbing and he was down. He didn't dare move, for the span of shadow was a thin one. His only break was that as yet, no one had reason to look his way. He waited, watching the hut that was his goal, wondering what had become of Solomon and the Neanderthal.

He hadn't long to speculate. Abruptly, the night was split with what sounded like the scream of a wendigo coming down from above the ruins. Without stopping to wonder how the two had managed that, he stepped out of the shadows and sprinted toward his goal. His leg held, but the pain was fully as bad as he had expected and he had to clench his teeth to keep from crying out.

There was no time to see if anyone had noticed him—though at least no shots had been fired. Still running, he crashed into the flimsy side of the structure and tore through, half entangling himself in the fiberplast. Several startled figures faced him, two armed but all taken totally by surprise.

Before anyone could draw a weapon, he had spotted his prey. She was the only one who could be Kessler—she even looked like her kinswoman, Téna bor Rijn. He was all Lost Rythan now and with a bound he had her.

But the woman he held was older than Téna. A lot older. Though she had been renewed several times, she must be two centuries subtime by now. And despite her age, she fought him, clawing for his eyes, cursing and hissing like a wild animal, stronger than he could have imagined.

Even so, he had to overcome his reluctance to manhandle an old woman by forcing himself to remember Shami's death. That gave him the resolution to pin her arms to her sides where, to his surprise, he felt the hardness of a holstered weapon at her waist. "Easy now," he said. "Tell your people to back off."

"Let go of me, you animal!" Twisting her head around, she sank her teeth into his arm.

He squeezed harder, knowing he was hurting her, forcing himself to a level of brutality that shamed him. He could feel the blood running down onto his hand.

All this time, he was aware of the others watching him, not daring to reach for weapons yet, waiting for some sign from their boss. "Tell them," he said. "I don't have to kill you. I can start by breaking your arm!"

Apparently she believed him. "Get back," she said.

Ard Matthew shifted his hold until he gripped her against him with one arm. He extracted her own gun from its holster with his free hand. Even helpless, it felt like trying to hold a snowtyger and he was careful not to get within range of her teeth again. He pointed the gun at the other three, two guards and what looked like a clerk. "Put your weapons on the floor," he said to the guards. "Tell them," he added to Kessler and gave her a rib cracking squeeze.

"Do it," she gasped, half snarling the words.

He motioned everyone back as he kicked the guns aside.

"Just who are you?" Kessler demanded. "That renegade Lost Rythan? The one who was supposed to be dead at the port? If you are, it's plain I have idiots working for me!"

"Ard Matthew Third-Blade," he told her politely. "Faring Guard."

"The hell you say! Faring Guard? So am I supposed to be under arrest?"

He wasn't quite sure how to answer this. Probably she didn't know he was alone, though she would already know that word was out about Windy-Go's colonists. It was natural to assume he represented the authorities. He only wished he did, but Faring Guards didn't have that kind of power.

But even more than all that, he wished he could sit down and ease his leg. He dared not let her know that he was injured, that it took all the will power he could muster to continue holding her as he was doing. But the sweat was pouring from him as he fought off wave after wave of pain.

"I will assume an affirmative," she said when he did not answer. "Or are you really a renegade after all? I know you worked for that Mong—and he's no paragon."

"He sold us out," Ard Matthew was unable to keep from saying. "Betrayed us. To you."

"Every man has his price."

He wanted to break her neck.

She must have mistaken his silence for something else because she relaxed once more. "You, too, I would guess," she ventured. "You have a price."

Still he did not say anything. He was too angry and in too much pain to speak.

"You know about the phessite, Third-Blade? You know what's at stake here?"

He managed to grunt an affirmative.

"Then you know that some of us are going to make a lot of money. Some of us are going to be rich beyond our dreams."

"You already are," he growled. "Rich."

She shrugged in his grip. "Don't underestimate my dreams," she said. "Or yours."

"It doesn't belong to you," he told her. "The phessite. It belongs to the colonists. To the citizens of Windy-Go."

"Those cavemen? What good is it to them? They are no more than beasts."

"They are not beasts!" he roared, pushed beyond endurance. "I have met them and they are as human as I am!"

She laughed a little at this. "Likely they are," she said and then broke off. Outside, a commotion had begun and they could hear the sounds of firing. But he had not heard a flyer. And he had no idea what Solomon and the Neanderthal were doing. Meanwhile, it could only be a matter of time before someone discovered the damage he had made to the back wall of the hut.

He did not take his eyes from the others in the room as he heard someone shout. "It's a slope-head! Up there!"

More firing.

He winced.

"Listen to me, Third-Blade," Kessler said, turning her face up to his. "They don't matter. When my people get here—you know I have another crew coming?—when they get here, we'll take care of the natives and clean up after ourselves. There won't be any evidence. You'll have a share in the profits. You can have Babe's share, in fact. His job, too if you want it."

The firing continued. This time he did hear a flier.

"My people," Kessler said. "They're coming in now."

"Where is Babe?" he demanded. "And Téna?"

"Locked up. I'll deal with them."

The wendigo sound came again. All things considered, that one Neanderthal was causing a lot of uproar—if he was the one making the sounds. And then he realized that one man could not be calling from all directions at once. And a moment later when Solomon came skidding in the door, he knew that something more was going on.

The archaeologist stared at Kessler who stared back at him in surprise. "That her?" he asked.

Ard Matthew nodded.

"Who is this?" Kessler demanded, no longer quite so sure of herself. "Your partner?" She glared at him. "Have you been trying to set me up?"

At that moment, there came a very human scream that ended in a sound that could only mean one thing. Someone had died violently. The Rythan looked at Solomon. "Was that—your friend?"

The other man shook his head. "They're coming in from the port. Her people. It was one of them."

Ard Matthew stared at him. "What do you mean?"

"The Kola are upset."

And then the sounds were all around them. With panicked looks, the two guards and the clerk made a run for the door and out into the night. Twisting herself from his loosened grip, Kessler tried to follow them. When Ard Matthew grabbed her, she kicked him in his bad leg and he fell, helpless in his sudden agony, losing his grip on the gun.

With one look back, Kessler turned and was gone.

She didn't get far. He heard her scream and then a sound that could only be a tomahawk striking flesh. He ran to the entrance and nearly tripped over a body. Two bodies. Kessler and one of the guards. He tried to look away, but could not help seeing the look of final terror on her face as blood and brains leaked from a broken skull.

"In the name of God, Solomon! What is going on here?"

"Ranesh brought them," the other man said. "They think these people are devils."

"They may behave like devils," the Rythan said, "but they are no more than sinners like you and me. Can't we stop the slaughter?"

Even as he spoke, he saw a Neanderthal cut down and another barely escape the same fate even as the shooter, one of Kessler's guards, was killed by an arrow in the eye. The scene was repeated all over the campsite. Already one of the huts was burning and he saw some of the company men fleeing into the tunnels. He doubted they would get far.

"We've got to find Babe and Téna," he said suddenly. "See if she has a key or something."

When Solomon only stood there, he handed him his gun and searched the body himself. There was nothing that might be a key, no electronic device of any sort. He stood up. "Come on," he said and led the way to the center of the camp.

At the first of the storage units, he paused and hammered on the locked door. "Babe?" he called. "Téna?"

There was no answer. He ran to the next, expecting at any moment to feel a bullet or a laser cut in his exposed flesh. Again, he pounded and again there was no answer. He noted that another of the huts was afire—the mess tent. A Neanderthal ran past waving a meat cleaver.

Only one unit left. He battered at the door and heard nothing from inside. For the first time he realized that there were no openings at all, no airways. How long could anyone survive in there? He looked around frantically, remembered the man with the cleaver and ran into the burning tent. Frantically he looked around the kitchen and seized another tool—a hammer that lay beside an opened crate. Ducking a flaming streamer of plastiwall, he ran back outside. There was no sign of Solomon.

He swung his tool at the lock, felt the impact run up his arm and into his shoulder. He swung again and yet again. With a tearing sound, the lock gave way and he grasped the door, pulling it open. He was met by a mound of supplies, crates of syntho steaks and some sort of pasta. There was no sign or any human occupant.

Quickly he rushed to one of the others. Swing and thunk. Swing again. He strained something in his arm. God knew he had swung a battle axe often enough back on Lost Rythar, but this was a matter of rending metal. Once more—

When he got the door open, the sight that met his eyes sent a chill of despair through him. Babe and Téna lay entwined, her face on his shoulder, his arms loosely clasped around her. They didn't seem to be breathing. A few half empty crates were scattered on the floor and there was nothing else.

With a groan of despair, he ran inside and knelt beside them. "Babe?" he whispered. "Téna?"

The bad air made him a little dizzy. Quickly he pulled the pair outside and let the night breeze blow over them. All the while he watched for some sign of life while around him, the flames and the screams continued as though this were an antechamber of hell.

Trembling, he reached down and touched Téna's face. "No," he said. "No!"

Suddenly Solomon was beside him and at the sight of the man's hopeful expression, he remembered—oh everything. He began to pray.

Beneath his hand, he felt a twitch. Or perhaps he imagined it. Beside the girl, Babe moved and opened his eyes. For some moments he stared up at the Rythan glassily, gasping in long draughts of air. Then as consciousness returned, he struggled to a sitting position and reached over to Téna. Ard Matthew moved back.

"*Ona zhivet*! She lives!" The words were no more than a whisper.

"See if you can get up," Ard Matthew told him. "We've got to get away from here. Into the tunnels if we can." The firing had moved off and there was less of it, but even so, they could not stay out in the open.

He helped Babe to his feet and then picked up Téna. "This way," he said and headed back for the wall. Of course he could not climb the way he had come in. "Help me, Solomon," he said. "How did you get in?"

The archaeologist led him back into the shadows and along the wall until a rockfall gave them egress to a fissure that had remained invisible until they were almost upon it. Once inside, Solomon took them into a niche where Ard Matthew put down his burden. Téna moaned and let Babe take her hands. "Boris? Where—?"

"You're safe now," Babe told her. "Everything is okay."

In the light of his torch, which he had somehow retained, Ard Matthew saw that Solomon had slipped away again and sighed. As the stimulants he had been given—so long ago, now—wore off, he felt suddenly weak. He found he could no longer hold himself upright. Slowly he felt his legs give way until he sank to a sitting position on the stone floor.

"You alright?" Babe rasped.

The Rythan nodded. If he wasn't alright, he had better be.

"Looks like the Neanderthals are fighters after all."

Ard Matthew made no answer to this. He was sorry in a way, to find that the primitive people were not the innocents he had taken them for. But of course it must be so, he reminded himself grimly, not only here among the stars but back on his homeworld where the price of survival was always paid in blood. Original Sin, the Star Brothers had called it—that great flaw that ran through all creation. He thought about the child, Kensh and mourning already the things the young tribesman must see and do as he grew to manhood, he felt darkness flow over him.

***

"Wake up, Third-Blade."

He groaned and turned his head aside. How long had he been out? And now of all times. He felt very weak.

"Dammit, Third-Blade. They're here!"

"Who?" he muttered. As consciousness slowly returned, it brought with it a headache and a very unsteady feeling in his middle.

"The troopers. You've got to talk to them."

"Me?"

"You're a Faring Guard, aren't you?"

He was that. But why he had to—

And then he finished waking up. "Right, Babe." He straightened himself. "How long have I been asleep?"

"A few hours, I think. The fight's over, but you'll have to tell them what happened. Solomon and I talked to Makena and the other leaders—the ones who weren't killed—and we told them that the troopers are on their side. Or should be. I hope they believed us."

"Right, Babe. I guess I represent the Star Brothers, too. Unless Father Bauer came with them?"

"We both represent the Star Brothers, Matthew," said another voice and he turned to see the priest standing beside him. He tried to get to his feet and stumbled. Babe caught him.

"You don't need to get up," the Star Brother said. "Just get your account on record." He handed the Rythan a disk. "Tell them how it was. They're listening."

Ard Matthew did so. From time to time, someone on the other end put a question and he answered as truthfully as he could. When it was over, he lay back. Someone had put a pad beneath him and he could smell meat cooking somewhere. He was ravenously hungry, but the priest only handed him a ration bar. He looked up at Babe.

"You don't want to know," Babe said. "Just don't accept any dinner from our friends—at least not for a few days."

Ard Matthew swallowed a bite of ration and coughed a little. He hoped Babe didn't mean what he thought he did, but wasn't going to ask. "Okay," he said. "What now?"

"Now you're leaving. I'll finish cleaning up here. They're going to appoint Téna acting president of the company and I'm her—assistant, I guess. Of course Kessler Corp is going to be dissolved but that's okay with both of us."

The Rythan looked up at him. "I'm glad, Babe," he said, wondering how he had ever taken Boris Oleg for nothing more than a company thug. "Yeah," he said. "Really glad."

***

The few Kessler personnel left on Windy-Go seemed at loose ends, some accepting contracts with other corporations, others still trying to recoup the money that was owed to them. Many of these were staying at the Port Hotel, drinking hard and running up bills on a still operating corporate account. But they were living on borrowed time and everyone knew it.

Ard Matthew sidestepped a pair of these as he limped down the hallway to the suite Babe and Téna had taken—also on the Kessler tab. As Babe said, he was collecting his hazard pay.

"But we'll be gone soon enough," Téna had assured the Lost Rythan and it was true. The Faring Guard was always in the market for instructors in a variety of fields, everything from espionage to demolition. Captain and Mrs. Oleg were going back to Sachsen where they would have diplomatic immunity under the auspices of the Star Brothers, and a chance to build a new life.

But Ard Matthew knew Babe had not got off scot free any more than he had. The Star Brothers were very particular about these things. Boris would be training with the Faring Guard for the first few weeks of his tenure at the motherhouse on Sachsen. And Ard Matthew knew very well how penitential that could be.

He reached the door and laid one hand on the panel. As he was recognized, someone called out, "Admit" and the door swung open. Inside, the little sitting room was a jumble of packages and luggage. Téna had been shopping.

"Are you leaving tonight?" the Lost Rythan asked in surprise as he surveyed the mess. The Star Brothers' ship, *Baltasar*, hung in orbit above Windy-Go along with another, a Net Central starship, People's Will. Ard Matthew had been summoned by his superior who awaited him aboard the *Baltasar*. He was not looking forward to that meeting, though it must be borne. He had done wrong and now he must face up to it.

"We're going with you," Téna told him. "We've been invited to travel on the *Baltasar*." She made it sound like a luxury liner and the Lost Rythan hadn't the heart to tell her how Spartan—how absolutely decrepit, the old hulk really was. She would find out soon enough.

"I am happy to hear that," he said aloud. For the first time, he saw how pretty Téna actually was. The Star Brother had consented to marry Téna and Boris once he determined that both were baptized and that Boris had no objection to conforming himself to the western version of Christianity, at least for the wedding.

The Lost Rythan found himself a seat on the only chair not covered with packing debris. It was, of course, too small for him and he had to stretch out his legs in order to sit. But that was alright. Though his wound was mostly healed, the leg remained stiff and had a tendency to swell at the end of the day.

"Beer?" Babe asked.

Ard Matthew gave him a very Lost Rythan look and the other man produced a bottle for each of them.

"Have you heard from Mr. Solomon?" Téna asked then.

Ard Matthew nodded. "He refused to leave when his university sent for him. He's applying for citizenship in the colony."

"And is he mentally competent to do that?"

The Rythan shrugged. "They need him to help with some of the colonial organization," he said. "Of course the Star Brothers are sorting things out for them with Net Central, but there are a lot of details that go into running a colony."

Babe grinned. "So it doesn't matter if he's got all his marbles," he said. "If the tribes want him, he stays." Ard Matthew noted the plural of "tribes". As it turned out, there had been more than one band of Neanderthals on Windy-Go. That was yet another headache for the Star Brothers.

"Did Mr. Solomon—marry that girl?" Téna asked suddenly. "Lish?"

Ard Matthew flushed. "Not—exactly," he said, repeating what he had heard. "I mean, not yet. They are not baptized." Though he had no doubt that the Star Brothers would succeed in evangelizing this world as they had so many others, that still lay in the future.

Presently, guessing that the other two still had much to do, he rose. "I've got to get my own things together," he said, though in fact he had already gathered his meager belongings from the apartment. All the time, he had kept wondering if he would meet his former boss, Saler Mong, but the broker had fled as soon as word got out of the breakup of Kessler Corp. Under the circumstances, the Rythan thought grimly, that was the best thing he could have done—for both of them.

Later, on the shuttle, he watched Boris and Téna as they sat together, planning their new life. He was sure the Star Brothers would leave nothing undone for their spiritual and physical welfare and if his own prayers were heard, their happiness and that of their future children was as secure as anything could be in this life.

He looked down at his linked hands, resting quietly in his lap. How scarred they were, how calloused and battered. Like his own soul.

And then, almost before he had time to so much as wonder what he would say to his superiors, he was passing through the link and onto the starship. And there was Gaed Alfred, all seven feet of him, looking sternly down at the prodigal. Ard Matthew stood his ground, meeting the eyes of his superior. It was one of the hardest things he had ever done.

And then it was over. Gaed Alfred smiled suddenly, beaming, as he reached out to seize Ard Matthew's shoulders, and draw him into a crushing embrace.

"Welcome back," he said and all of Lost Rythar was in his words and in his face. Ard Matthew was home.

ABOUT THE AUTHOR

Colleen Drippé has been producing fantasy and science fiction for quite a few years. Along with many short stories now being published as e-books, she is the author of six science fiction novels which can be found on Amazon.

OTHER BOOKS BY COLLEEN DRIPPÉ

Gelen
Sunrise on the Ice Wolf
Treelight
Vessel of Darkness
The Dawnstrikers
The Branded Ones
Sharan
Planet of the Winds

House Avers
Recall

Frightliner & Other Tales of the Undead (with Karina Fabian)

Please leave a review on Amazon. Just 20 words about what you thought about the book helps readers who are considering the book and helps the author with Amazon ranking.

Made in the USA
Columbia, SC
28 October 2024